KISS AND TELL

MAYA HUGHES

THANK YOU FOR READING

Maya Hughes

To 2021, which will forever be the lost year in my mind.

Cover Design: Najla Qamber

1

REID

Covered in sweat, barely able to catch my breath, I chugged the lime green sports drink from my bottle with my name scrawled across it in big block letters, "REID". It was the only way to ensure I wasn't gulping down someone else's backwash.

Not even the much needed drink slowed my pounding pulse. I had yardage marker paint crisscrossing the back of my jersey, and I'd be picking grass out of my teeth for the next week.

Our first practice had been a nightmare. Where the hell was Trevor? He was a senior and one of our most solid performers.

The August heat was no longer beating down on me, but the tension in the locker room still made it feel like I was trapped in a pressure cooker. Western Pennsylvania summer wasn't blistering, but after hours of practice, the heat sweltered under my uniform.

With the sweat soaking through my pads and into my jersey, I looked like I'd been sprayed by a firehose. Felt like I'd survived a battle, but the war was still undecided.

All around, my teammates streamed into the locker room that was bigger than some college gyms. Welcome to Division I football. The huge open space with the gold and orange bulldog printed on the carpet still smelled new even through the nearly impenetrable sweaty haze of sixty guys still panting hard after our first official practice. It was a locker room although there were no lockers.

We each had a cubby with our name on it, a padded seat, and storage above and below. Benches were placed around the main room with towel bins near the showers. Large glass windows overlooked the coaches' offices and the physiotherapy rooms. Ice baths, cryo tanks, physiotherapy tables, Icy Hot, ace bandages and athletic tape were neatly organized by the coaching and support staff that rivaled the player count.

"Riddick, do you need PT?" One of the physiotherapists checked in with me.

"No, I'm good." The aches and pains were part of the job, and I knew there were others who needed it more than me.

He nodded and moved on to another player. The whole place was a hive of activity. Only there was no honey in these combs—they were filled with blood, sweat and tears.

Training camp was only the beginning of Coach Mikelson's torture. But if I wanted to go pro, I had to be the best. If I wanted to buy my dad his own garage, I had to be the best. If I wanted people to scream my name, wear my jersey and never go back to being that scrawny kid who got tripped in the cafeteria, I had to be the best.

Coach Mikelson marched into the room, and everyone quieted. Even the guys in the showers turned them off while we waited. His eyes locked onto mine, and I steeled myself. Weakness was a liability. I'd gotten my spot as a starter and I didn't want him to have a doubt.

"It's your future, not mine." Coach scanned the room with a scowl and a glare. "I'll be here long after you've been shipped back to your no-name town where everyone will have forgotten how great you were in high school. I'll start over with another team in a few years, and you'll be nothing."

I swallowed past the thickness in my throat strangling me. I couldn't be nothing again. I wouldn't be. I'd clawed my way onto this team, and not winning wasn't an option.

"This is the last shot some of you have at ever being something. At anyone even remembering who you are. The championship is ours to lose, and I expect perfection out there!" He pointed in the direction of the field.

Now, determination flowed through me, and I clenched my fists, feeling the throb of my pulse in my veins.

After every losing season, he only brought the hammer down harder on us. If our best wasn't good enough, he'd push our bodies to the limit until we were faster, stronger, better. I scanned the room, looking for Trevor. Maybe he was injured, but he wasn't near any of the guys on crutches or nursing other pre-season damage.

One of my roommates and one of our linemen, Griff, stood a little in front of me. His hands were locked at his sides, and his face twitched. He scrunched his nose. Now wasn't the time for a sneeze attack. Griff slammed his eyes shut, muttered "fuck" under his breath and began his rapid-fire sneezing, which would probably burst a blood vessel in his head from holding them in.

Mikelson reached peak pissed off, whipped around and grabbed an orange and white water cooler. He launched it through the air toward the just-finished-sneezing Griff.

Guys jumped out of the way. My heart rate spiked

higher, and I gripped Griff's jersey and yanked him out of the way of the flying cooler.

Griff and I stumbled but recovered, knowing not to say a word throughout Mikelson's speech. The water cooler slammed to the ground, and what little bit of Gatorade left inside spilled onto the carpet.

I snapped back up straight and tried to get my heart rate under control. In some ways, it made all the shit he put us through easier to endure. He didn't normally single anyone out. He was an equal opportunity asshole.

Mikelson continued. Our movement hadn't drawn his attention away from his not-so-inspiring speech.

A hair of the tightness in my chest lessened.

"Thanks," Griff mumbled over his shoulder.

I leaned in and kept my lips as still as possible. "I've got your back, not just on the field, but in the face of incoming flying objects."

Gaze trained on the man who was supposed to be our god, Griff stood tall, and his lips twitched. A small sound escaped from his sealed mouth.

Beside me, Ezra's shadow loomed over us with a noise rumbling in his throat through his clenched teeth. His way of telling us to shut the hell up while we were in the middle of Mikelson ripping us a new asshole. Once we got back to the house, he'd probably lay into us both about the completely normal biological function Griff had been trying to suppress.

The almost imperceptible shake of Ezra's head was his version of punching Griff and me for talking. He—out of all my roommates—took the game most seriously and considering how determined we all were said a lot. It made him a beast on the field.

The veins on Coach Mikelson's neck throbbed a deep

red. "If you're not going to pay attention, I don't know why you're here. This is a dictatorship," he shouted. "You want to know why?"

No one was dumb enough to speak. He told us when he wanted to hear from us and not a moment before that.

"I have more trophies up on my wall than most of you will win in a lifetime. Do the work, follow my rules, and never stop giving me everything you've got, and maybe I'll keep you from wasting your talent and killing your future. But if you make a mistake, if you fuck things up, you're done."

Being benched, cut or—in the case of the staff and support team—fired, happened at least a few times a season for actual or perceived insubordination. But we all put up with it. It's what it took to be on a top team. We wanted to win.

Mikelson marched over to the table of clipboards and tablets all the coaching staff had laid out. "I will not have another failure this season." In a move we all saw coming, he flipped the whole thing, sending electronics and packets of paper flying. "Do you hear me?"

"Yes, Coach." The entire eighty-player squad shout had to be louder than the marching band blaring the fight song on game day.

"Today's practice was a disgrace, and we will not lose to Fulton U or anyone else again. Do you understand me?" He launched his clipboard, sending it sailing through the air.

"Yes, Coach," we responded in unison.

"The championship will be mine." He stood with his hands behind his back and bored holes into each of us. "This season, I want no excuses. Bulldogs on three. Then hit the showers."

The group chanted in unison. "One. Two. Three. Bulldogs."

And I was the loudest. I didn't care if he was a hardass, didn't care if he didn't care about our feelings. Showing up as the first-place losers—once again—wasn't what I'd signed up for. Unlike some players who complained about how he ran things, I'd put up with it all because I knew what was most important—winning.

The whole team broke out of statue mode and rushed back into the showers or started stripping down before Mikelson could lay into us again.

I whipped off my jersey.

"His." Beside me, Cole, our team center and my roommate, glanced over his shoulder, sucked his teeth and dropped to one knee to rip off his cleats. "His championship." A tall, lean guy who'd never had trouble using his spot on the team to score off the field, Cole always seemed to flip-flop between idolizing and hating Coach. In our three years as roommates, it felt like those swings had gotten even more mercurial. "We're only the ones out here busting our asses in four-hour practices, which break all kinds of rules." His face was set in a grim mask of determination to get through the rest of the pre-season without another team-wide punishment.

"Since when has Coach cared about rules?" I channeled my anger at every other team into each movement. The cool air snapped against my sweaty skin. I shook out my towel and wrapped it against my body.

"Two more seasons. Two more seasons, and we'll never have to see him again."

With the way Coach had been riding him season after season, he should've sounded happier about that. But he made it sound like he was running out of time for something.

I grabbed my soap. "With the way that vein in his neck and forehead are always bulging, maybe even sooner."

Cole huffed and shook his head. "Not that lucky."

Ezra ran a towel over his closely cropped hair. "How about we all agree not to screw around while Mikelson's talking so he doesn't make us run laps. If anyone does, I'll remove their spines and hang them in the locker room like a trophy."

2

REID

Ezra zipped up his bag on the floor at his feet, shaking his head. "Can't believe Trevor's gone."

"What happened?" Panic hit me as I scrubbed the towel over my head, soaking up the dampness from the shower and I froze. "Did something happen to him? He's on the injured list?" The room now smelled like sweat covered over with liniment and bar soap. Humidity seeped out of the twenty-stall shower room. Cole still sat on his seat, eyes closed, sweat dripping off him and his head resting against the wooden divider between his space and mine.

"No, not hurt. Mitchell's got his spot." Ezra looked up from tying his shoes and nodded toward the new addition to the starting lineup.

I relaxed that he hadn't gotten hurt and grabbed my shirt out of my cubby, then did a double take. "How the hell did Mitchell get his spot?"

Mitchell's blocks were sloppy, which meant everyone else on the line had to pick up his slack. He thought his size made up for speed and determination—it didn't.

Cole didn't open his eyes. "Trevor's out."

"No shit, but what happened? And are you planning on showering sometime today?" I jumped into my boxers before dropping the towel. Missing was an understatement. The last-minute change-up to the roster, not because of injury or a team sanction, was going to wreak havoc this season. Trevor was a senior with first-round pick plastered all over him. Our defense would suck without his size, skill and leadership on the field and experience. "That's a lot more pressure on you guys."

Cole gently rotated his shoulder. "Trevor wouldn't break up with his girlfriend. That's what happened."

"What the hell does him dating someone have to do with his spot?" I dumped one of my towels in the industrial-sized laundry bin, thankful that we weren't responsible for cleaning all our gear after practices.

"It's Coach Belton's daughter." Cole's eyes popped open, and he tugged off his drenched socks.

Ezra shoved his hat on. "Didn't Belton leave to be head coach at Alabama?" Belton had been a good counterbalance to Mikelson, but no one blamed him for leaving for a head coaching job, especially at Alabama—well, everyone except for Mikelson.

I pulled on my jeans. "The only way that would've been worse was if he'd gone to Fulton U."

Cole stood with a wince and picked the top towel off the stack of neatly folded ones. "But as usual with Mikelson, anyone who crosses him or even thinks of crossing him and anyone associated with them is fucking dead to him. And if you know what's good for you, they should be dead to you too."

I glanced over my shoulder. "Why didn't he just break up with her?" I whispered through gritted teeth. Annoyance shot through me. We wouldn't have him on the field, a senior, this season because of his girlfriend?

"Why *should* he break up with her?" Cole yanked off his socks.

"If he wants to play and go pro and that's the only option." I whipped my other towel into the bin. It snapped at the air. He'd put a girl over the team? "It seems like a no-brainer." His draft potential would take a dive, and our lineup took a hit. "We were there beside him during every practice because we wanted to win. The least he could've done is not screw us over. And for what?" Anger bristled through me. How stupid could he be? I shoved my feet into my shoes.

Cole jerked off his shirt. "Maybe there are more important things than football."

I zipped my bag so hard a piece of the zipper broke off between my fingers. "Name five."

Cole stared at me like I was insane.

My skin heated, and I shot up with indignation. "You've been playing this game since you were younger than I was, and you're telling me that if Mikelson walked in here and told you to punch me in the dick or you weren't playing this season, you wouldn't do it?"

"I'd do it even if he said I'd be benched for the rest of the year." Cole dragged another towel off the stack at the end of our row of benches. "Especially when you're acting like a dick."

"How am I acting like a dick? We all make sacrifices to get where we want to be." I slung the bag across my back. "I've solved this whole problem by not dating anyone."

Ezra grabbed his duffel bag. "I'm passing out for a few hours before Welcome Wagon. Do you guys want me to wait?" He dropped his pads and cleats in the designated bin. "I'll sleep in my car until you're ready."

Cole waved him off. "I brought my car."

"I'll walk." I leaned back, popping my spine. "If I don't stretch out after what he put us through today, I won't be able to run tomorrow."

Griff returned from the shower with a still red nose and flopped down on his seat. "You and your little one-man parades down the street."

Ezra rolled his eyes and tugged on the brim of his hat. "Seriously?"

"What?" I shrugged. "Can't help it if the walks clear my head, and there's the bonus of fans getting to wave to me when I walk by." Who was I to deny them that pleasure?

"They only care about us when we're winning," Cole said, shaking his head.

"Which is why I need to make sure I've got my parade route locked down for all the cheering this season."

"Way to jinx it," Ezra grumbled.

"Just telling the truth as I see it."

"If you want to walk, that's fine with me. I've got better shit to do." Ezra left the locker room, marching like the floor had pissed him off.

"Come on, Cole." Hollis, our quarterback and another of my roommates, marched out of the physiotherapy room and snapped a towel in his direction. "Get your ass in the shower. We don't want to jinx the season, so we've all got to be at Welcome Wagon." He wrapped a fresh towel around his waist.

Cole massaged his knee. "Doesn't participating after losing to Fulton U for the past two seasons make it seem more likely that we're actually jinxing ourselves?"

I stopped midstride with my foot dangling in the air.

We'd been at Welcome Wagon every year, and every year we had made it further in the play-offs only to lose. All eyes were on us during the campus tradition. The attention was magnetic. Maybe this time would be the time it worked.

"Better to get everyone cheering for us while we can." The mood on campus after last season made it hard to go to class. It had been hard to hold my head up and brought back all those old memories from high school before I bulked up and found my football family. After last season, there had been long, uncomfortable weeks where it felt like everyone was staring and not in a good way.

But the summer break seemed to have made a lot of people forget or at least have hope for what the new season would bring. I turned and spread my arms wide. "You know what this season will be like. I'm not giving up a single party opportunity. Who knows how many we'll get. Let's have some fun. Remember what that feels like?"

Cole glared and gritted his teeth, setting off a squeaking and grinding noise that made me want to explode my own ear drums. "I can't even feel my legs from the knee down. How am I supposed to have any fun?" His hip injury from the summer was slow to recover.

I held out my hand.

He grabbed onto it, locking his fingers around mine.

I pulled him up.

"With Mikelson"—he glanced over his shoulder—"on my ass, I don't remember what fun is anymore."

"Come on, you're at the center of it all. Other than all eyes on Hollis, they're all waiting for you to toss that snap." I raised my hands in the air like I was painting a picture of the adoring fans all cheering and screaming our names.

"For now." His eyes clouded, and his jaw clenched,

setting off the vein in his neck. "The target on my back just got a hell of a lot bigger."

"That's why this year, it's all about no distractions. You've got this. We've got this."

I finished up first and grabbed my stuff. The locker room had emptied out in record time. Cleaning crew wandered through picking up discarded athletic tape, bandages and everything else used to hold us together. Most of the guys would crash for a while before Welcome Wagon began. It was an off-the-books St. Francis University aka STFU tradition that the administration hated.

With a towel around his waist, Cole walked out of the showers. He looked dead on his feet.

"Hauser, the coach wants to see you," an assistant coach called out from the doorway leading to the coaches' offices.

"Fuck." He didn't even try to muffle it. "Can I at least get dressed first?"

The coach shot him an apologetic look. "He said now."

Gripping his towel tighter, Cole turned toward the offices.

"Do you want me to wait for you?" Cole might need to decompress after a talk with Mikelson or maybe just throw a few things. We'd all been there. Sitting alone after a meeting with Coach was an invitation for shitty things trying to pull you under. I don't know where he got his motivational advice from, but it might've been the 7th circle of hell.

"No use in both of us being miserable," he said and marched off.

I shoved through the doors to the outside and inhaled the first breath of the new school year and the official start of the season.

Stiff soreness worked its way through my muscles, but the football high was still there, humming through my veins. With a bottle in hand, I gulped water on the walk back to The Zoo. The moniker followed us wherever we lived, mainly due to the parties post-season. If there was one group of guys who knew how to blow off steam, it was football players who'd been avoiding booze for months and didn't have to wake up at 5 a.m. for practice the next day.

Cars lined up curbside in both directions—trunks brimmed with boxes and SUVs had couches strapped to the roofs and back windows you couldn't see out of. Horns honked as people were rushed to unload their crap and haul ass off campus.

Dad hung out for a few hours before the trip back home two weeks ago before the long trip back to Harvard, Mass. One perk of moving in for training camp was not having to deal with the gridlock madness that took over the campus for the weekend before classes started.

I ducked through one of the lawns with residence halls on four sides and got to our street. It wasn't as packed, since most of the people on the off-campus side had arrived early when their leases started to avoid the campus chaos. But the other half of the street teemed with brand new upperclassman moving all their things into the four-person apartment clusters.

I turned the corner down the street that ran the length of campus where I'd call home for the next two years. Our place was right on the dividing line between on- and off-campus. It was the best of both worlds and meant we didn't have to worry about leaving for the winter breaks or the summers.

My phone buzzed.

I grabbed it out of my pocket. "Hey, Dad."

"Hey, son. How'd practice go?"

"I'll let you know once the adrenaline fully wears off. I left the field a little while ago and I'm on my way home."

"Didn't practice start at eight this morning?"

"Yeah."

"It's nearly 1pm."

I stared up at the sky, squinting at the sun. Losing track of time during practice happened a lot. I could tell he was shaking his head even from the other end of the line.

"That coach," he grumbled.

"I wanted to play for the best." Not that Mikelson deserved me jumping to his defense, but for my own dad to think I couldn't handle the work it took to be a winner stung.

"You always wanted to be the best." His chiding tone shifted and rippled with amusement.

"At least I'm not that scrawny kid forcing you to play with me in the back yard anymore." My dad went to every game once I started playing for my high school team. His car was always the first one driving behind the team bus for away games, and he even came to practices when things were slow at the warehouse. Making him proud was half the reason I'd started playing to begin with.

We watched football every Sunday through high school. He knew all the stats, and hanging together after his long days during the week at work were some of my favorite memories from growing up.

"Hey, I happened to like that scrawny kid." His mock outrage for my former pathetic self shaved the sharpness off his doubts. "The young man he's turned into can be a pain in the ass sometimes though."

"Thanks, Dad."

"You know I speak the truth."

I laughed and crossed the street. "Most of the time. What's up?"

"A dad can't call his son?" Even though he sounded upbeat, exhaustion was threaded through each word.

"Of course, you can." We'd spent some time together over the summer, but between my workouts and his work schedule, it wasn't as much as either of us would've liked.

"Just checking in on you and wanted to make sure you had enough money. Did you need me to do another Costco run?"

"Dad, you're a few hundred miles away." I brushed my hand over my chin, squeezing my jaw tightly. I hated how much he sacrificed at the drop of a hat for me. "Don't worry —we have enough paper plates and toilet paper to last us into the next decade. And my meal plan for the dining hall plus the money you sent will be enough to get me through the semester."

"If you say so." But his skepticism was clear.

There were far fewer parents on this side of the road, plus some kiddie pools filled with beers out on the lawns and water guns sitting at the ready. I waved off a guy holding out a beer to me. Nothing helped me focus on my future more than talking to my dad.

"You know if you need anything all you have to do is call me up. I can always spare a few bucks for my favorite son."

I laughed at his go-to dad-joke praise. "I'm your only son. Don't worry so much. It's not so bad." In a couple years, I'd buy him his own garage and whatever else he needed. A few nights of hunger during college would be a blip in my rearview.

"Don't drive yourself into the ground too often."

Running out into a stadium filled with thousands of screaming fans in whatever city I might be in and staring up at the bright lights and cameras wasn't new, but doing it with some extra zeros in my bank account would feel a hell of a lot better.

"It's the only way to make sure I'm a top draft pick."

The risk of injury or Mikelson deciding he didn't like my face and benching me or kicking me off the team loomed with every breath. But it didn't stop the daydreams. The cars I'd drive. The way people would look at me. It was all I'd ever wanted.

"It's not a guarantee, son."

Shock gripped my chest, like a brick had been lobbed at me, the thud reverberating against my ribs. "You don't think I'll make the cut. I've been putting in—"

"I didn't say that." There was a long deep breath. "I'm just trying... I know you've wanted this since you were on the JV squad back in high school, but there are thousands of other players all doing the same thing. Even the hardest workers, even the people with the most talent, sometimes life comes down to luck, and I don't want you to feel like if you don't make it, your life is over."

Gritting my teeth, I slammed my eyes shut and leaned against a light pole ladened with STFU banners. The heated metal seared my back, giving me something physical to focus on. Him thinking I couldn't make it was like a bag of wrenches being dumped on my head.

I pushed off the pole and walked the last block before the house. I needed to keep moving. Forward as always. "It won't be because I'll make it." If I was the only one who had to believe in me to make my dream happen, then that's all I needed. Because I was so close and I wasn't giving up now.

"I know you will." He sighed. "Give me a call if you need anything."

"I will." I punched the phone closed as I passed the identical red brick houses with identical porches and identical stairs. I wasn't going to be like everyone else though. None of us were.

The Zoo had moved in, and once the season was over, everyone would know it.

We'd gotten the lease from another group of guys from the team who'd graduated, but we had to keep up the football player reputation. We'd already started planning for the Halloween party, aka Boo at The Zoo. Our one glimmer of bad behavior during the season, but with that rhyme, how could we pass it up?

I hit the curb at a jog.

"Reid!" An unmistakable high-pitched voice burst through the move in chatter on the busy street.

I spun around and shielded my eyes.

Across the street, Taylor and Ashley waved. Taylor wore a pink STFU jersey, and Ashley was in her faded new student orientation t-shirt from freshman year.

I walked over. I'd known them since we'd lived on the same floor freshman year.

"What's up?" Elbow to elbow, I tapped them a hello and then slid my palm around Taylor's and hooked her thumb. We pulled back for the finger explosion.

Ashley broke down a box and flattened it. "Sizing up the street for party potential?"

"Any good spots?" I rocked onto my heels with my hands in my pockets.

Taylor glanced up and down the road. "So far the party prospects are looking good. Kind of like our season."

"So that's why you're already moved in." I should've known she wouldn't pass up the chance to be here for the pre-season. The school revolved around football, and Taylor was here for it.

"I wasn't going to miss the first unofficial practice of the season." She tugged at the shoulders of her jersey. "How's your knee doing? And the shoulder? I saw a slight dip when I was watching you guys today." She was a bloodthirsty sports fan, and after our loss last season, the scrutiny had increased. Not that I minded.

"By watching, you mean spying?" Better to have people watching than not give a shit. "Practices are closed."

"Not if you've got trusty binoculars." She tapped the side of her head with a smirk.

Ashley's gaze shot to the sky. "You should see the notebook where she was scribbling the whole time."

"Die hard as ever, huh?" I turned to Ashley.

"I feel like it's even worse now."

"I'm just excited for the season." Taylor pointed her finger between the two of us. She was the type for a lot of guys on the team. She never had a hair out of place but didn't look plastic. And while she was perfectly styled to look killer in jeans and the jersey of her player of choice as she cheered in the stands at every home game, her knowledge of football caught a lot of people off guard. "And I'm warning you both, if anyone takes my seat in the student section, there will be blood."

I laughed. "Feeling less cutthroat than last season, huh? Weren't you threatening limb removal in September last year?" Since STFU football was practically an on-campus religion, there were strict protocols for who got season tickets and how the seating was assigned. And by assigned, I meant a bloodbath to get the best seats while also not getting thrown out of the stadium.

"Only slightly less. Maybe I'm mellowing with age." She snorted. Her interest in the game wasn't a front. She bled STFU orange and gold. She could recite stats better than most of the guys who were up in the booth commentating. "At least I'll only have to fight seniors for my spot, unlike last year when I had to fight juniors and seniors. But—bright side for everyone—we'll get to see you play more this year." Her hand landed on my shoulder.

I patted the back of it. "Don't jinx it." There was strictly friends energy between us, although she had a type. And her type was football players. But the intersection of her type and my type had run its course back during freshman year, which had led to an unfortunate kiss that felt like a wet duffel bag filled practice gear being smacked into my face.

It didn't stop us from being friends—hell, maybe it was why we were friends. It was a lot easier to be friends with someone when you knew the spark between you was as fiery as a pair of soggy after-practice cleats.

She elbowed me in the side. "Don't jinx it by even thinking there's anything to jinx. We already lost Trevor." Her head swept back and forth solemnly. "The bench isn't as deep as it once was. We can't lose anyone else—not even you."

"Will she be dragging you to the games again this year?" I asked Ashley as she stomped on another box.

"Probably, unless I can schedule my hikes for every Saturday until the season ends. But I don't feel like being stuck in the woods for four hours every week. Why can't your games be shorter?" She punched my shoulder.

My arm went numb. "Are you trying out for the team, Ashley?" I rubbed the spot, trying to get the blood flowing to my fingertips again. "That fucking hurt."

"Shouldn't you be a bit tougher now that you're officially first string?"

"Shouldn't you be making sure you're not injuring a star player right before the season starts?"

She sucked her teeth. "You're not a star yet."

"Thanks for the vote of confidence, but I will be." I bowed, waving my arm for extra flair before snapping upright. "How did you know I was starting this year? I thought the roster wasn't live until this weekend. And how did you know about Trevor? I just found out."

"It was posted all over the STFU Dirt account."

I groaned. "I thought it got shut down last year." The social media account had reported on a few of Mikelson's freak-outs, which led to even more team torture. Other campus gossip, from the petty to shocking, would spread in days, if not hours.

Ashley rubbed her hands together, looking comic-book diabolical. "Maybe. It's back up now, under a new name, but the same juicy gossip."

"Feels like a waste of time. And if they report on Mikelson again, he'll probably turn us to corpses on the practice field." How much time were people spending soaking up every illicit, on-campus whisper? I didn't have time for distractions like that.

Taylor propped her hands on her hips. "Come on, Reid. You know I need to know all the dirt first. And thank you for confirming the post. Ninety-nine percent of what's on there turns out to be true. Did you hear about Professor Hess? Turns out his sabbatical won't be super relaxing with the twins he'll be taking care of. The ones that belong to his favorite student from last fall and not his wife."

"You're going to rot your brain with that trash." Who cared what other people did?

"How else am I supposed to pass time between classes? But back to you—I'm sure you'll show everyone what you can do this year." Taylor's words might've sounded like flirtation to anyone listening in, but where football was concerned, she was dead serious. "I can't take another loss. We have to win this season." She gripped my arm, and her gaze drilled into my soul.

I pulled away.

Her intensity was just one more reason she would never make my list. I didn't want a hook-up who might try to murder me in my sleep after a missed pass. Not that she couldn't break into my room to do that anyway.

I picked some cardboard scraps Ashley left behind off the ground. "You two in a double?"

"Triple." Ashley flicked her fingers toward the brick building behind her. "But our new roommate is still moving in her stuff."

Walking over to the dumpster, I tossed the trash away. "Who is it? Not Megan." She'd been a one-woman, vomiting and screaming wrecking crew every weekend.

Ashley shook her head. "God, no. We managed to shake her after last year. Our new roommate is a transfer. She seems nice. As long as she's not an uber slob like Taylor, we won't have any problems."

"I'm not a slob," Taylor huffed.

"I'm just glad we have three singles." Ashley walked backward toward the apartment entrance. "And I don't have to extract your earrings from my sheets like bedbugs."

"Whatever." Taylor hurried after her. "I needed to find the perfect pair for Welcome Wagon." She looked over her shoulder and waved. "See you there, Reid?"

"Of course." I spread my arms wide. "It wouldn't be a true STFU school year without hundreds of people getting shit-faced at an oversized pond."

The pair disappeared through the archway.

"STFU!" a guy shouted through an open window. A few more opened, and the chants began.

I cupped my hands around my mouth and called, "Bull-dogs!" back, and they carried on with the fight song.

Spinning around, I rammed straight into a box. A person and a box, and the box went flying. At least it wasn't the person—no, not a person. A girl.

She stared at me with wide, unblinking eyes for a second before they darted down to her half-crushed box.

"Shit, sorry!" I sounded like a pathetic freshman on the wrong side of things already while she was hot and surely an upperclassman. "I swear I'm saving my gracefulness for this weekend."

"Obviously." Her head tilted, and her black braids brushed against her shoulders.

"I'm Reid. Let me help you with that." I gave her my not-all-jocks-are-assholes smile.

Instead of smiling back, her gaze dropped to the crumpled box, and suddenly she flung herself over it like she was falling on a grenade. "I got it. Don't worry about it."

Her whole body was spread out over the box like a starfish. Her non-STFU t-shirt rode up, showing off the sweet spot expanse of skin just above her jeans. "I got it. I'm good," she promised from the sidewalk.

A guy walked past, pushing a dresser on a hand cart.

"It's my fault. Let me help." Crouching beside her to grab the box, I bit back my groan as my muscles let me know how much they didn't appreciate this after a full practice.

"Thanks." She scrambled up and tried to wedge herself between me and the box. "But no thanks."

Two more guys walked past carrying a couch.

"Are you sure?" I shuffled back.

"No, don't worry. Thank you." She folded in on herself, and her gaze darted over her shoulder. "Damnit, this is going to take forever." Her arms flapped down at her sides when she crouched back down. "You're still here." She shielded her eyes from the sun and looked up at me.

I dragged my attention away from the curve of her ass less than a couple feet from my face. "Why are you acting so embarrassed? Is this a box full of dildos?"

A couple people walking past with TVs glanced at us.

Her grip tightened on the box. "I wish." She clamped her hand over her mouth and avoided my gaze, before peering up at me with flushed cheeks.

"I..." My voice dried up, and I got lost in those dark eyes of hers. At least three different shades of brown, they had a depth I hadn't been prepared for.

Brownie batter eyes filled with both humor and embarrassment stared back at me. She was stunning, sunrise-stunning in a girl next door kind of way. But it was her t-shirt that finally snapped me out of the stupor where I'd forgotten how to form words.

"Cool shirt," I blurted out way too loudly for how close we were.

She glanced down at the yellow and white Weyland-Yutani Corp logo on the black shirt and tugged it away from her chest. "You're a big Aliens fan?"

Freckles dotted the bridge of her nose, and some traveled up the center with a sprinkling on her forehead.

"I've seen it at least five times this semester already."

"Isn't today move-in day?"

"I got here earlier." I kept it vague. No need to pull out the football player card already. "And who isn't an Aliens franchise fan?"

Her hands rested on her thighs, just above where her jeans were ripped at the knees. "Five-year-old me. I couldn't sleep for a month after accidentally watching it one day on TV."

"Same." I cringed internally. Again with the blurting. Girls love guys who are piss themselves scared of movies, even if I was six at the time.

She jutted her chin out toward the box that got more mysterious by the second and sighed. "Were you mentioning something about helping?" She chewed on the corner of her bottom lip. "But you have to promise me you won't make fun of me."

I nodded, ready to shout, *what's in the box?*

"Promise." She held up her little finger.

Confusion crackled through me. "A pinkie promise?"

Her finger hovered in front of my face.

"Don't think I've made one of those in a long time."

Her lips scrunched right along with her nose. "The eternal bond of pinkie promises still stands."

I hooked my pinkie around hers and flushed at the brush of her skin against mine. "It's my fault your stuff fell in the first place. I promise."

Her smile brightened her whole face and made me forget half the aches that still needed nursing from practice. "We should probably get to it." Her gaze dropped back to our intertwined fingers. "I'm sure you've got somewhere to be."

"Right." I pulled my hand back and ripped my focus away.

She stepped out of the way and rolled the box over fully. A tinkling sound like a plastic waterfall accompanied the movement. Between the curb and the sidewalk, a rainbow slew of plastic blocks littered the grass.

"You're into Legos."

"Lego." She glanced over her shoulder at the other upperclassmen moving into their dorms and brushed the pieces into a small pile.

I grabbed a handful. "This is a lot more than one." I dumped them and a crap-ton of grass inside the box. The blades of green stuck out amongst the sharp edges of the multicolored pieces.

She dropped in another handful of pieces. "Lego is the plural of Lego, like deer and deer." She swept her arms across the grass, gathering up more. "It's a thing I do when I need my brain to turn off. Building helps me focus. I'm not just playing with them or anything."

"Who gives a fuck if you like to play with Legos?" I added another handful to the box.

She stared at me, squinting in the sun over my shoulder. "Come on—if your backpack opened up in the middle of campus and a bunch of Barbie dolls fell out, you wouldn't be the least bit embarrassed?"

"Probably, at least a little bit." I grinned. "But they don't make five-figure Barbie sets."

Her lips quirked up. "How would you know?" That smile of hers could melt a guy's heart. The heat beating down on me intensified under her teasing scrutiny. "Have you been searching for the perfect Barbie Dream Mansion?"

"Just a guess." I'd played with action figures way too late and had gotten teased like hell for it, just missing the cusp where superheroes were a thing everyone thought was cool. "But maybe you know better than I do. What else do you have in here?" I pulled back the flap of the box.

"My toy fixation ends with Lego." She slapped it closed. "So I can zone out for a few hours."

I stepped back and raised my hands in mock surrender. "No harm. No foul." My Lego building ended with—buildings. Tall, solid rectangles, nothing particularly interesting. "What are you building? Or do you just tinker?"

"The Death Star."

"Of course, it is."

Her eyes cut to mine, defensive and with a hint of hurt. "What's that supposed to mean?"

My heart lurched. "I didn't mean it in a bad way. Seems fitting for a nerd."

Her lips parted.

"And I should know. One of my best friends, Ezra, is one. He's got everything *Aliens, Predator, Dune, Terminator* and more all over his bedroom. I've watched all of them with him. I didn't mean it in a bad way."

"Not all nerds are the same, you know?"

"They aren't? Guess I shouldn't tell you he's been coveting a Terminator T-800 Lego bust for a while now."

She swatted my shoulder. "He has not."

I didn't hate the playful way she touched me. It made me want to lean in closer. "Definitely is." I pointed at my house across the street. "My roommates and I were planning on pitching in to get it for him for Christmas since those sets are so insanely expensive."

"I'm a fan of fandoms."

"Is that what we're called now?"

"We?" Her eyebrow lifted. "Outing yourself as a fellow nerd?"

I folded my arms across my chest. "I thought we were called fans of fandom?"

The way her lips pursed made me want to smooth them out with a kiss. That hit me like a sideswipe to my brain. I'd known her for all of six minutes. I'd obviously been without female company for a bit too long.

We switched to picking instead of scooping to get the scattered stranglers hiding in the grass.

"Did you just move in?" I grimaced. Thanks, Captain

Obvious. Not like she was moving boxes into a new apartment on move-in day. Real freaking smooth.

"It's my first day on campus."

"You're a transfer?" I glanced at her before going back to picking up the last of the pieces still embedded in the lawn. Did she know about Welcome Wagon? It would only be right for her to immerse herself in her new campus.

"That's usually how that works. I transferred from the University of Queensland."

I was so focused on the gentle brush of her hands across the grass and imagining them over the back of my hand that it took a few beats for her response to sink in.

I popped my head up. "Like in Australia?"

"Do you know of another?" She chuckled and dropped her handful of Lego into the box.

"I'm not hearing an Australian accent." If she came to Welcome Wagon, maybe we could hang out. I could make sure she didn't get shitty, watered-down beer.

"I'm not an Aussie."

"Reid, you good?" Cole called out from behind me. I squeezed the pieces in my palm so hard they stabbed me. Annoyance built with each of his footfalls closer. I'd never cared before about Cole showing up. He was one of my best friends.

He was also notorious for being an unreliable wingman —there was a 25% chance of him leaving with whoever you were talking to. For some reason, the thought of that happening with her really fucking sucked.

"Just helping our new neighbor," I shouted back, hoping he'd go inside the house.

He walked around the front of the car. "Oh hey, new neighbor. I'm Cole." He'd deepened his voice a hair.

"Leona." She smiled and held out her hand.

Shit. I hadn't even asked for her name or introduced myself, but Cole had.

I glared at him. "I'm helping Leona pick up some stuff she dropped." I gave her a wink, and she snorted like we already had an inside joke. It tempered some of my annoyance.

"Okay, some stuff I made her drop."

"This looks like a Millennium Falcon mix." He dropped to one knee.

I glared. Maybe I could push him into the slowly rolling traffic. Since when had he become a Lego expert?

"Close, it's the Death Star." She poured more into the box and flashed him a smile.

"You don't have to help. We've got it." I pointedly stared at him and tilted my head back toward the house.

He looked at me and back to her. "I don't mind." His smirk was punch-me-in-the-face gloating.

A bolt of annoyance streaked through my chest. The last thing I needed was Leona wandering down the stairs of The Zoo after a night out with Cole.

"Griff and Hollis were looking for you. They said to have you find them once you got home."

He glanced back at the house. "Really? Okay, I'll go check it out." He dusted his hands off on his jeans and stood with a wince and groan. "Nice meeting you, Leona. Are you coming to Welcome Wagon tonight?"

I slammed my lips shut, clenching my teeth. I wanted to punch him in the dick. I'd been working up to maybe asking her, and he'd swooped in and done it himself. Not that I wanted to go with her, but just make sure she knew it was happening and maybe have a friendly face to see if she went. I was being neighborly, and she was new.

"Is that a place or an event?" She folded over the flaps of

the box, sounding more distracted than when she'd been talking to me.

Some of the tightness in my chest loosened.

Cole walked backward across the street. "It's the unofficial kick-off to the school year. It's over by Poe Pond behind the Arboretum. There's an old covered wagon statue even though Pennsylvania isn't exactly on the Oregon Trail. It's tradition."

"Sounds like it could be fun." She lifted the box and rocked back and forth, shifting the contents and smiling. A small wave was all she could manage with her arms around the box.

I would not beat the shit out of Cole. I repeated that in my head over and over and glared at him until he was on the other side of the street.

"Are you going too?" She peered over at me, and I froze like I'd forgotten how my muscles worked.

I cleared my throat. "Most of my roommates would drag me there against my will no matter what." Shrugging, I tried to play it cool. "I'll probably be there."

"Cool, then maybe I'll see you there." Her smile brightened, and I couldn't stop my goofy grin in return.

"Maybe you will."

Her gaze lifted to the slamming door to The Zoo. "Is that one your house?"

"Yeah."

There was a flicker in her gaze, but I had no idea what it meant. "I guess we'll probably see each other pretty often then."

"Probably." My mouth felt dry. I cleared my throat. "Did you need help with the rest of your boxes?" I reached for it.

"I'm good. This was the last one. I'll see you around, neighbor." She turned and walked toward the brick archway that led to the center of the apartments built around a central, common grass area.

"See you, Leona." I backed away, this time checking behind me to make sure I wasn't going to ram into someone else. Somehow, I didn't think if I did it again that it would be nearly as enjoyable as it had been with her.

Inside the house, I kicked off my shoes.

Cole tossed a wrapped sandwich at me that he'd most likely stolen from the cafeteria. "If you wanted some alone time with our new neighbor, you didn't have to lie about Griff wanting me, you asshole. And after I got this for you on the way home."

"I wouldn't have had to lie if you could take a damn hint."

"You know that's not one of my strong suits." He cracked open his soda and gulped it down like it was juice. "I'm going to sleep. Practice wrecked me."

"What did Mikelson have to say to you?"

Cole stiffened. "More of the same bullshit he always does. I can't wait until he's not riding my case like this anymore." His tone was more hard-edged than Cole usually managed. He reserved that for people on his absolute shit list, and I'd only ever known one other person to sit there outside of Mikelson—Kennedy Campbell.

"But then we wouldn't have a common enemy." I unwrapped the turkey and cheese sandwich.

"There's a certain Philly rival team we could direct all our hate to."

Irritation blistered along my skin. A loss to Fulton U was not an option again. "We do that anyway." I devoured half the food in what felt like two bites without even tasting it. "Is everyone else already asleep?"

Cole nodded. "This shit is only going to get harder once

classes and study halls start. I'm not looking forward to it."

He dragged his hands down his face and up through his hair, pulling the dark brown mass up in odd angles. "I know one thing you're definitely looking forward to though. Seeing your new friend Leona." He sing-songed her name. "So close, right across the street."

He flicked the blinds open to peer at the brick building across from us, sending bright light streaming into the room. "She was pretty."

Beautiful. "Just chill with that. It was one conversation."

"If it was just one conversation, why were you trying to keep me from talking to her?"

I tensed, shifting my gaze. "I just didn't want you bothering her. She's new and doesn't need you hovering around her. Weirding her out." I chomped down on the remaining half of my sandwich.

"She didn't seem weirded out. She seemed to like it a lot actually. And if she's coming to Welcome Wagon, maybe I'll—"

My heart pounded so hard that my brain throbbed. "Would you stop! What did I say before about distractions? No distractions, right?"

"No distractions, hmm." He looked at me out of the corner of his eye. "If you say so. I'm going to go pass out. Don't leave without me." He ran up the stairs, shaking the whole house.

I finished my sandwich and couldn't stop myself from checking out the window again.

Leona came back outside and jumped into her car with her phone pressed against her ear. Where was she off to? I shook my head. I needed to get some sleep and stop fixating on my new neighbor. Although maybe I'd see her later— later tonight.

3

LEONA

I glanced across the street at the townhouse Reid had pointed to earlier, and my stomach fluttered like a school of kites had taken up residence in it. His laugh had been rich, like warm honey. And he'd invited me to the Welcome Wagon. Well, his roommate had, but I was counting his follow-up question as an invite.

Maybe settling in here wouldn't be too hard after all.

I hopped in my car just as my phone rang.

"Hey, Dad." The word felt like it stuck to the roof of my mouth. There was still weirdness calling him that, like re-learning how to ride a bike. Dad, not Frank, as I'd gotten used to calling him in the sporadic phone and video calls up until six months ago. "I'm on my way. Already moved in all my boxes, you don't have to come all the way here." I shoved my phone into the holder on my dashboard and drove in the direction of his house, but not before chancing another peek at the brick townhouse across the street.

"Move-in day is a big deal on campus. I'm sorry my meeting ran late. I wanted to help you." His words were laced with regret.

A twinge of guilt pinched me. That was the last thing I needed, but I knew how much it meant to him. "I'm twenty-one, Dad. I can handle it." Showing up as the new girl on campus who just happened to be President Oakes's daughter would've made me an instant pariah. Throwing in the dad wrinkle would either drive people away or bring the suck-ups out of the woodwork. I'd had enough of people only wanting to know me for what they could get from me.

"I know you can, but I still wanted to be there." There was an edge of sadness in his voice. We'd already missed so many experiences.

The simple words turned the guilt pinch into a full-on knife slipped between my ribs. "There will be plenty more chances. Lugging a bunch of boxes into my new apartment wasn't exactly exciting."

"It would be for me. I'm so happy you're so close. I don't want to miss a thing." His thick swallow echoed in my ear.

Regret panged in my chest. "You don't have to make my lunches for me and walk me to class every morning." The last thing I wanted to do was make him feel like he had to drop everything and come running if I needed anything. I'd disrupted his life enough and made my awful choices in the past—it felt wrong to show up making demands now.

"You did love it when I cut the crusts off your turkey and cheese sandwiches," he teased.

"When I was seven." I made it to the edge of campus and turned down a street I'd driven many times before. Slowly it was feeling like returning to a place I knew, not one where I had to keep checking the directions to make sure I was going the right way.

"You don't like turkey and cheese anymore?" A strand of sadness sliced through his words like he'd just found out I no longer believed in Santa.

"Who doesn't love turkey and cheese?" Driving down the long, winding, tree-lined driveway, I saw the stone exterior with green and white windows peeking from between the tree trunks. It was different from the house my mom, Andy and I lived in outside of Melbourne. The sprawling five-bedroom bungalow with a wraparound porch meant walking straight out into the edges of the vineyard and felt more laid back, while this house screamed stately. At least it no longer felt like I was walking into a stranger's house, but more like a close friend's.

"Are you sure you don't want to stay at the house? Your room here is a lot bigger and nicer than the on-campus apartments." His voice wasn't as somber now.

"I'm sure. It's much nicer, but I couldn't have friends over." I drove past the carriage houses that had been renovated into offices and drove around the circular driveway to the front steps.

"Why not?"

Switching the call back to my phone, I hopped out of the car. "Come on, Dad. Being introduced as the daughter of the president of the university doesn't feel like the best way to make new friends."

The front door opened before I could even tell him I'd arrived. Even after spending the summer here and seeing him every day, it was still hard to reconcile the dad I'd left behind seven years ago with this grayer version.

"Maybe you're right, but your room is ready for you, and over the breaks, you can stay here too. I know they shut down the dorms and apartments for cleaning. Unless you were planning on going back to your mother's." His body stiffened almost imperceptibly. He wore the same silver oval-rimmed glasses with a shorter, generic businessman's haircut. While some people's default clothes were a t-shirt and jeans, his was a button-down shirt and tie. His jacket probably wasn't too far away, draped over a chair or hooked on the back of his door. It was what happened when meetings could be called at a moment's notice.

I ended the call and walked around the car.

He jogged down the stairs and hesitated.

I opened my arms, and his spread wide, engulfing me. Our getting to know you phase over the past couple of months had been stifled by my intensive studying for online classes to meet the transfer requirements and his non-stop work schedule. There were still awkward moments where neither of us was sure how to act.

"I'll be here for Christmas, Dad."

He beamed, so happy it made my heart ache. "Great, the house is done up so beautifully for Christmas. And we'll have a huge tree. It'll be perfect."

Although he squeezed me extra tight, I didn't complain. A summer of dinners together most nights hadn't quite made up for the long time we'd gone without hugs like these. The guilt of all those years gnawed at the back of my mind.

"I'm sure it will be. I can't wait." Anxiety knotted my stomach thinking of flying back to Australia and setting foot in the house I'd previously called home. I released my grip on him, and he let go too.

What we needed was a chance to reclaim some of our missed years. The ones I'd chosen not to celebrate with him.

He walked me inside the house he'd lived in since being appointed as the St. Francis University president nearly six years ago, just five months after my mom and I left for Australia. To think of him bumping around this huge house all by himself, when we'd been meant to move in with him as a big happy family hurt my heart.

"Are you hungry? I was going to have a quick lunch before my afternoon meetings."

The vaulted ceilings with exposed, rich wood beams and oversized iron light fixtures suspended from the ceiling made the whole house feel part ski chalet and part medieval castle.

"More meetings?"

The circular rooms on either end of the house mimicking towers also helped with the fortress impression. I'd often tried to imagine over the past few months what it would have been like if I'd spent the past six years in this house. If this had been where I brought my friends back to hang out after school, or what the campus would feel like if I'd had years to explore it before applying as a student.

"If I didn't have all these meetings, how would I ever know what time it was?" He chuckled at his joke and rubbed his hands together. "I could whip you up a sandwich. There's still a bit of ham and cheese quiche in here or maybe some roast beef?"

He tugged the fridge open.

I wasn't too hungry, but I knew how much he wanted to make me food. "How about a turkey and cheese. No crusts."

His smile was infectious.

That was the right answer.

Rolling up his sleeves like he was about to go into surgery, he grabbed all the ingredients and set them out. We sat at the table with some lemonade and soft-baked chocolate chip cookies—score!—and talked about the new school year.

I was two bites into the second half of my sandwich when the front door banged open.

"Oakes!" The booming voice rattled the windows.

My heart lurched at the thunderous interruption.

Dad's lips tightened, and his gaze narrowed. He leaned back and dropped his napkin onto the table beside him.

I whipped around to stare at the person who barged in.

A tall, broad man in khakis, a polo shirt and a baseball cap, both embroidered with the St. Francis U bulldog mascot, stormed into the kitchen. "Where do you get off screwing with *my* team?" He jammed a rolled-up packet of papers into the center of his chest.

My dad seemed more annoyed than angry that a total stranger had just waltzed into his house, but not the least bit surprised.

Dad sighed. "You do know this is my home, William."

The man glared. "It's university property," he barked without a hint of shame.

"Would you like me to break into your university-provided home and see how it feels?" Dad never raised his voice, but this was the least diplomatic I'd heard him in all his interactions at work or elsewhere. He was always glad-handing and gracious.

"I'd like to see you try." He threw out the challenge.

Why had a university employee broken in and started yelling like a lunatic?

Dad's jaw clenched, and he folded his hands, placing them on the table. "To what do I owe the pleasure of this visit that couldn't wait until our meeting tomorrow?"

A thick stack of papers landed beside me with a thump. I jumped and dropped my hand into my lap. Old feelings of hearing my parents hushed arguing in the other room and pretending I couldn't hear them came flooding back. But I was in the middle this time—literally. There was no quick and easy escape.

"What the hell is this bullshit?"

Dad nudged the edge of the stack and ran his finger

under the word 'Budget' printed at the top. "I'm fairly certain you can read, William."

That was the closest I'd ever heard of my dad using snark.

The man glowered. "You slashed my budget."

"We've gone over this. A one percent decrease, as agreed, after your football budget came in ten percent under its generous budget for the previous year. Hardly a gutting." Dad leaned back, his calm returning. He reacted like this happened all the time, which put me less on edge that a random man had barged into my dad's house glowering and grumbling.

"Our end-of-the-season activities were cut short, but this year, they won't be. We need that money." His face flushed, and veins stood out prominently on his neck and forehead like he was a second away from an explosion.

"You mean because you lost and you didn't get your parade? We can cut back on streamers."

The man stepped forward, jabbing a finger at Dad. "My program deserves every cent." His voice boomed with bluster and venom.

I braced myself for him to throw a punch. Maybe I could grab my chair and fling it at him, but my dad seemed as calm as ever.

"Ticket sales account for a hefty portion of the budget as well as your salary, which, need I remind you, is bigger than mine. The botany department needed repairs to their green-house after the storm last year. If you hadn't been shouting over everyone else for half of the meeting, you'd have known that." Dad remained calm and even, which seemed to infuriate the man even more. Dad threw me a smile and gathered our plates, walking them to the sink. Growing up, he'd always been the relaxed one, even with his love of ties, blazers and cufflinks. My mom would freak out about every little thing, but Dad was always there to stop the churning waters around the rocking boat.

"Who the hell cares about flowers and plants?" William followed him, his footsteps rattling the glass in the cabinets.

"Bees," I mumbled and took the last bite of my sandwich.

The man's gaze shot to me. Either that mumble had been a little louder than I'd thought or he was attuned to even the slightest insult.

I shot him a warm smile, which seemed to do the trick, and his face flushed even redder.

That vein looked ready to jump from under his skin.

I picked up a gooey cookie while maintaining the smile and took a bite. It had been a while since I'd seen a grown man throw a temper tantrum. Usually, they were way too drunk at the vineyard after a wine tasting and way too loud about how much money they had intended to spend but weren't now that they'd been cut off by the bar. But this guy was taking meltdown to a whole new level.

William's eyes narrowed. "Dipping your ink in the university well?" His lips twisted in a self-satisfied grin.

Shocked revulsion smacked into me, and I scrunched up my face, not trying to hide my reaction.

Dad marched back over, stepping between us, and dropped his hand to my shoulder with a reassuring squeeze. "This is my daughter, Leona."

The man's fury dropped away for a second, and his gaze jumped from Dad back to me. "You have a daughter? I didn't know that."

"Polite conversation isn't your forte. She transferred in this year. She's a viticulture major." Dad said it with the kind of pride reserved for med student parents.

I sunk a little lower in my chair, wishing I'd made my escape earlier. Having Dad brag about me didn't freak me out too much. It often felt like he was making up for lost time, which he was, but it wasn't usually to a man staring at me like I was a half-crushed bug and he wanted to finish the job.

"What the hell is viticulture?"

That was the normal reaction most people had to my major.

"It's the study of soil and grapes to make wine."

William's furry, salt-and-pepper eyebrows dipped low like he'd never heard of the 6,000-year-old drink. "Like plants and shit. Interesting that your little budget diversion comes just as your daughter is transferring in."

My dad sighed. "That had nothing to do with it. Viticulture isn't the only major that uses that facility. The greenhouse wasn't safe to occupy. It needed to be repaired and updated, and I'm sure the boosters will spring for extra confetti, if you do win this year."

"When we win this year." The apparent football coach's voice sounded like ground glass.

"I hope you do."

The man snatched the stack of papers off the table and stormed out just like he'd stormed in. Did he walk into every room that way? The heavy wood door at the front of the house slammed behind him.

Tension left the room like air being let out of a balloon, but it wasn't back to the easiness of before his arrival.

"Is that one of the perks of being the president?"

He shook his head and chuckled, but his shoulders were still tight. "All that glitters isn't gold. Mikelson is one of my biggest headaches. But football is king around here, so there's not much I can do about it. His whole program is a necessary pain in the ass. Between his players' bad behavior and his, it's a wonder I don't have even more gray hair than I do now."

"His team causes problems on campus?" The athletes at my old college hadn't been any rowdier than the rest of the student body, though things could get crazy when there was a rugby match.

"Constantly." His jaw clenched, and he dropped into the seat beside me. "They're a hundredth of the school population, and it seems like the whole program takes up at least a quarter of every nightmare fire that needs to be put out. We have nationally ranked programs in everything from computer science to viticulture." He gestured to me. "But football is all anyone talks about. It brings attention to the school, but half the time, I feel like it overshadows all the other great things taking place on campus."

"With a coach like that, I'm surprised they aren't hearing every word he says from three states over." I ducked my head to catch his eye. "Football season's only a few months, right? Is it happening right now?" My sports knowledge was pretty lacking. I still didn't understand Aussie rules football or rugby, and I'd seen far more of those games in the past seven years than I had American football.

He laughed. "You've been away too long. For the die-hard fans, it's year-round, which isn't a bad thing when it comes to fundraising efforts."

A rhythmic knock on the entryway to the kitchen put a smile on Dad's face.

I'd learned that knock over the past few months.

Amy, Dad's executive assistant, strode into the kitchen. A much different arrival than our previous not-guest. Today, she wore a black pantsuit and a cream top with one of those floppy fabric ties that I could never hope to get right. Her light brown hair was neatly tucked into a low bun at the base of her neck.

She and I had spent a lot of time together over the past few months, and I still wasn't sure how old she was. Mid-to-late thirties maybe.

"Dr. Oakes, are you ready for your two o'clock?"

He glanced down at his watch and pulled his jacket off the back of the dining room chair. "Yes, I am, Amy."

"Good to see you as always, Leona." Her smile was warm and looser than her more public façade. She was probably the only person better than Dad at appearing even-keeled, never seeming to get flustered.

"Hey, Amy."

"How was it settling into your new apartment?" Her full attention was on me, like me moving into a campus apartment was an event she'd been waiting ages to hear all about.

"It's fine. I only had a few minutes to talk to my new roommates and put their numbers in my phone, but they seem nice." Although their bickering made me feel like I'd be third-wheeling it a lot this semester.

Her smile dimmed a hint. "I'm sorry I wasn't able to reserve you your own apartment. With the late transfer approval, most of the campus housing was already taken."

"No problem. It's my fault for leaving it so late."

Dad bent over and kissed my temple. "It's never too late, dear." He smoothed down his tie and buttoned his jacket. "Are you going to hang out here? Maybe have dinner with me later?" There was a hopefulness in his eyes.

The guilt wall was back. My mind flashed to the guy who'd knocked into me earlier and helped me clean up. Reid. He'd—well, his roommate had mentioned Welcome Wagon, and in between the bickering, my roommates had too. It seemed like it could be just the kind of college experience I'd been looking for. But dinner with Dad was never a bad thing, and he was so excited. "Su—"

Amy butted in, cringed a little and faced Dad. "You're booked through nine this evening for the honors student welcome dinner." Her apologetic gaze flicked to mine.

His schedule was always packed and would only get busier now that the semester had started.

His face fell. "Right. I forgot." He'd be lost without her.

"Don't worry, Dad." I scooted my chair back and hugged him. "I was hoping to do some of the new student activities and get oriented with campus anyway. It's totally fine."

He straightened his tie. "Maintenance came by to change the locks on the house. They do it at the start of every year, so the new set of keys is on the desk in my office. Make sure you grab them before you go. Let's make a standing dinner date, and Amy can make sure my calendar is always empty. And you know you can always stop by my office anytime."

"I know." Although it was only Amy here, the heat of embarrassment crept up from under my chin. I hated how much he needed to reassure me that I could come see him anytime, and I hated how much I needed the reassurances.

"I'm just so happy to have you here. I don't want to waste a single opportunity."

"We won't." I swallowed past the lump lodged in my throat. "But you're busy running this whole place, and I'll be busy once classes start. We'll figure it out."

He nodded, gave me another hug and followed Amy out of the house.

I wandered down the hall toward his office. The walls were lined with artists' renderings of the campus at various stages in history as well as pictures of groundbreakings and new buildings. Other than the kitchen, the first floor felt like a museum. The spaces were meant to hold large groups of people, but upstairs the living areas felt more comfortable. The second floor was a place I'd come to think of as home.

Inside the office, I spotted the keys on the desk beside a silver-framed picture of the two of us when I was seven and way too big to be on his shoulders, but there I was.

A wall of emotion swamped me. Back then, the biggest thing I'd worried about was what toy to blow my allowance on. My childhood perception of my parents was that they were infallible and had all the answers to the universe's great questions. I'd believed they were both the best people in the world.

I'd been half right.

There were other photos of him shaking hands with dignitaries and other important people, but at least half of the pictures on his desk and hanging on the wall in frames were of the two of us.

The gnawing guilt built up again, and I blinked back tears.

My phone buzzed, snapping me out of my trip down memory lane. I checked the text.

Taylor: Hey, it's Taylor. We're going to go to Welcome Wagon in a couple hours. Want to come with us?

There were those words again. Welcome Wagon. No one at the transfer orientation had mentioned it, but everyone kept bringing it up. It sounded like a big deal. At least as the third wheel, I hadn't been forgotten. It would be easier to show up with other people and also not feel like I was wandering around looking for Reid. If we bumped into each other, we bumped into each other. It wasn't like I'd be looking forward to saying hi to him with his smile that made my stomach feel as if I were ready to take flight.

Me: Sure, I'm on my way back to the apartment.

Of course, he had said he'd be there. Probably with a line of women vying for his attention. This was a massive campus, but he and his friend had struck me as the kind of gorgeous that didn't go unnoticed. And I wasn't here to throw myself at the first hot guy who spoke to me.

But maybe I'd wear one of my better t-shirts tonight. Just in case...

4

REID

Hundreds of bodies streamed toward the pond, which was more like a shallow lake. It was an oval that was split into five quadrants for this party. Seniors and athletes filtered to the left to take up our spots, while everyone else had to walk around the whole rest of the pond.

I scanned the crowd, kicking myself for not getting Leona's number. Would she show? She'd seemed unsure before heading into her apartment. Maybe I should've picked her up.

Three sprayers shot water high into the air, rippling the waist-deep pond. There were students on the shore ready to jump under the falling water with shower caps, bars of soap, and rubber ducks. Welcome Wagon was ridiculous and random, and I loved it.

A thrill rushed through me as I soaked in the whole scene. Being named to the starting lineup was one thing, but kicking off Welcome Wagon made everything feel real for the first time. All eyes on us, just like they should be.

I stood straighter and walked over to the rest of the guys.

"Cole and Reid, are you going to The Deadwood later?" A junior who I'd had classes with before appeared in front of us, walking arm in arm with her roommate. "I'd love for you to show me around." Her gaze raked over me like I was a juicy steak. Did I bask in it? Maybe a little.

Cole laughed. "Everyone knows we're not allowed in there during the season."

Her smile widened, and she leaned in, holding her hand up to one side of her mouth. "We heard there might be another place where all you guys are hanging out. A secret spot?" The play for her invite to the no-invite club was beyond shameless.

Cole and I exchanged looks and shook our heads. I hoped my look of confusion was half as good as his because right now, Cole had *me* convinced he didn't even know his own name. The rumors had always flown around about a possible hang-out spot for the STFU football team, and it was a testament to team loyalty that no one had broken the pact yet. Outsiders were only allowed in by a full vote of everyone in attendance, and that had happened on rare occasions.

"No, I haven't heard anything about that," I said.

Cole straightened the yellow duck float around his waist. "If you find out, let me know. I want in on it."

Both their shoulders dropped, and their frowns were almost comical, but the junior brightened a second later. "Will you find us later?"

I waved my pool noodle noncommittally. "We'll try." Not happening. This was a chance to hang with the team. And maybe a new neighbor I wanted to be sure was settling in okay.

That seemed to be enough of a chance for them, and they rushed back to their herd of friends farther down the hill.

"What was that?" Cole's gaze darted my way with a shit-eating grin.

"What was what?" Why had he been in my face with these big grins all afternoon?

"No invites to The Library."

I glanced behind me. "Isn't the whole point to keep that quiet?"

"Sure, but that doesn't mean you haven't been known to show off, especially when it comes to a certain type of classmate." He glanced back to the colorful pack of women screaming "woo!" at nothing in particular with arms raised over their head, sliding in the damp grass in their flip-flops.

The Library was what the football team's hidden, invite-only hangout had been dubbed. Not that a bunch of football players talking about going to the library wouldn't *also* raise a lot of red flags. But the word didn't jump out to people on campus and draw more attention when we made plans out in the open. With Coach on our asses about non-football-related activities and not wanting to deal with the mob scene at campus bars, the alternative was a welcome respite.

"Remember what I said about distractions? What happened to Griff? If there hadn't been an injury during training camp, he'd be second string this season. I don't want that to happen to any of us."

"Oh, now that you're first string, you're more selective?"

"Always have been, unlike you." I shrugged and tried not to think too much about my new neighbor, who'd driven off earlier today. "Stop trying to piss me off, and let's enjoy the party."

"Don't we always?" He grinned and grabbed me, charging forward into the sea of people who welcomed us with high fives, fist bumps, offered drinks neither of us took and enough rounds of the fight song to burn it into our brains if it weren't already tattooed there.

Seniors on the team flowed down the hill in waves, some making as much noise as possible to signal their arrival. Not that we weren't just as guilty. The fawning adoration of legions of fellow students cheering us on was a perk I didn't pass on. Not when the alternative was those same people turning around and sneering after a loss. Better get our fill while it was possible.

All five of us from The Zoo had gotten our gold wristbands and grabbed spots close to the shore that still provided an easy escape, if needed. Being at the center of the crowd and soaking up all the attention was a perk of the game I'd bask in until I couldn't anymore. Scrutiny off the field freaked out some guys, like Ezra, but not me, not when I'd experienced the alternative of being invisible or, worse, being the object of ridicule.

Even glares after a loss didn't compare to people sneering at you and hating on you just for existing. Being a part of the team meant I never had to experience that on my own again. Of all the sports teams on campus, football was the biggest. The end of last season had been another demoralizing loss, but my roommates and I were all starting this year. For some reason, that made me believe this season would be magic. The electricity that crackled in the air during training camp had to mean this was finally our year. Losing to Fulton U wasn't an option yet again.

We all only had two more years to prove ourselves and secure a pro spot, which was nothing short of a miracle for even the best and most dedicated players, but it had to happen for all of us. I wasn't letting the possibility of anything else enter my mind.

The Grilling Society, a campus club devoted to all things chargrilled and delicious, had at least twelve grills going between the junior and senior section behind the crowd to stop everyone from getting a face full of meaty fumes from all the charcoal pumping out smoke. Lines stretched on thirty students deep, but we had our servings brought to us on platters—poor freshmen.

Face paint, body paint, costumes—everyone was out in full force for the first big event on campus. The team had their own spot next to the seniors by the edge of the manmade pond.

Kegs had been rolled out, and there was a cordoned-off area complete with wristbands for upperclassman. No one wanted to get busted serving minors out in the open. The expulsions and suspensions of Christmas past weren't experiences anyone wanted visited on them after Mikelson booted them off the team. Guys had lost their scholarships and couldn't finish their degrees.

Music rumbled through speakers with a full DJ set-up. We organized the hell out of our chaos. It was one of the few nights campus police let this kind of madness slide.

Welcome Wagon began decades ago when the practice field had been closer to the pond and the team would dive in to cool off after the inferno of the locker room back before they had AC during their first official practices of the season. That had been the winningest team in STFU history. They'd clinched six consecutive bowl game titles.

In the decades after, others came to watch, then participation and the party grew up around it. Our current play-off situation wasn't anywhere near what it had been in the past, but that didn't stop everyone from showing up year after year. It was bigger than us now.

The edge of the pond where all the ducks crapped was left open for the late coming freshmen who would find out about this or had older siblings who'd clued them into it.

Sophomores had the area beside them where the runoff made the ground soggy and muddy. They'd be slipping and sliding into the pond by the time midnight rolled around, pretending to be drunk or actually scoring booze from an idiot upperclassman.

Juniors were out of the muck on the higher ground, closer to the grills and kegs.

Seniors took up the fully elevated spot beside the metal wagon statue with their own grills, kegs, and an entire bar complete with a bartender in a bowtie one of the frats had wheeled out. They must've been hard up for pledges. Some of the partygoers were in *Oregon Trail*-worthy gear inside the statue, but I was sure the beer hats weren't standard issue back then.

The athletes' section butted up against the senior section, meaning we got access to everything they set up.

"Reid and Cole, you going to keep Hollis safe this year?" a guy called out, raising his cup high in the air.

"You know it," I shouted back. Being part of on-the-field protection for Hollis had pros and cons. It meant that even on a sixty-person team, people could pick me out in a crowd. It also meant any sack was met with daggers from my class-mates, alumni, people at the drive-through and some professors. Left tackle was a high visibility position, espe-cially when I fucked up. This season, I was determined not to fuck up. I wouldn't let my team down, let my dad down. I wouldn't let myself down by failing.

Lawn chairs were out, and the sun was headed for the

horizon, so things hadn't devolved into absolute debauchery yet. I couldn't keep my gaze from scanning the new arrivals, looking for a face I'd only seen for a few minutes.

Griff waved me over with a drink in hand. Ezra glanced up, keeping his hands in his pockets and his hat shading his eyes.

Hollis, Griff, Ezra, Cole and I were assigned side-by-side triples freshman year, and we had worked as a tight-knit unit ever since, even when we were playing on different strings.

Hollis came up beside me and grabbed the noodle I'd looped across the back of my neck. "Planning on floating around for a while?"

I yanked it back and hit him with it. "Or using it to save some drunk asshole who doesn't remember to stand up."

Students called all our names and those of the rest of our teammates from all sides, as though us acknowledging them elevated their campus cred. Fans wearing jerseys or body paint with our numbers on them descended on the rest of the team. I was infinitely more recognizable with Hollis beside me. With Cole added in, we were the merry three of the offensive line.

Ezra walked over, holding up his phone with a count-down clock already running. "We're all out of here in an hour." His intensity served him well on the field, but off it, he paced like a caged animal, determined to break free at the first chance.

Hollis rested his hand on Ezra's shoulder. "Calm down. It will be okay. Things will not get out of hand."

Ezra tilted his head. "Like last year, when the captain of the basketball team had to get twelve stitches in his scrotum?"

We all winced and shifted. Vicarious nausea rolled

through me. Hollis gained his voice back first. "It was a freak accident."

"Or the year before when the captain of the lacrosse team had to get eight stitches in his forehead?"

"He was being a drunk asshole."

Ezra stared at the water like he thought it might've been stocked with man-eating piranha since last year. "Doesn't matter. The pattern is escalating and might be turning into a curse. It's moving up the ranks in terms of sport and severity of the injury. We get into the water and we get out, then we're gone." He jerked his thumb back toward the hill as people were pouring over on their way to the party.

He'd always been the stoic, worrier of the group.

I took a cup of beer held out for me. "This season can't be cursed. We're all here together. We've got this. The only curse will be you giving yourself an ulcer before we lift that championship trophy overhead at the end of this season." The stars were aligning. Why couldn't he see that? This was finally our time.

Ezra turned to me with a stony look. "Way to curse us before we've even played our first game."

Hollis shook his shoulder. "You worry too much."

"You don't worry enough." Ezra drank from his cup but kept his eyes darting around. He probably expected a rampaging bull to burst through the throngs of people any second.

Hollis handed him another cup like he'd materialized it out of thin air. "We'll go before it gets too late. We've got study hall in the morning before practice anyway."

Everyone groaned.

The two-hour study hall was required three days a week. Coupled with classes, practices and traveling for games, time to eat and sleep were at a premium, which was another reason distractions weren't often welcome during the season. But that didn't stop me from scanning the crowd, searching for a certain Lego aficionado.

Long shadows were cast down the hill. The sun hung just above the horizon. Anticipation swelled in the crowd. Lanterns and glow sticks began to shine, creating a surreal swaying sea effect.

Near the dividing line between the juniors and seniors, I spotted her. It wasn't her dark brown hair or her jeans that I noticed first, but her smile and the black t-shirt with large block writing across the front of it. *So say we all.*

I laughed to myself. Ezra had forced us all to watch *Battlestar Galactica* during training camp, when we could all barely move after our workout sessions. Well, forced us to watch the first episode, then we'd all been dying to finish the rest and binged the entire series in less than a week.

With her red plastic cup in hand, Leona laughed at whatever the person in front of her said. Her hair wasn't in a ponytail anymore. It was half-up and half-down, and the bottom section brushed against the tops of her shoulders.

Cole looped his arm around my shoulder. "It's got to be a girl you're looking at or a batch of fresh burgers off the grill because you're practically drooling." He handed me a cup. "Can it be? I see a sight for the sorest of eyes." He pressed his hand against his forehead and continued his stupid Shakespearean speech. "Our newest neighbor, the fair Leona, seems to have caught your eye."

I shoved my elbow into his side.

"Oof, how is it my fault you like a girl? Some might even call her a distraction."

"Fuck, I hate you. And I didn't say I liked her." Sure, I'd been wondering if she'd show up. And yes, seeing her laughing and smiling with the people around her made me wonder what had made her crack up like that. But it didn't mean I liked her. Even if I did, it didn't mean things would be more than casual at best.

"You didn't have to. It's written all over your face, just like that time you passed out sophomore year with your shoes on and Griff broke out the Sharpies again."

It had taken me an hour with alcohol wipes and raw, burning skin to get the ink off my face. "I still owe him payback for that." I rubbed absently at my cheek.

"Good luck with that. Stop changing the topic. Are you going to go talk to her?"

I took a gulp from my cup and shrugged. "Maybe, in a few. She's talking to people. I'm not just going to rush up to her like an eager freshman...to say what? It's not a big deal."

"Just go over and ask her if she wants some help building the Death Star."

"Why are you pushing me to go over there right now?" I wanted to punch him so hard, but we didn't need any unnecessary injuries this season. I definitely couldn't go bounding toward her like an excited puppy. That kind of over-enthusiasm was a surefire way to turn her off.

"Stop stalling." He nudged me forward.

I dug my heels in. "Stop pushing and leave it alone." But I couldn't stop looking over at her.

She threw her head back, exposing the delicate lines of her throat. How would it feel to run my lips over the soft skin there?

"Just go talk to her." He nudged me forward again. "Ask her how her move-in went. Ask her if she has classes tomorrow. You act like this is the first time you've ever talked to the opposite sex. You had no issue talking to those girls on the hill less than an hour ago."

"Because I didn't care if they actually liked me or not."

His smile widened at my accidental confession.

Even from this far away, she had me blurting shit out I had no right to be thinking, let alone saying. Cole wasn't going to let up though.

"Fine, I'll go talk to her. Just let me get another drink."

5

LEONA

Taylor approached with three red plastic cups with foam spilling over the lips. She and Ashley had introduced me to so many people with more names than I'd ever have a chance of remembering, and I was ready for a break.

"I'll pay for the next round." I waved my wallet in the air.

Ashley reached for a drink and held it in front of my face. "Don't worry about it. Consider it a campus-warming present."

"But we all moved into campus together."

"But it's your first time moving onto campus. Just let us be gracious hosts, Leona." Taylor scrunched her face in mock anger and handed me my drink.

Space was at a premium in the throng of bodies swaying and dancing to the competing music coming from different sides of the lake that everyone called a pond.

"Are you all moved in?" Ashley threw her hair up into a messy ponytail, and I handed her back the cup with her name written on it in marker.

"I didn't have too much—just a couple boxes and my two suitcases."

"You didn't move in your entire walk-in closet like Taylor?"

Taylor leaned in and spoke right next to Ashley's cheek. "I don't want to hear a damn thing when you need to borrow a skirt or a dress."

Ashley shoved her back. "It was a joke. Just kidding. I keep my closet manageable just by stealing your stuff when I need to."

Taylor playfully narrowed her gaze. "Yes, I have a lot of shit, but I have a perfectly good explanation for it."

Ashley tilted her head and raised an eyebrow, waving her hand in a *go on* motion. "And that would be..."

"I love clothes and don't give a crap what anyone else thinks about it." She broke into laughter, and we joined in.

"You're just lucky you got me as a roomie and I always let you have my extra drawer space."

"Why else do you think I keep living with you?" Taylor sipped from her cup.

"That and my dazzling personality." Ashley made spirit fingers in front of her face.

"And spare closet space."

"And surly disposition."

"And free space under your bed. You really don't maximize your available storage."

"Why would I spend my money buying things when you already have ten of everything?" Ashley tapped her cup to Taylor's. Then her hand shot out and gripped my wrist. "Speaking of ten of everything, tell me you didn't throw out your boxes."

They both stared at me intently.

"Not yet. Was I supposed to keep them?"

"Thank god. We both totally forgot we need them for homecoming."

"You need my moving boxes for homecoming?"

"Yes, for the float. We'll have to dumpster dive to find more. So stupid we forgot." Taylor turned to Ashley. "This year, we're winning. I don't care what we have to do, but short of lighting our competitors on fire, we're not losing the damn thing."

Ashley touched my shoulder. "She means our competitors' floats—not the actual people. And we're not going to do that this year. Every year, there are teams of ten that work together to create floats for homecoming. You can only use cardboard, string, glue, paint and tissue paper. It's a tradition."

"You guys love your traditions." My neon orange wristband scraped against my skin. With my red plastic cup and the blanket of beer odor wafting over the crowd, this event was turning out to be even more outrageous than I'd anticipated.

Taylor squealed. "We do. It makes everything that much more fun."

"And cutthroat, it seems." I laughed into my drink.

Ashley's eyes widened, and she stage-whispered, "You have no idea." Straightening, her lips pinched to a quick smile with a glance over her shoulder at Taylor. "We'd love to have you on our team. We only have nine right now, so it's perfect. The build is over a couple weeks. Everyone chips in when they have time, and we also have to have security shifts overnight to protect it. Sabotage is kind of another tradition, but I promise I'll keep Firestarter over here on a tight leash."

"I'd love to. When it comes to building things, I'm your girl." The campus I'd barely explored over the past month had changed so much already, now that everyone was here. At my old uni, it had been a lot of the same people I'd gone to high school with, so it hadn't ever felt like a truly alien place. But my fears about striking out on my own here were fading with how welcoming Ashley and Taylor were being. There were also the neighbors across the road, well, one in particular.

Taylor flung her arms around me. "Perfect!"

"Is that a slip and slide?" I ducked to peer around the heads of the people in front of me.

"Oh yeah, they're a bit late with it this year," Taylor said.

"I wonder if they'll get out those clear hamster ball things again."

Ashley pinched the bridge of her nose. "If they do, they need to keep it out of the pond. I'm not doing another water rescue for some idiot who thinks they can walk on water."

Taylor tapped her cup to Ashley's. "STFU Dirt said the crew team was going to bring their boats out onto the water."

"Was that why the boathouse was locked when we were driving across the bridge this morning?"

"Probably. Let's not have to fish anyone out, or they're going to shut this whole thing down."

"How long's it been going on for?" I asked.

Taylor and Ashley's eyebrows scrunched.

Ashley scrubbed her fingers across her chin. "Eighty years, I think."

"Really?"

Taylor nodded. "Obviously, it was less debaucherous back then. It was only a handful of guys, no women allowed." She crossed her arms and put on a stern face. "But it was the first year they had three of the teams on campus win championships. Thus, the tradition was born. I never asked you about your major."

"Viticulture, the study of grapes to make wine. I'm in the horticulture department." This was usually when the Harry Potter jokes came in.

Ashley stared at me with a stunned look. "I didn't even know we had that as a major."

Someone knocked into me, but in an ocean of bodies, it wasn't the strangest thing. Going to secondary school just outside of Melbourne hadn't quite prepared me for the American collegiate experience. Being able to drink at eighteen meant this level of alcohol-fueled insanity was usually reserved for first years or rugby matches or Aussie rules matches or hell, even cricket matches. Okay, maybe this wasn't completely out of the norm when it came to celebrating a good time, but it did make me feel like I was in a movie.

The area assigned to third years was filled with people, and there were even more coming down the grassy slope that led to the water, but oddly no one was in the pond. People stood around with comically small inner tubes, a few mermaid tails, and a bikini top here and there, but most were in their regular summer clothes.

"Does anyone actually swim?"

"Not until we get the signal. I'm just happy that we're juniors now, and I won't be digging duck crap from under my toenails this time around."

People behind me rocked forward, and voices were raised, not in anger, but it didn't seem to be pointed in my direction. The whole space was getting messier and messier as people exuded a pulsing energy of excitement and anticipation. It was easy to get swept up into the random chants and yelling and just letting go.

"An easy solution is sensible footwear." Ashley pointed to her hiking boots. "I don't have to worry about anyone stepping on my toes or rogue animal turds."

"When they make those in pink, then I'll think about it."

"I'll bedazzle you a pair for next year."

The music was cranked up, dueling from both sides of the pond. The tinny sounds of the freshman side were overwhelmed by the sound system from the upper-classman portion of the banks. Was that an actual DJ booth?

Taylor raised her hand high and waved. "Why is he being so weird? He kept looking at us but wasn't coming to say hi. Maybe he'll score us booze from the primo bar."

Ashley stood on her tiptoes. "He's headed over now."

The crowd was so tight that it took me pretty much forever to turn around, and when I did, I nearly slammed into someone's chest.

Not just any someone.

"Hey, Reid." It came out more breathless than I intended. A flickery flutter filled my stomach that had nothing to do with the watery beer I'd barely finished.

"They've met." There were hushed whispers from Ashley and Taylor behind me.

"Hey, Leona. You came." His eyes were bright and clear, not the glassy drunk version more people in the crowd were showing.

"I did. It's tradition, right? You and Cole got me inter-ested, and then my new roommates sold me on showing up."

He glanced over my shoulder and nodded to them. "I'm glad they convinced you."

"Hey, Reid." They chorused from over my shoulder, and their bodies pushed me forward, nearly toe to toe with Reid.

"Did you guys need more drinks?" His question was for all of us, but his gaze was trained on me. There was a hint of a dimple on his cheek, or maybe it was a cheekbone and jaw muscle fight causing a slight indent against those powerful features. His lips looked soft with a defined little dip above his cupid's bow. Had that spot always been so hot?

In an ocean of people, having his undivided attention heated my skin like the temperature had been jacked up a full five degrees—Celsius.

I glanced down at my nearly full cup. "I don't—"

"Sure!" The girls chirped. One of them knocked the cup out of my hand, and the sloshing beer barely missed Reid. "Maybe Leona could help you carry them."

"Hey, that cost you five bucks."

Their hands were at my back, shoving me forward, straight into his chest. "Sorry, not sorry."

Why were they pawning me off on him? Was he the campus weirdo? They all seemed to know each other, which felt like this could be a set-up. My guard shot up at how all this was coming together. Had they figured out who my dad was?

His hands gripped my shoulders and steadied me. "Thanks for the suggestion…"

I braced my hands against his chest. The room to move had been cut down in the past minute, which might've had a bit to do with the pushy roommates behind me. Looking up, I stared into his pale green eyes. "Sorry."

"You don't have to keep apologizing." He moved beside me and guided me through the crowd, which didn't seem to jostle him nearly as much as I'd been.

"I will when I stop ramming into you." My laugh was

overly loud, and I felt like a heat lamp had been flicked on under my skin.

"I don't mind. Are you ready for classes to start?" He walked past the kegs in kiddie pools, now surrounded by mud.

"No, but that won't stop them from starting. It'll take me a bit of time to get acquainted with the system here, but I'm sure it'll all be fine."

"What made you transfer all the way from Australia?"

"I moved to be closer to my dad. We haven't seen much of each other since I was younger, and I thought it was time." The clean and easy answer that didn't encompass the absolute bonkers reality of the relationship I had with my parents.

"He lives close by then?"

"Not too far, so we get to see each other regularly." Keeping details vague was harder than I'd thought it'd be. How long before other people on campus thought I was hiding a big secret because I was so nonspecific in everything I said? Not that I wasn't hiding a big secret. Obviously, I hadn't thought this whole thing through aside from getting to campus.

"That's cool. My dad's in Boston, so I don't get to see him much. He tries to make it to campus a few times a year to see me though."

He stopped in front of a bar that looked like it belonged in a club, not in the middle of a field. "What would you like?"

"You don't have to pay for me. Or for Ashley or Taylor. I have cash, and I owe them a round anyway." I held up my blue wallet by the strap dangling from my wrist.

With a flick of his arm, he touched me and leaned in.

His thumb brushed along the sensitive skin at the inside of my elbow. Cue jelly leg time.

Once again, his smile was killer, all lips and jaw and cheekbone working in perfect concert to render me speechless. "Don't worry about it. It's gratis." He held up his gold wristband.

"How does that work?" No wonder everyone was so happy. There was free booze for all these people. I'd thought Taylor and Ashley were just being nice by buying me the first two beers, but they were free. Suddenly, them not caring about spilling my other beer made more sense. "Who pays for everyone to drink?"

He ducked his head, almost like he was hesitant to let me know. "Not everyone gets free drinks." His gaze slid to mine.

And now Taylor and Ashley not caring about spilling my other drink made less sense. This still felt like a set-up. The good feelings were too good. Was Reid trying to make up for knocking me over earlier? He seemed nice. It felt like something an actual nice guy might do for a new girl on campus.

"Then how do *you* get free drinks?" I raised an eyebrow.

"Friends and friends of friends." He got all flustered in a way that only made him cuter. It softened the hotness, made it less blinding.

"Must be good friends."

"The best. What did you want to drink?"

"Beer is fine. I have no idea what Taylor and Ashley might want."

"They're good with beer, unless there's a margarita machine around here, and I don't think they went all out this year to have one behind the bar." He already knew my roommates and what they liked to drink. It felt like the perfect situation for a set-up, only I wasn't sure what kind.

Everyone had been so nice to me so far. Was a shoe going to drop in my future?

The space around the pond was even more packed than before. The crowd swelled with laughter, cheering, hugs and people reuniting after a summer away.

At such a big school, I figured I'd blend in, but it felt like everyone already knew each other. Around me, people regular-hugged and bro-hugged, welcoming each other back to campus.

The bartender who looked like a fellow student filled the cups from a tap, leaving a foam head wobbling on top.

Did I know anyone else on campus other than my dad and Amy?

"Is your roommate here too? Cole?" I took my cup and Ashley's while Reid grabbed the other two.

His head jerked, and the beer sloshed in the cups, but he kept even the foam on top from spilling over. "He is here. Why?"

Had I just stuck my foot in my mouth? Now he probably thought I liked his friend. Shit! How many times had I been in everyone else's shadow, thinking the guy who'd been talking to me really liked me when he had only been doing it to get a friend's number?

I dropped my hand to his arm, right above his wrist, and squeezed it a little with my pinky in the most awkward move ever. "No reason. That's great you didn't have to come alone either. You were both so nice earlier today, that's all."

Some of the tension leaked out of his body. "Why wouldn't we be nice?"

I lifted my drink to my lips and sipped from it, staring at him over the lip of the cup. "It's weird being new, and I'm sure you both have tons of friends on campus. Don't feel like you have to hang out with me. I'm totally not a clinger."

A crooked smile brought out the almost dimple on his cheek. "I didn't think you were. Plus, it's good to meet new people. How else would I learn new things like the correct plural of Lego?"

I cringed, hiding behind the two cups I carried. "That's going to be hard to live down, isn't it?"

"Oh yeah." He winked at me and gulped down some of his beer.

The curl of his lips filled my stomach with a lightness that made me feel like I was seconds from being lifted off the ground.

"Does everyone just hang out here until midnight or are we waiting for a starter pistol or a bullhorn siren?"

A familiar face appeared over Reid's shoulder. "Where the hell have you been?" Cole grabbed the back of Reid's shirt, who stumbled and recovered without spilling a drop of his beer. Practiced hands in action. "Hey, Leona."

"Hi, Cole." I offered up a small wave of one red cup.

Reid shook off his grasp. "What the hell? You almost made me tank these beers."

"That's what you get for holding us up. We've got three minutes until go time."

"Fine, let me give these to Taylor and Ashley, and I'll be right back," Reid barked but turned to me with a sheepish smile. "Sorry, he's pushy."

"What exactly are you late for?"

"We can drop these off, and then I'll show you."

I didn't expect that what he'd be showing me was at least forty guys stripping down. Taylor, Ashley and I were at the center of our own up close and personal stripper show. My fingers tightened and crumpled my half-full cup, leaking the drink down over my palm. I chugged the rest before I ended up wearing it.

My roommates didn't seem fazed about the clothes dropping to the ground at our feet.

Reid braced his hand on a tree and tugged off his trainers.

I leaned in, hoping I didn't sound totally freaked out. "What exactly is going on?"

Reid grinned and unbuckled his belt.

I kept my gaze locked onto his face like a tractor beam, fighting the urge to let it drift lower. Even from here, he was all hard-planed muscles and bunching tendons. Not that I was looking, but all the guys around me, now in their boxers, were ripped. What the hell? Was that a requirement for this school?

"It's the Welcome Wagon tradition, although no one really knows why we still do it."

"That didn't answer my question. What the hell are you doing?"

"It's tradition, Leona." Taylor piped up like that explained all this. She had her hands full of shirts.

Someone stumbled forward, catching himself against the tree Reid was leaning on.

"Did anyone ever think maybe the reason we keep losing is because we're all infected with some kind of water-borne parasite that's fucking with our heads?" A guy tugged off his hat showing dark brown hair—cut close to his head, but I could tell it would be curly if he grew it out —and tugged off his boots and let them flop to the ground.

"This is Ezra."

Another guy dumped his clothes on the pile. "Don't mind him. He's been a real pain in the ass lately."

Reid laughed. "Ezra and Hollis, meet Leona."

Hollis had breathtaking eyes. Even from five feet away in

low light, the crystal-clear blue of his eyes was stunning and contrasted with his chestnut hair.

Ezra glared at Reid before dropping his pants.

A sharp breath escaped my lips.

He had on trunks. That was partly sad and a total relief.

Checking out the rest of them, I saw that they all did, which made more sense. For some reason, a group of guys getting butt naked had been where my mind went, but there weren't many guys who'd want that level of scrutiny in front of a few hundred people.

Everyone around the pond was staring at the slowly stripping squad of men. It was a much less acrobatic version of Magic Mike, but that didn't stop the catcalling and whooping from the crowd.

No one else seemed to think this was anything other than totally normal.

Reid balled his clothes up. "What are you complaining about?" He glanced back at his friend. "Last time, I only got back half my clothes."

Ashley waved her hands overhead. "That's why Taylor, Leona and I are here to keep you guys from campus humiliation."

Reid whipped his shirt overhead and grinned at her. "Why do you think I got you those beers?"

The flutters in my stomach turned to a lurch. Was that why he'd gotten me a beer? And beers for Taylor and Ashley? So we'd be clothes babysitters? My giddiness took a nosedive as I worked through all the ways I'd been reading the signals wrong. Come on, Leona. He's being friendly. Don't be one of those people who confuses every guy being nice with a guy flirting.

It didn't mean I couldn't still check him out. He was built

like a rugby player. Tall and lean with muscles that weren't overly bulky, but there was no missing them.

The first splash of water yanked me out of ogle mode.

"Thanks, guys. You're lifesavers." He dropped his trainers beside me.

Our fingers touched. A tingle traveled across my skin and up my arm. "No problem." My lips felt numb, and the warm bubbly feeling was back.

Cole stepped up. "If anyone doesn't want their shit stolen, these ladies are on clothes duty." He slapped his neatly folded bundle of clothes into my arms, followed by another and another, until I felt like I'd been immersed in a pile of denim and cotton. There were boots and trainers around us where it looked like I was being sacrificed to the Nike and Timberland gods.

"STFU Bulldogs!" A guy with sandy blond hair stood at the edge of the water, facing the crowd with his hands cupped around his mouth to act as a megaphone. A chain dangled from his neck with a key attached to the end. "What season is it?"

"Our season!" Everyone shouted back. The group swelled, and the power of hundreds of students cheering all at once electrified the air.

"What time is it?"

"Our time!"

"Whose world is it?"

"Our world!"

"Then let's do this right." He backed up and flung himself back first into the water, flying through the air and landing at least eight feet from the wall he'd launched from. The distance he covered was incredibly important when the rest of the guys stripped down to just their boxers or swimming trunks and jumped in behind him.

That seemed to kick things off, and the entire pond was flooded with bodies. Water splashed everywhere, turning the previously trampled areas around the water into a mucky, muddy mess, but no one seemed to care. If anything, people were smiling even more.

I leaned over to Ashley. "Does this happen every year?"

"It's tradition." Her grin widened when a shower of wet rubber ducks landed at our clothes-covered feet. They were various sizes and shapes.

"What the hell do the ducks have to do with anything?"

They both shrugged, and I said the word along with them, already realizing that half the batshit crazy things that happened on this campus were chalked up to "tradition."

"My dad definitely didn't mention this when he told me about this place. Why don't they have it in the brochure?"

Taylor draped a pair of jeans around her neck like a scarf and dammit, it actually worked on her. "It's not exactly university approved. Is your dad an STFU alum?"

In the lake, the splashing created waves that rolled up onto the freshman shore, soaking blankets and drowning Bluetooth speakers from unsuspecting partygoers. Screams and shouts got louder.

"Something like that." With slips like that, I might as well hire a skywriter to announce my dad was President Oakes. "And I can see why it's not university approved." A guy trudged out of the water with a bloody nose, still laughing and pumping one fist overhead. Another was trying to stem the blood flow.

I sucked in a sharp breath through my teeth and recoiled.

Someone rushed up with a tampon and shoved it into his nose, and he went back into the water.

"Are you shitting me?" Taylor shook her head.

Were there water-borne brain-eating amoebas around here?

"Isn't that going to lead to an infection in his nose or brain or something?" I looked to Taylor, not wanting to watch the bloody faced guy anymore.

"Now you know why we party before they get into the water. After, it's a bit of a shitshow." She stood on her tiptoes, better able to see over heads in her wedged heels. "Thank god, they're on their way back."

Reid, Cole and most of the first guys into the water all rushed back out, using the ladder or hoisting themselves up onto the small dock and across the concrete platform that ran into the grass.

A giant stack of towels appeared to be floating in the air before I spotted the legs under the pile. All the guys took them, slowly revealing the underclassmen that acted as towel boys.

Wet bodies toweling off surrounded me, Taylor and Ashley. Droplets of water were flung into the air and dotted my skin.

Reid smiled in that stomach somersault way of his. "Thanks for keeping our stuff safe."

A hulking guy behind him, Ezra, grabbed his hat. His size was on par with the other guy standing behind him. His hair had maybe a fingertip of growth, and he had light brown eyes, like caramel sauce. Ezra shoved it on before snatching up his clothes and shoes from the pile between Ashley and me.

"That's Griffin, but he'll hate you forever if you call him that. He's Griff."

"Hi, Griff." I waved, and he waved back absently while struggling to pull his shirt back over his head. His hair was light brown, and he rocked a bit of stubble. The muscles rippling on him included a few I didn't think I'd even known existed.

"You've met Cole and Hollis already, so that's all the roommates." He lifted his head and struggled to pull his jeans up.

People were knocking into each other as they dragged clothes back onto their wet bodies.

"That's a lot of roommates." I was jostled and he reached out to steady me.

"We're going to get stuck on the bottom of a pile if we don't get out of here. Can you grab my shoes? Once I put them on, we can bail."

"We can? As in you and me?" He wanted us to bail together? I checked over my shoulder for Ashley and Taylor. They were at the center of what looked like a half-naked throng of worshipers coming to take their bounty.

I scooped up Reid's shoes and followed him as he jumped, trying to button his jeans. He didn't seem to hear me as he redressed in the melee currently unfolding.

He grabbed my hand, pulling me along with him so I wasn't lost in the deluge of wet bodies flooding around us.

We ended up at the back of the wagon statue. "Sorry you got roped into clothes babysitting duty."

"I don't mind, and it wasn't for too long. I still don't understand what all of this is, but it looks like everyone's having fun." Even the guy with the bloodied nose had been smiling the whole time, tampon in his nostril and all.

Reid's head poked through his shirt, and he grinned at me.

The flutters were reaching a fevered pitch.

"They'll take any chance they can to party." Stepping in closer, he checked over his shoulder. "It'll be total chaos until just before dawn, but it's tradition, so we had to get in the water as soon as the sun dipped completely below the horizon."

I got a sprinkle of pond water that flicked over me from his hair. "Taylor and Ashley told me it's been going on for a long time."

Reid's arm popped out of his sleeve, and his face turned pensive. "Everyone feels like it gives them some good luck for the seas—school year to come."

Holding out his shoes, I laughed. "I guess that's as good a reason to do it than any other."

He took them from my hands, and our fingers brushed together. His were damp and his touch lingered on my skin. Keeping his eyes on me, he bent and tugged on one shoe. For the second one, he stumbled forward.

I raised my hands to catch him, before realizing there was no way I could stop the slab of man hurtling toward me. His hand landed on the wagon statue at my back with a thud, and his body lurched forward, chest to chest with me.

I curled inward, preparing to be squashed between him and the bronze wagon, but there was no pancake moment. He caught himself.

The fabric of our shirts pressed together.

His body nearly covered mine, and his mouth was inches away.

"Whoops." A nervous laugh leaped from my throat.

"I tripped."

I licked my lips. "I saw."

His gaze darted down at the movement, then traced its way back up to my eyes. He might as well have trailed his fingers over my whole body. I shivered.

"Leona—"

Whatever he was going to say was cut off by a swarm of bodies. "Let's go. Smith just broke his damn ankle. We're out of here before it gets worse." Ezra's hands clamped around Reid's shoulders and pulled him away. His friends marched up the hill, away from the party.

"Bye, Leona," he shouted and waved above his head.

The whisper of his lips, so close to mine, lingered. I brushed my fingers along my mouth and couldn't keep the dopey smile from breaking through. "Bye, Reid."

6

REID

Metal clanked, guys ran with resistance bands around their waists and dragging sleds behind them and the conditioning staff walked through the weight room, checking form and making notes about everyone's progress.

I finished my dumbbell rows and set them back in line with the others. "Fucking Trevor, man."

Cole dropped his weights beside mine with a clank. "He's not even here."

"That's the problem. He should be here." His replacement, Mitchell, spent more time drinking than he did working. We were nearing the end of our ninety-minute workout, and Mitchell was skulking out the door.

"His whole life is supposed to revolve around the team?"

I grabbed a heavier set of weights and slid them onto the bar above the padded bench. "Yes, why wouldn't it?"

Cole shook his head and stepped into the spotting position. "Is there nothing else you care about other than football?"

"Food's pretty high up there." I shrugged and laid back,

gripping the bar, pushing it up and engaging my muscles for a clean, controlled drop to my chest.

"What about your Lego princess?"

My grip faltered, and Cole tightened his to keep the bar from smashing me in my face. "Leona? What about her?"

"You act like I wasn't there during Welcome Wagon. You couldn't take your eyes off her. It wasn't just me who saw it. I said go talk to her, but getting her drinks, having her watch your clothes, leaning in extra close behind the statue? None of that seems like the actions of a guy who doesn't do attachments. A guy who hates distractions."

"She's new. She's our neighbor. I'm just trying to be a good host."

"I missed the sign-up for the welcome committee."

"You're an asshole."

He gritted his teeth, taking the weight of the bar. "Takes one to know one."

"Real mature."

"Says the guy acting like he's not into a girl because she's got cooties."

"Are we finished with this workout?" I asked. "I feel like we're done."

"Just because you're finished with the conversation doesn't mean the workout is over. We still have pull-ups to do."

I braced my hands on my hips and dropped my head. "Shit."

"Your favorite."

"You could've reminded me before I did the bench press." I dragged my towel down over my face and across my neck.

"It's not my fault you still don't know the routine yet."

Cole walked over to the pull-up stand that had sandbags on each of the legs to keep it from moving.

I flexed my fingers and jumped, catching the rubberized hand grips. I bent my knees, locked my ankles and hefted my body weight.

Cole leaped up and took the same form next to me, dragging his body up until his chin made it over the horizontal bar at the top.

"Last one to drop steals the extra round of food for the other." I lowered myself, exhaling.

"You think you can beat me?"

"I know I can."

"You're on."

My forearms ached, my shoulders screamed, and my back was on fire, but I kept going. We hit twelve reps when Cole looked over.

"Getting tired?" he asked.

The summer between freshman and sophomore year of high school, I shot up four inches and worked out in the gym my dad set up in the garage for hours every day. Pull-ups were my barometer of progress in packing muscle onto my scrawny frame. When I'd started, doing two was a struggle. By the end of that summer, I could do five reps of twelve but every time I gripped the bars, I always had that initial burst of fear that my arms would turn to string beans again, and I'd be the one on the sidelines watching the game happening all over again.

"Nope."

"Me neither."

Ten more reps, and my arms were shaking.

The sweat patches on Cole's shirt were larger than the dry ones. Beads of sweat rolled down my sides.

"You give?" Cole grunted.

"I could do this all day." I relocked my ankles.

A hand gripped my ankle and tugged—hard. "Are you two trying to injure yourselves before you play your first game?" The gruff grouse from the head conditioning coach, Coach Wilkins, broke the deadlock.

Both of us dropped to the hard black mat, panting and trying to keep our smiles contained or we'd be doing a cardio crash course.

"Sorry, Coach," we mumbled in unison.

"Did you finish all your reps?"

"Yes, Coach."

He glared at us both and scribbled on his clipboard. "Get your asses out of here before I change my mind." He pointed toward the locker room.

"Thanks, Coach." We rushed out of the room, not wanting to jinx the lucky break.

After a shower and quick change, I slung my duffels over my shoulder. My stomach knotted and rumbled. Lunch, which had only been three hours ago, felt like it had been three days ago. "Let's eat. I'm fucking starving."

Cole picked up his bag. "Ezra's on cooking duty for nine tonight."

"He'd better not burn any this time." We chipped in for late evening fuel since our dining plan only allowed three meals each day. Burning a few thousand calories in practices meant our food requirements went well beyond what could be consumed in three quick visits to the dining hall. It also meant that, from time to time, we dipped into the territory of petty theft to keep the late-night hunger pangs away.

"If he does, he can eat them. Although that would probably be incentive for him to burn more."

In the dining hall, we both grabbed trays. "I can't wait until Neptune Night." The masses descended on the cafeteria for the one night of seafood insanity that had become the stuff of legends.

I pushed my tray along on the metal rail that ran along the front of all the food stations. Nabbing three burgers and a red and white paper tray of fries, I took another with grilled chicken and a side of roasted broccoli.

"Griff, Ezra and Hollis are over there." Cole gestured with his chin.

"Good, they can take some of this food back if they're done first."

We took two empty seats at the round tables close to the drink refill station most people forgot about. Or maybe it was not wanting to wade through ten partially occupied tables filled with ravenous football players.

"Root beer?"

Cole looked at me like I'd gone insane. "Of course."

"Anyone else need a refill?" Three more hard red plastic cups were shoved in my direction. That's what I got for asking. After a balancing act of refills, I slid all five cups onto the table.

I hacked through my chicken and stabbed some broccoli. "Classes start tomorrow. You know what that means."

Griff dunked a chocolate chip cookie into a mug of milk. "If we're not failing, why the hell do they care if we go to study hall or not?"

Hollis braced his hands behind his head and rocked his chair back on two legs. "Some would say having study hall three times a week is the reason most of the team isn't failing."

"Like anyone cares." Griff took another cookie from the crumbled napkin in front of him.

Ezra poked his straw through the ice in his cup. "Some

of us would like to get at least a degree out of all the shit Mikelson puts us through."

"Do you think anyone who is first string won't get a pick-up next year? Even if it's in the fifth round, none of us are getting left behind."

Hollis huffed. "The best from the team that always gets within a completed pass of winning playoffs, but keeps botching it."

"What the hell crawled up your ass? Do you need another couple of cookies?"

Hollis dropped his chair down to all four legs. "All I'm trying to say is it's competitive and there are no guarantees."

Cole dropped his fork. "You think I don't know that? The only reason I am where I am is because someone got a compound fracture that ended their career my freshman year. It could be over at any minute for any of us, but I'm not going to play this game with that sitting on my shoulder every minute."

Hollis stared at him before shoving back from the table. "I'm out of here." And then he was gone.

Ezra poached the last of his cookies. "Wasn't I the designated hot head of the group?"

I stared at the mountain of food I wouldn't be able to finish before my stomach exploded. "Shit, I forgot to ask him to take the food."

Everyone turned to me with disapproving stares.

"What? I'm being practical."

Griff twirled a ceremonial coin-flip coin over the backs of his fingers. "He's probably not going back to the house, but I'm about to head out. Do you have a container or do I need to grab a million napkins?"

"I planned ahead." I grabbed a gallon-sized plastic bag out of my duffel and kept an eye out while I scooped the proteins and vegetables inside. It wouldn't win any awards for presentation once it got back to the house, but it was better than nothing and it was free. Well, paid for with blood and sweat out on the field.

The school year had officially started, which meant the balancing act of keeping everything running its course, but I had to hope that course intersected with Leona's. I couldn't stop thinking about her and how good it had felt to almost kiss her. The real thing would be even sweeter. I'd make sure of it.

7

LEONA

The top floor of the main campus building was quieter than most other places on campus. But it made sense since it was mainly administrative offices, not ones built for the barrage of students that descended on campus now that classes had started.

My footsteps were silent on the classic patterned carpet runners down the wood floors that didn't let out a single creak. There were stained glass windows and wood everywhere. It felt like I'd been transported back to the 1800s.

There wasn't anyone in the waiting area outside of my dad's office, so I knocked and peeked inside. It was empty, which was unusual. All summer there had been faculty and staff wandering the halls, but they were busy now. Classes were officially in session.

His on-campus office was much grander than the one in the house. It was all solid mahogany that looked like it was polished daily. The massive desk felt like it belonged in Washington, D.C., not Pennsylvania. The carpet was soft and padded, a stark contrast to the industrial kind slapped over concrete in student housing.

I set my backpack against the front of his desk.

There was another framed picture of the two of us next to his monitor. This time it was me holding his arm and leaning against him right after my middle school graduation. The summer before everything fell apart.

"Good to see you, Leona."

I jumped and flailed, knocking over the frame.

Amy walked briskly into the room with a leather folder in hand. She always looked a split second away from breaking into a sprint in her sensible heels and pantsuit.

"Hi, Amy. I was looking for my dad." I righted the picture.

She checked her watch and her phone, probably synchronizing watches for her next mission. "He's on his way and has ten minutes before his next meeting. I know he'd be happy to see you." With a quick, efficient move, she tucked a stray hair behind her ear.

Not a minute later, Dad walked in and his face lit up. "Leona, you're here."

"In the flesh."

He hugged me, then shrugged off his jacket, hanging it up before taking a seat.

"To what do I owe this pleasure."

Amy moved in and out with leather folios and brought in a new flower arrangement for the small seating area opposite the desk.

"I was wandering around campus and saw the building, so I thought I'd stop by. I also got a little lost and needed to regroup. This place is huge." It felt kind of embarrassing to admit I'd run to daddy when I got turned around and made a beeline for the one building I remembered and knew I could cool off in that wouldn't be brimming with students.

"I'm happy when you got turned around, you thought to

come here." The corners of his eyes crinkled. "Where are you headed to next?"

Amy moved around Dad's desk, picking up papers and setting out new ones with yellow *sign here* stickies attached to them.

"Bacterial Physiology and then onto Winery Design in the Marshall Building."

He asked Amy for a map.

She grabbed one from the stack on her desk for visitors and he circled the building not far from here. "How are the classes going?"

"It's only the first day, but from reading all the syllabi, the class structure is a little different than I'm used to, but I'm sure I'll have it all figured out...by summer break." I mustered a laugh.

"I'm sure you'll catch on long before then. Probably even as early as Christmas," he teased, but then his face sobered. "Are you planning on going back to Australia this summer?"

That was a landmine topic I'd been avoiding whenever possible.

"I was thinking about it." And hated every time I did. When I was on campus, it was easy to pretend the past was in the past. It was part of the reason I'd wanted an apartment and not to stay at Dad's. But my avoidance would only last so long. "I don't have any other vineyard connections here."

"Yet. Don't count yourself out. You have the whole year to make some, and I could always pull—"

Amy's pen clicked from her seat beside the desk, and she scribbled furiously on her notepad. Glancing over my shoulder at her, I hated that she might think I was trying to get Daddy to call in a few favors for me.

"Dad, you don't need to do that. I need to figure this out

myself."

"What does your mother think?" He said it like he actually wanted to know without the bitterness and venom I felt his words should've held. Or maybe that was just me.

My stomach roiled. The loaded topic just got heavier. What would my mom think? Did I even care?

Amy hopped up from her seat. "I'll wait outside and buzz you when your ten thirty is here."

As much as Amy probably already knew about my dad after spending so much time together, I was relieved we didn't have to have this part of the conversation in front of her.

"I haven't talked to her."

"In how long?"

"Since the day I applied to transfer." I ran my fingers along the metal tacks pressed into the leather seat, holding the upholstery in place.

"Leona…" Disappointment rippled through his voice.

"What? She doesn't get a say in anything I do anymore." I snatched up my backpack and slid it onto my shoulders.

He sighed and leaned back in his chair. "I didn't say she did, but not talking to her—do you think that's the best way to handle this? You're going to have to speak with her at some point."

"I know that." Although I'd put it off as long as I could. "But me not going there doesn't have to be a bad thing. I thought you'd be happy if I decided to stay. She deserves that and more." I sat on the edge of the leather seat in front of his desk.

"Leona…" He sighed. "What happened between me and your mother had nothing to do with you, and I'd never want you to turn away from her out of misplaced loyalty to me."

Misplaced loyalty. "How can you be so calm?" He was

going into reasonable mode, and I hated it. I hated that he wasn't nearly as angry as I was. "Isn't that how we got into this whole thing in the first place?" I shot up from my chair and slammed my palms against his desk. "If you had just told me— If you would've said something..." I hung my head. "I'm sorry. I know you had your reasons."

He placed his hand over mine. "This is all new, and you're dealing with a lot." A long, heavy pause. "How about we have dinner? I have an event I'd love you to come to tomorrow afternoon, if you're free. Once we're finished, we can grab food and just...hang out." He said it like it was a foreign word he'd have to look up in the dictionary.

I looked up and raised an eyebrow. "Do you know how to hang out?"

His chest puffed up, and he leaned from side to side in his impression of— I don't even know what. A 1950s greaser? "You don't think I'm hip."

I covered my eyes and tried to hold in my laugh.

There was a light knock at the door. "Dr. Oakes, your ten thirty is here."

"Sure, I can come tomorrow. I only have morning classes. What's the event?"

"It's an award ceremony. You can help me hand out the envelopes and plaques. It's always a bit of a circus and can take forever, so it'll be nice to have you there to help out."

"Are you sure there isn't someone more qualified to handle that?"

"Of course not. It'll be nice to have non-stuffy company to talk to while we wait through all the speeches."

"You don't think people might be weirded out by me appearing out of thin air." Being up on stage with my dad wasn't exactly keeping a low profile. I was still feeling out the campus and meeting new people. Blowing my cover this early might mean sitting alone in my apartment for the next two years, or worse, being inundated with insincere people trying to get close to me to get to my dad.

"I'm fairly certain you'd walk into the room, unless they've taught you new skills and powers in Australia that I'm not aware of."

"No, just your basic safety against murderous animals and a healthy fear of ever going outside without sunscreen and a hat."

"I'd like you to be there, if you're not busy." He folded his hand over mine. "I know you're trying to not draw too much attention when it comes to being my daughter."

I opened my mouth, but he plowed ahead.

"You don't need to get on the mic and shout about it. But there will be a lot more of these events, and I'd like you to be there for them."

"Are you sure it won't be awkward if I'm there?"

"Not at all. It'll be great for you to see the old man in action." He stood straighter, like he was heading into a boxing ring, not an award ceremony, but I knew it was for my benefit.

I laughed. "Of course, Dad. I'd be happy to go. What should I wear?"

"Business casual will work."

I eyed his white button-down shirt, light sweater vest and tie along with black pants and shiny black shoes.

"Student business casual. Not my version. You could even wear jeans. Most of the other attendees will be."

"If you say so."

I walked out of the office, and Amy let in his next appointment. Behind her desk, there was a stack of envelopes and certificates.

She rushed back out, grabbed her phone and tapped out

a message before sitting down and clicking away on her computer and then picking up the envelopes. The woman was a whirlwind of productivity.

"Did you need help?"

She jolted. "Sorry, Leona. I didn't know you were still here."

"You seem a bit busy."

"We lost our work-study students and won't get a new batch for another week. And the other staff are wrapped up in all the beginning of the school year events, so I'm handling a lot of the things everyone else normally does." The knotted hairstyle at the base of her neck wasn't nearly as pristine as it normally was. This was the most undone I'd ever seen her, and I felt bad that I'd been so absorbed in my own worries that I hadn't even noticed.

"Can I help?" She'd done so much to help me get settled stateside, which I imagined wasn't in her job description at all. The least I could do was try to lessen her stress, if I could.

Her eyes widened, and her head whipped around like I'd offered her drugs or suggested she take up drinking on the job. "What? No, of course not. I'd never. It's my job. You have class to get to."

"I have another forty minutes until my class starts, and the building is the next one over."

Her shoulders sagged. "That would be amazing. I need to get all these stuffed for tomorrow."

"Do I need to do it here or can I take them home if I don't finish before I have to go?"

Her fingers froze on the stacks. "If you promise you'll be able to bring them back in the morning, then there's no reason you can't."

"Is eight a.m. early enough? My first class is at eight

twenty."

"That's perfect."

We worked side by side before the timer I hadn't even noticed she set went off. We'd made a dent but weren't even halfway through.

Amy scrounged up a box for me to take everything home with me, only I didn't think about needing to take everything to my next classes. Having already committed, I gripped the edges of the box and my backpack, and headed out to the building Dad had circled on the map.

Both classes were, thankfully, in the same building, which kept my lugging to a minimum, but I couldn't say I was graceful about it. Sweat circles had begun to form under my arms, and my backpack had probably created a nice sweat 'V' going down my back. It was supposed to be winter, dammit. My body wasn't prepared to go from Australia winter straight to humid Pennsylvania summer like this.

In my blur of sweat and hoping I didn't get lost while figuring out what the hell to do next, I nearly walked past him.

But it would be hard to miss the sandy brown hair, emerald green eyes and cut-a-steak sharp jawline, especially not when he was smiling in my direction.

I glanced over my shoulder twice to make sure there was no one else behind me. "Reid, what are you doing here?"

He pushed off the brick pillar outside of the Marshall Life Sciences Building. "I thought I saw you and wanted to see how you were adjusting. Time zones, campus, and isn't it winter in Australia right now?"

My cheeks flushed as he stepped up beside me. It wasn't like I hadn't talked to guys as hot as him before, but the somersaults in my stomach had never been this prominent before. "Things are going well. I arrived a couple months before classes started to hang out with my dad before I moved into the apartment. And classes are great so far. The curriculum is different, but not too different."

"Where are you headed to next?"

I pulled up my phone. "Lunch in a place that serves food, wherever that might be." I glanced around like a large glowing neon sign would appear mid-air with an arrow that said FOOD. "I'm not picky. This campus is massive. I was going to go home to eat, but it'll take me at least twenty minutes to get back to my apartment on campus transport and thirty minutes to my next class." I shifted the box to my side.

"Don't you have a car?" He said it like he already knew the answer. Had he been paying attention? He went out of his way to hang out with me at Welcome Wagon, but I figured that was residual guilt over plowing into me on the sidewalk.

"Yeah, but getting those parking permits is nearly impossible. The parking office said some people get on the waitlist during their freshman year and never get a tag." I wasn't going to complain to my dad to get one. It didn't feel right to fall straight into *I'm the president's daughter and deserve special attention* mode when I'd only just started to think of myself as his daughter again.

"I can drive you if you wanted to grab food from your apartment."

Peering over, I smiled. The somersaults were a full gymnastics floor routine in my stomach. Alone in an enclosed space with Reid, the electric charge I felt around him was going to short out my brain. "How did you get a hang tag? I thought only seniors had a shot at getting one."

He raised his hand and squeezed the back of his neck, which smeared his skin in ink.

"You got a little..." I grabbed his hand. There was smudged black ink all over it.

His body jerked, and he tried to take his hand again, but I held tight.

Sustainable Vineyard Development
Fermented Foods
Distilled Beverage Technology
Winery Design

The first three had lines marking the name of the class and room number.

I glanced up at him, and his face looked like it had been pushed in front of a flamethrower. His eyes were squeezed shut when he exhaled a deep breath.

"I swear I'm not a stalker." He looked at me with pained embarrassment.

Those were viticulture classes. My classes. Well, not my exact ones, but various ones in my major. Had he been trying to find me? The warmth along my skin turned to tingling. That electric charge was cranked up a notch. "That sounds like exactly what a stalker would say." Adjusting the box in my arms, I laughed.

He dropped his head into his hands. "I'll leave now."

I grabbed his arm, nearly toppling my box. "I'm flattered."

He stopped his retreat and whipped back around to face me.

"Sure, I've never had a guy rush all over campus to find my class before. What was so important you needed to talk to me about?"

Guys had always been friendly to me for *a reason*, like wanting to get close to my best friend or meeting my step-dad. But the near kiss at Welcome Wagon hadn't felt patronizing. It had felt real. Like he was really into me.

"Nothing specific. Let me take that for you." He took the box from me. "My car is over there." His chin lifted, pointing toward the parking lots behind the building.

I followed him with a barely stifled grin. Did he like me? Holy crap, this hot guy actually liked *me*. I'd never even been on a real date. Was that even a thing anymore? It felt like hang out and hook up was more the way things went now. And here he was hunting me down on campus. Maybe I should've been dumping Lego all over my lawn from the time I started high school.

The perfect glow-up shadow I'd been living under since we moved to Australia had been enough to block out any and all male attention. Not that my friends did it on purpose. It just seemed I was completely over-look-able. The side effect had been always paling in comparison to everyone around me and being the plucky sidekick who had to be appeased to get to anyone who wasn't me. A real self-esteem booster right there.

"Nothing specific had you track me down all over campus?" Some of the warm fuzzy feelings melted away. There had to be an angle.

"Maybe it was the tiniest bit specific." His smile was disarmingly handsome. And he likely knew exactly how well it worked to get him what he wanted. So the question kept ringing in my ears. What did he want with me?

"Care to share with the class?" I asked.

"Not yet."

On the drive over, Reid gave me a very different version of the campus tour Amy had taken me on.

"And our house's unofficial name is The Zoo."

"Do I want to know?"

He shifted into park. "What can I say? We throw great

parties. The Halloween party and the ones we have after—later in the year."

"Parties? That's why it's called The Zoo?" I squinted and gave him my best skeptical look.

He grinned, but there was a slight ruddiness to his neck. "What? You think it's from the smell?"

I feigned innocence and shrugged.

"It's not 100% derived from the smell, but throwing five guys together in a house is bound to generate a few." His cupid's bow was perfectly placed. So symmetrical, I wanted to pull out a ruler to measure it. Or maybe that was just to distract myself from my nerves. The drive over had loosened some of the tension of waiting for the shoe to drop.

His attention had been on me the whole time, other than a few waves when cars honked as we passed. He was apparently popular on campus.

The older, embedded fears about being used didn't have a reason to surface so far. If anything, he was probably on guard about me hanging out with him due to his popularity. It was a relief. My guard could finally be lowered.

He got out of the car and grabbed my box from the back seat.

We walked up the path toward the apartment courtyard. The butterfly wings were flapping hard now. It wasn't like I'd never been alone with a guy or anything, but I'd never had someone go out of their way to spend time with me. At least it never felt that way before.

Taylor and Ashley came through the archway. "Hey, Leona. Hey, Reid. What are you doing on this side of the street?"

Was it me or was there a different inflection on his name than there had been on mine?

"Taylor. Ashley. Just helping Leona with this." He shifted

the box, hefting it higher.

"Looking forward to this weekend? I know I am." Taylor stared at him intently with a half smirk.

Reid smiled. "Of course. Are you joining, Ashley?"

She rolled her eyes. "As if I have a choice. Don't disappoint us."

Their conversation confused the hell out of me, and then it hit me like a fist to my gut. Why would this be any different than things had been before? Why suddenly would this hot, seemingly popular guy want to talk to me? The whole reason we met in the first place was because he'd been talking to Taylor and Ashley and hadn't noticed me.

They kept talking until both my roommates walked off, and I was left with Reid. Suddenly, I felt like there should be a glowing L hovering in front of my forehead.

I grabbed the box, trying to take it from him and also brace myself for the crushing disappointment. "Which one is it?" Then I was hit with another thought. "Or is it both?"

That would be new.

His forehead scrunched. "Which one? Or both of what?"

"Which of them are you trying to get to? Never mind, it doesn't matter. Thanks for the ride." I turned and walked toward the apartment, humiliation burning through me with every step. Stupid, stupid Leona.

He jogged in front of me. "You think I searched all over campus to track you down to trick you into getting your help in hooking up with one of your roommates?"

I stopped at how well he'd pieced together everything running through my head. "You didn't?"

"You think almost kissing you at Welcome Wagon was a great way to get to your roommates that I've known since freshman year?"

Suddenly, I felt like a complete moron.

His shoulders dipped, and he scrubbed his inky hand over the back of his neck. "I've seriously lost my touch if it's taken you this long to realize I've been flirting with you."

I narrowed my gaze, suspicion and skepticism analyzing his every word, move and breath. "You have?"

"Yeah, it's not every day I help someone pick up a million Lego." He winked at not adding the S. "Or entrust them with my clothes while I go jump in a lake."

"Oh." Was this what flirting looked like? "You like me?"

He chuckled. "You're going to make me come out and say it, huh?"

I gripped the handles on the cardboard box tighter. "Since you're the one who tracked me down, I'd say it's only fair."

His head ducked in a low, heavy nod, but his eyes stayed on me. "Yes, I like you."

"I like you too." I hurried past him, not knowing what else I was supposed to do.

He'd just come right out and said it. Even when I posed the question, I'd expected some hedging or maybe a noncommittal answer. Some stammering and evasion before telling me the real reason they'd invited me to a party, hoping I'd bring one of my friends along or requesting another favor. But there had been none of that.

"You're going to drop that bomb and then walk away from me?" He rushed up beside me.

I swallowed, trying to remember how to use my tongue. "I thought we were going to have lunch. Did you still want some?"

He grinned and took the box from me. "Lead the way."

Our arms brushed, and I'm sure we looked like two grinning idiots, but the well of happiness inside my chest had turned into a geyser.

8

REID

Leona let us into her apartment. It was a standard campus apartment, although Taylor had already worked her magic on the space. Freshman year, she'd had the most decked-out room in the whole dorm, complete with fabric draped on the walls and rugs to go over the crappy, barely thick enough to cover the concrete kind that came standard in on-campus places.

But there were touches of Leona in here. An Xenomorph Funko Pop by the TV and the wine stacked on the counter, which wasn't the standard two-buck chuck most college students drank.

"I have pizza and...pizza," she said. "Sorry, that's not much of a choice. I should've probably asked before you drove all the way over here."

I set the box down. "Who doesn't love pizza, especially free pizza? What is all that anyway?" I shook the box in my arms. "You've got a campus job already?"

She took the box from me and set it on the kitchen counter. "Something like that. It's not official or anything, but I offered to help. We need to eat first, then we can do this, so we don't get pizza grease on these pretty cream envelopes. How long do you have? Don't you have class?"

"Not until three." Between practice, lifting and study halls, early mornings were non-stop, so the break between all that and actual classes helped my mind switch from athlete to student mode.

"Your first class is at three? That must be nice. The only seats in every one of my required classes started at 8:20. I don't know who I pissed off at the Registrar's Office to deserve this fate. It must be nice to sleep in."

"Just because my first class is at three doesn't mean I'm not up early too." My defensiveness shot up. So many people thought we had everything handed to us and didn't put in any work. The number of nights I fell into bed and was asleep before I bounced on the mattress was higher than I could count.

Her eyes went wide, and she shook her head, sweeping her hands out in front of her like she was trying to clear the air. "Sorry, I didn't mean anything by it. Speaking when hangry is a terrible idea for me. We can eat, and then I need to get to work on the envelopes. I promised I'd have this done by tomorrow morning."

I cringed and mentally kicked myself in the balls repeatedly. "Sorry for snapping. It was a dick move."

She stared back at me sheepishly. "No, it's my fault. My joking skills could use some fine tuning."

"I can help. It's the least I could do." For snapping her head off at the simple comment.

"You don't have to."

"I know." Had I once been called smooth? Right now, I felt like a turtle on its back, baking under the sun.

"Then let's eat, so we can get to work." She tucked a strand of hair behind her ear and smiled at me. The soft spread of her lips sent my blood humming through my veins. "We have two slices of pepperoni and half a pizza of Hawaiian."

"I'll take the Hawaiian," we both said at the same time.

"It's okay—you can have the pepperoni." Again perfectly in sync.

"No, it's okay. I like Hawaiian." Were we sharing the same brain now?

"Jinx." The width of my smile made my cheeks ache. Did I look like a dopey idiot? Probably. Did I care? Not one bit. "Do you like Hawaiian or were you just being nice?"

"I love Hawaiian." She got a dreamy-eyed look that shone with sincerity.

"Seriously? Me too. The guys never let me order it, not even on half a pizza, so I almost never get to have it."

"Then you're in luck." She split four slices between two paper plates. "Because we can polish off the rest of this." Turning away from me, she wedged both plates into the microwave.

I couldn't help myself and checked her out. It would be tempting to slide my hand into her back pocket and give her ass a squeeze. Instead, I dropped onto a dining room chair and shoved them under my legs to keep those thoughts from turning into actions, which would get my ass booted from her apartment.

"Perfect," I mumbled.

"What did you want to drink?" She opened the fridge. "There's beer, lemonade, water, apple juice. I could open a bottle of wine."

"No need to roll out the red carpet. Water's good." Not to mention drinking during the season was a Mikelson no-no. Not that we all didn't break some of his rules from time to time, but this one also kept us at peak performance most of the time.

She made a noise in the back of her throat.

"Were you thinking I'd say beer?"

"Maybe," she admitted.

"It's not even two in the afternoon yet."

"You should hear the guys across the courtyard at noon. They must start at eight a.m. to get that blotto by two in the afternoon."

"Contrary to your first impression of college life, some of us have classes to pass and other things to get done and can't be shitfaced 24/7, although I'm sure there are some people who manage it." Despite all the fawning and limelight that came with being on the team, there was a sliver of envy for people who had nothing to worry about other than classes and didn't burn through calories so fast that they went to bed hungry even after stuffing themselves full three meals a day.

She tossed me a bottle of water and poured herself a glass of lemonade.

We sat on the couch with our reheated pizza and chatted while we ate.

"Koalas aren't high all the time?"

She laughed and shook her head. "I'm pretty sure if eucalyptus could get anyone high, Aussies would have found a way."

"Well damn. Here I am thinking those little guys are just hanging out enjoying the sun, baked out of their minds. Highly disappointing."

"Sorry to burst your bubble." Her voice was filled with amusement.

"And you've never been attacked by anything there?"

"It's not like wildlife is literally waiting to attack us the minute we walk out the door." She ripped into the last bit of her pizza.

"That's not what I've heard."

"The rumors about Australia had been greatly exaggerated."

"Ah, so the jellyfish aren't that bad, huh?"

Her eyes widened. "No, box jellyfish will freaking kill you, and you've got to heed the warning flags they put up at the beach."

"Not so exaggerated after all."

"Okay, maybe not all."

"How did you end up there anyway?"

Her gaze dropped. "My parents got divorced right before I started freshman year of high school." She shredded what was left of her crust with her fingers. "My mom remarried, and I went with her and my stepdad to Australia. It's where he's from."

"Your dad was cool with that? With you being so far away?" That had to be hard on both of them. It sucked not seeing my dad for months at a time while I was in school, but we weren't continents away from each other.

She shrugged and lowered her gaze before looking back at me. "Not really, but I made it very clear I wanted to go with her, so he respected my wishes." There was a hint of regret in her voice. A slight waver.

"But you're here now to spend time with him? Is that why you transferred?"

Her smile made it clear she liked being closer to her dad. He probably didn't live too far from campus. Maybe he even worked here.

"Yeah, but it's a long, boring story." She waved her crust shred like she was trying to ward off old memories. "What about you?"

This was what I got for going down the getting-to-know-you path. It was always a real fun killer, but I wasn't going to lie to her. "Short story. My mom died from cancer when I was two. It's just me and my dad since then." They were lines I'd said a hundred times when people asked about my family life. Usually followed by an "I'm sorry," which usually means *I'm sorry I brought it up and now I don't know what the hell to say next.*

"I'm sorry you didn't get to know her." She rubbed her hand over my knee. And she meant it. The awkwardness of spilling my guts about my mom's premature death didn't feel half as awkward when she stared at me with those big brown eyes. She squeezed my knee in reassurance, but the increased pressure wasn't centered around her sincerity for my life situation.

A flood of adrenaline rushed through me, lighting each cell under her touch on fire.

I stared at the floor to refocus on what I'd been talking about before she touched me. "My dad told me all about her. He was always taking pictures and video of her, so I at least got to know her a little bit. She wrote me journals and journals of her thoughts. Even though she didn't get to see me grow up, I got more of her than a lot of people in my position." There was always a hint of sadness when I thought about my mom, but sometimes it felt like a loss that had happened to someone else. Like a close friend or family member—if I'd had any others of those. She'd always been gone, so it was hard to truly know what I was missing. I revisited the pictures or videos whenever the longing hit me.

"Wow." She sat back, pulling her hand off my leg, and moved it to the space between us on the couch.

The loss of the gentle pressure and warmth was like the air being sucked out of the room.

"Sorry, it's kind of a downer, I know." I covered her hand with mine, fighting against the urge to brush my fingers along the smooth skin on the back of her hand. It felt impossibly soft under my rough and callused fingers.

"It's no big deal. Sorry, if I—just sorry." Her chin dipped, and her gaze fell to the couch.

I didn't want her to be sorry. "There's nothing to be sorry about." Dropping my head, I craned my neck until I could see her eyes.

She nodded, seeming less uncertain than before. The rigidity in her shoulder muscles relaxed with her parted lips. Parted lips I wanted to taste.

But kissing a girl right after the whole spiel about my dead mom didn't exactly set the mood I was going for. What mood was I going for?

"Should we get working on your project?" Let's not focus on sad, Reid. I almost never told anyone more than a few words about my mom. Most people were happy to change the subject and not hear a sad story anyway. The guys obviously knew, but it wasn't exactly a fun subject to bring up, which made it even crazier that I'd done it at all. For some reason, it was easy to talk to her.

"Right, I almost forgot about it. We've got about an hour before I need to be at my next class. If I've memorized the bus schedule correctly, that gives us half an hour to get this all done." She pulled the box over to the beat-to-hell coffee table covered with a pale blue cloth that couldn't hide all the chipped edges. I'm sure Taylor was out shopping for a new tablecloth or, hell, a new table right now.

Leona flipped off the box lid.

"I can give you a ride. That'll buy us at least another

fifteen minutes." I'd truly lost my ability to flirt, if even after saying I liked her, she thought I'd just let her find her own way back to campus. Who the hell were the guys she'd hooked up with before? That was like blowing lighter fluid on an ember of jealousy I hadn't even known had been lit. Thinking about her with other guys was a mistake. Get a fucking grip, Reid. This was what? Day six since I'd seen her. But the pull was undeniable...

"I didn't want to presume." Lifting out the envelopes and certificates, she peered up at me.

"It's no problem. I've got my afternoon classes, so I'm headed that way anyway."

"Of course, I didn't think you were making a special trip just for me." She was flustered, which made her even more adorable. On her knees on the other side of the table, she arranged all the papers, but I couldn't wait any longer. I also couldn't let her doubt I'd meant everything I'd said already.

"Hey, Leona."

Her head popped up. "Yeah?"

I leaned over the stack of empty envelopes, messing up her neatly arranged piles.

She didn't jerk back or move a muscle.

I ran my finger along her jaw.

Her eyelids fluttered, and she sucked in a sharp breath through her parted lips.

"I'm going to kiss you now."

"That's what I hoped you were going to do." Her teasing sexy smile sent my pulse thrumming in anticipation.

Shifting forward until the side of the table dug into my stomach, I pressed my lips against hers.

She gasped like, even though I'd warned her, she was still surprised. Her lemonade taste, citrusy and sweet, made me crave more.

I held onto the sides of her face and deepened the kiss. Our tongues danced, lips greedy, and electricity jolted through me.

Her fingers gripped the front of my t-shirt like she didn't want me to stop. Good because I hadn't planned on it.

My hand slid to the back of her neck, and she whimpered, which sent the blood rushing from my head to regions lower. If we didn't stop now, things were going to race forward at warp speed, and I wanted to savor this —savor her.

Breaking apart, she stared back at me with giddy, glassy eyes. "Wow."

"I was just thinking the same thing."

She ducked her head, suddenly shy. "That was phenomenal."

"You sure know how to inflate a guy's ego."

"It was well earned." Her smile blinded me. She was flushed and flustered and beautiful. Clearing her throat, she dropped her gaze back to the envelopes. "We should probably get to work."

"Probably." But it wasn't without a couple more stolen kisses in her apartment and on the drive back to campus, which was probably why she jumped out of my car already three minutes late to her next class.

And it meant I was more fixated on her lips in those last few moments than figuring out when I'd get to see her next. But she was right across the street. Maybe I'd take her to dinner later to repay her for the pizza lunch. Players were allowed in The Deadwood before it became a bar only at 9pm.

Walking into my afternoon classes, I was more relaxed and content than I'd been in a long time. And it was all thanks to one Lego-loving transfer.

Relationships had never been something I'd entertained. I'd been laser-focused on my goals. No distractions. I'd seen more than one guy derailed by relationship drama, but things with Leona weren't like that. They were so natural and uncomplicated it was hard to see how things could be less right. It wasn't until I found myself grinning for no reason that I stopped dead in my tracks—so quickly that someone rammed into my back.

What the hell was I doing with Leona? What were we? Did I want there to be a *we*? My adamant *no distractions* stance might've been a bit overblown. If we kept things casual, if I didn't let myself get sidetracked or lose focus on what had always been the goal, then there was nothing wrong with hanging out with someone I clicked with.

Then the tension in my muscles loosened again. Maybe a little distraction wasn't a horrible idea. Besides, Leona was one I didn't think I'd be able to avoid even if I wanted to—and I didn't.

9

LEONA

Racing into class and sliding into the back row of the sixty-person classroom wasn't nearly as embarrassing as it would normally be since I was still all flustered and fluttery after my kiss, correction, kisses with Reid.

Holy shit, we made out. I made out with my hot neighbor who's totally into me, not one of my roommates.

The giddy, light feeling practically carried me past the three people I had to scoot past to find an empty seat. Who knew Plant Biochemistry was so popular?

"We have a strict door closed at the beginning of class policy, Ms..."

I froze in front of the empty chair I'd been trying to slide into. "Oakes. I'm sorry. I didn't know."

"Someone didn't read the syllabus I emailed to everyone last week."

Scorching embarrassment threatened to turn me to ash. "I must've missed it. I'm sorry, Professor Dawes."

"Well, Ms. Oakes—" He stood a bit straighter. "You wouldn't happen to be—"

My heart leaped, punching straight at my uvula. Panic must've been rolling off me in waves.

"I'm very sorry I was late, and it won't happen again. If I'm late in the future, which I don't plan on being, then I'll keep the door firmly shut. I apologize for interrupting."

His mouth opened and closed a few times, and I prayed he wouldn't say anything else, but the looks had already started.

There were more than a couple pointed stares in my direction as I sank into my seat.

But Professor Dawes launched back into his rundown of class expectations, and no one else wanted to be caught in his crosshairs, so the talking and whispering died down quickly. If I was lucky, by the end of class, everyone would forget about the girl with the same name as the president. Although, it wasn't like word wouldn't get around.

A minimum of twelve more hours of anonymity before I went to this event my dad wanted me to go to. Maybe there wouldn't be too many people there and gossip didn't travel quickly, but from the freaking social media account blasting campus gossip from the juicy to the mundane complete with pictures or graphics to add to the virality, I didn't expect I'd fly under the radar for long.

The trip back to my apartment was a lot less exciting than the last time since I wasn't in the passenger seat of Reid's car. Not that I should get used to it or anything. It was a kiss—well, a few kisses—and they were blindingly glorious, but that didn't mean they were for him. For all I knew, he thought they were meh.

Don't get your hopes up, Leona. Get out of the dream world you're building for yourself in your head.

"Who the hell makes their own pasta sauce in college?"

Taylor's voice blared through the apartment the second I opened the front door.

"Who the hell has twenty pairs of heels in college?" Ashley shouted back.

"Hey, guys."

"Hey, Leona." They answered in unison like they hadn't been in the middle of a screaming match. "How were classes? We heard you were late to Biochem."

My bag dropped straight off my shoulder. "What? How the hell did you hear that?"

"STFU Dirt. The post went up a little while ago."

I slumped into one of the chairs around the dining table. "Already?"

"Yeah, sorry about that." Ashley rolled her spatula along her palm. "It wasn't a hit piece or a headline or anything, but the comments can get wild from time to time. At least there wasn't a picture, just a drawing."

"Yet. There wasn't a picture yet." She showed me the artist's representation that looked more like a carnival caricature than a court sketch artist's.

Great, I banged my head against the wall. "Is my head really that big?"

Taylor slipped her hand in front of it, trying to cushion the blows. "It's not so bad."

"What happens when everyone on campus knows who I am, and they avoid me like the plague?" I groaned and turned around, with the back of my head resting against the cabinet.

Taylor gnawed on a piece of raw pasta. "We know who you are and we're not avoiding you."

"That's because you don't have a choice."

Ashley tasted some of the sauce bubbling in the pot.

"Not true. We knew you were President Oakes's daughter when you were assigned to our apartment."

My head shot up, surprise rippling through me. "What? How'd you know?"

She shrugged. "Same last name, plus it's not every day the director of housing emails and copies the president's assistant on that email telling us we'll be having a new roommate assigned to our apartment."

I slapped my hand to my forehead. "They didn't. I'm sorry they did that." So much for joining campus just like any other student.

Taylor waved her pasta at me. "Don't worry about it. We figured it out, but we weren't going to treat you any differently than anyone else. Once people know, it won't be a big deal."

"You hope it won't be a big deal. I don't want to take anyone else down with me." I laughed, trying to shrug off the weight on my chest.

Ashley held out a spoon with a little sauce on it. "What do you think?"

The full flavor with mixed spices hit me. "It's delicious."

"See, Taylor. Totally worth it."

"Don't encourage her," Taylor grumbled not-so-under her breath.

I laughed and rinsed off the spoon.

Ashley went back to stirring and added in another dash of seasoning. "No one thinks you're running around with a notepad scribbling down every infraction and reporting it to your dad. Trust me, it won't be a big deal. No one will care."

"I hope you're right."

10

REID

We marched into the room with the ceremony already in progress. There were five long rows near the front for the team. All eyes were on us. This was what happened when Mikelson got carried away in yet another session of berating us for our practice performance.

The whole football team and coaching staff sat in the on-campus theater along with other sports teams in seats built for people half our size. It was stuffy, with old creaky wood and carpeting a thousand times nicer than anything in student housing. Normally, guest speakers spoke on the stage, and new student groups were invited in along with their parents to butter them up within the storied walls.

The small wooden seats were squeaky and made our entrance even more disruptive—because sixty guys showing up late wasn't noticeable enough. But the movement of other sports teams across the stage hadn't stopped at all since our arrival. At least that served as a bit of a distraction.

Hollis shifted uncomfortably beside me, tugging at his tie like it was trying to strangle him. Cole sat on my other side, looking like he didn't hate being in his suit. I'd have much preferred being at home in my sweats, but at least I wasn't in a suit for a disciplinary violation or another booster event where alums reminisced about their glory days at STFU while drinking their tenth martini of the evening.

The director of athletics continued his announcements. Track and field came next, then lacrosse, baseball, basketball and a soccer award. The football team was always saved for the end.

Dr. Oakes took the stage.

There was no love lost between Mikelson and President Oakes. Though Coach Mikelson didn't find much love anywhere for anything other than football. If he hadn't led his team to three consecutive bowl game championships, but not national championships, he'd probably be gone right now.

"We're happy to have everyone back on campus. New and old members of the St. Francis University family. One of the reasons we're all excited for this upcoming year is to see our St. Francis Bulldogs take another shot at a championship. I know you're ready for it, and I'm sure the team is too. We do have a new national record for our quarterback and the whole team, so I'd love for them to come up here."

All the guys stood, looking just as uncomfortable as I did. It was one thing to be out on the field playing or celebrating after a game where confetti and stages appeared out of thin air, but all the eyes on us now were full of expectation for what was to come. There was no blocking it out now.

"Our former St. Francis University turned pro quarterback, left us last season and broke the record for most games gaining 400 yards or more, and we all know that's a team effort. So we'd like to commemorate this record and hang this on the trophy wall with all the other St. Francis Bulldog achievements and where I know you'd all like to have another trophy added to the collection amassed by Coach Mikelson."

The stands rumbled with the pent-up energy people hadn't been able to expel since football season ended.

"We have these tokens for you all to show our appreciation for what this team brings to the campus community and how you will all continue to do that in the future as respectfully as possible."

My row walked toward the stage for the photo op.

As the line moved along, a couple guys looked back in my direction. I wiped at my mouth and nose. Did I have something on my face? Most of us were a similar height, so I couldn't see over anyone's heads to find out what the hell they all kept looking at.

Cole went up before me. His legs locked, and he stumbled forward. His head jerked, and he looked at me, wide-eyed, over his shoulder.

"What?" I whispered through clenched teeth.

He didn't say a word and kept walking, so I stepped forward to shake Dr. Oakes's hand and moved forward to take the small box with the engraved plaque from the woman standing beside him. Only it wasn't any woman. It was Leona.

She started and stared back at me, the plaque suspended in mid-air.

I got that rush for the end zone feeling. Like I'd been waiting to see her for a year, although it was only yesterday I'd touched her lips and watched her dash off to class.

My hand hung inches away from the polished wood. "Leona?"

"Reid."

"What are you doing here?" we both asked at the same time.

"I'm on the football team." I swept my hands out at the line of other guys who'd just been announced. "What are you doing here?"

Her gaze flicked to the man several paces behind me who continued to shake hands. "That's my dad."

Time slowed down, and a sound escaped my throat.

Ezra bumped into me.

My chest was tight. This wasn't good. This was the opposite of good. This was a disaster.

Ezra reached around me and took the plaque from her hands, then nudged me along until my legs began working enough to get me back to my seat.

"Was that President Oakes's daughter?" he asked.

Cole leaned in. "Yeah, you figured that out too?"

I glanced at Oakes, who'd finished congratulating the players and was now shaking hands with Coach Mikelson. Coach stared at him like he wanted to throw a punch while Oakes stared back with a barely contained disdain. My gaze shot to Leona, who stared back at me as dumbfounded as I was.

Coach walked past Oakes and took his plaque from Leona like she'd coated it in shit before handing it off.

Fuck, this was bad. This was monumentally bad.

Ezra turned to me and slapped the plaque against my chest with a look in his eyes that, for the first time in months, didn't seem clouded with a glower. Instead this seemed to be the funniest shit he'd ever seen. "Looks like things just got interesting."

The end of the ceremony was filled with more talking and clapping, but I sat in my seat after being tugged down into it by Cole and stared at Leona sitting on stage beside her dad. Her dad, President Oakes. President Oakes was her dad.

I walked out of the auditorium toward the parking lot with the rest of the guys. The collar of my shirt felt like it was trying to strangle me.

No one said a word as we walked to the car. I could barely focus on putting one foot in front of the other and stepped out from between a row of cars following Cole, who was way ahead of me.

A car horn blared, and I whipped around and flipped them off. "Watch where the fuck you're going!" I was losing it, and some asshole was trying to mow me down. I stared at the windshield beyond my hand.

Leona was on the left of my still extended finger and her dad, President Oakes, was on the right with his hands tight around the steering wheel and a face-melting glare to match.

"Fuck."

Ezra grabbed my shoulders and hefted me out of the line of traffic. "You can say that again."

11

LEONA

Reid was a football player. He was on the team. The gold wristband and high fives before he made it to me at Welcome Wagon made much more sense now.

He was also standing in front of my dad's car, flipping us both off.

One of his roommates, Ezra, tugged him away, and his hand finally dropped.

"The disrespect. And I don't mean that I'm the president of the university, but just a fellow human being. These players have no respect for anyone or anything that's not connected with football. He leaps out in front of the car and then has the audacity to be so vulgar. That player in particular, his face is burned into my memory now. They're late. They don't care. They don't apologize."

My phone buzzed wildly in my bag. I grabbed it as the screen flooded with notifications.

Reid: I'm so sorry.

Reid: I didn't know it was you, even if I had, I'm so sorry.

Reid: It was a knee jerk reaction and if I haven't said it already, I'm so sorry.

Reid: Can you please tell President Oakes that?

I swallowed and glanced at my dad, still speaking as animatedly as I'd ever seen him about the rudeness of the whole team. And how they were singlehandedly destroying the very fabric of our campus culture of consideration and civility.

Me: I'll talk to you later.

I tucked my phone back in my bag and slumped against the seat.

How had I not seen it? The body, the swagger, the looks.

I'd thought word had gotten out that I was the president's daughter, but no, they were all focused on the football player I'd been unknowingly hanging out with. Part of a team my father detested with the fire of a hundred suns.

Dad didn't require much actual conversation from me for the rest of the ride and well into dinner, where I choked down a bit of chicken alfredo.

"And another football player was written up for theft." Dad set down his phone. "I swear, it happens at least twenty times a semester, and those are only the reports that make it to me. Many of the staff don't even report it, although I'd said they're not to get any more special treatment than they already do."

"I'm sure it's not that bad."

"Last year, a group of them plastered the Chancellor's Building steps in vomit. Seventy students covered the entire space in biohazard and tried to leave it behind for the poor custodial staff to handle. I demanded that they clean it up themselves, and you'd have thought I told Mikelson I wanted their fingernails removed. It's complete and total disrespect, and it feels as though it's only getting worse."

Maybe the fire of a thousand suns.

I poked at my nearly untouched pasta.

"Have you had any run-ins yet?"

The drawn-out silence finally ripped me out of the internal screaming with my hair on fire that had been happening in my head. "Sorry, what was that?"

"You haven't had any run-ins with the football team, have you? There might be some players in off-campus housing near your apartment."

I cleared my throat. "I'm not sure. I've met some of my neighbors from the off-campus townhouses, and they've all been nice, very helpful, very respectful. A few of the guys in the apartment cluster have been rowdy, but nothing outside of the norm for a college campus, I'd imagine."

He made a noise of discontent. "Coach Mikelson acts as if the whole campus should revolve around his team. He insisted they be given their awards last instead of the soccer team, which won their first national championship last season. I swear the man believes the whole campus should screech to a grinding halt for him and his players." He wiped his mouth with his napkin and dropped it to the table.

"Maybe they're not all that bad." It felt like I was hydroplaning in a car, and I had no idea how to stop it. Were you supposed to turn into the skid or out of it?

"With a coach like him drilling into them how important they are to this school, how could they not be? We've secured more research grants than ever before, and his team losing the national championship is what he thinks brings more to this campus than anyone else." He took a deep breath and looked at me. "You barely ate any of your food."

"Just saving room for dessert." I patted my still empty stomach that was looped in knot after knot.

"Did I tell you about the parent's farewell brunch where the players descended and stripped the whole buffet down like locusts? Some of the invited attendees hadn't even eaten yet. The poor kitchen staff had to work double-time to get more food out so they didn't go hungry."

"How about we talk about anything other than the football team?"

He shot me a chagrinned look and slid back from the table. "You're right. No sense in ruining our night talking about things that'll only leave a bad taste in our mouths. Is coffee ice cream still your favorite?"

"Absolutely." The careening car was back on the road.

"Sorry for spoiling our evening with all the talk about bad actors on campus. Let's talk about how you're settling in on campus. How are classes?"

"So far, so good. It's still early days. I'll let you know how I feel when midterms roll around."

"I'm sure you'll handle it all well. Your grades have always been excellent." He grabbed the bowls and opened the fridge.

"I can only hope." We were cruising along in safe territory, and hopefully no more trees jumped into the road.

I stood and found the ice cream scooper in one of the drawers, then pulled out a tall, wide glass and filled it with hot water.

"What's that for?"

"To make scooping easier."

He set the tub of ice cream in front of me. "Made any new friends?"

And the car had jumped the curb and was now careening toward a ditch.

I spilled some of the hot water on the counter and

submerged the ice cream scoop. "A few. There are so many new names and faces, it's hard to remember them all."

"That's the hazard of a campus this big, but I'm sure you'll find a solid group of friends to spend time with."

I dug into the tub of coffee ice cream. The metal slid across the coffee heaven with ease, curling into a perfect ball. "I'm sure I will. But it's been nice to get to know people and be surprised by how nice they can be."

"I hope that continues, and you're not blindsided by reckless individuals on campus. I won't pretend that there aren't any issues here and I want you to have the best experience possible."

After I finished serving our two scoops of ice cream each, I dropped the soupy glass and scoop into the sink.

The drive back to my apartment was filled with stormy, chaotic thoughts. What was I going to do about Reid? I'd finally met a guy I liked who liked me back. We'd kissed. It had been the kind of make-out session I'd read about and dreamed about and had never had before. And he was probably one of a handful of people on campus my dad would shit a brick about me having anything to do with.

I couldn't tell my dad I was dating him—not that we were dating, especially not after the "Watch where the fuck you're going!" incident. The panic of even considering telling my dad about Reid sent my heart rate spiking with the twisty-plummeting stomach feeling.

Plus, there was the way Reid's coach had glared at me when he walked up on stage. He hated my guts because my last name was Oakes, so that probably wasn't doing Reid any favors.

It's not like he and I had made any big plans or promises. Hell, we hadn't even planned the next time we'd see each other. We'd barely talked about much after the kiss—well, kisses—but it felt like it could be more than a flirtation. But right now...it didn't feel like it was possible for it to go any further. The heavy blanket of disappointment weighed down each step closer to the conversation I'd have to have with him.

A figure popped out of the brick archway leading to my apartment door.

I yelped and slammed my hand against my chest, digging my keys into my sternum.

Reid shot forward to keep me from pitching over into the bushes along the walkway. "Sorry, I didn't mean to scare you."

"Then why the hell were you lurking in the dark?" My voice took on a mixture of hysteria and relief.

"I was trying to be discreet."

"Discreet." The shoe had dropped and landed right on my baby toe.

He glanced over his shoulder like someone was lurking in the shadows to attack him at any moment. "I'm really sorry about before. Can we go inside?"

I folded my arms across my waist. "I don't think that would be a good idea."

He ran his hands down over his face. The dress shirt, which had looked freshly ironed earlier, was wrinkled. His face seemed taut and a lot less cheery and playful than the last time we'd been alone together.

"How long have you been waiting out here?"

"A while."

"Only to apologize?"

"Not only."

"But also to talk about who my dad is." It wasn't a question.

"Partially."

My stomach plummeted. I walked past him and shoved my key into the lock.

He dropped his hand over mine, stilling my escape. "Why didn't you tell me?"

"Why didn't you tell me you were a football player?"

His head rocked back. "What does me being a football player have to do with you being the president's daughter?"

"Everything apparently. Isn't that why you're here? I've met your coach and seen him and my dad in the same room together. They were probably five minutes from breaking out the boxing gloves. And us dating—" I fumbled, my keys falling out of my hand. "Not that we're dating. We made out a little. I'm not saying just because of that we're in a relationship or anything."

Some of the tension drained out of his face, and he bent down, while still holding my gaze, and snatched up the keys without even needing to look for them. "Has anyone told you you're cute when you're flustered?"

"Not lately." I reached for the keys, but he wrapped his hand around mine. Despite the chill in the air, his skin was hot, his touch gentle as the rough tips of his fingers sent shocks along my palm.

My heart rate skipped along like a stone across a lake before sinking.

"I like you, Leona."

"I like you too." I dropped my head. "But..." The words wouldn't surface. Dating Reid would mean lying to my dad. Maybe not outright, but being evasive whenever he asked me about school and making new friends and finding my footing here. After everything that happened between him and my mom, I couldn't do that to him. I couldn't be like her and lie.

His grip tightened on me for a flash before he relaxed. "But you're who you are, and I'm who I am. I take it after that incident in the parking lot, your dad isn't any more on board with the football team?"

I shook my head. "No, he's not. And I take it me being President Oakes' daughter wouldn't go over well with your coach?"

Reid let go of me and dragged his fingers through his hair. "He'd probably roast me over an open bonfire." His strangled laugh filled the widening gulf between us. "No, it wouldn't go well. One of the guys got bounced from the team because he wouldn't break up with a girlfriend who happened to be the daughter of a former assistant coach."

My stomach, which had once been filled with butterflies at the sight of him, knotted. "So we're on the same page then? I can tell how much you love football, and you don't want to risk that on dat—hanging out with me." I tried to keep my face and my smile easy, but it felt like sawdust was being shoved down my throat.

"Totally." He had a strange look on his face. The gears were turning, and I wasn't sure what it meant.

Damn, no hesitation. That hurt.

He scrambled forward. "I didn't mean it that way. I just meant...I'm sorry."

"What's there to be sorry for? No big deal. At all. We're in agreement. We're still neighbors. It's not like we have to go running screaming in the other direction if we see each other around. Right?" My laugh sounded as brittle as it felt.

His lips pressed together, and he said nothing.

"Right?"

"No, you're right. It's not a big deal."

Escape was my only thought. Coming to STFU was supposed to unravel the mistakes of my past, and here I was, longing to jump into a new one in my present.

I stepped up to the threshold, feeling like this was a door I didn't want to close, but I had to, not just for me, but for him. "See you around, Reid."

"See you around, Leona."

Turning, I moved inside and glanced at him over my shoulder.

He kept on walking without a look back.

I closed the door and pressed my back against the chilly metal, letting my head drop against it. This was better for both of us. Going beyond our flirtation and a kiss would complicate life for both of us.

No, there wasn't even an us. For Reid and me.

This was fine. A first-week flirtation. Totally fine. And I didn't regret my choice one bit. Absolutely not at all.

12

REID

I glanced back over my shoulder to get another look at her, but her front door was already closing. It was probably for the best. Scratch that—it was absolutely for the best.

Jogging across the street, I should've felt lighter than air. A bullet had been successfully dodged. No one had to know about my mid-day make-out with President Oakes's daughter. Not Mikelson, not even the guys.

When I'd gone over there to talk to her, I'd thought there would be some convincing I had to do or creative excuses, but she got it completely. Why'd that make it so much harder to climb the steps to my front door? If she got how important football was to me, then what the hell was my problem?

On the porch, I slapped myself in the face a few times. *Get it together, Reid.*

This was exactly where my *no distractions* mantra came from. I should be studying the playbook. Maybe getting in some homework, so I didn't have to worry about it before class tomorrow. This was a good thing. A perfect thing.

Inside the house, Ezra was watching one of the terrible *Terminator* sequels after *T2* that I'd pretended didn't exist with his guitar on his lap. Hollis walked in gnawing on a chicken breast on a fork—no plate, no napkin, just a full chicken breast on four tines.

I flopped onto the couch.

"If you drop that," I said, "you don't get to have another one."

He flipped me the bird. "I bought it. How'd your gentle letdown of the president's daughter go?"

I propped my feet up on the table. "Better than expected."

Ezra glared at me but went back to the movie with a plate of chicken and broccoli balanced on his lap. "No tears. No cursing."

"Not at all. Actually, she and I were on the same page about making a clean break."

He stopped mid-bite. "No shit?"

"No fucking shit. It seems she's just as happy to not go shouting from the rooftops that she even knew who I was."

Hollis leaned against the wall like there weren't four empty seats in the living room. "That makes one person on campus. I had to deal with two days of glares before I figured out some sophomore was running around telling everyone we were a thing after I picked up her backpack when it fell off the back of her chair in an English Comp lecture."

"Lucky me, then." I stared at the screen without seeing any of the action and explosions glowing in front of my face.

"You still know it would've been stupid, right? If Mikelson found out, you'd have been screwed."

Cole walked in, balancing his plate of pasta and seafood on top of a cup. "Who'd have been screwed?"

Ezra glared and upped the volume on the TV.

"Reid if Mikelson found out he had been banging the president's daughter."

Simmering, I gritted my teeth. "I didn't bang her. There was no banging."

"Then it looks like it all worked out."

"Why the hell was everyone so invested in whether or not I kept seeing Leona?"

Hollis tapped the now empty fork against his mouth. "Maybe because we need you in the starting lineup, and if you get benched this season and Fulton U kicks our asses again, we'll murder you in your sleep?"

"Oh, now you're all on the no-distractions train?"

Cole laughed with a mouthful of food. "Maybe someone's been drumming it into our heads, and it finally stuck."

I dropped my feet from the table. "Don't make a bigger deal about this than it needs to be."

Ezra, for all the time he pretended not to be listening to any of us, turned and exchanged looks with Cole and Hollis.

"Whatever, I'm getting some food. Did you leave any for me?" I shot up.

Ezra went back to the movie and strummed the guitar strings. "There's a catering tray of shrimp we need to finish tonight before it goes bad. There's also chicken breasts and broccoli, and if you can wrestle the box away from Griff, there's cereal, if you're up for carb-based hunger pangs at one am."

The old linoleum tiles in the kitchen squeaked with each step I took. Standing at the counter with his phone balanced at eye level inside an open cabinet, Griff held a punchbowl of Lucky Charms.

"Hungry?"

He jerked, sloshing milk onto the counter, and slammed the cabinet door closed.

I grabbed a plate from the tall stack of paper plates on the six-seater table rammed against the wall. "That wasn't suspicious at all."

"What wasn't?"

"You closing your phone in the cabinet so I couldn't see what was on it. You'd better not be watching porn where we eat." I opened the oven. Without grabbing the oven mitts, I tugged out the catering tray of garlic shrimp and chicken breasts that had been warming inside. The heat was more intense than I expected, and I dropped it onto the stovetop, blowing on my fingers.

"Why would you think that was a good idea?" He shoveled more cereal into his mouth.

"The oven's barely on."

"Tell that to your burned-off fingerprints."

"What's on your phone?" I jutted my chin toward the still closed cabinet.

"Nothing. Why are you so damn nosy? How'd things go with the president's daughter?"

"Now who's nosy?" I put a couple chicken breasts and a scoop of shrimp onto the plate.

Ezra had a part-time job in the summers with a catering company. Sometimes, when they did an event nearby, the owner took pity on us and let him take a couple trays of leftovers.

"This affects us all. She's the president's daughter. You know Mikelson would lose his mind if he figured out you let her borrow a pencil."

"It's handled."

"Handled as in you told her if she sees you on campus to run the other way?"

"No, handled as in we're neighbors. Enough said."

"You don't look happy about it."

I grabbed a bottle of water from the fridge and rolled it along my still toasty fingertips. "Would you lay off?"

"Wow." He dragged his fingers along his chin like he was observing the eighth wonder of the ancient world. "Is this what Reid Riddick looks like when he's in like?"

"Fuck you." I left the kitchen, but not before Griff's full-on belly laugh reached my ears. Not wanting to talk about the Leona situation anymore, I blew straight past the living room taking my food up to my room.

It wasn't until I finished my shrimp that it dawned on me that Griff might've just been pushing so I'd stop asking him what the hell he was doing with his phone. But after I trashed my plate and packed up my gear for the game tomorrow, I started to get annoyed with how relieved everyone had been once I told them I called it off with Leona.

I lay in bed with my hands propped behind my head and smiled at the memory of how flustered she got the first time I saw her. The look in her eyes as she tried to figure out what the hell everyone was doing at Welcome Wagon. The little gasp she made the first time I kissed her.

There wasn't time for much outside of football and classes, but I wanted to spend every spare waking moment with her. I'd suffer through a thousand paper cuts for another afternoon of talking music and movies and lemonade kisses.

I jerked my pillow from under my head and shoved it over my face, screaming into it. For once, I'd found someone I connected with as naturally as breathing, and she was the one person on campus who could derail everything I'd worked for. And somehow it didn't make me want her any less. But I had to. Not just for me, but for the team. For the win.

Cole jogged off the field beside me, cursing under his breath. Home field advantage was solidly in Maryland's court.

"I had him."

"You got him. He didn't touch Hollis."

"But he almost did." He marched over to the water bottle table and drank one down like he was trying to drown himself.

"This is the first game. Cole needs to calm the hell down, so he doesn't psych himself out for the rest of the season." Hollis ran a towel over his face, which was covered in sweat seconds after it had been wiped clean.

The support staff handed out water bottles to anyone who needed one.

"It's going to be a close one." We stared up at the scoreboard. Less than two points separated the teams, but we weren't in the lead. There were five minutes left in the fourth quarter.

"This is not how I wanted to start off the season." I dropped my head, and the sweat poured down my face like a curtain of water.

"At least we're having a better time than Mikelson." He lifted his chin to point farther down the sideline.

Mikelson was in a ref's face. The veins in his neck and forehead were more prominent than usual and his skin glowed bright red like he'd been left out on the beach all day.

"He's going to get us a penalty." Cole glared down the

line.

The play went forward with Maryland gaining less than two yards. Their time for a first down was almost over. We had three minutes if we could just get back on the field.

Hollis paced, rolling his neck. "There's still time. We can make it happen."

Mikelson once again charged forward, waving his clipboard.

At the shrill slice of a whistle, my stomach plummeted. The ref threw the flag and held up his hands to signal.

Our fears were confirmed with his booming voice over the in-stadium speakers. "Fifteen-yard penalty, St. Francis Coach for unsportsmanlike conduct. Maryland first down." The echo of the words reverberated long after they'd cut the mic.

The whole STFU student section and sidelines went off, but a quick glare from Mikelson had everyone stifling their anger.

Maryland picked up another first down.

I grabbed my hair and yanked at the roots. It was like watching a slow-motion car crash. Overhead the countdown clock ticked closer to the end of the game and our first loss of the season. That's not how any of us wanted to start things off.

I paced on the sidelines, barely able to hear anything over the screams of the Maryland crowd celebrating their victory even though there were thirty seconds left on the clock.

Maybe that's why they got a bit cocky instead of playing it safe. Their quarterback went for a pass instead of running it in for the final few yards and hammering the nail in the coffin home.

But our guys were there, hungry to not start this season

with a loss. The ball bounced from hand to hand before a pair gripped it firmly and tugged it close to his chest.

The whole bench was on their feet now, screaming.

I gripped the sleeve of Cole's jersey. Both of us stood frozen, staring at the field where Griff had intercepted the ball on Maryland's ten-yard line. The man was a walking fridge, like most defensive linemen. The whites of his eyes were comically large, but he moved like the flames of hell were chasing after him. And they were in the form of the Maryland offense. But the rest of the team was there for him, keeping the much faster guys off his ass as he charged the whole damn way up the field.

"Holy shit. He's—" I swallowed the words, not wanting to jinx him.

The clock ticked down the final seconds. If he got hit or went down, this was it—we'd lose.

Hollis chanted a low mantra of "Go!"

As one final opposing player dived for his legs, Griff leaped into the air and slammed hard into the ground.

Everyone sucked in a breath, like a single exhale would change the outcome.

The marker for the edge of the end zone was knocked over, and on the other side of the field, none of us had a good view.

Hands were twisted in towels and jerseys as the whole place fell silent.

"He was in." Cole turned to me with a smile so sure, I almost started celebrating.

The refs jogged together and conferred before the replay flashed up on the screen. His body crossed the plane of the line with both feet inbounds, and though his arms were outstretched, he maintained full control of the ball in both hands.

The ref's arms shot up over his head, and the touch-down announcement was drowned out by the insanity on the sidelines.

Hollis jumped up and down, using my shoulder pads to launch himself up. Cole tackled me from the side, and the whole team celebrated our first win snatched from the gnarled fingers of defeat.

Griff lay in the end zone for a long time, probably still not believing he'd done it.

During the sideline interviews, the locker room, the ride back to the hotel, everyone shouted about the final play like we'd been in the stands instead of on the sidelines the whole time. Had Leona watched the game? Had she seen me out on the field? What was she doing back on campus? My thoughts drifted to her on the bus ride back to the hotel.

Had Leona been roped into the STFU football mania? Had Taylor Clockwork Oranged her into watching the game? She'd been walking toward the campus when I was on my way to the team bus yesterday. My hand had been halfway up to wave to her before I shoved it into my pocket and kept my head down.

Our lobby was overrun with fans, and the party only dropped to a simmer when Mikelson and the rest of the coaching staff walked in. Once the elevator doors closed, the volume cranked right back up.

Dad: Tell Griff I said Congrats!

Me: Will do, Dad

Dad: Great game. Love you loads.

Me: Love you too.

He was probably running off to a second shift. Not much longer left until he could finally relax.

Most of the team joined in with the celebration. It

wouldn't be every game where our lineman ran in an eighty-yard touchdown.

Cole stood beside me and smiled at Griff like a proud dad. "Do you want to break that up or do I have to?"

Griff had been holding court for the past hour, recounting his final play like a *Sports Central* highlight reel.

"Why?" I tossed my empty soda can into the shiny metal domed trashcan. "Let him have his fun."

"He'll be having a lot less fun if he misses curfew and can't play next game."

"Shit." I checked the time. We had ten minutes left before we needed to be back in our rooms or face the Mikelson Wrath.

Hollis rushed through the lobby doors and headed straight for us. "What the hell are you guys doing down here? We've got curfew."

"Where the hell were you? I thought you were in the room," I said.

"Nowhere. Can someone grab him before he gets us all benched?"

"Griff." Cole cupped his hands around his mouth.

We waved our arms to get his attention.

His head popped up, and he grinned and jumped down off the table that looked ready to buckle at any moment.

I turned to one of the TVs hanging above the bar off the lobby and pointed toward it. "Griff's play's on right now."

The flow of people flooded in that direction.

Griff moved to join them, but I hooked his arm. "Curfew."

He snatched out his phone and cursed. "Why'd you guys wait so long?"

Cole slapped his shoulder. "We wanted to give you your time to shine. Now it's time to get upstairs, Cinderella."

In the elevator, Griff was still riding his high.

"I'm not getting any sleep tonight, am I?" Cole rubbed his hand over the back of his neck.

"Nope." Griff rocked back and forth to an imaginary song, shaking the whole car.

We got off on our floor, and the knocks from around the corner traveled down the carpeted hallway.

"Shit." I fumbled with my key and slapped it against the card reader.

Griff and Cole took off to their room. The beep of their door sounded a second after I threw open ours.

Hollis shoved me inside the room, and the door slammed shut behind us. Neither of us bothered turning on the light but scrambled to our bags and rummaged for clothes.

I kicked off my shoes, grabbed my sweats and took off all my clothes except my boxers. Hollis did the same thing beside me, banging his shoulder into the wall. I jumped into my sweats right at the knock on our door.

Ruffling my hair even more, I tugged on the handle and blocked the hall light with my hand. "Yeah, Coach?" The offensive coach stared at me with a stern look.

He peered into the room. "Lights out."

I kicked my clothes and shoes back behind the door. "It's been a long day. We were already asleep."

Hollis leaned against the wall in the open doorway, looking like he'd just rolled out of bed.

"Coach." He flicked his fingers from his forehead and yawned, which triggered my own yawn.

He scribbled down on his clipboard. "Six a.m. wake up to catch our flight home."

"The alarm's already set."

"Night." He nodded and walked off.

I let go of the door just as he knocked on the one next door. "Griff being the one to get us in trouble is certainly a new one."

Hollis flicked on the light beside his bed. "Yeah, normally it's you."

I snatched my clothes up off the floor. "Since when? I'm a fucking angel."

"Tell that to the literal dumpster fire you started."

"And put out!" I fished out my clothes for the flight and shoved the rest back inside. "The firework didn't go off for ten minutes. How was I supposed to know it was on a half hour delay timer?"

He laughed. "Do you think this is how the rest of the season's going to go?"

"Would that be so bad? Unexpected last-minute shit that ends up saving the day? It beats the alternative."

He sat up against the headboard with his knees up and his forearms resting on them. "If we lose again, he's going to be even worse next season."

I flopped onto my bed and knocked my head against the wall. It was two more years. Two more seasons, and I'd put up with him lighting us on fire if that's what it took to get drafted. It didn't mean I'd enjoy it, but the alternative of not making it was an impossibility. I'd worked too damn hard. Years in the gym. Running drills in my back yard until I passed out. I was so close now, and not even a little Mikelson madness could stop me.

"After he ran us for those eight miles last time and everyone started puking, I could barely feel my legs," I said. "My eyes were bloodshot for a week from puking so much."

"For some crazy reason, I thought hazing was banned." He scoffed.

"When it's your coach and under the pretense of 'practice'"—I threw up the air quotes—"then no one's got shit to say about it."

"Do you ever wonder what it would be like at another school? Like at Fulton U. Their coach seems like a hard ass, but not like Mikelson." His voice took on a faraway tone.

"Nah. You know why?" I rolled my head to the side to look at him.

"Why?" He shifted his head to stare back at me.

"Because then I wouldn't be on the team with you guys."

He laughed. "That was some legit sentimental shit, right there."

"I have my moments. But seriously. You guys are my family, and I wouldn't want to be anywhere else."

"Remind me of that if we have to do two a.m. runs again until I feel like I'm going to hack up a kidney."

"That's when you need your family most. When shit gets hard."

"The sentimentality is overwhelming. I'm beat. Did you actually set the alarm for six?"

I grabbed my phone. "Now I have."

"Night." Hollis turned off his light and rolled over.

Staring into the darkness, the words rang in my ears. I wouldn't want to be anywhere else. Sometimes things clicked, and you knew it was right. That was how I felt being around Leona, and maybe tomorrow I'd get to see her. That helped me close my eyes despite the post-win buzz humming through my veins. The faster I slept, the faster it would be tomorrow, and the faster I'd catch a glimpse that would have to be enough to tide me over until these feelings faded away.

Was this what people meant when they said someone had it bad? How about having it worse? Because I was definitely there.

13

LEONA

I rolled my pencil along my desk with the palm of my hand while analyzing the fermentation sample data. Different variables had been introduced to five samples, and now it was my job to gauge how that impacted product quality. When most people thought about what it took to run a vineyard, I don't think many thought of analyzing bacteria replication.

Reid would be back today. At least I thought he would be. Keeping up with classes was hard enough. I couldn't imagine throwing practices and traveling for football games into the mix.

But I can't say I was thinking much about football at all. More about how my dreams often centered around our last kiss. Who'd have thought I'd have to fly halfway around the world to finally be kissed like that? I guess it made sense that it would be how I'd have to lean on those memories for the foreseeable future. And I'd travel twice that far to feel it again.

Focus, Leona. Schoolwork, then I could drift off into the fantasy world of making out with the only guy who'd ever made it feel like there was a crackling fire being stoked under my skin. Although that was just torturing myself, since we weren't a thing and couldn't be a thing.

I'd finally gotten everything unpacked in my room. My extra-long twin bed was pushed under the window. The desk and chair were on the other wall, less than an arm's span away. A closet and dresser were all that was left. I hadn't hung anything on the walls yet, unlike Taylor, who'd transformed her room with fairy lights, scarves on the walls, area rugs and matching bedding and pillows that made her space feel like she'd lived there for years already.

She'd worked her magic on the bathroom and living room, so I hadn't had to buy anything extra. We had a full kitchen complete with a KitchenAid stand mixer. She didn't travel light and had already told me everything was mine to use, so I'd pitched in with buying extra groceries and cleaning duty.

My phone vibrated beside me. I tapped the screen without looking up, not wanting to lose my spot in the data.

"Hey, Dad, what's up?" He was the only person who'd called me during normal waking hours in months. Calling my phone a phone was a stretch since I hated talking on it.

"Leona." A familiar feminine voice, not my father's, came from the speaker.

Another reason I'd avoided the whole voice communication part of my phone. A rush of cold spilled over me. "Mom."

"So you do remember my voice."

"It's almost 1 a.m. there. Why are you calling me so late? Is everything okay?"

"It's good to know you still care, and yes, everything here is fine."

"Then why are you calling?" I slouched back in my chair

and folded my arms over my chest.

"Since you avoid my calls whenever we have a natural overlap in time zones, I thought I'd give this a try, and lo and behold, it worked. I am, in fact, speaking to my daughter, who is alive and well." There was a strained tease in her words. Forced and attempting the easy, playfulness we'd lost.

"Why are you calling me?"

"I wanted to hear your voice."

"And now you have."

A heavy sigh weighted down her end of the line. "Will you ever speak to me again?"

"I'm speaking to you right now." I didn't try to keep the irritation out of my voice.

"You know what I mean."

"I know." My fingers went back to the pencil, rolling it along the dented and dinged wood in a rhythmic pattern. It hadn't always been this way. Talking to my mom had been easier when we moved to Australia. Before the divorce Dad and I had always been closer, but now talking to her felt like there was a stranger on the other line trying to convince me to buy an extended warranty on my car. Funny how feelings changed over time, flip-flopping and then back again.

"Andrew said 'hi' and he misses you."

My stepdad had always been wonderful to me. But I cringed now at how I'd spoken to my dad about him. How the few phone calls of my dad's that I had taken were filled with all the new things I was learning from Andrew, how much fun I was having in our new beautiful house and how he'd take me for ice cream or any other dig I could get in.

With a throat that felt like a collapsed straw, I croaked out a response. "Tell him I said 'hi.'"

"We—he wanted to know if you were still coming back

in the summer? Or if you'd changed your mind about staying here for the Christmas break? You know how good Andrew's steaks are on the patio after you've opened your presents."

The picture she painted had been one of a holiday filled with presents, laughter and sun for the past six years, but now it turned my stomach. She thought those memories were still so bright and cheery now?

"I already told you I'm staying with Dad this Christmas."

"Well, there's a ticket waiting for you, if you want."

"Don't waste Andrew's money."

Another long, drawn-out sigh. "Will you ever be able to forgive me?" She sounded small and frail, not the bubbly, sunshiny version of her that I'd grown up around.

I sucked in a long breath and tried to piece together the broken puzzle of my middle school years. The shouting match after never having heard my parents raise their voices at one another, and then the bombshell that blew it all apart. Cheating. Cheating had broken up their seemingly happy marriage. And she'd let me believe it had been my dad who'd done it.

He moved out that night, and less than a month later, Mom and I moved to Australia.

I'd been cold and cruel to my dad. I'd said things he didn't deserve, so the answer to her question—through her lies by omission—was hard to answer because I was still wrestling with that answer for myself.

"I don't know."

"Things have always been so black and white for you, but life is never that cut and dry."

"I'm pretty sure your vows were. And you had no problem with me cutting dad off for almost six years after believing your lies."

"I never said—"

"You never said differently though. I've got to go, and I'll let you know about the summer later. It's September— there's still a lot of time left until then."

"I'll let Andrew know. He'd love to hear from you too."

"I can't, Mom. I just need to handle this my own way." These were two people I loved, yet I felt I didn't know them at all. The betrayal burned like a glowing coal in the center of my chest. All our happy memories and time together—it all felt like a big lie.

"Of course. I love you, Leona."

"Bye, Mom." I ended the call and paced around my room before going to the box stashed in my closet. After throwing a pillow down on the floor, I tipped the box over. The plastic bricks fell out in a waterfall. While other people meticulously organized their Lego, sifting through the pile to find the perfect piece was part of the fun for me. With my back against the built-in drawers in my desk, I started building and had no idea what it would become. The minutes melted away as I snapped a tiny white two-stud skinny plate into my creation.

With the whole base level of my castle constructed, I glanced up and jumped, clutching my chest at the figure standing in my doorway. I flung my pillow on top of the scattered pieces on the floor as if she couldn't see what I'd been doing for however long she was watching me.

"You really are into playing with these things." Taylor stepped inside my room and crouched down, picking up the corner of the pillow.

"It helps me relax." I rolled my shoulders forward and ducked my head, not wanting to be known as the weird roommate who plays with toys in her room all alone.

She shrugged. "Not like I can judge. Painting my nails,

spending ungodly amounts of time doing my makeup, and watching STFU games from the '90s and memorizing stats helps chill me out. We've all got our quirks, right?"

"I guess we do."

"Whatever floats your boat." She stood and wiggled her fingers in a wave motion. "Speaking of floating, we're headed to our first float building session, if you wanted to join. We'll get everyone on schedule and get to work." She clapped her hands together and rubbed them. "First place will be ours. I can taste it. This is the year of winners. You coming with?" She jerked both thumbs over her shoulder.

"I'm coming. Let me grab my stuff." I slipped on my shoes, then grabbed my bag and my folded boxes from move-in day. "Hey, Taylor."

She glanced at me over her shoulder.

"Why didn't you tell me Reid was on the football team?"

Her confused laugh filled the hallway. "I didn't think I had to. I mean, this is STFU football we're talking about here. This campus eats, sleeps and breathes football. They can barely walk down the street without people staring and talking about them. Do you not like football players or something?"

"Or something."

"You didn't notice half the clothes we were babysitting at Welcome Wagon were jerseys."

I waved my arm in the air in the general direction of the pond-side party. "Half the people on campus wear those things. You wear them. I thought it was just a thing people did to support the team, not that everyone wearing them was on the team."

Her smile sagged a little.

Ashley stepped into the hallway with a toolbox.

"I didn't know it was a big deal for you to know he was

on the team. Was there any particular reason why? We saw you two chatting awfully closely at Wagon, and he dropped you off a few days ago. Is there something going on between the two of you?"

I sputtered, absolutely failing at a poker face. "What? No. Don't be crazy. That's crazy. Of course not." The fewer people who knew Reid and I had kissed, the better. Eventually, people would find out who my dad was, and I didn't need to feed the rumor mill or that STFU Dirt account that posted new gossip at least twenty times a day.

They exchanged looks.

Maybe that was a little too much. "No, I was surprised, that's all. It's no big deal."

"If you say so."

Following behind the two of them, I toyed with the frayed strap of my bag.

"We're taking Ashley's car," Taylor announced when we hit the curb.

"What the hell? Are you paying for gas now? I drove you to class all week."

"We're in the same classes—you were going there anyway."

I waved my keys in the air dangling them from my fingers. "I can drive." At least focusing on the road would mean less time to think about Reid.

"Aww, Leona, you're so sweet and considerate," Ashley said sugar-sweet before poking her tongue out at Taylor.

They directed me to a garage at the far end of campus. There were a few other cars parked outside.

"Good, they're here already. I talked one of the agricultural manufacturing guys into letting us use one of the bays. There are only two other teams building here, so we're safer from sabotage, but we can't get lazy," Taylor warned before we got out.

"You guys take this really seriously."

Ashley leaned forward between the two seats. "You have no idea."

Taylor walked to the door beside the closed garage door. The used-to-be white building was a story and a half high with dusty-looking windows along the top. The fluorescent lighting flickered inside. If not for the music and voices coming from inside, it would've made the perfect horror movie filming location.

I followed Ashley through the doorway. Even more laughter and shouting came from inside. Whoever was here already was having a great time.

"And we have our final float crew member bringing all her building skills!"

I stepped into the overly lit room to cheers like I'd been shoved out on stage in a game show.

A metal clank followed my entrance.

"Leona."

After only hearing that voice a few times, I knew it instantly.

Turning, I locked eyes with a stunned Reid. At his feet, a can of paint slowly glugged out onto the floor.

"Dude!" Cole slapped Reid's chest and ducked down, picking up the can now half-covered in fluorescent blue paint. "Hey, Leona. Good to see you again."

Taylor swung around to me. "Guys, this is Leona. You already know Reid and Cole, Hollis, Griff, and Ezra. That's Maggie and Bryn."

Everyone waved back to me, but the guys all glanced at each other.

I waved, feeling like a shop window mannequin wanting to disappear. Accepting this invite was probably a mistake.

Ashley leaped into action, breaking the strained silence. "Taylor came up with an awesome design. If we can pull this off and keep the sabotage to a minimum, we're going to kick ass this year."

I was locked in place, unable to move toward the rest of the group because I could feel his gaze on me. I guess I was taking the tips from *Jurassic Park* literally and maybe hoping that if I didn't move, no one would remember I was even here.

Reid was still frozen, staring at the side of my face.

We were statues of awkwardness. At least I wasn't the only one unsure of what the hell to do.

The rest of the group gathered around the waist-high stack of cardboard boxes.

I flicked my gaze at Reid, who slowly moved toward them.

Breaking away, I stepped in front of him and kept my voice low. "If it'll be a problem to have me here, let me know, and I can go." I stared at the concrete between us.

The edges of his trainers were smudged with blue paint.

His body was rigid in front of me. "No, it's fine. We talked about it already. I'm good, if you're good."

I lifted my head. "Are you sure? Seriously, it's not a big deal. I know I'm a last-minute addition and these traditions mean a lot to all of you."

He shook his shoulders and seemed to reset his whole demeanor, slipping back into the more carefree version I'd met before. "Traditions you should get to enjoy too. I promise it's not a problem." He held up his pinkie with a smile that didn't make his almost dimples pop out, but he was trying.

My heart skipped into a full sprint before I reined it in.

If he was trying, I could too.

"I promise too. Friends." I locked my finger around his. The warm weight of his finger sent a flare spiraling up my arm.

"Friends. There's a bunch of us anyway. It's not like we're going to be on top of each other or anything." He winced. "I didn't—"

"I know."

We stood in front of each other.

I stared into his smiling eyes, but it felt like the facade was paper-thin. Did my face look the same? I was one gentle breeze away from letting loose all the tumultuous feelings raging inside me.

Ashley's voice broke through the connection. "Let's get to work, people. We have two weeks until homecoming, and these jerks have an away game this weekend." She handed out pieces of the design to pairs. I was matched up with one of the girls I hadn't met before. "You two are build buddies." Relief washed over me that at least I wouldn't be shoulder-to-shoulder with Reid throughout this whole thing.

I glanced over at Reid, and his Adam's apple bobbed. As much as I wanted to reassure him this wouldn't be awkward and we could work together with no issue, I didn't know if I could pull off that lie. And now that we wouldn't be paired up, it meant I didn't have to.

We started by reviewing schedules for when everyone could come in and who could work together for night security.

"You guys weren't joking about this." I popped open a can of soda.

All the heads swung in my direction, completely stone-faced. Ashley spoke up. "The prize is $10,000."

The soda shot out my nose, burning my nasal passages all the way up. "Are you kidding me?" I glanced around at everyone.

"Nope. It's no joke."

With that, everyone got to work constructing the base of our creature, which sat over Reid's car. He had an older convertible, and he'd offered up being without it for the next two weeks so we didn't have to try to lift this thing and set it on top, possibly getting the dimensions wrong. It also meant he wouldn't have to offer me a ride during that time. Probably hoping it wouldn't take more than that to erase our few days of flirtation from his memories of the school year.

"Sorry, I'm late. But I brought another ten boxes." The door slammed, shaking the flimsy structure we were all in, and a girl stood there with a stack of boxes she'd had to tilt at an angle to get through the door.

"Damnit." Our new arrival drew the word out like it had twenty-two syllables.

Cole walked around the wall of cardboard we'd already constructed. "Fuck no. Kennedy? Absolutely fucking not." He slammed down the tins of paint he'd be carrying.

The new arrival—Kennedy, apparently—was a little taller than me with her curly, black hair perched on top of her head in an effortless bun that looked like an actual hairstyle, unlike whenever I tried it. Her jeans hugged her generous curves, and the t-shirt and blazer combo didn't look overdone. Although we were all sweating in this chilly garage trying to dodge cardboard-sized paper cuts, she still looked like she'd fit in, just looking fabulous while doing it.

And she and Cole clearly didn't get along at all.

"Don't you know this makes me want to be on this team even more? Oh, Cole doesn't want me here? Let me go scamper away and hide." She bent her knees and shook them while opening her eyes wide and batting her eyelashes. "Want to know what I think of that?" She held up one beautifully manicured finger with a bored look in her eyes.

Taylor walked between the two of them and pressed her hands against their chests. "Would you two chill out? One bad hook-up, and you're both ready to go scorched Earth."

They both jerked. "Who said we hooked up?" Their reply was in unison along with their glares.

"Come on, no one harbors that much animosity without dating unless they've had sex."

Kennedy crossed her arms over her chest with a sly smirk. "He wishes."

Cole's face turned beet red. "I'm not working with her."

Taylor clapped her hands in front of their faces. "A thousand dollars, people. Get it together. Fine, you don't have to be paired up. Reid, Leona, are you cool working together? You're the only other two who have a security duty schedule that matches up."

"Sure," Reid called out and nodded toward me. "We're good with that, right, Leona?"

I nodded, not sure what else to say, and squeaked out an "of course." Just great. So much for trying to keep my distance. And as much as I knew that was best for both of us, I really didn't want to.

He was a temptation I'd never faced before. My feelings weren't unrequited, they weren't being driven deep down because he had his eyes set on my best friend or a spot at the vineyard or me being his new tutor to pass biology or chemistry. Working beside him was like a beautifully wrapped present that had been shoved in my Christmas stocking, but I didn't get to open it.

14

REID

Torture. The past eleven days had been absolute torture. Night after night spent within inches of Leona after classes. The away game only had us off-campus for one building night. It had been sweet relief with a sour aftertaste. The only thing harder than being close to Leona was not being near her.

My spot against the wall was surrounded by cardboard shavings. Somehow, I'd been put in charge of sculpting the dragon head. I worked on the eyes, picking apart the thick, stiff cardboard with a blade.

"I did some research last night. If we interlock the tail segments like this, they'll be sturdier, and we could move it up and down." Leona showed off her technique, which everyone worked on replicating with whatever cardboard they had on hand.

Cole jumped onto the metal folding chair, skidding it across the concrete floor. "Lego Queen for the win!" He hopped down and high-fived her. Fanning the small pieces of cardboard like a wad of cash, he laughed. "I can already smell the steaks cooking after we win."

"At least you don't want to spend it on stupid shit. Can we get to work?" Ezra snatched the cardboard from his hands and stalked off.

"What crawled up his ass?" Cole looked over his shoulder.

I picked up a box cutter. "Like you've been absolutely wonderful to be around lately."

"What the hell makes you say that? I've been fantastic."

The door opened, and Kennedy walked inside. "Hey, everyone, I've got coffee and donuts." She held up a cardboard carafe of coffee plus cups stuffed with stir sticks and sugar packets with a wide grin.

The room exploded in cheers, except for Cole.

She seemed cool. I'd seen her around campus and had a few Gen. Ed. classes with her freshman and sophomore year, but I'd need to find out from Cole if we were hating her guts for a particular crime against him or if we were all on board with a general dislike and avoidance. Not that her showing up with food to a bunch of hungry guys wasn't buying her at least a few points on the scoreboard.

Kennedy cupped her hands and shouted from across the room way louder than needed. "Cole, don't look so sad. There's a sorry biscotti in the bottom of the bag reserved especially for you."

He glared at her with his shoulders bunched tight.

Leona walked over to me with two cups and a couple donuts wrapped in napkins. "Two sugar and no milk, right?"

She held out the cup on her way down to a spot on the floor beside me.

I slid the cup from her grasp. Our fingertips brushed. "How'd you remember?"

"And I got you a glazed. I didn't know what kind you liked."

"You didn't have to." Being this close to her was killing my restraint. The first time I saw another guy flirting with her, I'd have to go on a five-mile run.

A tiny smile tugged at her cheeks. "You're my build buddy. What kind of buddy would I be if I didn't remember how you took your coffee after the IV drip we've been running for the past week, and snag a couple donuts before Griff and Hollis devoured them all?"

I rubbed my eyes. "If we calculate this per hour of work we're putting in, I don't know if it's even worth it." The mental shackles I'd locked around my muscles to keep my fingers from brushing back a stray hair on the side of her face probably offered a better workout than the gym.

She blew on her coffee and peeked up at me. Tonight, she was sporting a "Game Over, Man" hoodie with Bill Paxton's immortal line emblazoned on the front. Ezra had immediately asked her where she'd bought it. "True, but isn't that half the fun of traditions like this? Getting everyone together and doing silly things until you're sleep-drunk?" Her plump lips, resting on the rim of the cup, curved up at the edges.

"Part of the fun." Who knew drinking coffee could turn me on? Sure as hell not me. Or maybe it was her. Maybe it was the forbidden rearing its head in a way it never had before. But it didn't feel like this was only about the chase. This pull toward her had happened long before I discovered who her dad was.

"Are you ready for your game on Saturday? The whole float parade is after that, right?"

"Yeah, which will be even better when it's celebrating a win."

"Confident about that?"

"Half of winning is not letting anything get in your head.

The game is against the team that beat us for the national championship last year. If we go in thinking it could go either way, it could. If we go in knowing we'll win, then it's our game to be lost and drag the whole campus down with us."

"That's got to be rough. This place seems to revolve around football."

"Not much else going on in a college town like this. Plus some people have been STFU fans for generations. It's in their blood over half the campus—even the town."

"That's a lot of pressure."

I shrugged. "I've been playing football since I was four-teen and wanting to play it since long before that. Probably when I was seven or eight. It comes with the territory." Being in the spotlight was a hell of a lot better than sitting under the bleachers while wishing you were on the field.

"You've known you wanted to be a football player that long?"

"Sure. Haven't you always had things you wanted to do from that age?"

"Kind of."

"Were you always into wine?"

She peered at me with an adorable, scrunch-faced laugh. "There aren't many eight-year-olds into wine. In fact, I think that's illegal in most places." She knocked her shoulder into mine, then wrapped one arm around her bent knees and took a bite of her donut with the other. The crispy glaze and chocolate coating caught on the edge of her mouth. "I was surrounded by wine for almost six years. Walking the rows of vines in the vine-yard. Helping with harvesting even though it was more likely I was getting in the way. Testing vintages in their barrels. It was more about circumstance than a love for it."

Her shrug wasn't as bouncy as the others before. A weight settled over her when she talked about wine.

"But you enjoy it?"

"I do. And apparently I don't suck at it, so it seems like a waste to not pursue it."

"I've only ever had wine once." I winced, remembering the pungent, bitter taste that lingered on my tongue and how it turned my teeth purple.

"That good, huh?"

"It was disgusting. A fancy old bottle a booster served us last year."

She laughed and took another bite of her donut. "Let me tell you a secret." Leaning in, her sweet breath fanned across my face. "Some wine sucks. And some people just pretend to like it even if they really don't. The level of pretentiousness in the wine world can be overwhelming, but my step —" She froze and cleared her throat. "Someone I know in the wine world once said the best bottle of wine is one you enjoy drinking."

"I'll have to keep that in mind."

Leona licked some stray sprinkles and glaze off her fingers. My blood buzzed in my veins, imagining her tongue on me.

"We're going to need more of this tomorrow when we're on security detail," she said.

"Break's over, everyone, let's get to work." Ashley snapped me out of my dangerous thoughts, and we went back to our box cutters, paint or glue.

We worked into the night with hair dryers going to dry the glue and paint and save some time. It wasn't until almost eleven that we wrapped it up. Kennedy and Hollis stayed behind to watch the float.

Cole drove us back home since my car was buried under an avalanche of cardboard.

"Are you ever going to tell us what the hell happened between you and Kennedy?" I asked.

He jerked the wheel so hard he almost slammed into a fire hydrant. "Nothing happened. Why? What did she say?"

"Like that was a totally normal reaction for someone who'd done nothing with her."

His grip tightened on the steering wheel, and he leaned back, trying to look casual and failing. "It's nothing."

"Didn't you two hook up at the end of last year?"

"No, we didn't."

"I think I remember you two dancing, and then disappearing upstairs." I walked my fingers through the air.

"Do you keep track of everyone at every party? You need to get your eyes checked. Even if we did go upstairs, maybe I was showing her to the bathroom."

"Sounds like every other time you've ever gone upstairs with a girl at a party. Bathroom escorting."

"We didn't hook up, so drop it."

"Are—"

"We've got bigger things to focus on. This float bullshit is enough of a distraction. I'm not adding Kennedy to the mix." His shout reverberated inside the car. A vein pulsed in the side of his neck.

"Weren't you the one who wanted to put a float team together this year?"

"For the cash. I should've known better than leaving it up to Ashley and Taylor. I thought they'd still be rooming with Meg and didn't think they'd invite an actual succubus."

"Wow, language. Now I know for sure something happened between you two. You barely like to call anyone other than us assholes, but you call her a succubus."

"I don't want to talk about it."

"You know it'll come out eventually. Maybe STFU Dirt will be hot on the trail."

He ran the car up onto the curb trying to park in front of our house. After throwing it into park, his grimace flashed in the streetlights. "If I smell a whiff of anything about me in that thing, I'll destroy every server on campus."

"Not an overreaction or anything." I climbed out of the car.

"How about you and Leona? You two looked pretty cozy with your coffee and donuts." He stared at me over the roof.

I shrugged. "We're on a team together and getting along. What's wrong with that?"

"Nothing as long as you're not getting *distracted*." He waved his fingers in front of him like that was a spooky word.

"I'm not. We're both keeping things friendly."

"Have fun being friendly on security detail tomorrow night."

He stormed into the house.

I locked his car before following behind him. A full night alone with Leona. I'd managed to dodge security detail last week when Griff and Taylor had taken our spot, but this time I was the only other one free. I didn't want to see our hard work destroyed, so there wasn't another option. Not that I didn't want to be around her, but all alone and under the cover of darkness, it would be harder to remember exactly why we'd made the choice we made.

~

"You made it." She stood up from the far corner of the garage in a black pea coat with a gray wool hat pulled down over her ears. Even from here, she looked cold already.

"Sorry I'm late."

"Don't worry. Cole, Hollis, Kennedy and Ashley left a little while ago." She rubbed her bare hands together.

"I know. I saw them back at the house before Griff dropped me off."

"Of course. Sorry." She clasped her hands in front of her and stared at the float while sneaking a glance at me. At least I wasn't the only nervous one. "We've got some sleeping bags, plastic Adirondack chairs and a small heater, which I couldn't figure out how to turn on. It's supposed to keep things from freezing too much. I'm not sure if Ashley meant the paint or us. There's also an electric kettle for coffee and a thermos filled with hot chocolate."

I walked around the float, trying to focus on our work. The tissue paper was dulled a little once we glued it to the cardboard, but the dragon didn't look half bad. The head I'd worked hard on was even better with Leona's help. She was a pro at making seemingly unforgiving materials bend to our artistic will. The tail was covered in purple, blues and greens. Someone could sit in the backseat of my car and move it back and forth while I drove, looking out through the small window cut out at the front of the dragon's chest.

"This is the best one we've ever built." I ran my fingers over the tissue paper scales.

"Really?" Leona stood so close beside me that our jackets brushed against each other. And I hated it. I hated that the closest I could get to her right now was through eight layers of clothes between us.

Stop torturing yourself, Reid.

Stepping away, I picked up the thermos and sniffed it.

"Ezra gave us the good stuff. He must've gotten his some-times-boss to hand over the extra deluxe mix from one of their big parties."

Grabbing two cups, I filled them and let the steam roll over my gloved hands.

"I think he felt bad for us since it's supposed to be so cold tonight. I didn't think it would be this bad since it's only September."

"Your seasons have also got to be all messed up, aren't they?" I handed her a cup of the hot chocolate.

She wrapped her bare fingers around the cup and shivered.

"You don't have gloves."

"I didn't know I needed them." She took a sip. "It's a lot colder when we're not running around battling against card-board well into the night. It's been like kindergarten on steroids with all the tracing, cutting and gluing."

"Half of the traditions in this place could be described that way. Maybe it's why everyone loves them so much. Wait until we get to the prank war."

"Prank war?"

I tugged my gloves off and held them out to her. "You should take these."

"No, I'll be fine. I can tuck my fingers up into my sleeves. Me sucking at prepping for a night out here shouldn't mean your hands have to freeze."

"It's not a big deal."

"It is to me."

I stared into her eyes, not trying to hide how much I didn't want her suffering out here. "Please take them."

Her lips parted, and her gaze dropped to my extended glove. "How about we split them? I'll take one and you take one."

"Leona..."

"Or I take none."

"Fine, deal."

We finished our drinks and settled in for the night. While talking, we kept the music low to ensure we could hear any approaching cars or other sounds that might be a saboteur. A few bays over, the other team had gone quiet hours ago.

I scrubbed my hands over my face, trying to keep the tug of sleep from dragging me under. The biting cold helped some, but at a certain point, there wasn't much that could keep me from passing out after hours of practice and classes zapping the last of my energy reserves.

The main thing keeping me up at this point was minute stacked on top of minute with Leona.

She shot up from her chair. "What was that?"

15

LEONA

The rattle jolted me from my seat. My heart raced like we were about to be mobbed.

"You heard something?" Reid stepped in front of me and looked back.

"Yeah, what do we do?" My whisper came out just as panicked as I was.

"Finally, I was wondering if this year was really going to be that boring."

"What the hell are you talking about?"

"Why do you think we have security detail to begin with?" His eyes shined with excitement. "We're going to show them the Smaug isn't to be fucked with."

"How are we going to do that?"

He grinned and pulled his hat down lower on his head. Shoving his hands into his coat pockets, he stepped closer to the sounds. There was a thump and scrape almost too low to hear.

I gripped his jacket, the cold polyester bunched under my hold. Keeping close behind him, I stepped on the back of his shoes—twice.

"It'll be okay." He covered my hand with his and squeezed it.

My heart pounded like a jackrabbit in a shoebox. "Who is it?"

"Another team, most likely."

He pulled his other hand out of his pocket and tugged an object I couldn't identify in the low light from it.

"What's that?"

"A deterrent." Prying my fingers off his arm, he motioned for me to stand behind him against the corrugated steel wall without touching it.

He held up one hand and mouthed the countdown as well as lowering his fingers. A distinct flicking noise came from his other hand. At one, he lit the string that had been in one hand and jerked open the door, tossing what had been in his hand into the darkness, then slammed the door closed again.

He whipped around and covered me, sandwiching my ears between his palms.

An insanely loud round of pops battled with shouts and banging from the other side of the wall. The screams and yelps topped the rhythmic blasts that shot bits of light under the closed door.

When all the popping ended, there were only the voices. Pissed-off voices.

"What the fuck?" a woman screeched.

In the gap between the wall and the concrete floor, white paint pooled.

I tugged on his shoulder and pointed to the creeping paint. Had I been sleepy before? No more, my heart pounded in my chest.

Reid glanced over his shoulder, then released his arms

from around me. He stomped over to the door and flung it open.

Keeping close, I held onto the back of his jacket and peered around him. Was it an ax murderer? A cougar or a bobcat or a different animal from the woods surrounding the garages? My eyes took a second to adjust.

In the near pitch black hallway, lit only by the outdoor lights, two people stood in old-school sheet ghost costumes. Only they weren't covered in a white sheet. It looked like they'd been doused by cans of paint from above.

"You broke in here to sabotage us." Reid leaned against the doorway and watched them struggle. He didn't seem all that surprised or pissed off.

They'd come to use paint to deface and maybe destroy our float. My fear transformed into anger that these assholes had come to damage all our hard work.

I stepped forward, feeling bolder now that I knew we weren't going to end up in a horror movie. "That's what you get for trying to take down Smaug."

The pair wiped at their faces to keep the paint out of their eyes.

I leaped forward, but Reid held onto my waist and lifted me off the ground.

"I hope it stings like a motherfucker," I yelled at them.

"You don't want to get paint on your clothes." Laughing, he tugged me backward and looped his arm around my shoulder to keep me in place.

"What the hell were you thinking showing up here in the middle of the night, scaring the crap out of us?"

His touch calmed some of my fiery anger.

"You didn't have to try to kill us." The taller one whipped his arm out, trying to shake some of the paint off.

Reid shrugged and taunted, "Scare is more like it. And

none of this would've happened if you hadn't shown up to try to destroy what we've built."

"We were doing recon."

"With five gallons of black and white paint. Bull-fuck-ing-shit."

The two grumbled and glowered, shouting about the paint that burned their eyes and noses.

"How the hell are we going to get in my car like this?" More paint splatters hit the floor.

Taking pity on them, Reid grabbed a roll of paper towels and chucked it at them. "Maybe you'll think twice about trying to screw over someone else's hard work just because you're not good enough to win."

"Sabotage is half the fun."

Reid crossed his arms over his chest like the whole *let me chuck some firecrackers out here* was a normal night for him.

"Are you having fun right now?"

The two would-be saboteurs trudged away, their retreat much louder than when they'd tried to sneak in.

Headlights flashed in the windows high overhead, and then the quiet was back.

"You guys weren't kidding about people trying to mess with your floats," I said as we settled back into our Adiron-dack chairs.

The paint would've made a mess of the tissue paper and paint we'd spent nearly two weeks on. Who knows what other kind of damage they could've done with a couple well placed punches or kicks, not to mention Reid's car was under all this cardboard. If I were him, I wouldn't be half as calm.

First my dad with Reid's coach, and now Reid himself. Why were all the guys around me making me feel like I was a bloodthirsty maniac with their calmness in high pressure situations?

"What? Did you think this was all an elaborate plot to pair the two of us up alone at night?" His Adam's apple bobbed, and the whites of his eyes seemed to triple. "I didn't mean—"

My body hummed at the thought of a night alone with him. I was the opposite of opposed to a night alone with him. Too bad this was the closest I'd get. "I know. And no, I didn't think it was a plot. I thought maybe you guys were being overly paranoid, but it turns out I was wrong." Covering my mouth, I yawned and huffed my warm breath onto my exposed hand. "Does this mean we're most likely safe from another attempt?"

"Most likely." He yawned. "The paint trail out front will ward off any others who were thinking about it."

"Good, I'm tired. I don't know how you're still up. Don't you have practice for hours every morning?"

He looked like that last blast of adrenaline had drained him. His eyes drooped, and sleepiness had crept into his voice now that the high of the attack had worn off. "Most days, and I'm used to it by now. It's the work you have to put in to win, so I suck it up and just do it."

I kicked off my shoes on the concrete and stepped onto the stack of cardboard laid out for a little bit of a barrier to keep off the freezing floor. Not wanting to lose all my warmth, I wriggled down in the sleeping bag still in my coat.

"At least we have the heater?"

Reid dropped down beside me and got into his bag. "It would suck to be out here without it. We've got to protect our prized dragon." His sleepy chuckle warmed me some against the encroaching cold.

I rolled over and propped my head up on my arm. "Do you think we have a chance of winning?"

"The best we've ever had. Losing sucks, especially because second prize is a $50 gift card to the campus gift shop where you can barely buy a t-shirt for that much."

"That's a steep drop from first prize."

"Something you'll learn after being here long enough— second place is first loser to a lot of people. The money is a big deal for a lot of us, but also bragging rights. That's almost as good, but I can't eat bragging rights."

"You guys don't have scholarships that cover your food?" My dad had mentioned how generous the scholarships were to the athletes, including money for room and board, which included a dining plan.

"We get the three meal a day plan with our scholarship. The unlimited meal plan would be an 'inappropriate' incentive according to the national sports bigwigs. But even with an unlimited plan, most dining halls are closed by 10 p.m., except for Neptune Night. So if we've got practice early mornings, then workouts, then study hall, then classes until late, it doesn't leave much time to eat. Maybe for normal people, but we're burning calories at an insane rate, which means midnight snacks sometimes become midnight necessities, if we want anything in the tank for morning practice."

"I had no idea. I guess I see all that food at the dining hall and never thought about the hours or how much work you guys are putting in every day. So your big plans for the money are..."

"Mainly food. We load up the house. Griff's been bankrolling us for a while, probably from his parents. Ezra scores us leftover food from an old catering job whenever he can, but we spend a lot on food."

"I never thought of that." My plans had been... I didn't

even know what my plans were. I hadn't thought about it and didn't know there was a prize when Taylor and Ashley first invited me along. I'd been planning on getting a Xenomorph Lego set to work on over Christmas break, but that felt silly in comparison to food.

"Most people don't. It's why the dining hall people usually give us a break when we sneak food out as long as we're mildly discreet about it. One time we tried to get a whole tub of ice cream out to a player who'd broken his femur, but we got busted." He laughed, probably happy that at least they'd gotten busted trying to do something for a teammate who needed a pick-me-up.

"You all sound like a tight-knit group." I was glad he wasn't going through all this alone. He was lucky to have the team and the guys. I'd always been an outsider. Moving to Australia right as high school was beginning and trying to find my place there only to come back here to entrenched friend groups that were already solid made me a little jealous of what he had, but thankful he wasn't soldiering on alone through all the work it took to get where he was headed. And he'd folded me right into his group to the point that it was like I'd always belonged.

"The guys are my family. Football's always been that way for me. When you're all pouring your blood, sweat and tears out on the field together, there's nothing like knowing they have your back." He rested his hands behind his head and tilted his chin to hold my gaze.

I shivered, maybe from the cold or maybe from the look. Tingles flowed through me even as I tried to keep my teeth from chattering. The heater was pouring molten heat onto the top of my head, but the rest of me felt like ice. "Is your plan to go pro?"

He huffed out a laugh, and I swore I saw it in the air.

"Absolutely. Then again, it's everyone's plan. But we know we won't all make it. These last two years are the most important." The lightness in his voice gave way to determination. "All the hours in the gym and on the field come down to a few handfuls of games over five months."

"You seem like you love the pressure." In my world, it was a slow build to pressure. At every step, we tasted the wine to determine if a barrel had gone bad, but it wasn't like there was only one shot to get it right. A barrel could be tossed, but to have an entire season come down to a couple of hours on a field—that was a lot of weight and expectation to bear that felt heavy even to me, and I wasn't the one counting on it for my career.

"I love being the best," he said. "It makes all the pain worth it for a few minutes of glory standing on the field while the whole place erupts." His voice was laced with a faraway tone.

He lived and breathed football. He was dedicated to it. He was not going to let anything get in the way of his goals. His quick acceptance of my idea to break things off made even more sense now. I was someone he barely knew. Football he loved.

My chest tightened. I couldn't compete with that. Not that I wanted to, but even if I did, he wouldn't be swayed. And he shouldn't. After the parade, I'd need to put even more distance between us. I didn't want to be a reason for him to regret a single second of the hard work he'd put in.

"Night, Reid. I'm going to get some sleep."

"Night, Leona."

Curled up in a ball, I dropped into a fitful sleep. I hadn't even realized I'd passed out until I jerked, jolting awake with a violent shiver. My body felt like I'd been dunked into a frozen lake.

Reid's body was closer to mine. "The heater died. You've been shivering harder and harder." His breath gathered in the space between us.

"Ho-how long until morning?" My goose bumps had goose bumps. The fingers on one hand were numb. I couldn't speak properly through my shudders.

"A few hours."

"How come you're not a chattering mess?"

"It's my stadium jacket. It's extra warm in the sleeping bag."

A sound of longing escaped my lips.

"Come on, we can join the bags together and share some body heat."

My first instinct was to deny his request—snuggled up nice and warm beside Reid wasn't exactly on the *put some distance between us* list, but I could barely move. I nodded, trying to keep my chattering teeth from biting my tongue.

"I'll do it," he said. "You keep your hands inside your coat."

He got to work, unzipping his bag and mine and threading the zippers together. Satisfied with his work, he crawled in beside me. His knees knocked into mine.

I wiggled my fingers out from under my coat sleeves and sunk them into the warm lining of the sleeping bag.

My feet found their way over to his warm sock covered ones. With my hands tucked under my chin, I scooted closer to the heat from his side.

"You're almost a block of ice." He took my ungloved hand from under my chin and rubbed his across the front and back.

"Tell me about it." My exposed fingers were too frozen to even feel his touch. I might as well have taped some ice cubes to my hand and called it a day. Slowly the warmth moved in, and then his icy bare hand touched my warm one.

"Your hand is freezing too." I wrapped mine around his. We took turns massaging the freeze out of our fingers.

Slowly, I thawed, no longer feeling like my brain was rattling in my skull with shivers.

"Only a couple hours left."

I nodded, tucking my chin against my chest. "Thanks, Reid."

"Don't worry about it, Leona." His words sounded strained.

That didn't surprise me, considering how cold it was.

Slowly I drifted into a much warmer sleep, like a switch had finally been flicked.

Hours later, I woke, not like I had the first time.

This time, I was tucked in, nice and snuggly, pressed against Reid's chest. His head was propped on the top of mine. The room wasn't pitch black anymore. Sun came pouring through the windows above us, lighting up the ceiling.

Our hands were intertwined, our bare fingers protected from the cold by our bodies and the gloves.

I inhaled deeply and sunk deeper against him, knowing I shouldn't let myself. He smelled like grass and leather and Icy Hot, but there was also an underlying sweetness. I was tempted to press my nose to his chest and suck in a lungful of Reid.

I wished we weren't in a freezing cold garage, but back in my bed after we'd passed out watching *District 9* or *The Abyss*. Or maybe after taking things a bit further.

He yawned, rubbing his hand down my back. "Hey, we made it."

I scooted back a little and looked up at him, trying not to

be self-conscious about my morning breath. "We did. Thanks for not letting me freeze."

"What kind of teammate would I be if I let you turn into a popsicle?"

"A terrible one. Now I know why the guys keep you around. You'll do anything for the team." I meant it as a tease, but it was also a reminder of why we couldn't be together.

"I will." He didn't unlock his hand from around mine. The smooth glove glided over the back of my hand.

Staring into his eyes, all the feelings I'd been trying to suppress came rushing back. They flooded my veins and sparked my nerve endings.

His head dipped lower so our foreheads almost touched. I'd never thought mine was sensitive before, but now I could feel every graze and skim.

Our noses brushed, and I swore I could feel the flutter of his eyelashes.

It would be so easy to give in. "Reid—"

"What the hell happened out here?" Taylor's voice broke his glacially slow advance toward my lips.

His eyes widened, and we jumped apart as far as we could while still trapped in the bag. We fumbled for the zippers to escape, and then we were free.

The outside air was ice-block cold compared to the sleeping bag cocoon.

I smoothed down my hair and pulled off the glove, tossing it to Reid.

"Why's the whole hallway covered in paint?"

He snatched it out of the air and shoved it into his pocket before ducking to throw his shoes on. Next, we worked together unzipping the sleeping bags and trying to erase any evidence of our night snuggled up together. "It was me teaching those sabotaging assholes a lesson," he shouted as he rolled up the bags.

My heart raced at a sprint. I shoved my feet into my shoes, then kicked my bag to the opposite side of the cardboard platform and surveyed the area for anything else that might draw attention to how we'd spent the night.

The door banged open, and Taylor stepped through with Cole and Griff right behind her.

Cole handed us both a cup of steaming coffee. "Other than that, it was all good? No surprises?"

"All good."

I dropped my gaze and darted a quick glance at Reid. "Nope, other than that, it was quiet. No issues. Kinda boring actually."

Reid glanced over at me.

My coffee steam heated my lip, but I took a sip of it anyway and grimaced at the sharp bitterness of the black coffee.

"Here you go, Leona." Reid held out a couple of creamers and six sugars.

"You noticed I like a little coffee with my sugar?" I set down the cup and took the packets and mini cups from him with a half-frozen smile. My skin was tightening up now that I was no longer in the cocoon of warmth with Reid.

"Yeah, I noticed."

The tummy trampoline was back and bouncing higher than ever. Keeping my head down, I fixed my coffee and warmed my now bare hands on the cup. *Down, girl!*

Taylor tugged her pink hat down over her ears and shivered. "You two can head back if you want to get some real rest. We've only got one more day of babysitting, and then we're good. Bryn and Kennedy said they'll take the final shift during the game if you wanted to go to your very first STFU football fanatics frenzy."

I glanced over at Reid, who'd brought his cup up but froze at the mention of the game.

"Sure, I'd love to go and see just what all the fuss is about."

16

REID

The night laid out on the cardboard "mattress" in two barely held together sleeping bags shouldn't have been as good as it was. And waking up with my arm around her might as well have killed me right then and there. Why was I torturing myself? Why couldn't I just leave things alone and stay friendly but evasive when it came to her?

Probably because I'd never had feelings like this before. A need to be near her. A need to see her. A need to touch her.

And she was up in the stands at the front of the student section right beside Ashley and Taylor, who'd probably dragged them both here at 8 a.m. to get the prime seats. Every time defense was on the field, I couldn't stop myself from finding them in the crowd. Normally, I was laser-focused during a game, but for a couple of seconds every turnover, I let myself seek her out. Nothing ever distracted me like this, but somehow she had. I still wasn't sure how I felt about that, but I needed to know if she was here.

Homecoming was always insanity. There were alumni,

new and old, who'd been out tailgating for hours already. The stands were a sea of orange and gold, waving and rising and falling like a multi-limbed ocean. It was a big game for the campus and the town surrounding it. Hotels had been sold out for months, all for fans' chances to be here.

Leona leaned over while Taylor shouted and pointed wildly at the field. Probably at the scoreboard showing our one-point deficit. The first game Leona came to see me, and we were on the cusp of a loss.

Bodies banged into me, and a hand grabbed my jersey. I whipped my head around.

Cole tugged me forward. "What the hell? Let's go."

Grabbing my helmet, I shoved it on and took my spot, totally disoriented about what play we were doing.

Focus, Reid. I smacked my hand against my helmet, trying to rattle my brain and get my head in the game. One bad play was all it took, and I wouldn't be the one to drop the ball.

We lined up for the kick return to start our drive up the field in the last play. The clock was down to the final minute.

We all lined up, ready for the catch and demolition of the opposing team to get us as close to the end zone as possible.

Blocking was what I was good at, and I'd hold off whoever came my way to give one of my teammates the opening they needed to chew up some yardage.

At the whistle, their ball was set, and the kick launched. The ball sailed through the air in a perfect spiral. There wasn't a wobble in it.

I glanced one more time at the stands.

When I looked back, the ball was wide, lifted by the intense wind pounding us out on the open field.

And in that moment, I knew what I had to do.

The running backs hadn't had time to get to me, not with the other team encroaching, already set to block.

I plucked the ball out of the air and wrapped my arms around it, holding it close to my chest when I took off. I charged forward. Blood thrummed in my ears, but I could still hear the stands going wild.

The opposing team had all been on the other side of the field with our power runners waiting for that ball, so it took a while before they were on me, but not too long.

I wasn't as fast as most guys on the team, but I had a couple of seconds lead time and I would take advantage of it. If my heart exploded in the end zone, I wasn't giving up.

A defensive lineman sprinted for me and lunged for my legs. The fifty-yard line was coming up, and the whole sideline was going insane, running right along with me.

Pushing off with my back foot, I leaped through the air. It made me vulnerable for a mid-air tackle, but my brain was running the analysis on this whole play, and my body was reacting instinctively.

The forty.

But I landed without being taken down and kept going. I pumped my arms and kept my knees high.

The thirty.

A spin to dodge a tackle. A quick slam of the brakes to dodge another from my right.

The twenty.

I dug my cleats in deep. The clash and clank of shoulder pads and helmets just outside of my peripheral told me my team had my back.

The ten and the end zone was within sight. The uprights glowed overhead like a waiting welcome home hug.

I wanted to check over my shoulder, but that would slow

me a fraction of an inch. A body banged into me, throwing off my gait. I corrected and sprang through the air.

Another body plowed into me, knocking me off balance. I recovered without a glance behind me.

Pumping my legs faster, I used every bit of strength to propel myself toward the end zone line. I hit the ground with a thud. Bodies landed on me, grinding my face mask into the grass.

A whistle cut through the pounding in my ears and groans of guys all around me. Sunlight was no longer blocked out by bodies, and I panted, keeping still for the ref to come over and make the call.

He stared down at me and blew his whistle. The shrill screech drew everyone's attention, and his arms shot up overhead.

Touchdown.

The stadium rumbled, and even in the center of the field, I could feel the bombastic celebration from the stands.

I dropped the ball and rolled over, screaming into the air. For this moment, I soaked it all in. The way the whole place came to life around me because of my play. My eyes snapped open.

Cole and Hollis stood over me and held out their hands, shouting and bouncing around.

Grabbing them, I let them help me up.

I stood and pointed at the stands filled with cheering fans. Quarterbacks, wide receivers, running backs, they were the positions that got all the glory. They were the ones everyone watched, and after years of trying to turn myself into them, I had to choose to be on a team that would win, not a team that would have me in one of those positions. I chose the team over my need to be in the spotlight, but damn, when it swung in my direction, did I love every second of it.

"Thanks for letting us rest our legs for the party that's going to explode out of this place after that play." Cole grinned and knocked his helmet into mine.

On the sidelines, Griff and Ezra punched me in the chest.

Griff grabbed onto my jersey. "Asshole, I barely had time to get a damn drink."

"Sorry. Next time I'll be more considerate. At least you only have fifteen more seconds before we call this thing."

Unable to help myself, I looked for Leona in the stands. Taylor jumped up and down so hard and fast I was a little afraid she was going to rip an arm off. But Leona wasn't looking at the final, last-ditch efforts to run down the clock. She was staring at me, smiling like we'd just seen each other walking across campus and she wanted to say *hi*, not that there was a season-defining game happening behind me.

The end of game horn blasted, and the stands went wild all over again. But in the center of chaos, I held her gaze, and she held mine.

Students poured onto the field from the stands, blitzing past the security guards' semi-attempts to stop them. Rushing the field for homecoming was as big a tradition as the twenty other traditions that took over the school. I could barely stand as people jumped onto me to celebrate and scream about how awesome that play was. It wasn't the worst way to end a game.

Long arms wrapped around me, and a wave of blond hair fluttered in front of me. Taylor tackled me like she was trying out for the team.

"That's what I'm talking about, Reid. That play." She held up her fingers to make an imaginary camera. "I've committed it to my stats memory. I'll relive that every damn day." Her grin was infectious.

"Thanks, Tay."

Ashley hugged me next. "I couldn't not hug you after that, even though you're a sweaty mess." She stopped playing it cool. "Because that was the most insane thing I've seen all season!"

Over their shoulders, Leona stayed a step away and waved. "Great play. I swore the stands were going to disintegrate once you finally hit the end zone."

All around us, students and teammates celebrated, but the two of us stood like strangers an arm's length away. Taylor and Ashley threw themselves into the chaos and celebration.

I glanced over my right shoulder and stepped in closer to Leona. "Th—"

"That was one hell of a play, young man." From my left, an older man in an STFU jersey with a rolled-up wad of paper in his hand gripped my shoulder and shook me.

"Thanks."

"I wish I could've been down here to rush the field with all the rest of the students instead of stuck up in the box with the stuffy Governing Board, but I needed to get down here to tell you that was one hell of a play." He beamed, and while he was in his seventies with white hair that was thinning on top, he looked like he was ready to go running with the rest of the team straight into the locker room to celebrate.

Leona still stood a couple of feet away, looking completely lost in the madness, abandoned by her roommates to the post-win mania.

"Thank you, sir." I shook his hand and hoped that would be enough to get him to move onto the next player, so I could finally have a second with Leona. Maybe find an empty hall in the tunnels under the stadium to show her how happy I was to have her here showing her support to me—I mean *the team*.

"Davenport, good to see you down here." The voice sent shivers down my spine that had nothing to do with the sweat chilling my overheated body. "Riddick."

"Coach."

"Mikelson." Davenport settled his hand onto Coach's shoulder. "That was one hell of play Riddick had here. And it wasn't the first he's had all season. Why hasn't he been first string all this time?" He shook me and Coach at the same time.

I braced myself for Coach to unleash his wrath on the older man, manhandling him.

But he smiled. A genuine smile, which creeped me the hell out.

"You know you've got to break these players and build them back up to get the best out of them. Reid here was on the second string for a long time, but he finally got with the program, and now you see what that can do."

The crowd around us created a five-foot bubble away from Coach like a patch of burned grass.

"If he and the rest of these linemen keep making plays like that, then a win is ours to lose this year."

"We're always working for the win, but you know from time to time the budget constraints make that hard. That president—"

"Come on, Will. No need to bring the post-win celebration down."

Coach nodded and turned his head.

I could tell the exact moment he spotted Leona.

"What the hell are you doing here? Spying for that spineless father of yours?"

I rocked back on my heels like I'd just been tackled from behind. Had he just spoken to her that way?

Her shoulders set back, and she glared, full of a fury I didn't think she had. With a clenched jaw, she bit out, "Enjoying a win, just like everyone else."

"Some nerve you have showing up here with that father of yours trying to dismantle my program. Or are you here to cause a disruption in my team?"

I ground my teeth, wanting to rip his damn head off for speaking to her that way. I shot forward, ready to get between them.

Davenport held onto his shoulder. "Will, now's not the time."

The vein in Mikelson's neck bulged, and he shook his head. "You're right. Let's head into the locker room." With that quiet phrase, all the players knew the celebration was over, and we fell in line.

I glanced over my shoulder at Leona.

She stared at him with a glower and her fists clenched at her sides.

Every step was a struggle. Like a rope tightening around my body, dragging me away from her, to leave her alone— undefended. But I was well trained by now and knew that not obeying Coach would make things worse for everyone.

As Coach and Davenport walked, the people left on the sidelines parted in front of them like they had the plague.

"Will, you keep winning games like that with players like him, and I'll write you a check big enough to keep this program running no matter the budget cuts," Davenport said.

Everyone who hadn't already broken off for an early exit to the shower was in the hallway, silently walking while Mikelson and Davenport spoke about our futures. He kept going on and on about the way I'd crossed the end zone, and how everyone in his box had been on their feet, screaming my name.

The big play and the win soured in my stomach as I thought about the way Mikelson spoke to Leona. I'd put up with so much shit from him to me and the rest of the team, but for some reason, those few sentences to her made me forget how much of his bullshit I was willing to take.

17

LEONA

The walk over to the parade route helped calm me down. Bloodthirsty didn't cut it with the way Reid's coach had talked to me. But the way he'd talked about my dad hit hardest, maybe because I was more sensitive to that after learning the truth about my parents' divorce.

I had no clue how Reid put up with that impossible asshole, let alone pulled off the physical feats on the field with that jerk breathing down his neck.

A shadow fell over me.

"Over here." The deep baritone rumbled in my left ear.

I jumped and whirled around.

"Jesus, Ezra, you scared me."

He tugged down the brim of his hat and shoved one hand into his pockets. "Sorry." He gripped the shoulder strap of his backpack, looking incredibly uncomfortable. "Our float's over here." He lifted his chin over his shoulder.

"Thanks." I followed him away from the street as he cut behind the throngs of people flocking to the area, walking along the backs of the set-ups facing the parade.

The crowd from the stadium must've come straight here. When everyone talked about a parade, for some reason, I hadn't thought they meant an actual parade with hundreds if not a few thousand spectators along the route. I ducked my head and folded my arms over my chest, gripping my coat tighter. Did anyone know who I was yet? Maybe this was a bad idea.

Lining the street were sports fans in their jerseys, and some even had their faces painted. The ordinances about public drinking must not have been too firmly enforced since we passed people with red plastic cups, oversized water bottles and an actual keg on the street. The overly friendly man with an STFU hat offered me a beer with a huge smile and nudged it toward Ezra when I turned it down.

Tents with folding chairs lined the route, as well as tables ready for beer pong and grills.

A couple people shouted Ezra's name as we walked past, and he stopped and took smile-less pictures or signed their jerseys. Even with the hat on, it wasn't hard to spot him. He looked like he wanted to melt away into the trampled grass.

Reid never seemed to shy away from the attention. He'd basked in it after the play and had been pointing at the stands trying to get everyone to scream louder once he got off the ground. It had to be hard for Ezra to not like the attention and yet be at the center of it as all the football players seemed to be.

"This is insane."

"The people who can't get tailgating spots at the stadium will show up here early, stake their claim and watch the game from TVs."

Sure enough, under one canopy, a group had transplanted their living room—TV, rug, couch and end tables.

"How do they get all this here?"

"RVs, trucks, however they can."

"I guess it's weird having all these people come up to you after a win like that."

He smiled. The first real one I'd seen on him. "Reid did good." The genuine pride in his voice was unmistakable. "It never hurts to have another W. We're the fifth float back."

The whole area buzzed with exhilaration. Not as high as during the game, but still intense. Some of the cardboard creations were amazing, some were little more than cardboard strapped to the sides of a car. Or in one case, a bike. That felt like a cop-out, if I'd ever seen one. Apparently, I'd been on the team who came to win and wasn't taking any chances. Smaug was the best I could see down the line of floats.

Taylor wore a scaley, reflective dress.

Ashley had on a shimmery top.

Kennedy had a full wing cape made of multicolored panels that looked like small scales along with her bright blue bandage dress. And I was in my jeans, sweatshirt and coat after leaving the game and getting my first real taste of homecoming before the parade. I swear, it was less than twenty minutes ago that they'd said they'd meet me at the float.

"Why didn't you guys tell me you were dressing up? When the hell did you even have a chance to get changed and do your makeup?" I'd been welcomed into their group so easily, and this was the first time I felt left out.

Griff gave Taylor a boost onto her edge of Smaug.

They exchanged glances, and Ashley was lifted next by Griff. "We figured you'd want to ride inside with Reid to help him with navigation."

Alone in the dragon cave with Reid. My cheeks flushed,

and my skin tingled at the mention of his name. I turned and stared down the completely straight, although crowded, street that was the parade route. "Help with navigation?" It felt like a set-up.

Reid and I had been good at keeping things friendly but not too close. Had we been obvious? Could everyone else in the group sense something going on with us?

"Plus, you didn't bring any candy." Kennedy unzipped the backpack at her feet. It was filled to the brim with the tiny, shiny wrappers of bite-sized Snickers and other treats.

"Candy I also wasn't told I needed to bring." Jerk faces. My frustration mounted.

"Plus, we figured with your dad and Coach Mikelson being judges along the parade route, it might be best to maybe keep you out of sight."

I gulped. Yikes, I'd forgotten about that. Wouldn't want that to hurt the team's chances and be yet another thing I'd forgotten to tell my dad about.

"Oh, would you look at that, we're starting soon. Better get inside." Taylor crouched down and lifted the flap covering the open passenger side of the car.

Suddenly feeling like the whole team had been looking out for me, I squeezed through the door and collapsed into my seat. Right beside Reid, who was already inside and had probably heard the whole exchange. Yet another reminder of who my dad was and why that would get him in deep shit if anyone found out we were this close.

"Hey, Leona. Sorry you got stuck with me inside the Smaug underbelly." His gaze flicked to mine, riddled with nervousness.

Things were different now that we weren't huddling together for warmth and protecting Smaug.

"It's not a big deal. We've been stuck together before."

Why'd I have to bring that up? "I didn't want everyone else to think I'd flaked on putting in the extra effort." I closed the door behind me and sank into my seat.

"No one thinks that. They're just being cautious." He glanced over at me. "Since the coach is here—and your dad."

"They seem to be everywhere, aren't they?"

Muffled cheers and the movement of the float in front of ours signaled the beginning of the parade. There were eye-level rectangles cut out of the structure around us.

Under this dragon with a ton of brightly painted and tissue-papered cardboard, we were in a cave all alone.

I leaned through the middle of the two front seats to move Smaug's tail up and down. The rest of the back seat was taken up by the massive support structure required to keep the whole thing from collapsing under the weight of three people on top.

It also brought me boob-to-shoulder with Reid. I felt like I was breathing down his neck with the long stretch to the back of the car.

The little divot on the side of his cheek deepened, and his gaze flicked to the side.

"It's a bit of a tight fit." I laughed, trying to make this less awkward and failing spectacularly. Every brush against my coat or nudge of his elbow led to a shortened breath. Hopefully, I didn't pass out from a lack of oxygen while wedged into the gap in the seats right beside him.

"I don't mind." He made a sound like he was trying to claw the words back into his throat.

"This is kind of weird, huh?"

"A little." He shifted the car into drive, and we rolled forward. "But I don't mind."

My stomach and pelvis were brushed by his elbow on the gear shifter. "Anything for the win, right?"

The car moved at around five miles an hour, so running alongside it and with the other people in the parade wouldn't have been hard, but I liked being tucked inside with Reid.

Music blasted above us from speakers Taylor had rigged up. She wasn't taking a single chance when it came to securing the number one spot.

"I'm sorry about Coach." Reid spoke over the music. "He can be..."

I was relieved he brought up his coach. It gave me something else to focus on that wasn't how good he smelled, all freshly showered after the game. Cedar, liniment and soap. I looked over my shoulder. "A tyrant. A total, irrational asshole."

"And then some." His hands tightened on the steering wheel. "I'm sorry about what he said."

"You have nothing to be sorry about. I'm sorry he's your coach and you have to deal with him day in and day out." Facing the back, I moved the tail up and down and from side to side, trying to keep time with the music, but this lever was unwieldy.

"It could be worse. At least we get the wins."

My arm was already tired, resting on the back of the seat.

A rain of glittery candy moved past the openings I looked through. On the street, adults, students and kids caught the candy in midair or scooped it up off the ground. Music, dancing, laughter and silly happiness filled every angle I could see.

It relaxed me, and maybe that's why my guard lowered.

His hair was still damp, and I planted my chin on my

shoulder to keep from sniffing him more. "Are all coaches like him? The ones that win a lot?"

His laugh came out more like a huff. "No, we're just lucky. Not that most coaches aren't intense. Bobby Knight used to fling folding chairs onto the court back when they were on top of the world. A lot of times it takes crazy intensity and determination to push people to do their best. Sometimes it comes out like Mikelson, and other times it's different..."

Different how? Worse? It was hard to imagine it getting worse than Mikelson, although it had to suck for Reid knowing there were other coaches out there who were better. Who weren't spitting mad assholes.

"You've put up with a lot to get where you are, and that play today. I didn't get a chance to congratulate you out on the field." Ashley and Taylor jumped on him with hugs and congratulations, and it had felt like that would be a step too close for us. Like the moment we touched in public, everyone would know about our kiss and the night snuggled up together and the feelings I'd been trying to hide.

His head swung toward me. "Coach definitely ruined the moment."

Our eyes locked, and the closeness was a lot like when we were huddled up together in the garage. But nothing about our situation had changed.

Swallowing, I blurted out the first thing that came to mind. "I can see even more now why you were on board with not seeing each other once you found out who I was. He'd probably make your life a living hell."

"Probably." His jaw ticked.

"If he found out I was in here with you, he'd be pissed."

"Probably." His gaze blazed with an intensity that wasn't just anger about his dickhead of a coach.

"It's probably why everyone thought it was best to have me down here with you."

"Probably." The word seemed to have lost all meaning.

"I don't want to screw up all your hard work and sacrifices. It's probably why it makes sense for us not to be seen around each other after this is over." I choked on the words and forced them out past the lump lodged in my throat.

Instead of the probably I'd expected, he turned his whole body.

"No one else is here right now. It's just me and you."

A shuddering inhale, and our lips were on each other. I didn't know who kissed who first, but the sensations that poured through our lips meeting made me want more. It made me want everything. The way his mouth moved over mine. His tongue brushed against my lips, demanding and needy at the same time, which sent the fluttering deep in my stomach and turned it into a hungry clench for more.

Screams from above broke through our cocoon.

"You're veering! Turn left! What the hell! Pay attention."

Someone banged on the side of Smaug.

Reid course-corrected, and we were no longer headed straight for the living room transplanted to the side of the street.

I still tasted him on my lips. Peppermint and heat.

We drove in silence. The minutes ticked away, so did the end of the parade route. Once it was over, everything would be different—one way or another.

"What are we going to do?" I rested my head on his shoulder.

His hand dropped onto my thigh. "I don't know."

We'd been fighting this from the moment we found out. We'd been trying to put distance between us, but our orbits had never allowed us to get too far from one another.

"Once the parade's over," I said with a complete lack of certainty, "we can try again. We can back off and just walk the other way if we see each other."

He squeezed my thigh and looked over at me. "What if I don't want to?" His Adam's apple bobbed.

"Reid!" A shout came from outside. We were inches from rear-ending the float in front of us.

"What the hell are you two doing in there? Pay attention."

We both tried to refocus on the task at hand. I moved the tail.

He drove straight and tried not to run anyone over.

But anytime we came to a stop, our lips met again. The magnet was fully charged, and we weren't escaping this.

The end of the parade route couldn't come soon enough, and finally we were parked and ready for the judging, still tucked into the car.

My phone beeped with a text.

Amy: Can you come over earlier for dinner with your dad? There's been a change in his schedule and he didn't want you to go hungry.

Me: Sure, I can come over now, if that works.

Amy: Sure, sorry I'm messaging you. He's been slammed all day with all the homecoming events and an emergency meeting has been put on his schedule for later. He's on his way back to the house now.

Me: No problem. See you soon.

Reid looked down at my phone that glowed inside the darkened interior.

I shoved it into my pocket. "I've got to go. My dad left early, so he won't see me."

He nodded with a grim look on his face. "We'll let you know how it goes."

"Taylor and Ashley's screams will be heard across campus when we win. I know we will. Because we've got the best team out there."

His smile wiped away the furrow of his brow. "They'll be pissed if we don't win."

"And you won't be? You're pretty competitive."

"I managed to enjoy it this year for more than the win." His gaze lifted to mine, and my stomach fluttered.

"See you soon, Reid." I opened the door.

"See you, Leona," he called out as it slammed behind me.

I rushed up the steps to the house and opened the unlocked front door. Inside there were banker's boxes of papers and people speed walking from room to room. I'd never seen most of them before. It wasn't unusual to see a few different people in the house from time to time, but this was a steady stream of people all looking hurried and worried.

I walked into the kitchen, which was empty of university staff, and grabbed a spot at the island. The smells of tomato sauce, cheese and garlic enveloped me. I wanted to curl up inside a loaf of garlic bread right now.

After my afternoon at the game then in the car with Reid, I didn't want to have to hide that part of my life from my dad. Reid's coach didn't need to know about us, but keeping secrets from my dad didn't sit right. It lodged a huge, gravelly boulder right in my chest.

Keeping secrets was what led to our nearly six-year estrangement, and I didn't want to add more to that.

The kitchen door was shoved open.

"But the academic programs and the research. We've

brought in nearly double the research funding we had last year. There are grants in the tens of millions. The scholarships we'll be able to provide and the talent who'll see us in an even better light—"

Dad inhaled and brushed his hand over his forehead. "I know athletics are important. I know people love football, but we're a university—it can't just be about a game. What about the careers students will have when they leave, the good they can do—I don't mean in the pros." He glanced up and jumped. "Sorry, I've got to go. My daughter is here. We can speak about this later tonight." Ending the call, he set the phone down on the china cabinet beside the door.

"I didn't know you were here." His arms enveloped me in a big hug. He swayed me and kissed the top of my head. "I thought we were doing dinner later."

"Amy sent a message and said you wanted to move it earlier because of a meeting, and she didn't want me to be waiting around for you."

"She's too good to me." His eyes widened. "I meant at her job. She's too good at her job sometimes. It's an emergency meeting, and I was going to probably rush through dinner to get to it or call later to push dinner back. I'd hoped it wouldn't happen around this time. I'm sorry I didn't let you know earlier."

"Don't worry about it, Dad. Does it have anything to do with what you were talking about on the phone?"

He walked to the oven and pulled out a dish of chicken parmesan and a tray of garlic bread. "Unfortunately, due to how well the football team has been doing this year, the board has called into question the campus synergy."

I grabbed plates, cups, utensils and set them out for us. "What's that in plain English?"

He placed a bottle of sparkling water on the table then

looked away. "It means, if the team wins this season, I'm probably out of a job."

Shooting up from my seat, I nearly knocked the stool over. "Out? What do you mean out?"

He slid into his seat, much calmer than I'd have expected for the bomb he just dropped. But the weight of what was going on had settled on his shoulders. I wondered if the calm he was projecting right now was a veneer to hide how he truly felt. "It happens all the time. They'd most likely give me a year for a graceful exit." He patted my shoulder. "So don't worry, you'd still get to graduate before I left."

"Who gives a crap about graduation? How could they just kick you out like that after you've given everything to this place? You barely have a social life, you're in meetings all the time and having dinners and going to every event. You've done a whole lot for this campus, and they could just get rid of you?" And for an asshole like Mikelson? It made me wish I'd said a few different words to him down on the field after the game.

"More like making it known that it would be in my best interest to find another university position." His lips pursed, and he shook his head. "The politics of it all can be more tiring than the job sometimes." An undercurrent of disappointment ran through his words.

"Dad..." My idea about easing into the conversation about Reid soured in my stomach.

The smells of delicious food were no longer appetizing.

I picked at a piece of warm garlic bread. My phone buzzed in my pocket.

Lego Stomper: We won!

Lego Stomper: When can I see you?

The lump lodged in my throat tripled in size.

The better Reid did, the closer my dad came to losing his

job, but the closer he'd be to achieving his dream after being under the thumb of an absolute asshole. It was an untenable situation, but I couldn't keep myself from replying. The way Reid made me feel couldn't be ignored. As much as I'd tried to stay away, it felt like we were being tugged together, pulled closer, and after spending almost two weeks with him daily, I didn't want to not know him anymore.

Me: Tomorrow. I'll let you know once I get home.

Dad took a bite of his chicken parmesan. "At least I know, no matter what. My Leona-Loo won't abandon her dear old dad." He squeezed my hand, fisted around my silverware. "It's hard to be one of the only people on campus who haven't been swept up in the STFU sports mania. How are you finding it all? Making new friends?"

I coughed and held my napkin up to my mouth. Yes, that was me. His daughter who hadn't just been at an STFU football game and took part in the homecoming parade and hadn't spent over two weeks working on the float with a team partially made up of football players.

Guilt clawed at my gut. Right now wasn't the right time to tell him about Reid. There was no guarantee that we'd even be interested in each other after a week.

"It's been great. My roommates are nice, and they've been welcoming. They've included me in activities, but I've also been busy with class, so I haven't had much time for anything else."

"I knew you'd be responsible. I'm so glad I can trust that you're not one of those wild kids who's out there getting involved in all the madness that takes over campus this time of year."

"You know me, Dad." I smiled through cheeks that felt as delicate as blown glass. "I'll keep myself far away from all that kind of stuff and focus on school. It's why I came here, right? To get my degree and finally spend more time with you."

He hugged me, and we finished our meal, where I choked down every bite. He didn't need to know. It wasn't so much keeping it a secret, just not adding another worry to his already piled-high plate. I was doing him a favor. Why make him worry when he didn't have to?

18

LEONA

After checking myself out in the mirror for the twentieth time, I'd broken out the Lego to keep my hands busy before I ripped out more hair by redoing it for the eighth time. Reid was coming over tonight. He'd asked to see me on the first day we wouldn't be forced to spend time together. Not that there had been anything forced about the kiss under Smaug.

I picked up another off-white piece and snapped it into place. The base had taken me hours so far, and I wasn't even a third of the way finished, but the monotony of it helped me clear my mind and kept me from pacing across my bedroom floor until I'd burned a groove into it.

My brain focused on fitting each piece into the perfect spot.

A knock at the front door tugged me from my build. I glanced up at the clock.

"One second," I shouted, although I doubted he could hear me. Pushing another piece into place, I hopped up and stared down at the mess. There was no hiding this. I nudged the base toward the space under my bed. I should've set an alarm.

Another knock, and I flew down the short hallway.

Without looking through the peephole, I swung the door open.

"Reid." My heart fluttered. I waited to lift off the ground, but I remained solidly in place.

His gaze locked onto mine, and my smile burst free.

"You're here." Was my smile as goofy as it felt?

"It's the right time, isn't it?"

I nodded and stepped aside, so he could walk in. Unable to help myself, I peered outside to see if anyone else was around, but the courtyard was empty. Not being seen together was probably a safer way to handle this until we figured out what *this* was. Extra pressure and scrutiny or fallout from Coach Mikelson wasn't what either of us wanted.

"Sorry, the time got away from me," I said.

"Are Ashley and Taylor home?"

Closing the door, I turned to face him. "No, they won't be back for a couple—"

His lips cut off my words.

He'd bridged the gap between us, and my back was pressed against the metal safety door. His hands pressed into the door behind me on either side of my head, caging me against him, not that there was anywhere else I wanted to go. His mouth was searing and hungry and different than yesterday. It was more in every conceivable way.

He tasted like mint.

The tingles spread throughout my body, turning into sparklers under my skin. Hot and bright, the charge ignited every nerve ending. The firm but somehow soft feel of his lips sent the tingles traveling lower, and I gasped, squeezing my thighs together.

His hands moved from the door to the sides of my neck. His thumbs brushing against my skin fired off even more flares.

He shifted his hands off me and rested his forehead against mine. "I know this is crazy. I know we said we wouldn't, but I can't stop thinking about you. It's been keeping me up at night how much I wanted to touch you like this again. To kiss you again." His eyes burned with a fierceness that sent shivers streaking down my spine.

I swallowed, trying to keep myself from blurting out the first thing that came to mind. "Same."

His fingers skimmed across my shoulders.

Goose bumps rose along my arms, and my breath shuddered under the intensity of his gaze. "Sorry about that. I've just been wanting to do that, like really kiss you, for way too long."

"I wasn't complaining. What would you have done if I'd said Ashley and Taylor were here?"

"Probably paid them $20 each to go grab us sandwiches over at Killken's."

"Isn't that on the other side of campus?"

"Exactly."

Without thinking, I led him back to my bedroom. My body was on autopilot and knew what it wanted.

His smiling gaze flicked to the Lego bricks all over the floor like I was a four-year-old who'd thrown a tantrum. "You really do play with them."

I should've kept him out in the living room. Stupid autopilot. "Only when I need to shut my brain off for a while." Like when I knew he'd be here, and I still wasn't even sure what I wanted from him—or what he wanted from me. The nerves were back in full force, and I felt like I had no idea what I was doing. Probably because I had no idea what I was doing. For some reason, I'd thought I'd know what would happen once he showed up, but now my stomach was in knots.

"I could use that. Mind if I join you?" He gestured to the spot across from where I'd been sitting in front of my bed.

"Not at all." Lego, I could do. Fidgeting and building with my hands would also help my mind slow down. We could talk just like we'd been talking over the past two weeks, only this time we were alone. Just like the security night we valiantly protected Smaug and I slept in his arms. Great, now the taste of him still lingered on my lips, and the memory of him pressed against me sent a scrawl of heat creeping up my neck to the bottoms of my cheeks.

I stepped over him and sat on my spot.

He toed off his sneakers. The white of his socks seemed brighter against the dark denim of his jeans. He dropped down, resting his back against my bed frame. The duvet acted as a pillow against his back, but the concrete carpeted floor wasn't exactly forgiving.

"You can use one of these so your ass doesn't go numb." Why did I mention his ass? My neck got hot, and I was acutely aware of how close we were.

I leaned forward, reaching past him to my bed to grab a pillow for him to sit on. Lego could be downright diabolical when they wanted to be, and one took that exact moment to leap from the pile and drive straight into my palm.

I jerked and pitched forward, nearly knocking heads with him.

But he caught me. His hands shot to my sides.

My t-shirt rode up in the stretch, so his palms collided with my skin.

The tumble didn't feel nearly as embarrassing anymore. Now the flames of awkwardness were fanning a different type of heat.

"I got you."

My legs were stretched on top of his crossed legs like he'd decided to dip me while dancing, only he was sitting. Staring up, I gazed into his eyes. The same ones I'd been looking into while snuggled up in the sleeping bag. My heart raced. My body hummed, and my lips parted.

His solid body was still cradling mine. His head dipped lower, and once again, our mouths were inches apart.

I breathed in shallow puffs, and my fingers wrapped tighter around the pillow I'd forgotten I'd been reaching for a second ago.

The brake lines had been cut, and there was no stopping the feelings welling inside my chest and pooling in my stomach. I grabbed the front of his shirt and pulled him down to me.

Our mouths met again. My lips moved over his with frenzied intensity.

His tongue pushed inside my mouth, punctuating our wordless sentences with toe-curling need. It spilled over into a blanket of suffocating lust and made me forget everything else.

He shifted, and my legs were no longer over him, but under him.

The pillow I'd grabbed and had fallen to the floor was behind my head.

My jean-clad legs parted, and his weight settled between them.

His kisses were hungry on my lips, my neck and the hollow of my throat. And his hands were under my shirt, skimming against my ribs until goose bumps broke out.

I was just as insatiable against the scruff on his jawline. My fingers were buried in his hair when he pressed up and stared into my eyes. "I want you, Leona."

A rational part of me listed out all the reasons we shouldn't do this. We barely knew each other. We'd only kissed a few times. We were moving too fast. But the rational part of my brain was about to be locked outside the front door because I didn't care. "I want you too."

I threaded my fingers through his hair again and kissed along his neck.

Above me, he shuddered, and his eyes closed for a second before refocusing on mine. "How long did you say Taylor and Ashley were gone?"

"Two hours." My fingers dropped from his hair to the button of his jeans.

"That works for me." His practiced fingers slid my jeans down over my butt, leaving my underwear on.

A tiny bit of panic shot through me. Was this really happening? I wanted it. I wanted him. But after all this time, I was a little freaked out there'd be a glowing V down there when I finally got naked. Could he tell? Would he be able to tell?

"It's not a big deal or anything..."

His lips traced along the underside of my chin, and his hands worked over my skin, heightening every touch. "I wouldn't say that." He cupped and squeezed my ass.

But a part of the rationality had found an open window to climb through, and I couldn't ignore it. I didn't want this to stop but also thought I might prep him for me sucking at it. I chuckled. "I just meant I've never done this before."

His fingers froze on the clasps of my bra. "What?" He jerked up like I'd planted my foot in the center of his chest.

My stomach lurched. Maybe I should've kept that to myself.

"I—I've never done this before."

He moved back, so his entire body weight was off me.

"It's not a big deal. I just wanted you to know, you know, in case it wasn't..." I wanted a hole to open, swallow me up and save me from this awkwardness.

His body moved even farther away. "Shit!" He jerked, and a string of curses fell from his lips.

And I scrambled up, feeling naked although I was only half-naked. Embarrassment leapt to humiliation. I grabbed my jeans and shoved my legs back into them. "It—" But when I looked at him, he wasn't looking at me at all.

He'd fallen into the Lego pile. Each move of his knee landed him on another one. "Sorry." He yelped. "I didn't. I wasn't saying that about what you said, but I think one of these damn things is embedded in my heel."

Some of the tightness in my chest loosened that he wasn't freaking out over my confession. Well, he wasn't *only* freaking out over me telling him I was still a virgin.

I swept my arms across the Lego to get them out of his path.

No longer in Dante's inferno of Lego torture, he looked around like he expected them to jump at him. Assured they were no longer plotting their revenge, he turned and held out his hand to me.

Fighting against my embarrassment, I hesitated for a second before I took it and let him lift me up.

"When you say you haven't done this before, what exactly did you mean?"

"I meant sex. I've done other things, just not that." My

skin was on fire, and not in a hot way, but in a kill-me-now way.

I stared at my hand still wrapped in his. "That's not going to be a deal breaker, is it? Do you want to leave now?"

19

REID

I held her hand. My feet and knees burned with Lego-induced sharp, stabbing pains, but that didn't compare to her uncertainty.

Sure, I was freaking the hell out, but that damn sure didn't mean I wanted to leave.

I let out the breath that had been trapped in my lungs.

"No, I'm not freaked out. And I don't want to go unless you want me to go." I tipped her chin up. "Do you want me to go?"

She shook her head. "No. Does that mean..." Her hands reached for the hem of her shirt.

I stilled them, holding onto both at her waist. "But it doesn't mean I expect that. It's not why I came over. I wanted to see you. It's not about sex." And it wasn't, but this changed everything. She wanted me to be her first, which meant all other guys who came after me, as much as I fucking hated thinking of her with anyone else right now, would be compared to me. I'd make it good for her, better than good, spec-fucking-tacular. I wanted to be the best for her. A measurement no one else could live up to.

"It's not?" Her stricken look was accompanied by a slow blink. "Like not ever?"

I ducked my head and laughed. "I meant, it's not *just* about sex." Letting go of her hands, I took a step away and squeezed the back of my neck.

I looked up at her and gestured to the floor and her room. "I didn't mean not ever, but not right this moment. Sorry if I was rushing things." This was hard. This was new. Things were a lot easier when you got straight to taking your clothes off, but I didn't want to do that with Leona, even before I found out. I wouldn't be the guy she remembered fumbling her first time and making it an experience she cringed to think about or, worst of all, regretted.

"Would you be saying this if I weren't a virgin?" Her eyes were lit with a combative fire.

I took her chin and rubbed my thumb in small circles. "I honestly don't know, but you are, so it's what I'm saying. Would you prefer I didn't care and mauled you on top of soul-piercing Lego blocks?"

Her gaze softened. "No, but it doesn't have to be a big deal. I don't need rose petals and a candle-lit gauzy room filled with saxophone music." Her hands flailed around, punctuating her point. "It's not that I've been saving myself. It just never felt right before."

"And this feels right? A hard concrete floor in a Lego hazard zone? I don't even want to know what it would feel like to roll over onto one of those things bare assed."

She laughed, tension slowly ebbing from her shoulders. "That's not what I meant."

I leaned in and kissed her again, holding onto her chin. "I know what you meant. And I really didn't come over here for sex. I just got carried away earlier when I knew no one was around to interrupt us."

"So you're saying..." She stepped in closer and ran her hands over my chest.

Damn, this was hard, and I was halfway to being there myself, thinking about what she wanted. "Is that how you think things go for me? I show up, tell you I want you and demand sex?"

"I'm not saying I'd mind." Her playful shrug tugged at my heart.

"I mind. It's not how I want things to go."

"How do you want things to go?"

I scrubbed my hands over my face. "I don't want to rush you."

She stepped in so close, it was hard to think. "I don't feel rushed."

"Okay, I feel rushed."

"You feel rushed? Are you a virgin?" She peered up at me. Her dark eyes glowed with curiosity.

"What? No, of course not. Not that it would be a bad thing if I were. But I need to prepare."

Her lips pursed, and she stepped back. Folding her arms across her chest, she tilted her head. "Reid, you're killing me. What are you going to be googling, a how-to guide on devirginization?"

It might've been an entry in my search history a few minutes after I left her. Damn, was I looking like a fumbling first year with this. But I wasn't going to rush this.

"Three dates. Give me three dates, then we can sleep together." I might as well have said twenty dates. Apparently, torturing myself on the field wasn't enough. She'd be turning every night's dream into the taunt of not being able to have her from this moment until our third date.

"Isn't that supposed to be *my* line?"

"This could be my standard MO. This could be how I court any fair maiden I'm attracted to."

"If I asked around campus, I'm sure the descriptions would be horse-drawn carriage rides, waltzes and chaperoned visits while they took harpsichord lessons."

"Something like that, but how I've done things in the past doesn't matter. How I want to do things with you does. Three dates." If she said no, I wasn't sure I'd have a second line of defense to not royally screw this up. "How's that sound?"

"Like you're stalling, but I'll allow it. Maybe by the end of date two, I'll have decided I can't freaking stand you and walk to the other side of the street whenever our paths cross."

That was a helmet to the sternum. As much as I didn't like that, if I wasn't the right guy for her, I didn't want her to be with me, and I was determined to be the right guy.

"Then wouldn't you be happy you had the second date to confirm how much you hated the sight of me?"

"What exactly counts as a date?"

"Food. Drinks, alcoholic or not. And spending time together."

Her gaze narrowed, and her lips scrunched to one side as she looked me up and down. She unfolded her arms and sighed. A long-suffering one that made her chest rise and fall dramatically, drawing my gaze straight to her chest. She held out her pinkie. "This maiden accepts your offer."

I hooked hers with mine and curled my wrist to press my lips against the back of her hand.

She stepped in close enough to nestle our hands in her cleavage. Her lips brushed against my ear, and a shudder raced down my spine. "That doesn't mean I'm going to make this easy for you."

My eyes drifted closed. Digging deep for self-control, I tightened the internal reins so I didn't back her against the wall and do everything that had been racing through my head when it came to getting her naked.

"I'd expect nothing less." And I had to hope I could keep myself from screwing it up. Whether she thought it was a big deal or not, I'd make sure she'd never have a second of regret when it came to our night together. If I had any say about it, it would be the first of many.

Yesterday, we'd had out first loss of the season, and we all knew we'd be paying for it. My legs felt like a figment of my imagination, and although it was freezing, I'd need an ice bath to stop the swelling in my left calf. But Cole...Cole had gotten it worse than anyone.

His fingers sunk into the dirt, gripping at the grass. He wiped his mouth with the back of his hand. A puddle of puke soaked into the frigid grass.

Almost everyone else had left the field. In our last game, Cole's snap to Hollis had slipped after a projectile had been flung onto the field. The ref had already thrown a flag on the defense for encroachment gaining us a 5-yard penalty. The failed snap had no negative impact on thee game. Everyone else who had a botched play had been ridden hard during practice, whether it was a win or a loss, as was the Mikelson Motivation, but today Cole was a split second in shutting up once Mikelson began talking, which led to the current torture we were witnessing.

He'd been doing the cone footwork drill for the past forty minutes, non-stop. The freezing air was locking up all our muscles, and with the sun setting, I could see my breath hanging in front of my face although it was only October.

Mikelson blew two sharp bursts on his whistle. "Again."

Cole glared at Coach and braced his hands on his knees before standing fully upright.

"Coach, I'd like to take his place." I stepped forward. He'd be useless to us for our next game if his legs didn't fucking work. "I was part of the play with the incomplete snap."

Mickelson swung around to face me with the vein in his forehead joining the one in his neck. His mouth twisted like he was prepared to spew lava. "Think you're a fucking hotshot now after one good play."

I steeled myself and didn't drop my gaze. "No, Coach, but I'm his teammate, so I should be out there with him."

"I say who should be out there and who shouldn't." His gaze bored into mine like an unstoppable drill. "He can't even complete a simple snap. Maybe he should be in another position. We're finding out right now."

Cole shook his head in a nearly imperceptible motion.

"Yes, Coach." I clenched my fists around the face mask to my helmet and bit my tongue as another whistle blast ripped through the air.

Cole moved past the seven cones, juking like he was cutting past a defender, and caught the ball thrown by one of the assistant coaches.

Though I was stuck on the sidelines, I stared at my teammate on the field, running and cheering him on through gritted teeth. I made sure I was in his line of sight so he didn't feel like he was alone out there.

He made it through three more, pushing himself. Most people would've passed out and stayed down. But not Cole.

One of the assistant coaches told Mikelson about a

meeting he'd be late for if he didn't leave soon. That was the only reason he ended the torture.

Cole stood straight and walked off the field, heading toward the locker room. I followed behind him.

A hand gripped my pads and spun me around. Mikelson stood in front of me full of bluster and fury. "Don't you ever interfere with my coaching. Do you understand?" Spittle showered over my face.

Rage burned in my stomach, and I slammed the door shut on it, not wanting to make things worse.

"A couple good plays doesn't make you invincible, and it sure as hell doesn't make you untouchable. Do you understand me?"

"Yes, Coach." My jaw ached, and my fingers bit into my face mask, bending the molded plastic in my grip.

I turned and walked down the cold concrete hall toward the locker room.

Halfway down, Cole leaned against the wall, looking like he could barely stand.

I jogged forward and wrapped his arm around my neck, hefting him upright.

"Reid—"

"Shut the hell up. I'm helping you, and I don't want to hear a damn thing about it. The strength and conditioning team is going to have a field day with you."

He groaned. "Don't do what you did out there again. There's no use both of us getting on his bad side."

"I couldn't just let him keep grinding you down like that."

A humorless laugh wobbled from his throat. "I'm used to it."

We hobbled into the locker room, which was relatively

quiet. Inside our lockers, we both got out our shorts and changed.

He was already inside the ice bath by the time I got there.

I checked in with the recovery coach and slid into the tub filled with ice cubes and freezing water. The ice felt like it was traveling up my veins from my toes past my knees, racing for the warmth in my groin until it hit my lungs. Quick, sharp breaths escaped me as I finally hit the bottom and tried to keep my muscles relaxed.

"How long are you in for?" I asked.

"Twelve."

"Shit."

"You're telling me." He jutted his chin toward me. "What about you?"

"Seven."

"Lucky bastard." Cole's arms were braced on the ledge of the bath while he stared at the blank wall in front of him.

"You okay, man?"

"What does it matter?" There was a thread of despair in his voice. Normally Cole seemed to let shit roll off his back, especially when it came to Mikelson. His determination not to let anything affect him was probably why we'd always done so well together on the field. But this level of dejection... Coach might've finally cracked him.

"Of course it matters. What the hell are you talking about?"

"He only did it because we've got five days until our next game."

Checking over my shoulder at the empty room, I leaned in closer. "I don't care if we have five years until our next game. That was bullshit. None of it was about making you better."

"What does it change?"

Helplessness hit dead center in my chest.

Cole squeezed his eyes shut. "Exactly. We put up with it because we don't have a choice. At least, I don't have to feel like I dragged you down with me." He clenched his teeth.

"I'm your teammate and I'm your friend, which means I'm driving your car home. I'll wait for you to finish all your recovery work."

That he didn't argue with me told me everything I needed to know about how much he was hurting.

By the time we got home, the rest of the guys had already taken off their ice packs and there were grilled steaks in the oven. "Who got steak money?" I stabbed a couple and shook them onto my plate.

"Griff rolled in here with half a cow," Hollis shouted through the meat in his mouth.

Cole took an ice pack out of the freezer and rested it on his shoulder.

"Still hurting?"

He grunted and took out the last couple steaks for himself, a pile of broccoli and some instant mashed potatoes.

"Good eating until the money runs out."

Cole and I grabbed our water and collapsed onto the couch. Ezra silently strummed his guitar and had on *True Lies* like we hadn't all watched it a million times, but how could you go wrong with the action classic?

My phone buzzed in my pocket. Shifting, I fished it out and stared at the screen, tilting it away from the guys.

L: Would now be a good time to come over? Ashley and Taylor will be gone for a while.

I shot up, making Cole spill water on his shirt.

"What the hell?"

"Sorry." I took a massive bite of my steak. "I've got to go."

"Where the hell to? You haven't even eaten yet." Ezra pointed to my plate balanced on the arm of the couch.

"Just a thing I need to do."

"A thing that involves leaving food behind?"

The whole room stared at me. I cleared my throat and slowed down, trying not to draw even more attention to myself. "It's not a big deal." I grabbed my coat and put it back on.

Cole shouted, "We're going to eat your food."

At least he sounded more like himself. "Fine, and I'll shave off one of your eyebrows in your sleep."

"As if I sleep." He laughed like a super villain.

I closed the door behind me and rushed down the stairs. I made it to the center of the street before checking behind me.

The blinds snapped closed. Nosy assholes.

If I ran straight to Leona's that would get us both busted. I turned right and walked down the block, then around to the front of Leona's apartment block that faced campus and entered there.

As shitty as practice was, sitting at Leona's dining room table was a nice distraction. More than a distraction. Finding time alone had been difficult, but once she said Taylor and Ashley would be gone for a few hours, we'd found our window.

We hadn't had much of a chance to be alone, so everything more than a few minutes alone felt clandestine. Like I should've had to repel down through the ceiling to kiss her upside down a la Spiderman.

"You do remember when I said I'm not big into wine."

"I remember." She nodded with a smile and uncorked another bottle. On the table, there were two small, sliced loaves of bread, grapes, strawberries and a little cheese.

"You're not going to be offended, right?" The last thing I needed was to get blitzed off my ass on wine and give in, making her first time with a sloppy drunk with deep purple teeth.

She was teasing, but I was strong enough to resist. I'd faced even bigger challenges in my life, but never one so tempting.

"No offense will be taken by you not liking what I recommend." Her eyes were wide as she swept her hands back and forth in front of her.

"But you're thinking you can win me over to the wine side? What would that do for my reputation? I can't show up with a bottle of—" I picked up the closest bottle to me. "I'm not even going to attempt to pronounce that."

She laughed. "It's a cabernet sauvignon."

"Oh, is that all."

"Don't worry about the names. Just try to have fun with it. And I won't be offended. You don't have to love everything, but if we can find one wine you enjoy, I'll consider it totally worth it."

She poured yet another minuscule amount into one of the eight wine glasses sitting on the table in front of me. "What college student even has this many wine glasses?"

"The ones who like to drink wine. Ashley and Taylor will be the very happy recipients of what remains of the bottles, if there aren't any you like."

"I'm sure they will. You're much more likely to find ones who drink Natty Light."

Her face scrunched up into a mask of horror. "I don't

know how anyone drinks that stuff. It tastes like watered down and carbonated pee."

"Had a lot of experience with drinking pee then?"

Her nose wrinkled even more. "Gross."

"You're the one who brought it up."

She shoved my shoulder. "You know what I mean."

"After choking down a few gallons of it, you get used to it."

"Well, hopefully, you won't have to choke any of this down." She raised a glass and rotated her hand, holding it up to my face.

"Do I have to smell it and pretend I smell oak and other random things?"

"Just drink it and tell me what you think."

"Do I need a spit bucket?"

She pressed the glass up to my lips. "Stop stalling. It's not poisoned. Just drink."

I took the glass from her and eyed it. With a deep breath, I lifted it to my mouth and gulped down the whole thing. I braced for the bitterness, but it wasn't there. At least what I could taste of it. Most went straight down my throat.

"Did it even touch your tongue?"

"Does it even matter?"

"Of course it does. If I was just looking to get you drunk, I could've opened a bottle of Bacardi 151 and poured shots directly into your mouth."

I clapped my hands together. "Now we're talking. Bring on the 151."

"Do you really not want to try?" Her shoulders drooped in disappointment. She moved to sit back.

Lunging forward, I grabbed her hands. "I'm being an asshole. Of course, I want to try. This is me covering for the fact that I don't want to look like a total moron. I'm out of my depth here, Leona."

She smiled with a hint of skepticism in her eyes.

I'd do whatever it took to wipe the last of that look away.

She gestured to the next glass. "Just relax and try to have fun."

I lifted it and took a sip of the red wine. It wasn't bad. There wasn't that sharp, acrid, tongue-numbing bitterness I'd had with other wines I tried. Holding the glass up, I checked out the color in the glass. "Not bad."

She brightened like I'd told her this was the best thing I'd ever tasted.

I'd be willing to choke down whatever else she served me and test out my acting skills to get that reaction every time.

Her diabolical grin should've clued me in to her big plans, but maybe I *was* just a dumb jock. She lifted out of her seat and straddled me, her thighs on either side of my legs, and lowered her mouth to mine.

The bright, flavorful taste of crisp wine hit my lips, and as our tongues mingled, more of the taste filled my mouth.

She sat back, hips squirming on mine. "How'd you like that one?"

My dick was trapped in my jeans, against my leg and hating my inseam at this moment. "It was the best so far."

"I thought you'd say that."

And that was how the rest of the blissfully torturous wine tasting went. I had no idea wine could be so alluring, but Leona had certainly found a way to keep me open to experimenting with it.

"Now what do you think about wine?"

"I never want to drink anything else."

"Somehow I think that would get in the way of your

playing." She shot up straight, her ass pushing even harder against my lap. "Aren't you not supposed to drink during the season? I didn't even think of that." She pitched to the side, but I clamped my hands around her waist.

"It's not that we're not allowed to drink—it's that most people don't think it's worth it. And this was hardly a night out on a bender. Ten gulps of wine aren't going to knock me out, especially when I'm tasting it off your lips."

Her arms looped around the back of my neck and her body pressed close. "Was it worth it?" A trail of kisses was dotted along my neck, and her hands brushed along my ribs under my shirt.

I shuddered and gripped her hips. Her mouth was sin, and my control was slipping. "Yes."

The grind of her ass on my lap was a maddening tease. "Still want to hold out for three dates?" She leaned back and bit her bottom lip. The move put off every bit of the hot as hell vibe she was going for.

But my plan was forming. I needed more time. "Absolutely." The words sounded like they'd been choked out of me. My brain knew this wasn't the plan, but my body was ready to eject my brain at this point.

"Are you sure?" A deeper and longer circle with her hips. The friction, pressure and heat threatened to undo all the big ideas I had.

"Y—" It came out with a squeak. I cleared my throat. "Yes, absolutely."

Taking her by the waist, I lifted her off me and scooted back.

She stepped forward with her legs on either side of one of my thighs and my head once again between both her arms, but at this angle, my face was also at chest height. The full curves of her breasts were within licking distance.

"And this counts as date number one." She bent and kissed the tip of my nose.

"No, this doesn't—"

"Drinks and food." She swept her hand through the air over the table to wine, bread, cheese and fruit. "It counts."

"You tricked me."

"You know it. And teasing you will be even more fun than I imagined."

I groaned. I was dead. I was an absolute dead man.

21

LEONA

Reid was exactly the kind of situation I'd talk over with my mom. She was always the one reassuring me when yet another guy would pass me over for a prettier friend or the guy I'd brought to the house spent more time angling for an internship or a job with Andy. But she wasn't here now.

And I wasn't sure I wanted her to be.

The screen connected the call. A swirling black and white circle got bigger and smaller, almost as a reminder for me to breathe.

After dodging her calls since the first week of classes, I'd agreed to the video call.

The fuzzy image sharpened, and her picture came into focus.

I folded my arms across my chest, against the lump forming beneath my sternum. I shouldn't miss her this much. It hurt and felt like a betrayal to want to hear her voice and spill my guts. My anger was still there, but it was hard to wipe away twenty-one years of her just being my mom.

"Leona, I wasn't sure you'd answer." Uncertainty was etched deep in the lines of her face.

I bristled, using that to reinforce the reasons I hadn't wanted to have this call. "I promised I would, and I did. You wanted to talk to me so here I am." Holding off for longer would've been better. For some reason, seeing her sitting in the house I'd called home for so long, with pictures of the three of us hung on the walls behind her, made me want to scream. Rage all over again and end the call right now.

"Is this how the whole call will be?" Her shoulders slumped with defeat.

She didn't get to be the sad one. She didn't get to pretend I was being the jerk in this situation.

"I answered. I don't know what else you want from me."

She sighed, her frown deepening before she sat straighter and looked directly into the camera. "How are classes?"

"They're good. I'm a half sophomore, half junior since I left partially through second year, but we've made my schedule work."

"It's wonderful your dad was able to help with that."

"Was there a doubt he would? He's always been great like that."

She nodded. "He has."

Her admitting it made me want to reach through and shake her. *If you knew he was great, then why did you cheat on him?*

"Have you been making friends? How is it living on campus?"

"My roommates are nice. Classes range from not too bad to challenging. The campus is big on football and their traditions."

Her gaze darted over the top of the computer screen. "Andrew wanted to say hi."

His familiar face dropped into sight behind her. My stepfather waved and ducked down beside my mom. The two of them together. I'd been so happy to see them happy. There wasn't ever any stepdad tension, and he'd always been great to me. But it had all been built on a lie. Betrayal. And it felt like I'd joined right in, like what they'd done hadn't been monumentally fucked up.

"Leona Luna, we've missed you." His smile looked as porcelain frail as my mom's.

Tears burned in my eyes, but I managed to croak, "Hi, Andy."

"Everyone misses you around here. The last barrels you worked on before you left will be waiting for you to taste test when you come back. Your mom's been trying to sneak a taste but I won't let her."

They both laughed, although it sounded brittle—forced.

I hated how they had each other. Cheaters never prospered, right? Except they did. They did time and time again. The two of them had been living in wedded bliss since less than a year after the divorce. Before, I'd been happy she found someone to make her happy, but now I realized they were all stolen moments.

"But you can try it when you're back?" Mom stared intently into the screen. "For Christmas? We've got a new pizza oven for the patio and we could get the steaks you love for the grill."

Silence filled the call, and I gripped the edge of the desk, trying not to blow up. Her manipulation tactics weren't even sneaky. *Remember the good times, Leona.* But every time I did, I thought of how Dad had been all alone through the whole thing. She wasn't alone. Andy was there.

"Leona, I think you're frozen."

"I told you already, I'm staying with Dad."

"Are you sure—"

"Mom, I'm staying with Dad."

Andy patted her shoulder and waved to me. "I'll let you two talk." He disappeared from the frame.

"How about over the winter once the school year is over?" Her voice took on a pleading edge, eyes boring into the camera that linked us over thousands of miles.

I scrubbed my hands over my face. "I don't know when I'm coming back. I don't even know if I am coming back."

She gasped. "What do you mean not coming back? It's your home."

"It's not."

"It has been for the past six years."

"That was before." Before I knew of all the lies that made it possible. The lies. The hurt. The betrayal.

"Think of all the memories we have here. How many wonderful times."

All tainted by the knowledge that they were built on the worst kind of lie.

"I need time, Mom. I'll decide what I'm going to do and let you know. It's not your choice."

"I miss you. I'm not used to you being so far away." She was trying to play the sadness card, and all it did was stoke my anger.

"Imagine how Dad felt."

Her lips snapped shut. "Leona—"

"Don't Leona me. You cheated and then turned me against him."

"I never—"

"You never told me the truth."

"Because I knew you'd react this way." Her frustration seeped through.

Welcome to the club. "And that's a bad thing? How is it a bad thing? You cheated on him. Left him. Took me with you and then didn't do a thing when I wanted nothing to do with Dad."

"How was I supposed to explain it to you?"

"By never cheating in the first place. That would've been a great way to avoid the whole mess to begin with."

"I can't undo the past."

"But you'll sit there and try to make me feel guilty because I don't want to have a happy, family Christmas with you and Andy."

"As you get older, you'll realize everything isn't so black and white. Sometimes things just happen, and you have no control over them."

"Or some things are methodically planned and executed to cover your tracks. Like how Andrew just so happened to have a beautiful new grand piano in his house when we couldn't afford one. Around when you suddenly decided I should take it up? One we were able to use for my piano lessons. It was so convenient that you found an instructor for me who could come to his house."

Mom stared back at me with a stricken look.

"Funny how you didn't give a crap about piano lessons for me once we moved. You figured since I'd been blind for so long that I wouldn't figure out how you'd used me to cover your affair." I slammed my fist against my desk.

"Sweetheart—"

"No!" Tears burned in my eyes. "No, you don't get to try to make this better. You cheated on Dad and let me close him out like I did thinking he'd cheated on you. I was so happy Andy was there for you and helped you when it was the two of you all along."

I wiped angrily at the tears spilling down my cheeks.

"You moved us away and left Dad all alone."

"I—" Her face crumpled. "I didn't want to lose you."

"You should've thought about that before you cheated and lied." I slammed the laptop closed.

A faint knock sent me lunging for the tissues. I wiped at my face and the door opened before I could say come in.

"Lee-lee." Taylor stuck her head in my room with her perfectly glossy lips all pursed to one side of her mouth with worry.

"Hey, Taylor. What did you need?" I wedged my hands between both my knees with my tissues balled up between them.

"Sounds like you were a little upset." She stepped inside in shredded jeans, black knee-high boots and a long sleeve halter top, which showcased her shoulders and collarbones. Dressed like that, there was an equal likelihood she was going to hang out watching TV or go out. She never dressed for anyone other than herself. Maybe that was why she could pull any outfit off so well. And she wasn't a red-eyed, screeching mess like me.

"I'm fine. Just a call with my mom."

"Do you want to talk about it?" She leaned against the edge of my bed.

"Not really."

Tracing her fingers over my bedspread, she looked up and grinned. "Want to go out and get shitfaced?"

My hands jerked from between my legs. Stay here and wallow or go out and party? "That's exactly what I want to do."

She straightened. "Good because if you said no, Ashley was going to come haul you out and make you go anyway."

"Was I that loud?" I wanted to crawl under my desk and hide.

She pinched her fingers together with a small gap between them and peered through it. "A little."

I dropped my head back and let out a groan. "Give me five minutes, and I'll be ready."

"Shots will be waiting." She closed the door behind her and left me alone with my swirling thoughts.

A distraction was what I needed. I plucked a pair of jeans and a shirt out of my drawers and threw them on.

Music rumbled my door hinges by the time I slipped my boots on.

Out in the living room, Ashley, Taylor and Kennedy belted out a song, using the necks of the wine bottles as mics.

I laughed and sang along to the last line.

"She's here!" They turned to me with their arms flung in the air. "Shots! Shots! Shots!"

"Hey, Kennedy." I hugged her.

She rocked jeans and a high-necked black top with sheer long sleeves and a sheer back. The keyhole at the front was perfectly placed to show off her assets that didn't even require the slightest hint of a push-up bra. The inside corners of her eyes were shimmery, and her nails were bright blue except for the pointer finger, which matched the metallic glitter of her eyes.

"I swear I could be wearing the exact same thing as the two of you and I'd look like a three-year-old dressed me."

Kennedy and Taylor laughed. They looked completely different, but also like they could both pose together on the cover of a magazine.

Ashley poured pineapple juice into the shot glasses along with blue Curacao and coconut-flavored rum, turning it into a turquoise swirl. She handed each one of us a glass.

"Don't worry, Leona. The two of us can be the non-fashion model crew when we go out. We'll pretend we're their assistants, and maybe they'll let us in."

Kennedy snorted. "As if Thyrst is choosy about who they let in."

"Good thing for us." Ashley clinked her glass against mine and downed it.

I lifted my glass and gulped down the bright blue. Prepared for the burn, I opened my eyes when all that lingered in my mouth was the sugary coconut and citrus taste. I smacked my lips together. "Damn, that's good."

"These are diabolical, Ashley." Kennedy rubbed her hands together. "Which means I want even more."

"It goes down too easy, doesn't it?" Taylor licked her lips without disturbing her lipstick.

Ashley took my glass and poured another round.

"Where are we going?"

"Phyrst Thyrst," they said in unison.

"Which means these will be the strongest drinks we get all night."

Ashley motioned to the bright glasses lined up on the counter, and we all picked up our glasses again.

Kennedy held her shot out in front of her. "To a night of debauchery we'll all have fuzzy memories of tomorrow."

"To a night out we won't forget, except for all the parts we do."

We clinked our glasses together.

After squeezing into a taxi, we got to the bar, which was already bursting with people. Groups were milling around in front of the building.

"Will we be able to get in?" I stepped out of the taxi and looked up at the glowing sign with its unique spelling.

Ashley turned laughing. "With these two?" Her hands shot out toward Taylor and Kennedy. "They'd build a booth for them. Why do you think I hang out with her? I get all the perks and don't have to spend half as long on my makeup."

Taylor spun around and stuck out her tongue. "You're lucky you make good drinks." She stood even taller in her boots and waved at someone inside. "Tables are at a premium, but it looks like they've got one with some room."

This was what I got for not wearing heels as tall as hers. I couldn't see anything through the mob of people. The entire bar was packed wall-to-wall with students. The dance floor, tables and bar were a humongous mass of movement, and it was hard to find a dividing line between each area.

"Yup, they waved us over. We're good to sit there."

I tried to look between heads.

"There."

She grabbed Ashley's hand, who grabbed Kennedy's, who took mine, and we wedged ourselves between the bodies in a human chain.

In a break in the crush of bodies, Taylor pointed to the semi-circular booth half-filled with football players. Not any football players, but our float-building buddies—including Reid.

The booths along the back seemed to mainly be filled with athletes. They all gave off a distinctly untouchable vibe. Local celebrity had its perks.

"Fuck, come on." Kennedy tugged on Taylor's arm. "There's got to be somewhere else."

"There's nowhere else. Do you want to have to stand around without a place for your drinks all night?"

"We could wait for someone else to leave."

"Or we could take the half-empty table right here." She stepped up to the booth.

The oversized booths seemed to have been made for the guys who were sitting on the outside edges, leaving the inside empty. Reid and Hollis stood, as did Ezra and Cole.

My heart raced, filling me with a glowing giddiness. Every time I saw him, it was like the volume was turned down on everything else around me. All the sights and sounds were slightly unfocused and muted so my vision tunneled on him until it all came rushing back. It was a split second when everything else fell away.

I didn't miss how Reid swapped with Hollis when we shimmied across the worn seating. He'd been on the end, but now he was on the inside. On the inside right next to me. Had anyone else noticed?

His knee brushed against my leg.

My lips twitched, and I tried to pay attention to the conversation and not give us away. I set my hand on the seat and brushed his pinkie. He crossed his over top of mine and darted a quick look my way. Our little secret.

I glanced around, but everyone else was staring at Kennedy and Cole, who both looked miserable.

"Where's Griff?"

As if I'd conjured him, he came back to the table with eight beers.

"You guys are lucky I saw you headed this way or it would have taken forever to get you a round." He slid the glasses across the table.

"How'd you even see us? That was less than three minutes ago." Ashley took the offered beer.

"My keen sense of observation." He winked.

Looking at the table, there now wasn't enough room to fit him. I tapped Ashley to squeeze in.

"No worries, Leona. I don't mind standing."

He sipped some of his drink and scanned the room filled with people. Once again, being on the taller side certainly had its benefits.

Ezra was sandwiched between Cole and Kennedy after Cole had forced him to swap so he wouldn't be sitting beside her.

"Griff, maybe you can scope out another free table for us, so you don't have to stand." Kennedy gulped half her beer. "Thanks for this." She raised her glass to him.

"You didn't have to sit here in the first place," Cole mumbled into his glass.

"We were invited to sit here, weren't we?"

"If we'd known you were with Taylor—" Cole's words were cut off by an elbow from Ezra. He glared at him and then Kennedy.

She looked at everyone else at the table other than Cole. "Maybe we should order some food? How about some nachos?"

"Maybe they're not big on unhealthy processed shit like you." Cole mimicked Kennedy's overly cheery tone.

Kennedy jerked back so hard some of her beer splattered to the table. She wiped the spilled drink up with a couple napkins, then focused on Cole. "Not nachos then? Anyone else feel like some overcooked pasta? A real limp noodle?" She swung her head around. "No, not anyone else's cup of tea? You're right, me neither." Her shoulders rose and fell dramatically, and she looked around like she was helpless to figure out our dilemma.

Cole shot back, "Why do you have to be such a bitch?"

Although the whole bar was rowdy and pulsing, silence descended on our table.

Kennedy's gaze narrowed. She popped up, climbed onto

the booth seat, and leaned over Hollis, who shrank back. "I don't know if you could be a bigger dick if you tried. But I'm sure you'll try, so I'm out of here."

Instead of waiting for anyone to move, she crawled up onto the table. Everyone picked up the drinks, making a path for her. If I'd tried to clamber over the table, I'd probably have looked like a cat with mittens on, but she made it look easy—not just easy, but damn good. Guys would pay good money for a show like that.

Griff held out a hand, and she slid off the table, adjusting her bra. "Thanks, Griff, for being a gentleman, and I owe you for the beer." She bent over the table and grabbed her glass before chugging the rest and pressing it against Griff's chest.

Cole's gaze didn't leave her retreating figure.

A guy smiled at her. She glanced over her shoulder, then took his hand, raising it over her head and led the two of them into the crowd that swallowed them up.

Ezra tugged on the brim of his cap and shook his head.

Taylor stood and punched Cole in the left pec. "What the fuck, Cole?"

"What?" he shouted like he had no idea why anyone would be mad at him.

"You two need to squash whatever is going on between you because it's getting painful to watch." She thumped back in her seat.

"She started it."

Ashley squeezed the bridge of her nose. "Are you five?"

Considering he folded his arms over his chest and pouted like a preschooler, it was possible.

Reid rubbed his hand over my knee.

A flush rushed up and down my legs. I checked around

the table to be sure no one else noticed I was seconds from combusting.

"We should dance," Ezra blurted.

The whole table froze for a second, then lit up at the escape option and shuffled out of their seats.

Hollis finished his cup and set it down. "Cole, you can watch our stuff."

Cole called out, but we were already disappearing into the throngs of people.

We were a motley group. Four guys and three girls. The back of Reid's hand brushed against mine. The fluttery shivers made me want to grab him and disappear in a dark alcove, but we were supposed to be keeping this quiet.

Taylor, Ashley, Griff, Hollis, Reid, Ezra and I created our own dancing pocket of awkward.

Instead of turning to Reid, I twirled around and danced with Ezra. The music thumped the floor, and between the bottles clanking and people shouting to be heard, leaning in and screaming in each other's ears was the only way to communicate.

Under the shadow Ezra's hat cast over his eyes, I saw them widen. He stared at me like I had a crazed cat in my hands, but didn't break the side to side shuffle he had going on.

"You don't like dancing, Ezra?"

"Not really."

"Why didn't you stay at the table with Cole?"

"He was being a dick."

I laughed. "Easy enough answer."

"It doesn't have to be hard." His absolute lack of filter was endearing. It might be why he wore the hat and liked to hang back. That kind of candidness could probably get him in real trouble.

"You're funny, Ezra."

The song changed, and Taylor and Ashley grabbed me to dance to it along with Reid and Griff, who was on my side of our group, wedged in between all the other dancing bodies.

"Leona's got moves," Griff teased.

"So do you, Mr. Football Player."

He raised his arms over his head in a ballet pose and spun on his tiptoes, knocking into everyone around him who looked angry for a split second before recognizing him and then cheering him on. "Of course I do."

"Will you be using that out on the field?"

"A perfect distraction technique. They'd have no idea what the hell was going on."

We danced through the next song before Reid swapped to the other side of our cluster, which happened to coincide with a song transition to something slower.

His fingers tickled the curve of my hip, and there was a look in his eyes that sent a flush skating across my skin. It would be so easy to give ourselves away. We were all so close, bumping and bouncing off each other as people moved through the space. It would be so easy to steal a kiss.

A guy banged into us both, skirting between us with his drinks raised overhead.

He smiled at me on his way to the bar, breaking through the moment with Reid. I wanted to throttle the guy. These chances were few and far between, and the guy was trying to flirt with me. I wanted to flip him off.

Reid leaned in, and his lips brushed across the shell of my ear. "Don't worry, Leona. I'll make it up to you later."

My body hummed in anticipation of exactly how he'd be making it up to me.

The song was over, and the group mixed up again.

Hollis didn't give a shit about looking cool out here, and maybe that made him look cooler. His moves were all over the place and kept me laughing, but I didn't miss the attention he got from other people on the dance floor, especially the women who looked like they were waiting for their chance to step in. I wanted to shout back, "He's all yours, ladies."

At one point, Cole showed up and apologized to everyone for being a jerk by buying another round of drinks.

Taylor leaned in and plucked two glasses from his balancing hold. "You owe Kennedy that apology."

"Sure, I'll go track her down right now." His monotone reply wasn't selling it.

A few minutes after midnight, we spilled out of the bar and onto the street filled with other students. The guys were all sober, but Taylor and Ashley had been happy to intercept all the drinks headed their way.

My stumbling steps into the apartment were met with giggles from the two of them.

"Leona's totally drunk." Ashley cackled with her arm draped around Hollis's shoulder.

"I know." Taylor flipped her head up from the fireman's carry Cole had her in. She smacked his butt. "That's for being mean to my friend."

"Ow, dammit, that hurt." He set her down on her feet.

Her fingers gripped the doorjamb to her room. She blew her hair off her face. "It's what you get for being an asshole. One day, she's going to take you seriously, and then you'll be really sorry."

Reid walked us past them to my room. His arm was wrapped around my waist. My feet felt funny, like they weren't quite connecting with the floor. Stupid heels.

He slipped my shoes off and opened a couple drawers before pulling out my favorite, most comfy pajama pants and a t-shirt.

"Why don't you get changed? I'll be right back." He closed the door behind him, and I threw off my clothes before fumbling with my pajama top. What the hell was wrong with these armholes?

He knocked gently before peeking his head inside, then he glanced behind him into the hallway.

I flailed my arms which wouldn't go down all the way from how this stupid shirt fit.

He laughed and walked in with a big glass of water before closing the door behind him. After setting down the glass, he was right in front of me.

"Let me help you with that."

His fingers skimmed over my stomach and up over my ticklish sides before he pulled my shirt up and back down over my head.

"Let's get you to bed. Taylor and Ashley are passed out already." He walked me over to my bed, and I pulled at the front of my shirt.

"You going to stay tonight?"

"Not tonight." He shoved the blankets down and swung my legs up into the bed before pulling the covers up over me.

"Here's some water and ibuprofen."

I nibbled the two white pills out of his palm and took the offered glass of water.

"You're nothing but trouble, you know that?" He tucked the blankets up to my shoulders.

"I know. Thanks for getting us home."

"Of course."

"Reid, you ready?" One of the guys called out from the hallway. "Is she okay?"

"She's fine. Just getting her some water. I have to go now."

"Thank you for tucking me in," I mumbled, my eyelids feeling like they were weighted down by barrels.

"Don't worry about it."

"And being so gentlemanly you make me want to scream."

He laughed. "I even surprised the hell out of myself with that one." His shadow blocked out the light. His fingers twined in my hair, brushing it away from my face, and his lips pressed gently against mine. "Night, Leona." The light flicked off.

"Night, Reid," I whispered as my bedroom door closed. Tonight, my hazy dreams would be of the guy who had no reason to want to risk his future to be with me, who I couldn't stop thinking about, who was determined to be my first and make it better than I could imagine. And I believed him.

22

REID

I burst through the wide-open glass doors, away from the handsy donor and her husband who had no idea about his wife's wandering hands while regaling us both with a mind-numbingly boring story about his glory days in STFU football. Not that he was on the field, but sitting in his father's club box cheering on the team. You'd have thought he was down in the grass and mud, pushing his body to the limit with how breathlessly he talked about back in his day.

Not only did we have to juggle practices, the weight room, study hall, classes and a sliver of a social life, but we also had to deal with booster events. We got to be paraded around on a night we might've wanted to do anything other than be here. Late-October and after yet another big win, we were the belles of the ball, and the boosters were happy signing checks that would go to help the team. I couldn't fault it, but it didn't mean I didn't need a damn breather every once in a while.

There were fewer people outside. The evenings were only getting colder, which meant people weren't willing to brave that in their cocktail attire. Me? I felt like I was under roasting lights inside the house.

A string quartet was on the slate patio. Propane patio heaters pumped out waves of warmed air, and waitstaff walked purposefully through the partygoers with trays dotted with minuscule bits of food, which we'd been barred from eating by Mikelson.

This wasn't my first time at the president's residence, but it was the first time being here since I'd met Leona, and the first time I didn't hate being stuck in a museum that masqueraded as a house. Unlike other schools where the booster events were a place for the players to get blitzed on someone else's dime, Mikelson would never let us have that kind of fun.

But knowing Leona would be here, if she wasn't here already, made it bearable. The second I had the opportunity, I'd roam under the pretense of mingling to look for her.

Cole nudged me from behind. "It would take thirty of those trays to make a dent in my stomach."

"Tell me we can go to The Library after this and order a burger. Screw the team diet. I'm starving."

"I'll let Ez, Hollis and Griff know. They got whisked off for some pictures a while ago, and I haven't seen them since. How much longer do we have to be here?"

"No idea." I wasn't wearing a watch, and our phones had been confiscated by Mikelson and the coaching staff on arrival. No one would want their main attraction distracted by phones.

"There's got to be a clock around here."

"We have to have been here for at least half of the required four hours already."

Another body bumped into my back. "It's been ninety minutes." Ezra walked around me and popped a bunch of pigs in a blanket into his mouth. They were so small in his palm they looked like aspirin.

"Where did you get the stash?"

He tugged open the pocket to his suit jacket.

"How did you get all those pigs in a blanket?"

He leaned in. "Terry's catering company is handling this, so he gave me a ziplock bag full of them and told me I could swing by to load up. Want some?" He leaned to the side, giving us easy access to his pocket.

"No, I can hold out until The Library. I'm not to the point where I need pocket appetizers."

"Yet." He inhaled a few more. The unmistakable meaty and flaky crust smell made my mouth water. "Cole?"

He glanced over his shoulder. "Fuck it." His hand disappeared into Ezra's pocket, and he scarfed down a bunch of the dough-wrapped mini hot dogs. "They have no right being this damn good." He covered his mouth with his arm.

"Mikelson," I warned.

Cole gulped down his water and probably swallowed a few of the pigs whole.

"If we're really lucky, he'll walk right past us."

His gaze locked onto the three of us, and he stomped in our direction.

My stomach clenched like someone had just landed a punch. Being under the Mikelson scrutiny never helped anyone. While we were all required to be in suits with squeaky, uncomfortable shoes and name tags with our numbers on them, he was in khakis and an STFU polo shirt and hat along with a plate of food.

"You're not supposed to be talking to each other. You're supposed to be talking to the donors. Can't hurt to make up some of the shortfall Oakes has stuck us with, so get out there and be personable." His hand curled over my shoulder in a tight grip, and he shoved us back inside the stifling room.

The next hand that touched me wasn't a punishing grip, but a gentle pat on the shoulder. It was the same man from the field after my big play.

"Mr. Davenport."

He smiled. "I'm sure you had to reach deep into the memory banks to find that one." He held out his hand.

I shook it. "No, sir. I remember you from after the game."

"I'm glad I made an impression. You certainly have. The whole board has been buzzing about the team this season, and your contributions haven't been missed. We're all expecting big things from you, Mr. Riddick, and the rest of your teammates."

"We look forward to not disappointing."

He nodded and tipped his glass in my direction before someone called his name, and he headed in the opposite direction.

I was five minutes deep into a conversation with an older man in a navy sports coat with a bad case of whiskey breath when the front door opened. One of the event staff stepped forward to take her coat and my tongue made a beeline straight for my esophagus.

Leona was stunning in the lavender dress.

"How about you? Have you enjoyed having your pick of girls on campus?" The older man beside me with the tumbler filled with amber liquid stared at me with a sloppy smile and nudged me with his elbow like we were part of a club together.

From across the room, her gaze collided with mine. Her lips flickered from casual smile to carnal desire. Freaking tease.

"Football takes up a lot of my time." I dragged my eyes

away from her, not wanting to give myself up with an erection in a room full of people. "So I don't do much other than that and study."

The older man stared at me like I'd suggested I slapped a few babies. "You only live once." Shaking his head, he walked away.

For the next twenty minutes, Leona and I danced around the room. Not actually, but moving from conversation to conversation, each one getting us a step closer to one another, until someone would drag us farther away. It was torture being this close to her and not able to show her how much I'd missed her or kiss those soft lips.

We were both in different conversations but had managed to get our backs to each other. Her fingers brushed against the back of my hand at my side. To anyone else, it was an accidental brush, but for me, it was napalm in my veins. The strain was getting too hard to control.

Her fingers skimming along my wrist had me clenching my jaw and trying to force the blood flow away from my dick.

"I think Mr. and Mrs. Felton could use another round." I grabbed on to a waiter, nearly toppling his tray just to get away from them and find somewhere to cool off for a few seconds.

Leaving the crowded room, I spotted a quiet bathroom away from all the noise, closed the door and turned on the faucet. I splashed water on my face and grabbed one of the fluffy towels stacked on a dark wood tray.

The door handle jiggled.

"Someone's in here." I dropped the towel from my face as the door opened.

Standing in front of me was the woman who'd been

torturing me all night. "Are you hiding in here?" Leona threaded her fingers through mine.

I let the towel fall into the basket with the others and pulled her forward, crushing her lips to mine.

She used the lapel of my jacket to keep me close.

Inhaling her scent, the erection I'd just managed to get under control was back, stronger than ever.

Her eyelids fluttered, and she ground herself against me.

I groaned, wondering if this was how we got caught. At the moment, I couldn't care less. But my stomach had other ideas. A deep rumbling growl that sounded more like a sea creature broke through the sexual tension cocooning us.

Her eyes dropped to my stomach. "Has everyone been talking to you so much you haven't had a chance to eat?"

"We're not allowed to eat."

Her plump and glistening lips parted. "What? There's got to be a football stadium's worth of food in there."

"And Mikelson doesn't want us getting distracted by eating or spilling all over our nice clothes."

She ran her fingers along the white buttons of my shirt. "Have I told you before that I hate your coach?"

"Join the club."

Her face set with determination, and I reached for her again, much preferring our party of two.

"Come with me." She grabbed my hand and opened the door.

My heart leaped into my throat, beating there to the point I thought a ribbit croak might burst from my mouth.

After looking both ways, she stepped out and tugged me along.

"Where are we going?"

"You'll see." She let go of my hand but stared back at me, and her direction was clear. Follow her. And I did, ducking into an alcove before squeezing past a velvet rope blocking off restricted areas of the house and tiptoeing up a set of back stairs then down a hall. Voices traveled throughout the house. From time to time, it sounded like someone was right ahead or behind us, but she'd creep closer and wave me forward. The whole place was an acoustic nightmare.

I kept my mind off how screwed I'd be if someone found me up here. How screwed I'd be if Mikelson found me with Leona. But it didn't stop me from taking each step forward.

Near another set of stairs, she opened a door. I looked down the hallway before rushing inside behind her.

She closed the door, and we both stood in darkness. The room was lit only by the lights outside on the ground level, which looked like old school street lamps. She clicked on a lamp on the desk by the door and walked back over to me, so close I could smell her strawberry-scented lotion.

"What exactly do you have planned for me now that you have me here?" I wasn't sure if I hoped for or feared what she had in mind. After hours of being on my best behavior, I wouldn't be against getting up to some mischief.

Her lips were fierce and hungry on mine, and I had no issues with whatever she wanted to do to me.

"I'll be right back," she promised. And then she was gone again.

I paced around the room. Without her close by, the epic levels of the shitstorm I was courting by being here were amplified.

Her room was a lot bigger than the one she had on campus. There was a wrought iron balcony through two glass double doors.

The large bed had a tufted navy fabric headboard. Her desk looked like an antique and seemed a little out of place with the ergonomic black chair in front of it. But it meant she used this room.

The door opened again, and it wasn't Leona walking inside.

My stomach dropped until the fear was wiped away when their faces registered through the terror. "Cole? Hollis? What the hell are you two doing here?"

Cole's face transformed into a relieved smile. "We're not exactly sure. Leona led us here and then disappeared. We thought something happened to you."

Hollis glanced around the room with wide eyes. "Where is this?"

"It's Leona's bedroom."

Cole spun around and quietly closed the door. "If anyone catches us up here, we're screwed." He laughed. "And not in the way I'm sure you thought you'd be screwed when she led you up here."

The door opened behind them, banging into Cole.

Leona stepped through the door with an unwieldy catering tray we'd seen Ezra palm time and time again.

"What are you doing?" I plucked it from her grasp and set it on the desk.

"I brought provisions. I asked them to load it up for me, and no one batted an eye. There's cloth napkins in there too, so you can cover your shirts. I didn't get forks or knives, but I figured you guys wouldn't mind," she rushed out.

I looped my arm around her waist and pulled her close. The soft fabric of her dress nearly melted under my fingertips.

Cole and Hollis had already started digging into the tray of food. The smells were sending my stomach into somersaults like it was going to climb out and take the food itself if I didn't hurry up.

"Thank you." I kissed her.

She leaned in before bolting straight and nodding to the guys.

"They know."

"They do?" Her voice squeaked, and panic flared in her eyes.

Cole covered his mouth with a napkin. "I definitely didn't think I got the same treatment as Reid on the dance floor."

Hollis ripped some chicken off a skewer. "Me, neither. Rude, Leona. But this food is starting to make up for it."

With a laugh, she buried her face in my chest. "I guess we weren't that good about playing it cool." She stared into my eyes, and I was the furthest thing from cool.

I wanted everyone gone so I could have a few more minutes alone with her. "I guess not."

She smirked. "Next time, I'll be sure to dance with them the exact same way."

"Wait, I didn—"

"Too late." She pushed me toward the food. "I'll get more trays and more guys. You figure out a system, and I'll keep the appetizers coming."

The system ended up being a rotation. Five guys would come up to her room at a time after being tapped on the shoulder and relieved of entertaining duty by the group previous that had left the room. That ensured there was no wasted time and always a group inside eating.

By the end of the night, Leona was the favorite person of every guy on the team. And I wasn't sure how I felt about that. Jealousy wasn't a good look, but feeding a starving sixty-person squad made the looks she was getting that of a newly ordained STFU saint.

23

LEONA

My arms ached after schlepping what felt like the thirtieth tray of food up the stairs, but it might've been closer to forty. I'd seen Reid and his roommates eat before, but a whole team of players—that was a sight to behold.

And his asshole coach didn't have any problems eating himself, as I'd seen on the few trips into the larger party to make an appearance and say hi to whoever my dad wanted to introduce me to.

The door to my bedroom opened, and a head popped out. One of the players I hadn't spoken more than a couple words to yet spotted me, and his eyes widened before he relaxed and smiled.

"Leona?"

I froze at the top of the steps. "Dad!" My face must've been all the signal he needed to get the point. The door closed gently, and my sweat glands cranked up.

Turning, I tried my best to hide the massive metal chaffing dish filled with food.

"What are you doing?" Dad walked halfway up the staircase.

I tried to look as innocent as possible. "Just stealing a little food. I love those crab Rangoon and asked the catering people if I could steal a few."

His gaze dropped to the massive dish in my hands. "A few?"

I shrugged and grinned so wide he could probably see my molars. "I really love them."

He chuckled. "I had no idea. Are you sure you want to keep them in your room? Surely, it'll smell terrible in the morning."

"I just wanted to stash them away until they started cleaning up and then I planned on bringing them back downstairs. Things are wrapping up soon, right?" I gripped the edges of the tray in a panic as he climbed the rest of the stairs to stand beside me.

"Not too long left. Are you tired?" His gaze scanned my face. "You had classes all day, didn't you?"

I faked a yawn into my shoulder.

"Here, let me take this."

The panic spiked to terror. "No, it's fine," I choked out. "I've got it."

"Don't be silly. It looks heavy. I wouldn't mind stealing one of these either. I never have much time to eat during these events with all the talking I do." He smiled and took the tray from me, walking to my room.

"Thanks so much for helping me bring this into my room, Dad," I announced like I was corralling drunk wine tasters off the patio at the vineyard.

He turned and stared at me like I'd lost my mind. Nope, just worried about the handful of football players currently in my room.

Overwhelming dread washed over me like a bucket of ice water. My breath locked in my chest. *This must be what being strangled feels like.*

Not missing a beat, Dad opened my door, and I braced myself for the onslaught of questions. But there were none. Only the rustling of foil being peeled back.

The absence of any other sounds ripped me from my fear spiral and turned to curiosity. The terrified kind of curiosity, like peeking from between your fingers during a scary movie.

I stepped into my bedroom, where nothing looked amiss. Out of the corner of my eye, I caught the lanyard on my closet door swaying the slightest bit. My chest loosened its death grip.

"These are delicious." Dad finished his bite-sized fried crab appetizer in two bites.

He held one out to me.

"Thanks." I choked down the still hot, creamy, crunchy snack and pasted on a smile, playing up the sounds of a tasty treat.

With a glance at his watch, he sighed. "I should get back down there so Mikelson doesn't railroad any more of these poor donors, not that they seem to mind being manhandled. Don't stay up here too long. I wouldn't mind a rescue." He kissed the side of my head and left me alone—well, not entirely—in my room.

I followed him to the door. "I'll be down in a few."

After waiting for him to disappear down the stairs, I jumped back into my room and closed the door. "We're good."

One guy with a shaved head popped up from behind the other side of my bed. Another with permanent bedhead and

Vans crawled out from under my bed, and two guys slipped out of my closet.

"That was some excellent hiding."

"This isn't our first rodeo, Leona." The guy with the shaved head winked. "Thanks for giving us the cover to hide."

"No problem." That was close. My heart was still racing, and my hands shook with the adrenaline high wearing off.

He grinned and took a few of the crab Rangoon. "Let's head back down. Hopefully the other guys didn't run into President Oakes on his way out."

"It seems you guys are pretty smooth at this stuff."

He chuckled. "We have our moments."

"Let me make sure the coast is clear."

In the hall, another few guys were headed this way. I got guys in and out, feeling like a coach in the weirdest game where instead of a field, there was a shiny wooden floor, and the opponents were donors with oversized wallets.

After the guests had left and the catering company packed up the food, filling the Viking fridge with more than could be eaten in a week, I wandered through the living room and picked up an abandoned cup. Reid had stolen another kiss before boarding the bus with the rest of the team. Who I was to him seemed to be an open secret with his teammates now. I wasn't sure how I felt about that. The more people who knew increased the odds of our secret getting out. If only Mikelson knew it was easier to buy everyone's allegiance with pigs in a blanket versus an iron fist.

Reid's text while the bus had been pulling away was cryptic to say the least. But he wanted to see me. With the away game they'd had over the weekend and mid-terms, we hadn't been able to see each other in what felt like a week.

"Leave it, Leona." Dad walked in with his tie off, which

meant he was practically ready to jump into bed. "The cleaning crew will be here in the morning to put everything back together, and Amy will take all the food into the office."

"I've got it." I tapped my fingers against the stem of the glass. "Did you need anything else? I was going to head back to campus." I hated not being able to tell him everything. I hated the lies of omission, but he had the weight of the world on his shoulders, and I didn't want to add more. Even that was a lie. I didn't want to face his anger over me dating a football player or worse, his disappointment.

I'd given him a lot of reasons to be disappointed in me and I wasn't willing to add another to that list.

"You didn't want to stay here tonight? It's late."

I forced a laugh and hoped it didn't sound it. "It's barely ten."

"I guess I've forgotten what it's like to be a college student on a Tuesday evening."

"Some bars on campus don't start trivia night until eleven."

"Ah, to be young." He covered his mouth and yawned. "Don't want your old dad ruining all your fun."

I spun around in front of the door, regret slamming into me that he thought I didn't want to spend time with him. A tug of war raged in my chest. "Dad, you're not ruining anything."

His arms wrapped around me in a bear hug. There wasn't any hesitation now. "It was a joke. Don't worry about me. I'm headed to bed. I'm glad you came tonight." He opened the front door. "It was nice to have someone I knew wasn't plotting my resignation while drinking my wine and chatting about football."

I blanched and swallowed past the lump in my throat. "I'm glad too. Night, Dad."

"Night, kiddo."

From the bottom step, I waved and walked to my car, which was halfway down the drive.

He stood in the open doorway while I got inside and pulled around the large circle at the front of the house. With a wave and a honk, I headed back down the treelined driveway.

I'd worried we'd never fall back into an easy father-daughter relationship like we'd had before, but we were getting there day by day. Although I didn't feel so great about the lies from tonight, it was best for everyone. Maybe repeating that to myself would make the lying easier. Knots tightened in my stomach.

After parking at my apartment, I pulled Reid's text back up. His instructions had been odd, and I wasn't sure what the hell I was getting myself into. After a few minutes of searching, I found the door. How many doors with Bulldog knockers could there be on campus?

I checked the message again and repeated the knocks as he'd typed out and waited. I tried it again.

The knocker was pulled in, and I jumped.

An eye peered out at me through a thick metal grate. The small door slammed shut again, and the main door opened. Darkness filled the area beyond.

Tiptoeing forward, I peered through the doorway, not sure what the hell I was going to find on the other side. All I saw was a dark hallway.

Behind me, the door slammed, and I stumbled and spun. Reid stood in front of the now closed door.

"Welcome to The Library."

The short hallway was made from stone and led to a stairwell. There were small lights in the ceiling, which seemed newer than everything else. It was colder than outside and reminded me of the wine cellars where barrels were stored, just less humid.

He stepped around me and walked toward the light at the end of the hallway, holding out his hand.

I interlocked my fingers with his and let him lead me as I followed behind him with tentative steps. As we walked, I started to make out music, voices and laughter until the sound reached a normal volume.

Reid checked over his shoulder to make sure I was still there and grinned.

"What is this place?" I asked.

"A team hang out."

He pulled me into the full light of the room at the end of the hall.

The second the light hit me, a huge cheer went up that rumbled under my feet. It was like a scene from an old medieval pub, and I expected everyone to be raising a grog of ale to toast my arrival.

"Leona!" was blasted at full volume by a chorus of smiling guys.

Two long, wooden tables reinforced that medieval feel, but the rest of the tables were normal rounds with chairs. The floor in here was a smoother slate, not the rough stone from the hall. In one corner, an old pinball machine, skee ball and hot shot basketball set up were lit up. In another, a large TV with a gaming system had a few guys playing at it.

There were five doorways leading out of the main room, but those doors were all closed.

"What is this?"

"It's a spot where the players can hang out and not worry about being hassled for a loss or a win. Going out to bars on campus can be a hell of a lot of fun, but sometimes we just want to chill and not have to reenact our game or have drunk people spill drinks all over us to celebrate."

"So you guys put this together?"

"Nah, it's been here for at least thirty years. There are six or seven different secret entrances on campus. We rotate which ones we use every year to keep anyone else from finding out about it."

"Thirty years?"

"It's not as if no one knows about it. It's just that they might not know the exact function. Maintenance is cool with marking this down as a storage space as long as we don't do anything too stupid and keep it relatively clean. The rookies handle a lot of that."

Spinning in a circle, I soaked it all in. "This is incredible."

"Did you want a drink? Or food? The Deadwood delivery should be here in a few minutes."

"The Deadwood delivers?"

"For us, they do."

"It looks like you guys have everything you need down here."

He motioned to one of the seats at the end of the long table, and I sat, still unable to believe this existed, let alone that it had been a secret for this long.

"Drink?" Reid asked. "We have some beer, although nothing on draft until after the season's over."

"You have your own kegs?"

He turned my shoulders to the nook in the back that I'd missed with a bar, complete with what looked like a freshman handing out sodas. "There are probably a few bottles back there. We try not to go batshit crazy during the season, but there are a lot of us."

"A beer would be great."

"Hey, bartender, what beers do you have?"

He ducked down behind the smooth wooden bar that looked like it would fit in at any pub. "We have Yuengling, Natty Light, Budweiser, Blue Moon, Yards, Michelob Ultra."

"A few bottles?"

He ducked his head with a chagrined smile. "Like I said, there are a lot of us."

"I'll take a Yuengling."

Reid grabbed a bottle of water for himself and the beer for me.

"You're going to make me drink alone?"

"What can I say? I'm an asshole like that."

"Food's here," a voice bellowed from the doorway I'd walked in earlier. Ezra marched in carrying a box with so many bags inside I could barely make out the top of his head. The smell of meaty fried food filled the room.

In seconds, he was descended upon and the box was empty.

Ezra looked down at the box and back at the room with a glare. "Hey, dickheads. No one left a bag for Leona."

All the guys turned in my direction, and in a flash, I had at least twenty bags of food stacked in front of me.

I plucked two from the top. "Thanks, guys. I don't think I could eat all of this."

And the bags disappeared all over again, leaving the two I'd held on my lap to protect them from the onslaught.

I handed Reid his.

"This wasn't at all what I expected when I found out you were a football player." I squinted over at him and unfolded the top of my bag.

"Were you imagining Jell-O wrestling and all-night ragers?"

I ripped open the bag, flattening it to use as a plate for my food. "Something like that."

"It's not that we're all Boy Scouts. But the guys all want to win, and going into games and practices hungover or eyes blazing from staying up partying isn't how to do it. During the off-season guys can lose their shit, but we're a team, and no one wants to be the guy who lets the rest of us down."

"I can see that. It's like one big extended family."

"Those doofuses are the closest I've ever had to brothers since I was an only child. It's how it's been with every team I've been on. A lot of them feel the same way. It's not just about the wins. I mean—don't get me wrong, it's a big part of it, but it's also about playing a game we love with people we trust to have our backs."

"That sounds awesome." I bit into my burger, spilling ketchup and grilled onions out onto my makeshift plate.

Reid held out a napkin and tried to contain his laughter. "It looks like you might need this more than me."

"Shove it." I covered my mouth with my hand and grabbed the napkin. "I was on waitress duty all night."

He pushed up from his side of the table and leaned over kissing my ketchup lips. "And we greatly appreciate it."

We hung out in the secret speakeasy for another hour. The team was nothing like I expected, but I could say that about a lot of my time at STFU—most of all when it came to the guy driving me back to my apartment. I'd never expected to meet a guy like Reid. As infuriating as his three-date rule was, it only made me want him more.

He drove since I'd had a couple drinks after my attempt at choking down a beer. Despite the fully stocked bar we'd just left, the only thing he drank besides water was the rest of my beer.

Sitting tucked into the seat beside him with the heat

cranked up, I wanted to pull down a side street and crawl onto his lap to show him just how hot his patience made him. "You know that counts as date number three, right?"

The car shot forward, before he eased off the gas and sputtered, "What? No, we haven't even really had an actual date yet."

"Wrong." I held up a finger, counting them off. "Wine tasting. The booster event and then our time at The Library."

"No, that doesn't count."

"You said food and drinks together in different locations. I'd say those all qualify." I crossed my arms over my chest, basking in the self-satisfaction.

"That—those were the rules."

"Try not to sound too happy about it. I'm not saying we have to do it tonight. I just...I want you to stop worrying that you're rushing me, okay?" I ran my hand over his knee. "The more you make me wait, the more I want it, so if your goal is for me to corner you and rip off your clothes, you're getting close."

He laughed. "I can't say I'd complain. But maybe not for the first time. Just give me a few more days, okay?" He lifted my hand and kissed the back of it.

"You can be very persuasive when you want to be."

He pulled down a street a few blocks from ours and put the car in park. "And don't think any of this means I don't want you, Leona." He turned and kissed me. A gripping-my-neck, fierce, greedy kiss that made my head swim. One where it was hard to catch my breath, and I was totally okay with suffocating.

The windows were steamy before long. "Because it's killing me to wait, but I have patience enough for both of us, even if it kills me." He kissed the tip of my nose and pulled back onto the main street with one hand while I was still trying to form words.

His thumb brushed across the hair at the base of my neck. "A few more days, Leona. And I swear, it'll be worth it."

I squeezed my thighs together. The heat from the kiss and his touch made it hard to keep still. But I believed him 100%, and I couldn't wait to find out what he had in store for me.

24

REID

The dining hall buzzed with activity at 10 a.m. Freshly showered and starving, half the team came to this one, which was closest to the practice field. Plus, they served until eleven, while most others only had heating lamp food from ten until noon.

Saying goodnight to Leona inside her apartment and leaving had been torture. She loved to tease, and damn if I didn't love to be teased. But my breaking point was close. Setting up the requirement for three dates was meant to buy me more time, but my inability to stay away from her meant it was already here.

My focus was now on making it a night she wouldn't forget.

Posters for the Pittsburgh game were pinned to announcement boards on the walls. We'd booked our own party bus, which happened to have a few extra seats for four. I'd brought it up to Taylor, and she'd jumped at the chance, keeping Leona from being the one to ask if they'd like to join in. All I needed was a wall of TV screens, a sinister cat and a spinning chair and I'd get my mastermind badge before the end of the semester.

Griff's plate was filled with eggs, hash browns and bacon. "I was ready to chew through the locker room bench. Did Coach have to drone on as long as he did about dedication? We're there at 6 a.m. How much more dedicated does he think we need to be?"

"We had our second loss of the season. He doesn't want a repeat."

"Our last game was a win. If he didn't try to run the legs off everyone, we'd have more to give when we played."

Carb loading was my favorite day of the week. I grabbed a short stack of pancakes, bacon and eggs. "If it gets results..." I shrugged, hating how the ends justified the means when it came to Mikelson. I didn't have to like it, but I liked winning.

Ezra got his hardboiled eggs, bacon and biscuits.

Cole picked up French toast sticks, home fries and bacon.

Between the four of us, we'd probably taken a full caseload of bacon.

We grabbed a round table and dug into our food, going over practice and our prep for the Pittsburgh trip.

I leaned over to Griff. "Are you sure your dad doesn't care?"

He shrugged. "He's literally got millions of points. How do you think we're all getting our rooms? I'd have done it no matter what, but if it's for Leona." He sucked through his teeth. "Of course. Let me know which room, and I'll get it all set up."

I nodded and went back to my food. The few minutes I'd danced with her weren't enough. The thumping bass and her body rubbing against mine had been the sweetest torture. I couldn't wait for another round.

Hollis rushed in and threw himself into the empty chair beside Ezra so forcefully that two legs came off the floor. He gripped the table and dropped his voice. "Did you hear about Mitchell?"

"No." Cole shoveled home fries into his mouth.

"What about him?" I mopped my pancake across a pool of syrup and added bacon to the fork.

Hollis grabbed his phone and slid it across the table.

In the picture on the screen was Leona from our night at Phyrst Thyrst beside Mitchell. Under the image was the caption, "President's daughter has dance-filled night out at campus hot spot."

I snatched it up. "Who the fuck took this?" My heart punched so far up my throat it kissed my tonsils.

Hollis shrugged. "No idea, but guess who just got bumped down to second string?"

I wanted to punch something. Mitchell was annoying as hell, so that sucked for him, but who had been spying on Leona? She couldn't even have fun out on campus without some asshole taking her picture and posting it with captions filled with complete lies.

Cole came out of his seat. "How the hell did Coach even find out about this? He's benching Mitchell because he's in a picture with Leona? They weren't even dancing together."

Hollis took bacon from Ezra's plate, who growled back at him. "Whether it's true or not, Mikelson was losing his shit when I walked past his office on the way here, and the roster was changed by the time I got to the parking lot."

"Are there other pictures?" Ezra glanced down at the phone and back up at Hollis.

Cole cursed under his breath and shot a glance my way.

"Sorry. She was sitting with the rest of us all night. I wanted to know if we should all prepare to be sitting out the rest of the season?"

I wanted to shove his plate of food into his face. "Is that all you can think about?"

He stared back at me. "You're telling me that's *not* what you're thinking about?"

"No, I'm thinking about some asshole out there taking pictures of Leona without her knowing."

"You're not thinking about how screwed you'd be if your dance with her was what was all over this account?" He waved the glowing screen in front of my face. Scratch shoving food in his face, I wanted him to be the one I punched over this.

"No, and it's fucked up that's where your head went." I snatched it away from him and slammed it down.

"Hey! That's my phone." Hollis shouted.

Cole's wide-eyed stare grated on my nerves. "Who are you? You should be shitting bricks right now. You've been working on making first string since you showed up here. It's all you've ever talked about. You've been one of the first ones in the gym and the last ones to leave. Dedication to the point of insanity or hurting yourself to get here, and now you're just willing to take this risk?" He ducked his head and stared intently, lowering his voice. "I like Leona as much as anyone else. She's great. She's funny. She's pretty. She's smart. But she's also President Oakes's daughter."

I shoved back. My chair screeched against the tiles. "You don't think I know that?" Anger dropkicked me in the chest. I yanked my duffel off the floor. Getting out of here was my only goal. I was seconds from losing it.

He caught my arm when I tried to march past.

I stared down at his fingers biting into me.

"I'm not trying to be a dick. I just don't want anyone else to end up on Coach's bad side more than they need to be. We're here to play this game and put up with all his shit to come out the other end. Don't throw it all away over a mistake."

"She's not a mistake." I shook off his hold and stormed out.

Cole's voice rang in my ears as he called out to me.

I peeled out of my parking spot and raced to the other side of campus. The whole time, it felt like I was trying to claw my way out of my own skin. Cole's words gnawed at my brain, buzzing like a swarm of wasps.

My car lurched to a stop at the curb outside the house. I strode across the street with fast, heavy steps and walked straight to the door I'd helped her stumble through a few nights ago. My knuckles stung from the sharp knock against the cold metal.

The door swung open, and Leona stood in the doorway. Her eyebrows drew together. "Reid, what—"

I stepped forward and held both sides of her face. Pressing her against the wall, I kissed her, deepening it and needing more of her sweet taste.

Her hands balled into fists in my shirt, pulling me closer.

I kicked the door closed and held us there. Our tongues danced, and my body hummed.

She leaned into my chest, and I broke the kiss, resting my forehead against hers.

Her eyes were clouded with confusion. "What are you doing here?"

I brushed my thumbs along her cheeks. "I needed to see you."

"How'd you know I'd be here?"

Her eyes were filled with amusement. Under my fingertips, her skin was smooth, warm.

"You don't think I have your schedule memorized by now?"

Her lips parted.

I wanted another kiss. I wanted even more, but a kiss would take the edge off.

A throat cleared to our left.

We weren't alone. My first reaction was to put Leona behind me, but then it dawned on me where we were.

Taylor stood in the hallway with her backpack halfway on like she'd been distracted by her roommate making out with me and blocking the door. I didn't want to hide this, and I hated that we had to keep it a secret from almost everyone.

Leona's face dropped, and she moved to step away, but there was nowhere for her to go since I had her backed into the wall.

I took her hand and threaded my fingers through hers. The guys knew—it only made sense for Taylor to know. At least when we hung out with our friends now, we wouldn't have to act like we barely knew each other.

Taylor glanced from our interlocked hands to back up at me.

"Ashley owes me twenty bucks. And I get to dress her in Pittsburgh." Taylor rubbed her hands together like the plotting wheels were turning.

Leona and I exchanged confused looks.

"Hey, Ash. The blue mini dress will look killer on you."

Ashley popped her head out of her door and threw her hands up. "Dammit! You guys couldn't have waited a few more days?" She turned to Taylor. "I'm not wearing it to the stadium. I'd like my knees not to turn into blocks of ice."

The two of them continued bickering as Taylor followed

Ashley into her room.

Leona leaned in closer, nibbling on the side of her bottom lip. "You're okay with them knowing?"

"Are you?" I probably should've checked with her on that part of my decision to show up here and kiss her out of the blue. But I hadn't been thinking of much more than my need to see her.

She rubbed her fingers over the backs of my knuckles. "I am. I hate lying to everyone." Her swallow was audible. We'd both agreed to not tell anyone, but I knew that this had been weighing on her more than she'd let on.

Pulling her closer, I wrapped my arms around her and kissed her again. "Think of it less as lying and more of keeping people out of your business."

Her arms came up and held onto mine. "I'll try."

Taylor popped out of Ashley's room. "Whatever you need to keep this quiet, we're happy to help. We don't want you ending up like Mitchell."

Fuck! News traveled fast. I didn't want to end up like Mitchell and I didn't want Leona to worry about that either.

Leona's head tilted when she turned to Taylor. "Who's Mitchell?"

I shot a look to Taylor with an almost imperceptible shake of my head. Knowing Leona, she'd call the whole thing off and never want to leave the apartment again. "No one. A guy on the team."

Taylor's mouth snapped shut. "You know football drama." She waved a dismissive hand through the air and closed Ashley's door. "On that note, some of us have to go to class. Out of the way, maker-outers."

Leona and I stepped out of the small entryway hall and into the kitchen.

The door closed, and the apartment was quiet again.

"How was practice?" She peered over at me with questions lingering in her gaze.

I shrugged. "The usual." Until I figured out a plan for dealing with whoever was running STFU Dirt, I didn't want her to worry. I'd shield her as much as I could.

"Nothing happened?" She folded her arms and leaned against the kitchen counter.

"Why would something have to have happened?"

"You don't normally show up here sweaty and frantic, kissing me in my doorway."

"Can't I want to see you?" I trailed my fingers down the inside of her forearm.

"Of course, you can. But I also have class in an hour, so we won't get much time to hang out."

"We have all the time in the world."

She gave me a sideways smile.

It eased the ball of tension that had begun to grow when Taylor mentioned Mitchell.

Walking her fingers up my chest, she narrowed her eyes, but her face stayed relaxed. "What's gotten into you?"

"I wanted to see you and wanted to make sure you were still going to the Pittsburgh game." I *had* wanted to see her. What led me to racing across campus to do that didn't matter right now.

"Like those two would let me back out. Why?" She looked at me with a curious smile. "I can't wait to see this caravan there. I'm sure it'll be insane."

Then it hit me. The guys might not even want her on the bus now. If Mitchell got benched for what looked like a dance, what might happen if whoever this gossip asshole was found out she was riding in the bus with a bunch of guys from the team?

"Did you want to ride with me?" I asked.

"Isn't there a party bus going?"

"Yeah, but I can drive. That way we won't have to deal with shouting over the blasting music and people getting rowdy."

"Isn't that half the fun?" Her arms draped over my shoulders, bringing her lips a hairbreadth away.

"I want to spend time with you—alone."

Her gaze intensified, and her fingers brushed along the back of my neck. "That's all you had to say. But I'll drive. You can rest."

"I don't—"

"You do. You would have played a game the night before."

"You have my whole schedule memorized."

Her lips pursed in mock annoyance. "Like I could miss a single game with how everyone talks about them. But maybe I do."

I braced my hands on the counter behind her, pressing us even closer together. "Don't look now, Leona, but I think you might be falling for me." I tried to make it sound like a tease, not a wish. Leona had thrown a wrench in my focus and become even more than a distraction. She was all I could see half the time. She was the first thing I thought about when I woke up and the last thing I thought about when I got into bed, only to hope I'd dream about her all night.

Her eyes widened, and she whispered, "I think I might be."

My heart slammed against my ribs, my breath stalled, and my brain felt like someone had tossed it onto a grill.

So hearing I wasn't the only one out of my depth here hit me harder than I expected.

My lips brushed against hers. "Me too."

25

LEONA

All around us, cars and buses were covered with streamers, foam writing and flashing lights that had to be a hazard.

"I thought everyone was only crazy for STFU football."

Students hung out of their cars, screaming and pumping their fists in the air like we were at the homecoming parade instead of driving down a highway. I kept my eyes alert to all the cars around me, not wanting to get cut off or run over an unfortunate classmate when they fell out of their car.

"It is STFU night at the stadium. People go crazy for anything with our name on it."

"I can see. But it must be nice to watch a game where there aren't any stakes for you."

"There's always stakes." Reid grinned. "But I get what you mean. It's a change of pace to be in the stands with everyone else cheering for my team." He lounged in his seat beside me, doing absolutely nothing but looking at me and still managing to be incredibly distracting. He had his seat leaned back, and his eyes were already drooping, although it was noon. "Thanks for driving. You didn't have to."

"I know. Don't feel like you need to stay awake on my account. Sleep, if you want."

"I'm good for now. Just taking in the view."

Chancing a glance, our gazes clashed.

A flush rushed through me. "Do you always stare like that?"

"Only at things I truly want."

"And that includes me?"

"I've got big plans for you, Leona."

A quiver of anticipation fired through my body. "You do?"

"Absolutely."

The cars and party buses around us sped up, leaving us in their wake of chaos. I wasn't in a rush to join up with the mob, not when it meant we'd have to once again pretend we barely knew each other. The deception was getting to me.

I checked the directions and took our last merge for a while. "We have an hour and a half to go. Did you want to pick the music?" I held out my phone.

It hung in the air.

"Reid?" Leaned back in the seat, his arms were folded, and he was sound asleep.

I set my phone down and brushed my fingers along his hair before refocusing on the road. I didn't mind riding in silence, not when he needed his rest. It wasn't easy being part of a team that seemed to shoulder the morale of the whole campus and every STFU alum. But his shoulders were pretty damn broad, and he loved all the attention and pressure.

After the couple hours long drive, I parked near the hotel Ashley and Taylor had booked. It wasn't a roadside motel but a big-name chain with floors reaching to the sky.

Other streamered and foamed cars were scattered

around in free weekend street parking. We weren't the only ones who'd booked in here.

I stared over at Reid again and turned off the car.

His eyelids lifted like old garage doors before snapping open. "Did I fall asleep?"

I chuckled. "Only twenty minutes in."

He scrubbed his hands down his face and raised his seat upright. "Shit, sorry. Not much of a navigator, huh?"

"I figured it out. Most people are staying in the same hotel, right?"

He nodded. "They give us a good rate for the game. One of the chain higher-ups is an alum."

"Those STFU connections pay off in spades." Was the higher-up one of the powerful people trying to take my dad's job from him? Every game the team won put Dad one step closer to losing the job he loved.

"You okay?" Reid touched my arm.

I gripped my keys tighter in my hand, letting the metal dig into my palm. "I'm fine. A little tired after the drive. Are you excited about the game?"

His look of concern immediately transformed into anticipation. "Always."

"The shuttles leave from the hotel in a couple hours. We should probably get checked in."

As if they were listening in, our phones buzzed.

He checked his. "I'm on the tenth floor."

"We're on the third floor."

Reid traced his fingers over the back of my hand. "After the game, I have a surprise for you."

A shiver of excitement raced across my skin. "What kind of surprise?"

He leaned forward. "If I told you, then it wouldn't be a surprise."

"We've had three dates."

"We have."

"We had a deal, or have you forgotten?"

"Not for a single moment." He kissed right where my shoulder met my neck, setting off even more sparks. "There's no rush, Leona."

Then why did I want to climb over the center console and mount him in this damn car?

"Says you."

He laughed. His breath breezed across my skin.

"If you're just going to tease me, then get out of my car."

"On one condition."

"What?" That had definitely come out pouty. How many women out there were pouting because their maybe boyfriend wasn't ready to bang at the drop of a hat?

"A kiss." The velvety smoothness of his voice was irresistible.

He wrapped his arm around my waist and pulled me closer.

Our lips met with a hungry intensity that made me forget where we were. Namely, on a busy street and in a rapidly steaming-up car.

I was lost in his kiss, and everything faded away—until three party buses pulled in, spilling STFU fans out onto the street.

They sang and danced and cheered. A few couples walked across the street toward the hotel. Most of them had the guy with his arm over his girlfriend's shoulder or they held hands. One guy carried his girlfriend. They all might've been dating or just having fun, but at least they didn't have to hide it.

"We should probably get out separately." Reid watched them through his window.

"I know."

His head dropped. "If you want to end this. I understand."

My heartbeat skipped before racing. "Do you want to stop? I know the risks are high. Taylor told me about the guy who got benched. She showed me the pictures." Regret and guilt twined in my stomach.

"I told her not to say anything."

"I should know the risks you're facing. And I'm sorry for that guy. I feel like I should bake him a tray of cookies for getting tangled up with me." Misery rolled through me.

He turned in his seat and pulled me into a hug. "This is why I didn't want her to tell you. I didn't want you to blame yourself."

"Is this why you suggested we drive separately? Did the guys not want me on the bus? I don't blame them if they didn't."

He let go of me and held onto my shoulders.

"I made the choice for them. I didn't even ask, and the guys would've loved to have you ride with us, but I wanted time alone with you without worrying who might see us. It has nothing to do with Mitchell. Plus, he's kind of a dick."

How could the whole situation not have to do with Mitchell? Mitchell's future could be in jeopardy because of a mistimed picture. What would've happened if the pictures had been with any of the other guys I danced with that night? I might as well be radioactive. Maybe it was best that I stayed away from half of the new friends I'd made since I got here.

"You're protecting your teammates. It's what makes you a great one." My tongue felt like it weighed one hundred pounds.

"Do not blame yourself."

I stared at the center console and breathed through the crushing sensation in my chest. There was no escape. The only way I could turn that wouldn't blow up in my face was the one way I couldn't force myself to move—away from Reid.

He tipped my chin up. "I have big plans for tonight, but if you're not feeling up for it, we can scrap the whole thing and hang out in your room watching movies and eating crap food." His Adam's apple bobbed. "Or we can call the whole thing off. It's not what I want—not even a little bit, but if you're not happy... All I want is for you to be happy, Leona." His gaze was intense, but not with pressure. His eyes were open and vulnerable as though his biggest fear was that I wanted to kick him out of my car and tell him it was over.

I wrapped my hands around his. "No, I don't want to call anything off. I just worry."

"Let me take care of it." He kissed me.

The street was quieter now.

"We should probably go in."

He nodded. "You can go first. I'll make sure I lock up."

"Okay, I'll see you at the game. We can surreptitiously wave to each other."

"I can't wait."

I could barely feel my cheeks. The Heinz Field stadium worked like a wind vortex, and even standing shoulder-to-shoulder with others in the stands, I felt like my nose might fall off. I hadn't been this cold since the night I was on security detail, but this time there was no Reid to keep me warm.

He was three rows ahead of us right at the railing and ten seats to my right.

"Come on, ref! Do you need me to go get you some new glasses?" Taylor bellowed and pointed at the spot on the field where the play ended. Apparently, STFU football wasn't the only team she got intense about.

A few people turned and laughed at Taylor's non-stop tirades. In her jersey-over-sweater combo with thigh-high boots, she didn't scream out-of-control football fan, except when, you know, she opened her mouth and literally screamed like an out-of-control football fan.

Ashley took a bite of her chicken tenders. "You're going to get us kicked out."

"Please. Those drunk guys who're about a quarter away from fighting are going to get kicked out way before I do." She cupped her hands around her mouth. "Come on, ref! LensCrafters only takes an hour. I can get you new ones before halftime."

I covered my mouth and laughed, catching Ashley's eye behind the still bellowing Taylor.

Ashley shook her head and laughed along with me. "We're going to get some food. Want anything?"

The play had started, and Taylor took off her bag and shoved it at Ashley without looking. "Hot dog, chili cheese fries and a cookie."

Ashley took the bag, and we climbed the stairs to the concourse, where the crowds were much lighter since everyone's attention was riveted to the field.

"Has she always loved football this much?" We waited in the short line at the concession area.

"Always. For half the year, she's the normal girly girl, and then football season rolls around, and she's a diehard, will-run-you-over-to-get-to-the-TV girly girl."

We ordered overpriced food and headed back to our seats.

I couldn't stop myself from checking Reid out. It didn't hurt that he was in the path of gameplay, so it didn't feel completely obvious.

"When are you guys meeting up?" Taylor leaned back without taking her eyes off the field.

"Later." My skin tingled and not because of the cold. Reid and I would be meeting tonight in a hotel room where there would be no interruptions, roommates, or anyone else other than us. And we'd had our three dates. The excitement and nervousness were two fuses lit and sparking their way through my chest.

"I can't say we won't miss you when we take over this city tonight, but I imagine you'll have a great night without us." Ashley winked and sipped from her cup.

"Something like that."

Reid turned back to look up, and his eyes locked onto mine.

The flood of warmth hit my veins. I hoped I was ready for what he had in store.

26

REID

Our seats were on the fifty-yard line right behind the Pittsburgh bench. Our feet were level with the heads of most of the players on the sidelines, but we could hear all the chatter. It was like our games, but different. They were the pros.

Another flag was thrown, and refs converged to confer.

Normally, the game had my entire focus, but this time my gaze kept being drawn to the stands. Tugged like the universe had dropped a glowing beacon only I could see.

Taylor bellowed louder than anyone else around us, so it was easy to find Leona. She laughed, watching Taylor. Her gaze skimmed across the seats until it landed on mine.

Her smile took on a secret slant, and she bit her bottom lip.

My blood thundered in my veins, beating back the November frost. Tonight was the night. The night I'd been waiting for since we collided, although I didn't know it then.

The stands came alive, and Griff's arm shot up, nearly knocking into me. Everyone around us was screaming and shouting. In a sea of fans celebrating, Leona and I shared a moment—a connection I hated to break.

Reluctantly, I turned back to the field.

"Did you see that?" Griff grabbed my shoulders and yanked me back and forth with one hand while balancing his container of food in the other. "That play was insane!" He raised a wing in the air triumphantly.

The running back did a celebration dance in the end zone.

"You're going to get wing sauce all over yourself."

"Like I care." He bit into the wing, which looked comically small in his hand. "Can you believe how close we are? One more season, and we could be out there. In two years, there could be guys just like us standing up here watching us out there." He raised his chin to the guys shoving their helmets on and jogging onto the field.

Cole scarfed down some bacon cheese fries. "I can't wait to look up in the stands and see people wearing my jersey." He watched the fans still celebrating in the stands.

"People wear your number now." I stole a fry.

He glared. "Yeah, but I'll know when they're wearing it, that at least I get a cut of that cash."

Griff tapped one of his wings against Cole's fry. "Hell yeah."

I leaned against the railing. The metal was so cold it seeped through my coat. "It's so close I can taste it."

"That's probably just one of Griff's buffalo sauce burps."

I screwed up my face. "You two are morons."

"These two morons are your best friends, so what does that say about you?"

"Hey, what about me?" Hollis jumped in, holding nachos in his bare hands.

Ezra stood with his arms crossed, eyes locked onto the field.

"Not feeling a little left out, Ez?" I leaned farther out.

"No." His stone face looked like it had been frozen by the rapidly dropping nighttime temperatures.

The rest of us exchanged glances before making it our mission for the rest of the game to get him to break. Offers of food and drink were made, but he didn't drop out of sentry mode. He was always like that when we watched a game. Once during freshman year, Cole had gotten him to eat a single tater tot. He watched the field like if he took his eyes off it for a second, he might miss a move that would be the key to unlocking fame and glory.

It wasn't until a commotion broke out behind us that he finally blinked and took his eyes off the turf.

While we mostly abstained from drinking, it wasn't the case for everyone in the STFU section. Two guys got loud behind us. Beer was splashed all over everyone in a three-row radius. More raised voices from people who didn't want to be showered in booze. The tension ratcheted even higher than on the field when two guys came to blows.

I checked on Leona.

She was several seats down and trying to see what was going on, but at least she was far away from the escalating conflict.

Everyone surrounding them dove out of the way or jumped into the melee to break the two apart. Phones were out recording the whole thing, and it was probably being live-streamed with commentary. Couldn't they just watch the game? All the highlights would be online by the time we left the stadium. It also meant if I so much as spoke to Leona, there was a chance of it being recorded.

Ezra turned with his jaw clenched and made it two

steps to intervene before a girl from two rows up was knocked down. She was headed for a nasty, face-first fall straight into the seats when he lunged with arms out and caught her. The two of them disappeared into the row behind us with his legs sticking up over our seats. We jumped forward in unison, trying to get them up before they were hurt.

If he was hurt... Stupid shit like this could end careers. A twisted knee, a broken ankle.

Another body rolled down and landed on top of them.

We scrambled to block any others from dropping down into the row behind us and keep anyone else from falling.

Security finally arrived and carted away the two who'd started the whole mess. Disgust shot through me at their drunken screaming and cheering like they were kings for showering everyone in beer and throwing wild haymakers. Couldn't they watch a game without screwing things up for the rest of us?

Hollis and Cole helped the girl up off Ezra, who was still playing the part of her not-so-soft pillow. More people recorded the aftermath and were scanning the crowd with their phones instead of helping.

"Are you okay?" Ezra shot up and rested his hand on her shoulder.

She nodded, holding onto her forehead with a small smile. "Thanks for breaking my fall." Blood, bright red, seeped through her fingers. I flinched at the volume pouring down the back of her hand and looked for something to help stem the flow. On the field, we were used to getting dinged up, but the hit she'd taken had been nasty.

"You're hurt." Ezra knocked over Cole's fries to get to the napkins underneath and moved her hand away to press them against her head.

The cut on her forehead bled like a mother because that's what head wounds did.

"Let's get you to First Aid." He took charge, not giving any of us a chance to even suggest coming with them.

He walked up the stairs with his arm around her waist so fast that he was practically carrying her and didn't look back. Phones followed their progress onto the concourse. Then Ezra and his rescuee were gone.

And I was jealous. Not of her getting hurt, but of how he didn't have to think twice about touching her in public. How he could hold her close and protect her, and she was a stranger to him.

I looked back a few rows to my left, where Leona was at least half an aisle from all the craziness.

She mouthed, "Are you okay?"

I wanted to climb over the seats between us and kiss her. I wanted to watch the game with my arm around her. I wanted to not have to keep our relationship a secret.

The horn blared, and the quarter began again. Half the sideline rushed back onto the field. The field where I wanted to be. The field I wouldn't make it to if Coach found out how I felt about her.

I nodded tightly, and she nodded back.

The score was 20-23 in the third quarter, and I'd never wanted a game to be over as quickly as I wanted this one to finish. Tonight I'd make up for the hours we were apart when I couldn't hold her and touch her. Tonight I'd make it the perfect experience for her, just like she was the perfect one for me.

27

LEONA

Exiting the elevator, I glanced down the hallway. It was empty, but I could hear the celebrations from lower floors. The space between the doors here was at least twice as wide as it was on the floor where I was staying with Ashley and Taylor. There also weren't any roving, screaming mobs of drunken students up here.

On shaky legs, I walked down the hall to the door with the same number from Reid's text.

Standing outside, I shook out my arms then my whole body, trying to banish the jittery nerves. Hadn't I been the one to tell Reid this was no big deal? It wasn't. People did this all the time. Most people long before me. It was like a Band-Aid you ripped off. No one needed anything special to rip off a Band-Aid.

Deep breath in. Deep breath out. I knocked on the door.

It opened, and Reid stood in the doorway, not looking one bit like I'd expected him to.

Instead of being in a t-shirt and jeans or a jersey or sweats or anything else that might've been appropriate for an STFU night out at the pros, he was in a suit.

And damn, he looked good in it. More than good. Mouthwatering.

I felt a bit underdressed in my gray skirt and high-necked shirt that zipped at the back.

"Hey."

"Hey." He stepped back and held out his arm to let me into the room. But this was not like the room I shared with Taylor and Ashley, where three or four people were crammed into two double beds. This was a suite. Reid stood in a living room that displayed a massive TV, a bar with crystal glasses—unlike the zip-tied mini bar in my room—and a dining table that would comfortably fit four but was set for two. Double doors behind him led to a balcony, and through an open doorway, I spied a king-sized bed.

"Reid! How did you afford this? This is crazy."

"Griff's dad travels a lot for work, and Griff asked him to use some of his points for this."

My throat pinched as I walked past him. "So Griff knows that we're going to..." I glanced over my shoulder.

He jerked forward. "No, I didn't tell him why. I just said I wanted to repay you for bailing us out at the booster event."

That helped some. I leaned against the back of the gray couch, running my hands along its buttery soft texture. My nerves were going haywire. Jittery anticipation made it hard to stay still. *Calm, Leona.* Deep breaths. "Now that you have me here, Mr. Riddick, what do you intend to do with me?"

His head tilted, and he stepped closer. His fingers slid down my arm. "You look beautiful."

I held my breath, anticipation zipping across my skin so quickly I expected sparks to shoot out of my fingertips. "Thanks, you too. Handsome, I mean." My skin heated.

"Thank you. Did you want a drink? I grabbed some provisions."

He slipped his suit jacket off and rolled his sleeves up his arms, exposing all the sinewy, veined forearm goodness.

I had no idea what provisions required him rolling up his sleeves, but I was onboard. A sound must've escaped my lips.

His head snapped up. "What's wrong?"

"Do they pull you guys aside in school and teach you how to do that?" I gestured to the perfectly rolled sleeve that gave off the *relaxed after a long day in the office, but ready to unbutton your shirt with his teeth* look he was pulling off, and if it was a question, I certainly was. Even more now.

"Teach us what?"

I shook my head. "Never mind."

His eyebrows pulled together as he lifted a bottle out of the ice bucket. I spotted the label. Actual Champagne, not sparkling wine.

I lunged for his hand that was working on the foil over the cork. "Reid, it's too expensive. Why...you should save that for a special occasion."

"What do you think this is?"

"You didn't have to."

"But I wanted to. We don't have to drink, if you don't want."

When I thought he couldn't get more gorgeous, this uncertainty was thrown into the mix, and it was the perfect mixture of rugged adorableness.

"I wouldn't mind one."

He unwrapped the metal from around the cork and popped it. A steady flow of bubbles shot from the opening.

"Shit!" He scrambled to get to the glasses, which were only tumblers.

Laughing, I rushed forward and grabbed them, holding the heavy crystal under the flow trying to catch the spilling alcohol. The bubbles quickly overflowed all over my hands. "It happens."

"That was real smooth." He set down the bottle and shook Champagne off his hands and forearms.

Ducking, I caught his eye. "Reid, relax. It's okay. I'm having fun. Are you having fun?"

His eyes pulsed with desire. "You know I am. I wanted tonight to be perfect." The timbre of his voice sent a sizzle of lust through my body.

"Who said it wasn't?" I ran a wet finger along his lip. "You don't have to be anything or anyone more than you are."

He groaned and sucked it into his mouth. "I know, but I wanted this to be special. Not a mess."

My heart pounded so hard I felt it in the soles of my feet. "It's special because you're here. It's special because you cared enough to try to make this a night I'd never forget."

The heated coil winding in my belly got hotter the more he stared at me and revealed his surprises for the evening.

A chime at the door sliced through the mounting tension.

"Now, we eat." He stepped back and grabbed a towel to wipe off his hands.

I rinsed mine in the small sink in the wet bar.

Reid opened the door to the room service attendant.

The guy didn't look much older than us. He pushed the cart over to the dining room table. "Would you like me to set the table or would you prefer I leave the cart?"

Smells from the covered plates were heavenly, throwing a delicious cloud of spices, and sugars in the air.

"You can leave it. Thanks." Reid shook the guy's hand with a bill slipped in there.

I brushed my hair behind my ear, trying not to let my nerves about where this was all leading get to me too much.

There were four silver covers on the cart. "Is someone else coming?"

"No, I wasn't sure what you might like." He pulled the covers off and stacked them on top of one another. "There's pasta, a steak and salmon."

"What about that one?" I lifted off the cover. A massive slice of chocolate cake with chocolate filling sat on its side, topped with whipped cream. A bowl of fresh strawberries wedged in next to it. I dragged my finger through one of the cream swirls.

His Adam's apple bobbed. "Dessert."

"What if we started with this one?" I picked up the plate and a fork. Slicing off a small piece, I slipped it into my mouth. My eyes fluttered closed. The smooth, dark chocolate exploded on my tongue. The cake was rich and fudgy, and it was warm, making it perfectly melty. "Oh my god, you've got to try this." I opened my eyes, and Reid swallowed audibly.

For some reason, his nervousness helped calm my nerves. The throbbing between my legs grew, thumping in time to my heartbeat. I wanted him.

I cut another small piece with the edge of my fork and walked closer. "Want some?"

He nodded and opened his mouth.

I fed him, and his eyes widened. "I told you."

"You weren't lying." He smiled and talked with his mouth half-closed.

"Would I lie?" I took another bite of the cake and smeared a little on the corner of my mouth and lips. "I made a bit of a mess. Could you help me with that?"

His gaze hooded, and he looked hungry for more than cake. "Tease."

My stomach flipped, the knots from earlier completely gone. "I don't know what you're talking about."

His lips were fierce on mine. He slid the plate from my grasp and sat it back on the cart. "I've wanted you since the first moment I saw you."

I pulled him closer.

His hands dropped to my waist and down to my ass, cupping it and lifting me until I sat on the table. The silverware and plates clattered. "You're making me lose my cool, Leona."

"You say that like it's a bad thing." I locked my legs around his waist, and he slid a hand along my back, up under my shirt.

His belt rubbed against the insides of my thighs.

"We were supposed to take things slow." He breathed against my shoulder.

"I don't remember signing on to that agreement." I walked my fingers along his shoulders and sunk them into his hair just above his ears.

"The three dates were supposed to make it easier." A ragged breath brushed across the curve of my neck.

"Reid."

His head lifted, and he stared into my eyes.

I cupped his cheeks and gently kissed his lips that still tasted of chocolate. "I'm ready."

He took my hand and helped me off the table.

We crossed the room with my hand in his like he was leading me out onto the dance floor.

"If you—"

I pressed my finger against his lips. "I won't. The more patient and understanding you are, the more I want to jump your bones. It's driving me all kinds of crazy, so please keep asking me if I'm sure I want to."

He swung me around like we were dancing to imaginary music. "You make it sound like a bad thing."

My stomach flutters were like an aviary filled with hummingbirds.

He sat on the edge of the bed and bent to take my foot, sliding my shoe off. His fingers were strong and warm against my toes, massaging them a little before he kissed his way up the inside of my calf. The trail ended just above my knee, and the firm strokes of his hands sent reverberations through my body.

My lips parted, my breath quickening. His fingers brushed higher up my inner thighs, making my knees buckle.

His hands wrapped around my waist.

He smirked. "Careful."

The torture was repeated with the other leg.

I stood in front of him, teetering on the edge of what came next, but I didn't feel scared. Vulnerable, yes, but there wasn't a flicker of doubt in my mind about what I wanted from him. Needed from him.

His hands slipped under the waistband of my plain black cotton underwear and skimmed along my skin.

The cool air traveled up under my skirt and against my heated core. The throb between my legs deepened. I swayed closer to him and braced my hands on his shoulders to keep myself upright.

His hand slid down from my bare ass to the back of my thighs. Callused and firm, his grip tightened and pulled me closer. The tips of his fingers brushed against my pussy. A tease. A taunt. A taste of what was to come.

I could feel myself coating his fingers as his hold circled to the inside of my thigh.

My body buzzed with desire. The noises that escaped me brimmed with need.

He shuddered, and in that moment, I felt powerful.

It was delicious knowing that I wasn't the only one who felt close to bursting. I rode a wave of anticipation that was skyscraper tall.

Stepping closer, I widened my legs, giving him access to me.

His gaze flicked up, and the craving in it made me light-headed.

He slid off the edge of the bed and sank to his knees in front of me. With slow movements, he pressed the hem of my skirt up, and his hands rested on the front of my legs.

Goose bumps broke out over my skin, and I clenched my fists against his shoulders to keep steady.

His fingers crept closer to the insides of my thighs once again. I trembled.

Perhaps sensing my difficulties standing still, he spun us around until the backs of my legs pressed against the bed.

I took in a shuddering breath.

He pressed his hand to my stomach, and I dropped to the edge of the bed with my skirt hiked up around my waist.

Lowering to his knees, he parted my thighs. Once again, his thumbs moved in maddening circles along them and crept higher.

My breath turned to pants when he parted my folds and skimmed his thumb across my clit. "I'm going to be selfish and have my dessert before we eat dinner."

"That would be acceptable." I released a shaky breath.

The corner of his mouth turned up. "I'll have to make

sure it's a hell of a lot better than acceptable." He leaned in and placed my legs over his shoulders.

I flopped back, giving myself over to the sensation.

He painted my pussy with his tongue, teasing every part of me with his mouth while his hands squeezed my ass before he sank two fingers inside of me.

I had one hand on his head, probably ripping out half his hair, and the other gripped the cool, plush duvet beneath me.

A heady rush of pleasure flooded my body. I moaned. Crackling electricity raced through me. The crest raced toward me faster than I could've anticipated, and I squeezed my thighs around his head. I clenched around his fingers, the orgasm tightening all my muscles and flooding me with pleasure.

He kept pumping his fingers into me. The noises of my wetness filled the room along with his name wrenched from my throat.

Through the come-down, my body still felt like it was floating.

He stood at the end of the bed, staring down at me like a satisfied demigod. "How was that?"

I attempted a shrug from my near boneless state. "I didn't mind."

He laughed and fell on top of me. "So what you're telling me is I need to work a bit harder?"

"Only if you want?" My heaving breaths probably destroyed my fake air of nonchalance.

"Oh, I want."

After popping back up, he unbuttoned the first few buttons and pulled his shirt off overhead, then undid his pants. The tent of his boxers drove the lightheadedness away, and I no longer wanted just the appetizer. I was ready for the whole meal.

I scooted back toward the headboard, and he followed around the edge of the bed, tracking my every move.

From his back pocket, he pulled out a condom and dropped it onto the duvet.

This was happening. It was actually happening.

My pulse quickened, beating so fast it hummed.

He leaned in and lifted me up, his fingers brushing against my shoulders and down my back. The rugged creases of his knuckles tickled my skin as he pulled the zipper on my shirt down.

Then I was surrounded by an Ikea's worth of cloud-soft pillows—naked.

He climbed into the bed and trailed his fingers down my neck. "I'm so fucking lucky."

My stomach somersaulted.

"No, I am." I pulled him down on top of me and wrapped my legs around his waist.

Using my heels, I pushed his boxers down over his firm ass and moaned when his cock sprang free and rubbed against my pussy.

He groaned, his hips jerking involuntarily. Fumbling on the bed beside me, he grabbed the condom and slipped it on.

I reached between us and wrapped my fingers around his solid length. Pumping my hand up and down, I brushed my thumb across his thick mushroom tip. "I'm ready."

With both arms braced on either side of my head, he rocked forward.

The head of his cock nudged at my entrance, and I shifted lower, not wanting to be patient anymore.

His shallow thrusts were maddeningly efficient at sending sizzling sparks flooding my system.

"More."

"You're killing me." He groaned and sank in farther.

"No, you're killing me. Don't be afraid." I cupped his cheek. "I'm not."

That seemed to be all the confirmation he needed. His hips snapped, sinking into me fully.

My back bowed off the bed, and I clung to him, losing my breath to the tight fit. The stretch and burn were soothed by the grind of his pelvis against my clit—a perfect friction that stole my breath in a new way.

I gasped like a fish tossed onto dry land. Squeezing him tightly, I sank my fingers into his back, urging him to move faster. Barreling toward the next crest made it hard to focus on anything other than how good this felt.

"I can't get enough of you," he whispered into my hair.

Then the train hit me. The freight train of pleasure, stealing my breath and vision as black dots swam in front of my eyes, swamped me. I clung to Reid.

He kept grinding and pumping into me harder, drawing out every last second of bliss.

I was blanketed in suffocating lust as my muscles tightened like a rubber band being pulled. White-hot currents of pleasure raced through me, and I thrust up against Reid, chasing the building crescendo.

He reached between us and brushed my clit with his thumb, setting me off.

I screamed against his neck, hugging him to me. His erratic tempo and thrusts made spots dance in front of my eyes. Pleasure cascaded through me, demolished me.

His body stiffened against mine.

The lock on my arms was broken when he pressed up

and bracketed my head with his arms and stared into my eyes like he had to see me.

He groaned and shuddered, rocking us both. His thrusts were less measured. Less controlled. He sank his fingers into my hair and buried his face in the crook of my neck. He drove into me harder and faster. Shameless, sloppy and sublime.

Under him, I stared up at the ceiling with wonder. My erratic heartbeats slowed to a warm glow in my chest.

He shifted and looked down at me. His eyes were beautiful, just like him. He dropped his forehead, resting it against mine. "Leona. You've ruined me."

I brushed my fingers through his hair. "I know." Because I felt exactly the same way. In the best possible way—completely undone by him.

28

REID

I t didn't take long for me to recover, not with Leona's fingers running down my side, tickling my chest. She'd been on top, and I got to watch her enjoying herself, finding her own pleasure. It also gave me access to her breasts, so it was a toss-up on my favorite position, and I was sure there were more ties to come.

Now that we were down to the final condom, I was back on top. The sensations shooting down the backs of my legs told me shower sex wouldn't be an option with her. Not when she made me crazy like this. Not when I could barely hold myself together without spilling into our last condom.

It didn't mean there weren't many more options on the list.

I stared at her beneath me, gripping the reins tight and not wanting this to end. This whole plan had been about making this a night she'd never forget, but rocking into her and drawing those gasps from her lips, I knew it wouldn't be possible for me to ever forget a single moment. Not that I'd ever want to.

Her legs hitched around my hips, tightening around me.

She clenched so hard around my dick that I groaned and cursed, the telltale spasms rocking my body as I kept a death grip on my control to hold on longer.

She was the most beautiful thing I'd ever seen. We were both sweaty messes, and I never wanted this moment to end. I snapped my hips harder, drawing even more delicious sounds from her.

Her fingers dug into my back, but I welcomed the pain for the split second of control it allowed me to gain.

"Reid!" she screamed and bucked under me.

Finally letting myself go, I braced my body on my knees and pounded into her, following her over the edge we'd been sprinting toward.

Sweaty, heart hammering and toes clenched, every muscle in my body locked before the explosive grip loosened.

I flopped down beside her.

Her sleepy laugh broke through the muted silence of the room. "Okay, that was definitely worth it."

I rolled over onto my side. "I'm glad you thought so."

Her hair was plastered to her forehead, and we were both still trying to control our breath.

"Let's take a shower."

Her eyes widened in alarm.

"Just a shower."

Her stomach rumbled.

"A shower, then we can eat."

She nodded and slid out of bed.

Once we got in the shower, there were a few detours into excessive cleaning territory regarding certain body parts, which may or may not have been with just our hands. But we made it out of the bathroom unscathed and sat in our robes, eating food that was now cold but still delicious.

Leona's feet were in my lap, and I had one hand on them, massaging them while I ate.

She cut up my steak and grinned at me like we had a secret. A new one to add to the mountain already piled up high.

And I had another one. I'd never felt this way about anyone before her and I didn't want to find out if I could feel this way about anyone after her. I only wanted her.

Room service rang the bell just after nine in the morning. The curtains were drawn, blocking out the morning sun. It was still too early, but I needed to make it back for my afternoon classes. Taylor and Ashley had dropped off Leona's bag right after the food arrived. With sly grins, they passed it off and said they'd see us back on campus.

I passed Leona the mini bottle of syrup. "You're sure you're okay with skipping your morning classes?"

"It was either that or wake up at five a.m. And after last night, I don't think my legs were working properly that early."

She sliced into a stack of huge French toast with extra syrup and bacon. I had a five-egg scramble and a side of bacon.

"Griff really came through in setting all this up," she said.

"I owe him big time."

"He's a good friend. Not good enough to offer you any of his wings, but still a good one." She smiled and took another bite of her food.

"Spying on me, were you?" I tickled her side.

Her body jerked, and she swatted at my arm.

"You were in my line of sight, so technically I couldn't keep my eyes off you." She set down her utensils and turned, fully facing me. "You weren't watching the game like everyone else was watching the game. You were so intense watching every move everyone made while they were on the field, even the guys on the sidelines. What were you thinking about while you were looking at them all?"

And I'd thought Ezra was the intense one. Although it felt like I spent half the game watching her, I had been soaking up every minute of play that I hadn't devoted to glancing over my shoulder at her in the stands.

"So many things. A lot about how close I was to being out there." The smells, the sounds, the feel of the place. If I closed my eyes, I could get the surround sound version of it, only with me at the center of the field.

Her fingers brushed along the back of my hand.

"About what I'd do once I signed my first contract." Standing in front of the giant screen next to the football commissioner as they handed me the hat of the team who'd drafted me and staring out at the round tables filled with other players all ready to sign the key to their futures.

"What's going to be the first thing you do once you sign? A huge party? A big vacation? A nice new car?"

My throat locked up. I hadn't shared my plans with anyone other than the guys, and even then, it had been in vague terms.

"None of that. I'll buy my dad his own garage. One that's got top of the line everything." He deserved it. I owed it to him. After that, I hadn't thought much about the money, but whatever happened, he'd get his garage.

"Is your dad a mechanic?" He had been. He hadn't been able to find steady work within a hundred-mile radius of our house since he got fired almost six years ago. The guilt had threatened to eat me alive. It still hadn't left after all this time.

"Not full-time. He works on cars on the side and helps out with easier-to-do fixes when he's not working." After being blacklisted from every shop and no money to start his own, he'd had to take up warehouse work.

"He must like it if he does it on his time off."

"He loves it. He's got a 1965 Chevy Malibu he's been working on for years." I'd helped him with some restoration work, but that had slowed down once he needed to pay for training camps and extra travel for me back in high school. Now, he didn't have the time or energy to do more than tinker every few weeks. He deserved so much more. How different would things have been for him, if I hadn't been the one to get my ass handed to me regularly.

"That's great you want to do that for him."

"He's sacrificed a lot for me. It's only fair I pay him back ten times as much." Working would be optional once I signed my pro contract. The time he spent on cars would be for the sheer love of it. I got to live my dream—it was time he lived his.

"It's cool you two are so close."

"I want him to be proud of me and all he sacrificed to get me here." Emotions welled in my chest, but I tightened my grip on them and forced a weak smile.

"I'm sure he knows." She slipped her hand under mine.

I cleared my throat. "We should get packed up."

She leaned over and rested her head on my shoulder. "Okay. Just give me two minutes."

I brushed my hand along her hair and inhaled deeply. "Take all the time you need."

We stayed like that for longer than two minutes, but I wasn't in a rush to move, not when her body was pressed against mine. Packing up didn't take long, and then it was time to leave. Our little reprieve from prying eyes was gone in a blink.

We left the room separately. I hated not being able to walk hand-in-hand with her to the front desk to check out, but the hotel was still crawling with classmates.

I walked around the block and met Leona once she was already in her car. The street was busier on a Monday, which meant we weren't as obvious among the other people on a city lunch rush.

I opened her door and held out my hand.

"Let me drive us back."

"You sure? I don't mind." Even after sleeping in, her eyes were still tired. "Especially since you actually have to go to class, and I'll just be going home to nap more."

"You need your rest." I hadn't missed her ginger movements in our room. That my overzealousness from last night gave her even the slightest discomfort was a lance to my chest. I'd do whatever was needed to make it right.

She took my hand and swapped seats.

I threw our bags in the back of her car, and we both got buckled in.

She was asleep before we pulled onto the highway. But her questions about my plans for the future brought up more about my past than I wanted to admit.

I didn't just want to give my dad his shop and anything else he wanted—he'd be the dad of a pro football player. Not the dad of that scrawny kid who had his ass kicked for sticking up for a kid even smaller than him, but of the professional athlete who had a stadium filled with screaming fans wearing my number.

But Leona didn't need to hear about how I'd come home bruised and bloodied. How I had to look Dad in the eye and tell him I hadn't been strong enough to defend another kid, let alone myself. The burning disappointment and shame that came along with it, and made me wish I'd gotten taken out by a car on the long walk home.

I'd have taken the beatings forever if it meant my dad hadn't gone to confront the bully's dad, who was also his boss, and ended up losing his job. The guy blacklisted Dad in our town, and we almost lost our house. The same one he'd moved into with my mom.

Instead of moving, he'd sent me to the school two towns over that had a great football team, and the rest was history. I'd expected the football players to be bullies like at my first school. Instead, they'd shut down anything that smelled like picking on smaller kids. I'd become a mascot of sorts for that team until I worked my ass off to play alongside them.

Every workout, every long run to build my stamina, every block and tackle and catch had all been to get me to this point, and I couldn't let him or the team down.

Leona mumbled and rolled toward me in her seat.

She was a complication I'd have never thought I'd get tangled up in, but now I couldn't walk away. There were only two more games left in the regular season and another month before the play-offs ended. We'd kept things a secret this long. Holding out a little longer wouldn't be hard. Only a few more weeks. We could make it.

29

LEONA

Campus was quiet, but the house was quieter.

Other than the gentle closing of the fridge and a drawer opening, there were no sounds.

Reid, Hollis, Ezra and Griff were in the living room, staring at nothing. Ezra leaned against the wall, running his fingers over the taut strings on the tuning pegs of his guitar, looking crestfallen, like he'd been forced to watch a puppy kicking contest.

It felt like an intrusion to be so close to them during this moment. Maybe they'd forgotten I was here, and I should leave.

Reid rested both elbows just above his knees, and his head was cradled in one hand. Tension radiated off him, the almost dimple on his cheek deepening as he worked his jaw.

I rested my hand on his leg and leaned in closer.

His body jerked, and then he covered my hand with his.

Cole walked out of the kitchen. The bottles wedged between each of his fingers clanked and clinked as he opened them all. He handed a beer to Reid.

Hollis gulped his down like he hadn't had a drink in

months. Considering how hard the guys went during the season, maybe he hadn't.

Reid sat up straighter but didn't drop my hand. Instead, he handed the beer to me and took the next one from Cole. "At least we'll get a chance to kick their asses again in play-offs. And Coach is having a much worse time than we are right now."

A rumble of laughter broke some of the tension.

Hollis looked up with a twitch of his lips. "He's got to be losing his fucking mind right now." He took the last sip of his beer.

Ezra pushed off the wall and raised his drink. "He's probably so pissed. Maybe that vein on his neck will finally burst."

"If only we could be that lucky." Reid's voice reverberated up my arm. He rubbed the back of my hand in small circles. "But he's going to work us so hard in the post-season. Prepare to be destroyed. It will make this season look like a cakewalk."

All the guys drank.

I took a sip of my beer, trying to douse the fire in my gut. I'd seen Reid and the rest of the guys wrapped up in ice packs after practice. The thought of them being worked even harder made me want to punch Mikelson in the mouth.

Hollis winced.

"True, but one thing I do know." Cole walked over and stood beside him, handing him another beer. "As much as it sucks that we lost our last game of the season, you know what sucks even more?"

Hollis's eyebrows dipped.

"You're it." He slapped Hollis on the shoulder and stood there grinning.

Everyone in the room froze and whipped out their phones.

Had I missed a text alert? I took out my phone, but the screen was blank.

"Shit! No." Hollis lunged for Cole, who stood with his arms folded and a wide grin.

"You know the rules, no tag backs."

"Fuck." Hollis moved to put his drink down.

"No drink dropping," Cole taunted.

Reid, Griff and Ezra all looked down at their beers and chugged them.

I chugged mine too. Whatever was going to happen, I should probably finish it now.

"And no breaking the house," Cole continued. "We'd like to get our security deposit back. No jumping from second stories or doing stupid shit to get yourselves injured."

All eyes looked at Ezra.

He stopped drinking. "I thought the window was open."

"Well, it wasn't, and you're lucky you didn't slice an artery and those bushes broke your fall."

"I promise I'll be low-key this year." He stood, trying to look casual, turned his beer upside down and bolted through the front door, nearly ripping the screen off the hinges. Outside, he vaulted over the hood of a car parked out front and took off running like he was going for a touchdown.

Where the hell was he going? What was happening?

"Fucker." Hollis chugged his beer while leaning forward like he was trying to give his body a head start.

Reid grabbed my hand and turned his bottle upside down. He pulled me toward the stairs.

"What's going on?"

Another curse from Hollis.

Reid took off and pushed me in front of him, right up the stairs. At the top of the steps, he quickly shut all the doors, then darted into Cole's room to close and lock the door and turn off the lights. We crouched behind the door. "Tradition."

"Is the whole campus doing this right now?" This place was next level when it came to play, and I didn't hate it.

"No, just in our house. From midnight the night after our last game of the season until midnight before the first day of post-season, we play tag." His excitement made him extra adorable.

"Seriously? You do this every year?"

"A few times a year. Mostly after the season is over, except for now. Campus is mostly empty, and it can get boring as hell waiting around for the games, so this is how we keep ourselves entertained."

Of course they had. Who'd have thought college guys would be so into a kids' game, but from the smile on his face, I could tell it was a fun release valve. "What are the rules?"

"No tag backs. Meaning you can't just tag back the same person who tagged you. There's a sixty-second countdown after each tag to give everyone a chance to get away. You can't drop your drink and run. You've got to stay where you are and finish it. The game shuts down from midnight to six a.m. every night, so we can get a little sleep. No using cars to evade capture and no tagging while a car is in motion. No tag on the field during practice or in the locker rooms."

Footsteps scrambled up the stairs.

My heart jackhammered, and my palms were clammy.

"Any other rules I should know about?"

"You can't be it, so you don't have to stick around for this craziness. It might get weird over the next week." He shot me a look of chagrin.

A door at the top of the stairs opened.

"I'm cool with weird," I whispered.

"This is going to be insane levels of weird."

Another doorknob turn.

I grabbed his hand. "I'm up for anything."

His grin was blinding in the dim light of Cole's bedroom.

"Then let's get out of here." He rushed to the other side of the room and shoved up the window. My breath clouded in the flood of freezing air.

Half-in and half-out, he extended his hand. "Follow me out. I'll make sure you don't fall. Or you can go down the stairs since he can't tag you."

"How many times do I have to say it? I'm game." With my heart racing, I slipped my hand into his and shivered. We scrambled out onto the roof, ducking to either side of the open window just as the door opened.

My breath came in sharp pants. I wasn't exactly afraid of heights, but I'd never been on a roof before. About three feet of shingles stuck out over the side of the house.

Reid lifted his finger to his lips.

I nodded. My shoes stuck to the shingles and I pressed my back against the siding next to the window, where my heart thumped through my back into the vinyl. My lips were pinched together so tightly, they were numb.

A hand shot out of the open window and smacked into my chest.

I yelped.

Hollis's head popped out. "Shit, sorry, Leona."

Reid used the element of surprise to grab my hand and bolted, pulling me past the open window.

"Dammit."

Showing off his athletic prowess, Reid lowered himself gracefully while I scooted my ass across the rough roof tiles.

"Cole said no windows."

"He said no jumping out of closed windows." He motioned his fingers, calling me forward.

I crawled toward him, trying not to panic about moving toward the edge of a freaking roof.

"He also said no jumping from the second floor." Hollis stepped one foot out the window to follow me before jumping back inside. The house shook with a thud.

"He went back inside. I think he tripped." There weren't any yelps or screams, so he wasn't hurt. I was relieved, plus it might buy us some time. And now I was feeling super competitive. It was easy to get caught up in the game, although I wasn't even technically playing.

"Dammit," Reid muttered.

"It's okay. You can leave me."

His hands locked onto my knees. "I'm not going anywhere without you, Leona."

He dropped down off the roof and beckoned me toward the edge. I rolled onto my stomach and let my feet slide into nothingness.

I was sandwiched between him and the gutters. The ice-cold metal pressed against my stomach and chest. Had I known what I was getting myself into when Reid grabbed my hand and we took off upstairs, I would have grabbed my coat.

My tiptoes touched the railing Reid was perched on.

"You good there?"

"Holding on." My fingers were tight around the gutter and the edge of the roof, and I tried to keep my wobbly footing on the railing.

He hopped down and gripped my thighs. His steadying

hold made me feel a little less like I was going to plummet to my death.

I peered over my shoulder.

"Let go. I've got you."

The front door banged open.

With adrenaline surging through my veins, I let go.

He wrapped his arms around my legs and guided me to the porch. Before I could even get oriented, he'd jumped over the railing and was scooping me up to pull me right along with him.

My hair flew into my face.

He brushed it away. "You good?"

I nodded.

Hollis lunged over the railing, narrowly missing us.

"One sec." Reid held up a finger and took off running past the houses on their block before disappearing around the corner.

"Son of a bitch." Hollis jumped over the railing and raced after him.

I stood outside, running my hands up and down my arms and rubbing my legs together, and tried to decide what to do next.

The front door opened, and Reid walked out with both our coats in hand. "I had to double back and hop a few fences. I came in through the kitchen."

A thrill rushed through me at the joy on his face.

I was freezing my ass off and so grateful to have my coat back. "Are you guys always this intense when you play?"

"Always." He slipped my coat around my shoulders and grabbed my hand. "How about we hang out at your place for a while?" His grin was infectious.

"Are you sure they won't find us there?"

"They might, but the door locks, and I'm sure we can

find a good reason to stay nice and warm inside." He tugged me forward and kissed me.

"I like your plan."

"I thought you might."

Slick steps rushed along the pavement.

We turned.

Hollis stood at the end of the block with his hands resting on his knees and giant puffs of condensed breath surrounding him. "I hate you both."

"Let's go." We took off running across the street.

30

REID

Classes were over and the holiday decorations all over campus fluttered above empty quads and buildings. Our street was less quiet, since no one got kicked out of their campus housing during the holidays for industrial level cleaning like the other side of the street, but with no classes and the pre-Christmas cold, most people stuck to their houses.

Practices were bitterly, bitingly cold, and the crunchy grass stabbed into our palms when we set up to run plays.

But I always had the sunshine escape, even on the dreariest of days, of Leona's arms. With most students gone, being seen outside together wasn't as much of a hazard. I usually hated this time of year, which only led to restlessness and wanting the place to fill up again. But lately, I didn't care if this break stretched on for another year.

We still couldn't hold hands or kiss like I'd wanted to so many times, but at least we weren't confined to our rooms. Unless we wanted to be. Like right now.

"What about your place?" I turned the car onto our street.

The sleet had picked up. "Taylor and Ashley have late finals. They don't leave until the day after tomorrow." Lights were still on in all the apartment windows facing the road.

"We can be quiet." I walked my fingers from her knee up her thigh. Tiny bits of ice mixed with rain pelted the roof and windows with little pings.

"They are in intensive study mode. Ashley left her plate in the microwave for too long, and the beeping went off twice, and Taylor put the entire thing in Ash's closet. If we value our lives, I'd stay away until they're done. Hell, I'm afraid to flush after I pee, they're both so quiet right now."

"My house..." I pulled up to the front of The Zoo, where no cars were parked along the curb. Dropping my arm along the back of Leona's seat, I checked the street then peered out the window. The house was dark. I didn't know where the other guys were and I didn't care. "Is empty."

We could relax together for as long as it took for someone to show and hope they weren't it.

"A movie and you know..." Her smile was every bit as sexy as it was adorable.

She didn't have to ask me twice. Every part of me was up for whatever "you know" she had in mind.

"Let me come around." I hopped out and jogged to her side of the car.

Sleet fell in stinging sheets.

She popped out and yelped, covering her head with her hands.

I tossed my jacket over her and raced us from my car to the porch while the freezing pellets stabbed at the backs of my hands. Inside, we took off our coats, and I stashed them and our shoes upstairs so we didn't give away that we were here. If anyone showed up and saw my car, they'd assume I was across the street at Leona's.

"Are you good with watching on my laptop upstairs? We can keep the lights off."

"Is this your attempt at seduction or are you hiding from tag?" She folded her arms across her chest and propped herself against the counter.

I leaned in, reaching past her to open the cabinet, and let my lips brush her ear. "Why not a bit of both?"

She made a small sound that sent a shockwave straight to my dick.

I stuck a bag of popcorn in the microwave.

"How much of this movie are we actually going to watch?" Leona laughed while flicking through options on her phone.

"There's only an hour left until midnight. After that, I'm untouchable."

"What if all this was just an elaborate plot from one of the guys who'd paid me twenty bucks to get you to let your guard down and trap you in the house?"

When the microwave timer beeped, I rubbed up against her. "Then I'd say I still end up the winner." I kissed her again, tracing my tongue along her lips and deepening it with my hand on the small of her back.

A shrill chirp sounded again, and I let her go.

She rocked forward onto her tiptoes trying to follow my lips. "Let's go upstairs."

I gathered the rest of the provisions. A couple cans of root beer, some smiley cookies that Leona had discovered as new favorites. Not that I blamed her. I could devour an entire package of the crunchy icing covered, but soft-baked sugar cookies in minutes, but I was happy to share.

"You got more of the cookies." Her voice shot up an octave.

"It's the way most businesses work. They tend to keep making products people love."

She walked upstairs with the still steaming bag of popcorn pinched between two fingers.

My focus was split between her face each time she looked back at me and the way her ass looked climbing the stairs. There could be a whole firing squad waiting for me, and I'd gladly go.

Without turning on the lights, I grabbed my computer.

She closed the door before flopping onto my bed. Seeing her in my space never got old. Her sock covered feet moved along my bed, wedging beneath the blankets, and she had her head propped up on one arm with strands of hair that had come loose from her ponytail draped across her hand. "Do you want action, adventure, or sci-fi?" Her brows were knitted together like this was the most serious decision she had to make all week.

"Are those the only options?" I sat the laptop beside her and dropped onto the bed.

"The only options I want to watch right now. Adrenaline pumping in the lead up to midnight." Her wanting gaze flicked to mine.

"Anything you want to watch is fine with me." I wouldn't be paying attention to the movie with her lying beside me anyway.

Fifteen minutes before midnight, the front door opened and slammed shut.

We shot up and looked at each other.

I closed the laptop and slid to the end of the bed.

"Who's it?" she whispered.

"I don't know, but I'm not going to be the last one caught. When we start back up during spring break, being it sucks with so many more people around and open buildings to hide in on campus."

"We've got less than ten minutes left." Outside, the pelting rain came down even harder. I wasn't taking her out into that just to avoid being tagged.

"We can hide in the closet." She tiptoed across the floor in silence and darted into the darkened space.

That was the last place we'd want to be if someone came in. We'd be trapped, but where Leona led, I was more than happy to follow. She'd gotten into the game, and I wouldn't take that from her. If I got tagged and couldn't get anyone else back before this break, it would be more than worth it to clean up after every party for the next three months.

We crouched low, and I pulled the door closed, relieved I'd kept it neat. Other than a couple pairs of sneakers, the floor was clean. My shirts hung above our heads. I pushed them to one side, wincing at the squeal of the hangers scraping along the metal rod.

"Are they coming upstairs?"

I strained to listen for movement. Downstairs, the microwave beeped, and faint, tinny voices came from the TV.

Her screen glow filled the dark space. "Ten minutes left. How do you think we should pass the time?"

A sliver of light from the streetlight shined from the gap in the door. She tugged on my belt.

Her take-charge attitude sent me from shocked to simmering. "It seems you have an idea, and I'm not going to say no."

My belt jangled. I grabbed the buckle to muffle the noise and tugged it off, lowering it quietly to the floor. We weren't exactly being stealthy, but at this point, I was more worried about being interrupted than being caught.

I jerked her forward, crushing my lips to hers.

She gasped against me.

I moved my hand from her back to her stomach and let my fingers dip inside the front of her leggings and over the waistband of her underwear. My dick strained in the confines of my jeans. The pounding in my veins all centered on my groin wanting to feel her again. To be inside her again.

She was hot and wet. With rhythm and pressure, my fingers worked her clit in ever-tightening circles.

I deepened the kiss, swallowing her moans.

Her legs shook, and she clutched at my arms. Then she sunk her cool hand into my jeans and palmed my cock, nearly making my legs buckle.

She worked her hand up and down my length, spreading the moisture from the head down over the shaft. Now it was my turn to groan. I gritted my teeth to keep quiet, but damn, it was getting near impossible.

I slipped two fingers inside her. The sounds and smell of her arousal filled the closet, driving me crazy.

She broke the kiss and panted against my cheek.

"I want you so bad," I growled.

"Then have me." She dragged me with her as she backed against the closet wall, only letting go of my cock to shove her leggings down. They tangled at her feet, and I was on her again.

Trying to be quiet in a dark closet heightened every gasp, moan and slap of skin. Every graze or brush felt like sensual fire.

Fumbling for my pocket, I breathed deep to calm myself and put the condom on with a clear head in the tiniest bit of light that filtered in. I yanked her close again, and my dick glided through her wet heat, drawing another groan from me. It was hard to rein myself in and not let go, but I wanted it to be good for her. I always wanted it to be good for her.

She shifted her hips, and I sank inside, choking back a moan. Her grip on my dick and the small sounds she tried to keep quiet would be the death of me.

Reaching overhead, she held onto the pole to steady herself against my deepening thrusts, and that sent all the blood rushing from my head.

Using my lips and hands all over her body, we worked together to bring her right to the needy edge. My hand gripped the back of her neck, and I tugged her down farther into me.

I thumped my fist against the wall behind her.

"We have to be quiet." She moaned and let out a throaty chuckle that was swallowed by a gasp when I sunk in completely, bottoming out.

"You can't feel this good and expect me to be quiet."

She locked her legs around my waist and used the pole for better leverage, rolling her hips against each of my thrusts and setting off sparks in front of my eyes.

"How about that?"

"Fuck, Leona. You're going to kill me." White hot currents of pleasure shot down the backs of my legs. I dropped my hand between us to circle her clit once again, needing her to come first.

She released a panting keen, and her legs tightened around me, holding me so close, I could barely move. I ground myself against her even harder.

Her whole body stiffened, and I finally let go. The head-rush made my vision swim, but she remained clear at the center of my gaze. I filled the condom, bracing myself on the wall behind her as my body spasmed.

Sweaty and breathless, we looked at each other in the dim light.

Leona sighed, then the whole closet collapsed on top of us. The pole ripped straight out of the wall, and we tumbled to the floor.

Beneath me, she trembled, and I pushed back, hoping I hadn't crushed her. "Are you okay?"

In the sliver of light, I could make out her face. Her shoulders shook with laughter, and tears spilled down her cheeks.

Then the closet door was wrenched open. Blinding light poured in, and Griff screamed like we'd sprayed him in the eyes with acid.

She yelped and grabbed onto me. I shouted and reached for the retreating wood barrier that banged against the wall while also trying to cover her.

Leona buried her face in my chest and kept laughing. At least she wasn't freaking out. It relaxed me a little, though I still didn't want Griff getting an eyeful of her.

I shifted in front of her, blocking the open doorway and grabbing for the edge of the door that was just out of fingertip reach.

He whipped around, slapping his hand over his eyes.

"You could've at least closed the door," I said.

He kicked his foot out behind him, trying to close it without looking. "What the hell are you doing in the closet?" he yelled.

"We were hiding." I gripped the edge of the door and closed it, trying to cover the embarrassment of literally being caught bare-assed naked by Griff. Damn, I'd better not get tagged after this.

"That looks like a lot more than hiding to me," he grumbled over his shoulder.

I helped untangle Leona's leggings and helped get her back into them. "Are you it?" I shouted through the door.

"You're banging in the closet because you don't want to be it?" His voice was full of disbelief.

With us both tucked back into our clothes, I opened the closet. "It started out that way."

Griff peeked over his shoulder from the doorway and relaxed. "I'm not even it, plus it's after midnight."

Having sex with Leona was one way to make the time pass in a snap. "Seriously?" I looked for a clock.

"Mission accomplished." Leona high-fived me.

Griff's head tilted. "You two are freaking weird, man. I'm going to bed. Whatever you're doing, keep it quiet." He closed the door behind us.

She covered her face and laughed even harder. "I can't believe he caught us. We'll never live this down. A decade from now, he'll be retelling this story in front of us in a bar somewhere."

I liked how she talked about us in the future like it was a foregone conclusion. I didn't hate that, not even a little.

"It's late and still sleeting. If you want to stay here with me, I'm cool with that." The words seemed to leap from my mouth without my brain checking in. I'd never had anyone sleep over before. I'd never wanted anyone else in my bed, in my own space, all night. But I wanted her there.

"Are you sure? It's not that far."

Now that it was on the table, I didn't want her to pass. I wanted to wake up beside her again. "I can't have you afraid to pee in your own house."

"I don't have pajamas."

I reached over and picked one of my shirts up from the open dresser drawer. "Problem solved."

Her lips were pinched with thoughtfulness.

Stepping closer, I used my thumb to drag her bottom lip out from between her teeth. "I'd really like it if you stayed over tonight. You'll be headed to your dad's for Christmas, and I'll have play-offs after that, and I want to see you as much as I can before then."

She nodded, her face brightening. "In that case, I'd love to."

After we both changed, I slipped into the bed beside her. My heart pounded. We were crossing over into unknown territory, although every step with her had been uncharted so far. I'd never been so caught up in someone before. She was the first, and I was pretty damn sure she would be the last.

She scooted closer and rested her head on my chest.

My arm was wrapped around her shoulder, and I skimmed my fingers over her skin exposed by the overly large t-shirt.

"I'm glad I stayed." She squeezed me tighter.

"I'm glad you did too."

31

LEONA

C hristmas Day felt weird. For one, I was wrapped up in wool socks and a sweater. The snow on the ground was much different than our sandals and barbecue Christmas back with my mom and Andy.

Then there were the Christmases when I was little and my parents were still together. I'd sit at the top of the steps, waiting until exactly 6 a.m. to run into their room and wake them up.

Had Mom and Andy made the orange and clove pomander decorations to hang all over the house? Had she made the big Christmas breakfast she always did since it was only the two of them?

A gentle knock broke through my early morning reminiscing.

My door opened, and Dad stood in the doorway in his full button-down pajamas, robe and slippers. "Merry Christmas, Leona-Loo."

The second reason it felt weird was that I was waking up in the same house as my dad with presents under the tree from Santa.

"Merry Christmas, Dad." I hopped out of bed and hugged him.

"It's almost nine. I was wondering if you'd secretly snuck away. I remember back when you were a kid, and your mom and I had to cover the stairs with wrapping paper to keep you from running down and sneaking a peek at your presents."

"It's been a while since I've woken up at the crack of dawn to check out the presents."

Dad headed downstairs, but before following him, I grabbed my phone to send Reid a text. One from him was already sitting in my messages. I replied with butterflies of excitement in my stomach and guilt weighing heavily in my chest. These feelings warring were building, getting stronger, and I had no idea how to fix any of it. I set down my phone and resolved to focus on making this a great Christmas with my dad even as I longed to see Reid.

In the kitchen, I stuck the French toast casserole we'd made the night before in the oven while Dad worked on his hot chocolate recipe.

We ate breakfast and watched *A Christmas Story*—or at least parts of it since it was on repeat—while we made hot chocolate and opened our gifts, which almost felt more like an afterthought than the main attraction they once were. It wasn't the present avalanche and giddy excitement of my childhood Christmases, but it didn't make the morning any less fun or special.

Dad liked the ties and collar stays I got him. He had to dress up so often that they seemed like the perfect gift.

I also gave him a new picture of the two of us from the summer. "I thought it would be nice to have a new one."

He hugged me tightly. "This is perfect. I know just the spot for it. Thank you."

He stared at me with a hint of apprehension before handing over my gifts.

I took them and opened the envelope first before ripping into the newspaper comic-wrapped one.

He got me a Lego store gift card, a scratch-off tracker of the 100 best sci-fi and action movies, and a history of wine book called *Cork Dork*.

"These are great, Dad."

"Your mom sent you a present." He held out a box with Snoopy Santas all over it. It had to have cost an arm and a leg to ship. "Have you talked to her yet?"

I took the box from him and squeezed it so tightly the wrapping paper tore. "It's already midnight there. I'll call her later." Like in March. I still wasn't sure how to talk to her.

After bingeing more Christmas movies and a turkey dinner for two for lunch, Dad began yawning. "I'm beat. After all that turkey and the excellent wine pairings from my in-house sommelier, I think I need a nap."

"Now you know why I don't wake at the crack of dawn. Go rest. I'll clean up here."

"I can help clean up." Another yawn.

"Dad, it's not a big deal." I grabbed his shoulders and turned him toward the stairs. "When's the last time you had enough free time for a nap?"

He perched his hand on his chin and looked off in the distance. "You're right. It's been a while. Normally, I travel over the breaks for fund-raising events, but it's been great to be home with you."

Guilt always found a way to blindside me like a car sideswiping me out of nowhere. He shouldn't have been alone.

I almost hated how happy he was to have me here. If he'd still been preoccupied or distant, I could pretend that things wouldn't have been different if I hadn't left and stayed away, but I knew they would've. Hopefully, we could regain even more of what had been lost.

"I'm glad you're taking a break too."

"I'll go grab twenty winks."

"Take as long as you want. Don't worry about me."

He kissed the top of my head and went upstairs.

I closed everything down and cleaned up in the kitchen, packing away the leftovers. Running my fingers along the banister that had been professionally decorated after Thanksgiving, I went back to the tree Dad and I had decorated earlier this week in the TV room tucked away from the more public spaces of the house. There were ornaments I'd made when I was smaller. Terrible glitter and clay monstrosities. Handprints of all sizes along with tin foil and string holding them all together. The house was beginning to feel more like a home. More like a place I might've lived in for longer than the next year and a half until graduation.

Back in my room, I sent Reid a text. I wished he could be here with me, eating loads of Christmas food and spending time with me instead of on his own without family. Although he had the guys, so at least he wasn't alone.

Me: How's your dining hall turkey?

A chirp rang outside.

I jerked my head up and sent another message.

Me: I wanted to give you your present.

There was another chirp from outside my window. That was not what I thought it was.

My pulse skyrocketed, and I rushed to the double doors leading out to the balcony that overlooked the back patio.

Yanking one open, I peered outside and didn't see anything. Walking farther out, I heard the cursing. "Fucking thorns. Looked a lot lower from the ground."

I slid across the pavers and slammed into the wrought iron railing. Peering over the edge of the balcony, I tried to swallow my heart back out of my throat.

Reid was climbing the ivy-covered trellis that ran the height of the house with a bright yellow box gripped between his teeth by its red ribbon.

"What the hell are you doing?" My voice was a shrill whisper.

He jerked and nearly lost his hold. "Are you trying to kill me, Leona?"

Covering my mouth, I bit back my scream. "Are you crazy? You're going to hurt yourself."

"One sec." After a few moments of hesitation, he flung himself at the railing, banging his hips and perhaps other important pieces of his anatomy into it.

I glanced over my shoulder at my still closed bedroom door. "Why did you climb all the way up here?"

"Why do you think?" He looked half pained and half proud of his insane stunt.

I grabbed onto him, and he flipped over, landing flat on his back. My heart thundered like I'd been the one scaling the side of the house. At least my dad's room was a few doors down and faced the front. "Have you lost your mind? I could've met you somewhere."

"I know, but I wanted to give you your Christmas present." His cheeks were flushed, and there was a thin sheen of perspiration on his forehead, even in the frigid air.

"The back door also works. I could've snuck you up the stairs by the kitchen." I wrapped my arms around his and tugged him forward.

He sat up, and the corner of his mouth quirked. "Where's the fun in that?" He pulled me down onto his lap and kissed me.

"The fun is in not breaking your neck." It had only been three days since I'd seen him, but I'd missed him.

"Don't you know by now I'm an expert at scaling buildings?"

"Tag has gone to your head. Who is it for the next time it starts?"

"Ezra."

"That's got to be like trying to escape the Terminator."

"You have no idea."

"Let's go inside before you get pneumonia, and I'm the asshole who got a star player sick. They'd have that splashed all over STFU Dirt with devil horns drawn on my picture."

I crawled off him, and he popped up like he hadn't just been dangling to his possible death minutes ago.

Inside, he set his coat on the back of my desk chair and set the box beside the wrapped one I'd left there. He walked his fingers along the smooth finish of the wood. "One of these days, maybe I'll be in your room when it's not sneaking around."

He laughed, but it hit at the center of my chest with a dull thump. All this sneaking around made me think of my mom. Had it been this easy for her? Felt this exciting? The circumstances were different, but there was still a whole barrel full of lies I was serving up left and right.

"One day." If his season went the way he hoped, he might not be visiting me here ever again. Dad kept calm as always, but the undercurrent of stress and tension was always there.

Shaking off the unwanted feelings, I flopped back on my bed.

"Where's your dad?"

"He's taking a nap. The turkey lunch took him out. How was your Christmas lunch?"

Reid laid down on the bed beside me but propped up on one arm. "Good. Santa even showed up with a giant red sack and handed out presents."

I laughed, imagining a bunch of eighteen to twenty-somethings perched on Santa's lap while he gave away gifts. "What did Santa give you for being a good boy?"

"If he only knew." His grin widened. "They gave away STFU swag. Hats, koozies, t-shirts, keychains."

"Is that what you got for me? Stolen Santa gifts."

His smile faltered. "Did you honestly think I'd have given you regifted crap?"

My hands shot out, and I rubbed them soothingly along his arm. "No, of course not. It was a joke." I slid off my bed. "I got you a present too."

He sat forward as his eyes lit up with excitement.

A tender nudge squeezed my heart. I brought over both boxes.

Sitting facing each other on my bed, I handed him his and kept mine.

"Did you wrap this?" I shook the box, which gave off nondescript, muted bumps.

"Me? No way. Ezra did."

"Ezra?" I slapped my hands over my mouth.

My brain couldn't process the thought of Ezra with his hat shadowing most of his face and gruff demeanor standing over a box and meticulously creasing and taping the wrapping paper then adding a bow. This was a bigger surprise than anything that could be in the box.

"Seriously? It's beautiful." I held it out and turned it around, still not believing he'd wrapped it. Not wanting to disturb the pretty bow and paper, I slipped it off and gently slid my fingers under the tape.

He shrugged. "He's got the patience and for some reason likes doing it. None of us are going to complain."

"Wow." I pulled open the top flap of the now naked box and found a small white shadow box frame inside.

With a curious look up at Reid, I wiggled the shadow box out and let out the cheesiest "Aww" there ever was. It was Reid and me in Lego form. His little guy had on a football helmet and an STFU jersey with his number on it. His plastic hand held a football.

Mine had her hair up, wore a *Terminator* t-shirt, and held a bottle of wine.

Underneath both, it said Reid + Leona.

"This is the most adorable thing I've ever seen in my life. How'd you get the STFU jersey on here?"

"My Googling skills are world-renowned." He interlocked his fingers and pretend cracked them. "There's more." He motioned to the box. "It's more a present for both of us though."

Inside, against the white interior of the box, were two little white cloth bags. "It's not like a cock ring or anything?" I eyed the innocuous-looking bags.

He huffed. "No, but I love where your mind went. I'll file that away for next Christmas."

Next Christmas. He saw us still being together next Christmas. It sent a rush through my veins. I wanted that too.

I slid the muslin bags out onto my palm and tugged open the first. My jaw dropped. It was the same little figurines from the shadow box but on keyrings.

He took the other one out and set it in my palm before closing my hand around the tiny plastic figures.

"Now, even when we're apart, we'll have a little reminder."

I flung my arms around his neck and climbed onto his lap. "God, it's hot when you're so damn sentimental." With our Lego figures keyring looped through my fingers, I kissed Reid.

There was a knock at the door, and then I was flying through the air. Reid rolled to the other side of the bed before I bounced once.

Reid disappeared behind my bed. He'd moved so quickly that I expected a flutter of papers scattering in his wake.

He popped back up from behind me and grabbed the boxes with our gifts, then vanished over the far side of my bed.

"Yeah, Dad?" He opened the door as I shoved the last of the wrapping paper into the nightstand drawer.

My heart pounded in my throat.

"I need to run out for a little while." He'd changed into a button-down shirt and gray pants. For him, this was practically leisure wear.

"Where are you going?" I crossed one arm over my chest and propped my chin on my hand. The perfect, not-at-all-suspicious picture of cool, calm and collected.

"There's an errand I needed to run." He waved his hand vaguely in the direction of the front door.

"An errand that has something to do with the box in your hand?" I nodded toward the red box with green ribbon wrapped around it that he tapped against his palm. My heart no longer felt like it was trying to climb out my throat and stuck to beating in my esophagus.

He looked down like he'd forgotten it was there. "Yes, it does." His fingers brushed over the shiny paper.

"Tell Amy I said Merry Christmas." I tried to keep the strain out of my voice. A gentle nudge almost imperceptibly rocked my bed.

It—I—" He sputtered. "I forgot to tell her before the break."

"And that's something you couldn't say over the phone?" I teased.

His mouth opened and snapped shut. The tips of his ears reddened. "She left in a hurry, and I was in meetings and I forgot to give this to her before the break began." He gestured to the present.

"You didn't make her wrap it herself, did you?"

His face morphed into mock shock. "No, I wrapped it myself. I'm not completely helpless without her."

"Not completely," I teased. How long would it take for those two to finally fess up to their feelings? Although the whole boss-employee situation complicated things. "Don't worry about me, Dad. I'll be fine here on my own."

"Did you want to come along?"

"No, of course not." Not when Reid was under my bed and not when Dad and Amy might have a chance to talk outside of work. "Have fun."

"It'll only be a quick visit. I might drop it on her doorstep."

"You should give it to her in person. Don't want the paper to get soggy."

He looked down at it with a thoughtful expression and ran a gentle finger over the bow.

"I'll see you later."

Instead of leaving, he rushed into the room.

Panic scorched through me. Could he see Reid on the other side of the bed?

He leaned over and pecked me on the cheek. "See you in a bit. I shouldn't be more than a couple hours."

The door closed behind him, and I waited to hear the front door close.

Apparently, I wasn't the only one listening out for the slam.

Rustling came from the other side of the bed. Behind me, the mattress dipped, and Reid's knees settled on either side of my hips. His shadow loomed overhead. A tingle tripped down my spine. My body hummed in anticipation of his touch.

His body weight pressed down against my back. Strong, solid, searing. His lips fell to my nape and shoulders.

Then my shirt was up and over my head.

I turned and did the same for him, running my hands over the muscles honed and put to work during every game and practice.

He reached for me, and I shot up, scrambling away from his grasp. "Hold that thought."

I flicked the lock on my door. "Better safe than sorry."

On his knees in the center of my bed, Reid was a heady sight. Then he lifted his hand and crooked his finger, beckoning me closer.

My pulse shot from cardio to predator evasion. Only this one I didn't want to evade. I was very much looking forward to him devouring me completely.

Sweaty and sated, I collapsed on top of Reid.

His arms came up around me, holding me close. "Merry Christmas, Leona."

I laughed against his neck, my lips tasting the salt on his skin. "Was that another of my gifts?"

His chest rumbled beneath me. "It's a present you can have year-round."

"Oh, trust me, I'll be unwrapping this gift as often as I can."

His heart beat out a rapid thump against my ear, and his arms tightened around me like he didn't want to let go.

I sighed, not wanting to kill the mood but also not wanting this to turn into a shitshow if my dad shortened his visit to Amy's like he'd threatened.

"I broke the heater."

Confusion sliced through all the warm fuzzy feelings. I sat up and looked at him. "Heater? What heater?"

"During our security night. I sabotaged it, so it wouldn't turn on." His hesitant smile was overwhelmingly endearing.

"You risked us getting frostbite on the off chance I was on board with jumping into a sleeping bag with you?"

"I hoped you would be."

"And if I hadn't been?" I shoved at his chest. "My toes could've fallen off."

"I'd have offered up the extra sleeping bag before I let that happen."

"Then you'd have frozen your ass off."

"It would've served me right for not being persuasive enough."

"I can't believe you."

"But can you believe I'm crazy about you?" He dragged me back down on top of him.

"I'm halfway there." I traced my fingers along his neck.

His eyes were hooded with desire all over again. "I know. I need to go."

I squeezed him tighter. "I'll be back in my apartment in a couple days."

He tipped my chin up. "I can't wait."

My phone pinged with a text. Panic gripped me. What if Dad was minutes away?

Dad: Headed home. I should be there in thirty minutes. Want to go to the movies?

We rushed to get dressed, which took longer than it should've since we couldn't stop touching each other.

"How about instead of going out the way you came, I walked him to the front door."

He nodded and laughed. "If I cut through the trees to the left of the house, I'll get back to my car."

"I can drive you to your car."

"Can't help yourself, huh? You've just got to have more of me." He grabbed me and cupped my ass, spinning us around to music only playing in his head.

I scrunched up my nose. "More like you can't keep your hands off me, and I don't want you to break your neck Spidermanning into my room to get your fix."

He threw his head back and laughed. "You got me there."

Fully dressed, I grabbed my keys and purse from the table.

We walked downstairs hand-in-hand, and I rested my head against his shoulder.

"Your present! You didn't even open it." I turned to rush back upstairs when he caught me around my waist.

He tickled his fingers along the hair at my temple. "Leona—" He cut himself off with another kiss.

The front door swung open, followed by a bellow of "Oakes!"

We jumped apart and stared at our new arrival.

Mikelson. Reid's coach stood in the doorway, gaping at us. After the months of being careful, after staying away from each other on campus, after not being able to let anyone outside of our small group of friends know we were dating, of all the places to get caught. Here in my foyer, his coach walked in on us making out.

"Riddick." Coach's growl made the hairs stand up on the back of my neck. He stared at me like he was inspecting shit on his shoe.

My throat closed, and I looked to Reid and back at Mikelson.

Reid's whole demeanor changed. No longer playful and relaxed, his back snapped straight, and his hands were balled into fists at his sides.

He stepped in front of me. "Coach."

"What the hell are you doing here? With her?"

"With all due respect, Coach. We're not on the field right now. It's none of your business."

I wanted to scream at the older man to get the hell out of my dad's house, but I didn't want to make this worse for Reid. I didn't even want to reach for his hand. Ashley and Taylor had told me about the unfortunate guy who'd gotten benched for the picture posted by STFU Dirt. I could only imagine how this would blow back on Reid.

My stomach was a churning, knotted mess.

"None of my business." His voice rattled the picture frames on the wall. "Disrespectful little shit. You're nothing without me, but it seems you need to be reminded of that." The coach stormed out, leaving the door wide open.

His stomping footsteps ended with a car door slamming and a gravel-filled peel out from the circular driveway.

I stood behind Reid, shivering from the cold blasting in through the open door.

Stepping forward, I touched his hand.

He flinched and looked over at me.

"That could've gone better," I said.

He nodded. It was tight and mechanical. His gaze was still trained on the empty doorway. "I need to go."

"Wait, I was going to drive you to your car."

He shook his head. "No. Let's just—I'll be fine." He turned and kissed me on the cheek, and then he was gone, closing the door softly behind him.

Rubbing my hands over my arms, I tried to not feel like I'd been standing in the same room with a ghost.

I collapsed onto the steps and rested my head against the spindles. It would be okay. Maybe it wouldn't be as bad as he expected. Maybe that other guy had done something else to piss the coach off, and that was why he'd been benched.

Maybe this wouldn't blow up in our faces like we'd suspected. How long until my dad found out? Would the coach throw this right into his face the next time he saw him? I bent at the waist and hugged myself.

This was turning into the nightmare we'd both warned ourselves about, but my Christmas wish was that we'd have each other even if it all went south. And I hoped that wasn't a pipe dream wiped away by Mikelson showing up. I hoped.

32

REID

My sneakers soaked up water with each step on the snow-covered grass and were soggy by the end of the long walk back to my car. On the way to Leona's, I'd barely noticed, but now they were like ice blocks strapped to my feet.

There were only a few other cars in the athletics department parking lot, but the Football Director spot was occupied.

I dropped my head to the steering wheel and slammed my fists into the dashboard until they ached. Playing with fire was fun, but the resulting burns would be deep. I'd known the risk. I'd known the reasons I should stop. I'd known one false move would be the end of my career. And I'd done it anyway.

My heart raced like I'd been doing sprints for the past hour.

I walked down the long hallway lined with jerseys of STFU alumni who'd gone pro. Those numbers mocked me with a future that was minutes away from being snatched from my grasp. Mikelson's office loomed ahead, and each step became heavier than the last.

I tried to swallow, but there was nothing there. My stomach was an after-practice mess that felt like I was one step away from dry heaving all over the hallway.

With my clammy, shaking palms squeezed tightly at my sides, I stood outside the frosted glass door of Coach's office, praying I could avoid the gut-bomb.

"Finally made it here, Riddick."

The hairs stood up on the back of my neck. I pushed open the door that hadn't even been closed all the way.

He'd been expecting me.

Maybe a part of me hoped I wouldn't find him here. That he had better things to do on Christmas Day and he'd forget all about me in a few hours.

He stood with his back to me, staring at the wall of artfully lit trophies that highlighted each of his major wins. Bowl game trophies, the national championship trophy and the coach's trophy, which was a crystal football on a black stand.

I stood in the center of his office with my hands behind my back. A wall clock ticked through the silence, its jerky second hand counting down the moments before the guillotine dropped.

He picked up a bottle of whiskey that sat behind a few tumblers and poured two glasses. Turning, he motioned for me to sit and placed the glass on the far end of the desk. The end closest to me.

"Have a seat. Try this whiskey. It's a fifteen-year-old. A beauty." He leaned back in his chair.

Was the drink poisoned? No, he'd poured some for himself and took a leisurely sip. The glass then? Had he coated the rim in cyanide?

I picked it up with a shaking hand, and the liquor splashed against the high edges of the cup.

This was more unnerving than if he'd punched me in the mouth the second I walked into the room.

"Have a drink. And sit down." Each word was spaced out with the Mikelson intensity. This wasn't a request.

I sat on the edge of the chair and sipped the amber liquid. It was biting and sharp under the initial smoothness. Nothing like the wines Leona had chosen for me.

Mikelson didn't give a shit about my enjoyment, of course. This was all a power play for him.

He picked up a cloth and dragged it over another polished crystal trophy on his desk. "How many of your teammates knew about this?"

I choked on my sip, suddenly feeling like I was trying to breathe through a throat packed with cotton balls.

He'd timed the question perfectly.

Pounding my chest against the burning, I gasped and blinked back the tears welling in my eyes. I could feel the heat of the alcohol in my nose, but it paled to the dread welling in my sternum like an ominous beast ready to pounce. "I don't know what you mean, sir," I wheezed.

He set down his glass with a thump. "Let's not play dumb. You're fraternizing with President Oakes's daughter. Dating her, hooking up with her, fucking her, whatever it is you kids want to call it."

My rage piqued that he'd ever speak about Leona that way. I gripped the wooden arm of the chair. How many other guys had sat here while Mikelson ripped into them? Tried to break them down?

"I'll repeat my question again. How many of your team-mates knew?"

"No one, sir." The words were laced with acid barbs I wished I could shoot straight at his damn throat.

"I find that hard to believe. You're all thick as thieves." He took another sip from his glass.

"No one knew, sir."

"I'll ask you again. Who on the team knew about this? You—well, you were obviously thinking with your dick, and it must be drunk to want to fuck her. But the rest of them, that's insubordination on a level I can't tolerate. An undermining I'll not allow to continue, and it needs to be ferreted out and lanced like a festering boil."

I held the glass so tightly the tendons in my wrist felt ready to snap. "No one else knew." Not only had I put my future in jeopardy, now he was trying to screw over the rest of the team. He wanted to win more than anything, but I didn't doubt he'd make an example of anyone he thought had helped me. It was better to keep my mouth shut and take the full brunt.

He shoved his chair back. "How about I make a deal with you? I'll let you play in the last two games of the post-season."

I kept my gaze trained straight ahead, but my heart rattled against my ribs like a prisoner trying to break free.

"If you give me names of who had direct knowledge of you fraternizing with President Oakes's daughter."

The words were out of my mouth without a second thought. "No one else knew. I kept it quiet and only ever went to her."

"That's the game you want to play? Have it your way. I won't kick you off the team for this indiscretion."

Hope flared in my chest. I'd had a great run this season, maybe...

He stood and walked around the desk. "You can sit your

ass on the bench. You think this team can't win without you? They don't need you. You think after a few hot plays that you're not replaceable. You're nothing. I want you to have a front-row seat to watch it all happen." His voice was laced with vitriol, and he jerked his door open. "Now get the fuck out of my office." The words were low and sinister.

An anvil was lodged in my throat, making it hard to breathe. I had to keep reminding myself to suck in a lungful of air and then release it. The entire hallway tilted, and I staggered to the side, slamming my shoulder into the wall.

It was over. It was all over. I'd courted disaster, and the time had finally come.

I'd rolled the dice and I'd lost—everything.

Every time anyone passed me sitting on the bench in my pristine uniform, their gaze locked with mine. They knew what the team misconduct announcement Mikelson had made for my replacement really meant. We'd seen it happen throughout the seasons, and I'd been dumb enough to get caught. Solidarity meant destruction under the Mikelson reign, and they didn't want his anger at me to rub off on them. It wouldn't unless they were rubbing up against President Oakes's daughter.

But I didn't blame them. We were all here for one reason —well, two. To win games and get our shot at the pros.

And the way the game was headed, they were all a step closer.

Ezra walked past on his way to the water and dropped his hand onto my shoulder. "You good?"

My chin cut down in a sharp nod. What was I supposed to say? The scoreboard should've had me pumping my fists into the air. We were up by six. The team skated to this win. If all went well in the next game, we'd probably face off against Fulton U for the championship. But they'd be doing it without me.

I'd worked my ass off to get to this point, and all I could do was watch it unfold in front of me. There wasn't a damn thing I could do.

From down the sideline, I could feel Mikelson's gaze boring into the side of my face. At least he hadn't marched me out to sit on the bench with a giant day-glow stay away sign hung around my neck. What he'd said in his office was coming true. They didn't need me.

Once I'd gotten home after the blow up from Mikelson, I'd looked into my options. They were bleak. Transferring was out. I'd have to sit out a year to be eligible again, which meant drawing college out for two more years, if I could even transfer. That upped my odds of injury before signing a big contract.

We were in our home stadium, and somewhere in the stands, Taylor, Ashley and Leona were cheering the team on, but I couldn't look. I couldn't force myself to turn around to check.

My hands were locked into fists, grinding against the bench beneath me. My jaw was so tight my teeth ached. My heart was a beat away from exploding.

So much had ridden on this season as my first to prove myself, and here I was, shooting myself in the foot at the finish line.

Cole knelt beside me to retie his already tied shoe. He kept his head down and yanked on one lace, untying them. "Don't let this get to you."

"How the hell am I supposed to do that?"

His lips slammed together, and he tied his laces with the

concentration of someone who'd just learned how. "At least we're winning."

That made it worse. "Yeah."

My stupidity and carelessness had led me here.

But Leona had been too tempting to let slip away. Every chance I had, I'd wanted to be near her. Every mistake had been made easier when she was around. And that was the problem.

The flashes of happiness with Leona had made this brutal season easier, but I didn't deserve easier. This was what happened when you split your focus. I leaned out for that brass ring too early, and now I was tumbling down the mountain.

The final sheer drop hadn't happened yet. But at the end, I'd be bloodied, battered and broken.

33

LEONA

Leaving the stadium after this win didn't feel like the others, despite the cheek-chapping wind and the cheers from everyone around me in STFU orange and gold. It didn't fill me with elation, even though I knew it was an important game for Reid and the team.

Now, I knew it meant my dad was closer to losing the job he loved. The magnifying glass was shoved right up to my face about how devastating my lies would be to him.

Every day I woke up and waited for his call or text asking me if it was true. Had I been going behind his back with the football player who'd flipped him off in the parking lot?

But the weight in my chest was made even heavier by the fact that I didn't know if that football player wanted anything to do with me anymore.

It had been three days since Reid's coach caught us kissing and three days since I'd seen Reid. His text responses had been short or non-existent.

I'd sat beside my dad in the movie theater, shoveling popcorn I couldn't taste into my mouth and waiting for a message from him, but none had come. Dad told me about the field house's groundbreaking ceremony next semester, but I could barely focus.

A few hours after the game, I knocked on the front door of The Zoo with one gloved hand and balanced two boxes in the other.

Ezra opened the door and stared down at me with his hat firmly in place. At least some things never changed. "Hey, Leona." His voice wasn't any different, but there was a new tension in him that made my stomach knot.

"Hey, Ezra." I waved like a dork, awkward in a way I hadn't normally felt coming over here.

Behind him, the whole house was quieter than I expected. Nothing like the celebrations going on around campus even though it was still half empty. There was a movie on the TV, food on the table in front of it, but they weren't all bouncing off the walls. They'd been happier the night they started playing tag, and they'd lost that game.

"Great game! Next stop, the final four." I forced a smile through my worry.

He grunted and stepped aside to let me in.

The rest of the guys were scattered around the living room with bottles of water and big plates of food, but none of them were talking.

"I know I don't know all the rules yet, but you did win, right?" My attempt at a joke fell flat.

Hollis nodded and tapped an ace bandage against his palm. "We did."

"Did someone get hurt?"

He looked down at the bandage in his hand. "No more than usual. We didn't all get to play, so things have been...." His gaze floated to the stairs. There was nothing accusatory in his tone, but the words still hit me.

I stalled, my foot lifted for another step, and the blood

drained out of my head. Somewhere deep down, no matter how shitty it made me, I'd hoped the reason he hadn't played was an injury or that he was sick. It would've also been the reason he hadn't gotten back to me. But that one sentence popped my little balloon of hope.

I was the reason Reid had been benched, just like he'd said would happen. "I'm sorry. I... It's all my fault." Spinning, I tried to escape.

Ezra's hand shot out, and he blocked my path to the door.

"We don't blame you, Leona. We just don't know if he's going to be up for a talk right now."

The somber mood was palpable, which made sense. They were still a team and friends. When one of them was down, they were all down. "I won't stay for long. I wanted him to know I'm here and give him these." I lifted both boxes. "He has all you guys, but I wanted him to know he has me too."

They all looked grim, like they were at a wake, and maybe it was the wake of our relationship they'd already gone into mourning over.

No one stopped me on the way up the stairs.

Their voices didn't rise above a low rumble.

I knocked on Reid's door and opened it before he said anything. "Hey."

He didn't look up from his spot on the edge of his bed. His elbows were resting on his legs, and he had his head in his hands. "Now's not a good time, Leona."

"That's what the guys said." My throat had a boulder lodged in it.

He didn't say anything else.

My fingers were sweaty against the orange cardboard box. I knelt in front of him, trying to get him to look at me, setting both gifts down. "I didn't get a chance to give you your present last time we saw each other. Someone might've distracted me." I covered his hands with mine and ducked my head to meet his gaze.

He sat up and slid his hands away. Pain radiated from my side as though someone had shoved a dagger between my ribs.

His gaze was flat, and he looked straight through me. A breath escaped him like he was sick and tired of me being here already.

I tried to shake it off. Maybe it was all in my head. "I—" The word came out strained, and I cleared my throat. "I got this for you too." My fingers shook on the orange box top beside his Christmas gift. I slipped out the orange and gold frosted cupcake with an STFU stamped in chocolate on top.

"I didn't want to tell the guys since they were all sold out of all of them except for one. So you get your special treat." I held it up balanced on my outstretched palms, trying to get him to smile.

"I'm not hungry." He leaned back even further.

"Reid—" My voice cracked. "I..." I was at a loss for words and didn't know how to deal with this new version of him. "I can't even begin to imagine what you're going through right now."

"Then stop trying to," he snapped.

The knife twisted.

"I know you're upset, but we both knew the risks." Inhale. Exhale. The corners of my eyes and back of my nose heated with swelling emotions. I wouldn't cry. I wouldn't.

"And I'm bearing the whole brunt of them. Is this cupcake supposed to make it all better?" He snatched it out of my hand, ripped off the paper and took a huge bite. "Wow, you're right. I feel so much better." His mocking tone burned. He dropped the cupcake icing side down on the wrapper like it was trash. "I should've just been eating these for the past few days, and I'd have never even felt what it was like to have my team out on the field without me."

I shot up as shock spread through my chest. "Aren't you glad they won, even if you couldn't play?"

He whirled to face me. "No! I wanted them to win with me." He jammed his finger in the center of his chest. "I wanted to be part of the team out there on the field to make play-off history and win the whole damn thing."

"Isn't them winning the most important thing, even if it's not with you?"

"No!" His voice boomed so loudly, I jumped.

"I never realized you were this selfish, but I'm seeing a much different side of you today."

"You think you know me? What makes you think you have a clue about who I am?"

Blood pounded in my ears, and indignation blazed through my chest. "Sorry, I thought all those long nights talking while snuggled up next to each other were exactly what that was. Getting to know who you are and showing you who I was."

He leaned in with his gaze narrowed. "If you knew anything about me, you wouldn't be here right now."

His angry words slammed into me, scorching my heart.

"What does that mean? Isn't this exactly what you do when you care about someone? You try to be there for them?"

"Not when they're the reason you've been fucked over." He stared at me like he hated me.

Pain flooded me, overflowing and splashing into the fire beneath the cauldron where all these feelings had been brewing. That hurt forged into anger.

"You're the one who broke the heater. You're the one who kissed me in the freaking dragon. You're the one who told me you wanted me. And made me want you!" How dare he about-face and accuse me, as though I was pursuing him and forcing him into a relationship.

He paced and raked his fingers through his hair. "I didn't think it would end up like this."

"You're the one who warned me. We decided together that it was worth the risk." I'd lied to my dad and done all I could to protect this secret, swallowing down my constant guilt for another hit of the Reid Riddick high.

"I changed my mind." His tone was flat, and he crossed his arms over his chest like his words were the final say in this.

His words carved at an already bleeding wound in my soul.

"Just like that." My arms flapped down to my sides, all the energy leached from me so I was nothing but a husk. "That's it? It's over?"

"Yeah. It's over. We shouldn't see each other anymore."

"Because you got benched." I was numb. I should've been better prepared for it. The secrets and lies had all been to stop this moment from happening, but here we were.

"No, it's not just about that."

My head whipped back. "What do you mean it's not about that?"

"It's just best." His jaw clenched. Those muscles I'd found mesmerizing before ticked like a bomb about to explode.

"I can take you saying you don't want to be with me because of what happened with your coach, but what lies are you telling yourself that it's not about football?"

"It's not only about that."

Outraged crashed inside my head, shifting my feelings from gasping to seething. "You mean to tell me that if your coach hadn't caught us, you were planning on breaking up with me anyway?"

His jaw clenched and unclenched.

"Exactly. Lie to me all you want, but you can't lie to yourself. If you'd played today and won, you'd be tackling me into bed and tearing my clothes off."

His gaze cut to mine. The intensity of the anger there sent mine skyrocketing.

"If you were just honest with me about it, I could respect you more," I spat back at him.

"What do you want me to say, Leona? That I'm angry? That I'm so fucking angry I want to burn everything down? That it's taking everything in me to keep me from trashing my own freaking room?" His fists clenched at his side so tightly his knuckles were drained of all color.

I felt like I was up to my neck in quicksand, treading and failing to keep my head above water. "Yes, at least it's honest."

"You want me to tell you how sitting there on the sidelines, a part of me wanted them to lose? I wanted to be so important to the team that they couldn't do it without me." Fury and pain were clear in his voice.

I shook but refused to wrap my arms around myself or shy away from facing him. The anguish in his eyes sliced at my heart. Even after the harsh words, I couldn't believe that all we shared meant nothing to him, like a switch had been flipped.

He slammed his fist into the wall. "This team has been my life for the past three years, and now I'm sitting on the sidelines again, watching it all pass me by."

Despite all the hurt he'd heaped on me, I still felt his

pain. To have something so important ripped away from you wasn't fair. "There's still two more games. Maybe—"

"Stop trying to fix this, Leona. There's no fixing it."

"I just want to be here for you."

"And I said I don't want you here. Did you think now that Mikelson knows I wouldn't want to hide anymore? Have you told your dad?"

My mouth snapped shut. Guilt and shame whirled in my stomach like a rotten cocktail.

"You're worried about Daddy being disappointed in you. This is my life, Leona! This is my future."

"I never wanted you to lose any of that," I shouted back, my voice breaking.

"I still have next season where I'll do whatever it takes to get back on the field." He pointed in the direction of the stadium. "Which means we don't know each other anymore."

I staggered back. "Just like that?" I snapped. Maybe the Reid I'd thought I'd known had been a lie all along. I'd been wrong so many times before. My dad. My mom. Andy. Friends. People I'd thought I could trust had betrayed me in more ways than one, so maybe I was just absolute shit at truly knowing anyone.

Because I definitely didn't know the guy standing in front of me.

"Did you think I'd actually choose you over football?" The words seemed to stun him, but they demolished me.

All the air whooshed out of my lungs. I was swimming underwater, and he'd just stolen my breath with a single question. My whole body ached.

Tears burned, making him a blurry mass filling my vision.

His face fell, and he reached for me. "Leona, I didn't

mean it. I'm sorry. Everything is so fucked up." Anguish was laced through every word, but so was the truth.

"Don't apologize for telling me how you feel. It's what I asked for, right?" I wanted to run away. I wanted to hide. I wanted this to all be a terrible nightmare.

He scrubbed his hands down over his face. "This isn't a good time for me right now."

I picked up the box abandoned on the floor and set it on his desk beside the door. "Tell your coach we're not together anymore. Tell him you hate my guts now." Because it seemed like it was the truth.

"Leona—"

"Maybe he'll let you play. Good luck with the rest of the season."

Tears burned my eyes and my cheeks. I flew down the stairs and out the front door croaking out a good luck to the rest of the guys.

The door had barely closed when someone called my name, but it wasn't his voice. It wasn't Reid.

I didn't look back the whole way to my apartment. Once inside, I slammed the door and collapsed with my back against the freezing cold metal. I wrapped my arms around my knees and hugged my legs to my chest.

34

REID

I paced on the sidelines, unable to look away from the field.

Fulton U's defense had been relentless, but we were stronger. The STFU offense was on the field, and we were up by three. They were at the fifty-yard line and it was third down. It was too close for comfort. Too close to ending our run for the championship.

The biting cold was made worse by sitting still in the shade on the sidelines and staring at a dream that had been so close.

I needed the game now more than ever. Everything had been a mess since Leona walked out my door. The words I'd shouted at her rang in my head like I'd smacked myself with a mallet. Standing in front of her, I'd lashed out, wanting her to feel the same pain I was. No matter how hard I tried, I couldn't stop myself from spewing the hateful words at her until she left.

I'd sunk to my knees and stayed there so long my legs fell asleep by the time the guys came to check on me. The silence had been painful, but it didn't compare to what I'd been living with for the three days since she'd left.

Football had been my respite for so long. Put in the work. Run the plays. Power through the pain so you could stand at the center of the field while confetti rained over you. But no matter what points were on the scoreboard, I couldn't stop the ache in the center of my chest.

This time it wasn't because I wasn't on the field. It was because I knew she wasn't up in the stands. So I clung to the anger. I clung to the unfairness and tried to put the look on her face out of my mind. If I let it in, it would bring me to my knees.

Guys were smiling and cheering, watching the plays intensely, like my life wasn't a pile of rubble sitting on the bench at the forty-yard line.

Shaking my head, I stared out at the field and willed the team to hold onto the lead for the victory they deserved. The victory they'd achieve without me.

The final pass flew through the air. Everyone on the bench shot up—including me—and we all screamed, shouting for the receiver to complete the pass.

Ezra grabbed onto my jersey so tightly the collar choked me. His gaze was transfixed on the field, and he might not even have known I was there.

The receiver turned and raised his arms in the air. The ball fell out of its arc and headed straight for him, center chest. Blocking happened all around him, and he ducked and dodged opponents. The ball that seemed to be in the air forever plummeted toward him.

The ball grazed the edges of his fingertips, so close to his grasp, when a defensive lineman plowed straight into him.

If I'd been out there, I could've stopped it. I could've

helped him complete the pass or recovered the ball. I'd have never let anyone get close enough to take him.

I cut my gaze down the sidelines to Mikelson, hating him with every breath and beat of my heart.

Silence burned through the air like a vacuum had descended on the stadium.

This time the slow-motion feeling was one of horror. My stomach dropped so deep it was like being on an out-of-control carnival ride.

The ball slipped straight out of his hands and into the opposing player's like he'd known it was going to happen. Their defense switched on a dime, blocking instead of tackling.

On the scoreboard, the clock glowed zero seconds remaining. This was the final play. Whatever happened here was the end for all of us.

Each step was one closer to our loss. The stands were half-silent, half-wild. Everyone at our back seemed to be holding their breath, then in a split second, they exploded, screaming for the player with the ball to be stopped.

The screams of joy and outrage merged, shaking the ground beneath my feet.

Mikelson stood feet away with his clipboard and his squad of assistant coaches.

On the field, diving tackles were sidestepped and blocked.

My vision tunneled. The unstoppable, head-on collision of our entire season ending mirrored the destruction I'd created in my own life, only now I was completely helpless. In my room, I might as well have been one of the guys blocking against my opponent, only it hadn't been a lineman I'd leveled, it had been Leona.

Every opening before the lineman slammed shut until

the moment he leaped through the air and smacked into the end zone marker. The refs conferred.

A mic was switched on, and the word boomed through the stadium as the head ref's arms shot up. "Touchdown!"

Our victory was plucked from the air and plunged straight into the serrated jaws of loss.

Silence pounded at my eardrums. Disbelief swallowed all the air from the stadium, gulping it down right along with our hope.

Mikelson turned and grabbed a bright orange water cooler, then launched it onto the field, spraying water everywhere. Next came the table flip. Paper cups were carried by the wind and flew all over everyone. This was a tantrum beyond all tantrums. I didn't see a man obsessed with excellence. This wasn't a man who was determined to work his team as hard as required in order to win. I saw a pathetic piece of shit who couldn't stand losing.

I stared down at my hands, clenching and unclenching my frozen fists. I let myself glance into the stands. Leona wasn't there, but my dad was. His face was a stoic mask of disappointment.

Hands grabbed my jersey and jerked me out of the way as a chair flew inches past my face.

My head whipped sideways while Mikelson continued his tirade.

Cole released his hold on me and stared at Mikelson. The emotions swirling off my friend were different than how the rest of the guys were reacting, but I couldn't place what it was. His Adam's apple bobbed, and the veins in his neck stood out a lot like Mikelson's, only he wasn't lashing out at everything and everyone.

Cole was destroyed. Welcome to the club. It looked like I'd gotten there a few days ahead of everyone else.

The rest of the team showered up, but I didn't need to. My skin was clammy, though it had nothing to do with exertion on the field. The locker room was filled with suffocating heartbreak. Despair permeated every inch of space. Escaping into the hallway, I leaned against the wall, closing my eyes and trying to forget everything that had just happened.

The chill from outside was concentrated out here, turning the cinderblock hallway into a wind tunnel. All around me, the sounds of celebration echoed like ghosts of what could've been. There was no escape from it. There was nowhere to turn.

A hand landed on my shoulder, and my eyes shot open. Disorientation gave way to recognition. Dad.

He wrapped his arms around me and squeezed me like only a dad could. I raised my arms and held onto him too, blinking back the welling moisture in my eyes.

"I'm sorry you came all this way to watch what happened out there." The burn of shame was as bad as it had been back in eighth grade. Each breath I took seemed to mash harder against the bruises and gashes inside me.

"I'm sorry it's the only game I got to see this season."

My shoulders sagged. Dread ricocheted inside of me. "I know. We should've been playing another one."

He patted me on the back and released me. "That's not what I meant. I should've been here for more before now."

"You're busy. Your schedule's always changing." The schedule I didn't want him to ever have to work again. He'd make his own hours. Be his own boss. But that dream was slipping through my fingers like grass clippings in the wind. Everything was collapsing around me, and I leaned against the wall so I didn't stagger under the weight of it.

"Still..." He shook his head. "That was a rough loss, son."

I dropped my head, unable to meet his gaze. The knot in my chest grew with each heartbeat. "I should've been out there."

He put his hand on my shoulder. "Why weren't you? Are you hurt? You never said anything about it."

Self-loathing rushed over me that I hadn't even thought to warn him. "I should've told you so you didn't waste the trip." I scrubbed my hands down over my face. But now I realized why. Why I hadn't wanted to break the news and tell him the truth. "I felt like if I didn't tell you, it wasn't really real. Mikelson benched me."

"Why? What happened? You've dedicated your every breath to this team. You won your first-string spot like I knew you would."

"I fucked up."

His body stiffened.

"I got mixed up with a girl." My stomach soured even talking about Leona like that. She was so much more than a girl, and what we'd had was beyond being *mixed up* with her. My throat tightened, and it was hard to think about her without breaking down.

I looked up at him.

His eyebrows were drawn together, and his head shook gently with mild confusion and concern. "Was she bad news? Get you involved in something illegal or against team policy?"

"She's President Oakes's daughter." She was all I thought about for months. In her own way, she'd pushed me to discover new things. She was the only person I felt like I could be totally myself around.

Silence. His hand fell from my shoulder. "I'm waiting for the mixed-up part."

"That's it. The coach and the president don't get along. Mikelson values loyalty above everything except for winning." My jaw tightened, and my fists clenched at my sides as anger reverberated through me once more. I held on to it to push aside the misery that was just waiting to tackle me back to the ground any second.

"He benched you during the biggest game of the season because you're dating the president's daughter?" Dad's eyes were filled with bewilderment and irritation.

I nodded, wishing numbness would set in to make this easier—less painful.

"Sounds to me like he values his ego over what's best for the team. You should've been out there." He bristled with indignation, just like a good dad should.

"I knew it was a possibility. Hell, it was a certainty, and I fucked up." I stared at the brushed concrete floor.

The locker room door flew open, and the coaching staff and team spilled out into the hall. Mikelson's voice boomed in the enclosed space. I'd probably have another mark against me for missing the beginning of his tirade.

"I've got to go." I couldn't look my father in the eye. "Love you, Dad. You've sacrificed everything to get me here. I'm sorry I let you down." I shot off the wall and hugged him tight for a flash before falling in line with the marching steps of the other players. Confessing everything to him didn't feel better. I couldn't hide from his disappointment now and pretend I hadn't fucked things up in every conceivable way. And there was no making any of it right.

"Reid!" My dad's voice was drowned out by the crashing waves in my head beating me against the jagged rock that had become my life.

The parking lot was still filled with revelers in their blue and yellow jerseys. They chanted the Fulton U fight song so loudly it shook the bus.

We'd lost. Our play-off run was ended. The championship had slipped through our fingers once again.

As we pulled out of the lot, FU fans celebrated and flipped us off.

The bus was funeral quiet during the long trip back to campus. The ride was our wake for the season and the blow to every player's draft potential.

Mikelson paced the aisles, grinding gravel into the still bleeding wounds we all carried. His voice was grenade loud in the bus. From the airport through takeoff to landing an hour and a half later, the fire of his words lashed through us.

Beside each player, he recounted every misstep. Every lost opportunity. Every failure.

Next to my seat, he stared down at me with his face contorted and moved on without another word. Somehow that was worse.

Staring ahead, I tried to retreat inside myself, but things were torn up in there too. Each time his gaze landed on me, I steeled myself so I didn't flinch.

We were lined up outside the bus in the campus stadium parking lot with our duffels over our shoulders when his voice finally gave out. That's the only reason he didn't have us there until midnight.

The drive to the house crammed into Cole's car was so silent that I wasn't sure any of us were breathing. Cole and Griff sat up front while Ezra, Hollis and I were wedged into the back. I stared out the window, taking in the dark, damp and dreary night as we rolled through the streets.

Campus was dead silent. The fan buses wouldn't arrive for a few more hours. More people who had witnessed our loss in person and could relay what it had felt like to be in the stadium when it happened.

Hollis dropped his head against the backseat headrest. "Maybe he ripped a few vocal cords tonight, and we don't have to hear his mouth for a while."

Griff grumbled, "If only we were that lucky. Tonight was the warm-up for how he plans on blowing up our lives for the next eight months. None of you remember last season?"

Cole turned down our street. "We all blocked it out. Just pretend it didn't happen, so we can drag our asses out there and repeat it all over again."

If only I had another do-over. If only I could repeat Christmas Day and how I'd handled things with Leona. I'd go back through this whole season taking the L, if it meant I could make that better.

Ezra checked his phone and leaned forward. "There's a bunch of food ready in the oven. I figured we'd be using it to celebrate or blow off steam. Steak, cheesy potatoes and no fucking broccoli."

I leaned back against the door. "You've had food in the oven since yesterday?"

He flicked the brim of his hat. "Yes, I'm a complete fucking moron."

My head was swimming with eight billion different thoughts, so maybe I'd missed how what he said made sense. "Then how's there hot food in our oven?"

"A friend did it for me." He turned off his phone screen.

Silence reigned in the car, this time not out of misery but shock.

Griff turned from the front seat. "Who's this friend we don't know about?"

Ezra leaned back, tugged down his hat, and folded his arms over his chest. "You guys aren't my only friends."

Cole looked at him through the rearview mirror. "Since when? You barely speak to anyone else, let alone hold a conversation long enough to have them qualify as a friend. And to trust them in our house when we're not there."

"It's not a big deal."

Hollis and Griff exchanged looks.

Whatever was going on with Ezra seemed to be giving him at least a sliver of comfort, and I didn't begrudge whatever it took to make that happen. Not that he wouldn't be pumped for every detail later.

Cole parked.

"Whatever. If you don't want the food, don't eat the food." Ezra climbed out of the car and slammed his door, rocking the whole thing.

The chance to tease him had been a momentary distraction. But then the fun blinked out like the lights being cut at the stadium and blanketing us in the dark emptiness again.

I popped Cole's trunk and handed off the guys' duffel bags then grabbed mine.

Halfway up the stairs to the porch, I glanced over my shoulder at the apartment block I hadn't had the guts to look at since the day Leona left my room. The lights were on. What was she doing? Who was she with? Was she hurting half as badly as I was?

It didn't feel possible.

I trudged the rest of the way up the stairs.

"Reid!"

I froze and shook my head. Turning, I dropped my bag off my shoulder.

Standing at the bottom of the wooden stairs was my dad.

"What are you doing here? Is something wrong? How— how'd you even get here?" His car idled at the curb with the headlights still on and the door open. Why would he be here when he'd just been halfway across the state? I tensed, preparing for another bomb. Maybe I'd jinxed myself by thinking things couldn't get worse.

"I drove." His lips quirked up in a semi-smile.

"Over four hours across the state." There wasn't any urgency or panic in his face. He stood there like he'd just felt like taking a multi-hour journey in the wrong direction of home on a whim.

"My son needed me." He jerked his head toward the car. "Come on. Let's go."

I dumped my bag inside, closed the door behind me and followed him to the street. "Dad, why don't we talk in the morning? You can have my bed, and I can crash on the couch."

"No, that's all right. I'm back into work tomorrow."

Back to a job he hated and wouldn't be able to leave because his son was a fuck-up. The guilt was back and kicked up the gnawing inside my chest another notch. "It's almost ten right now. You won't get in until almost five a.m."

"Then we'd better get a move on, so I can get some sleep before my shift at noon."

Bitter disappointment clawed at the back of my throat. He shouldn't have to live like this.

"Get in the car, son. Let's go for a drive."

I got into the car and kept my gaze straight ahead, unable to look at my dad.

He hopped in and drove us to an off-campus diner. It closed at midnight, so it didn't get hit with the campus crowd like the places that stayed open 24/7 or late enough to pick up the students needing to carb load after too much booze.

Inside, we sat at a booth. The place was mostly empty. A few older guys at the counter and three of the other thirty tables had people at them.

"I'll have a short stack, sausages, eggs scrambled hard and a pot of coffee."

The waitress took his menu and stared at me.

I hadn't even looked at it. Handing it back, I let my hands drop into my lap. "I'll just have a coffee."

"This late?" He scoffed. "You'll never get to sleep. He'll have the chocolate milk and the smiley."

When I thought the night couldn't get weirder, now my dad was ordering for me like I was in elementary school. "Dad, I'm not hungry and I haven't had chocolate milk since I was ten."

"Even more reason to get it now. Two chocolate milks to go with my coffee, please."

I sank deeper into the booth and tried to keep a grip on myself so I wasn't lost in the sea of despair threatening to swallow me up. If I lost it here, Dad might decide he needed to stay away from work longer, and it would put his job in jeopardy, and I could only destroy so many futures in a night. The limit had been reached. Adding another reason I'd fucked things up might throw me over the edge.

The waitress walked off and came back with a carafe of coffee and two off-white mugs. Dad stole mine.

I shot him a look.

"You'll never get to sleep if you start pounding caffeine right now and you look like you could use a solid night of rest." He filled his cup and added creamer and one sugar.

I dragged my fingers through my hair, massaging the pounding in my skull. "It's been a rough few weeks."

A tendril of steam broke over the tip of his nose as he took a sip. "Why didn't you tell me about them?"

Embarrassment. Disbelief. Failure. I didn't even have the words to articulate it all. It was hard enough thinking about everything that had happened, but saying the words...that felt impossible.

"You have enough on your plate."

"None of that matters if you're having a tough time. You've always had your eye on the prize to get you out of funks."

My head shot up, and I gritted my teeth. I let the anger mask my shame. "I told you I didn't want you to know I got benched, okay? That's why I didn't say anything."

His eyes bored into mine with an unreadable expression. "This girl you mentioned. You like her a lot?" He skated right past my anger, batting it aside like he could see straight through me.

My throat tightened, and I squeezed my fingers into my legs beneath the table. I couldn't deny it, not even to myself. "Yeah." I shoved my hands against my eyes to stem the moisture building there.

His face and voice gentled. "Love her?"

The word struck me like lightning, and I squeezed my eyes shut, nodding.

He made a noise of understanding. "Was she at the game?"

"No, she wouldn't be. She hates me now." My throat felt like gravel was being shoved down it.

He wouldn't understand.

From every story he'd told about Mom, their whole courtship had been sunshine and rainbows. They'd been high school sweethearts and blissfully happy.

"You really like her, probably love her, and she hates

you. Why would she hate you?" Confusion rang in his words like this should all be a simple situation.

"Because I broke up with her after the coach found out about us." I choked on the words, hating myself more.

He sank back in his seat. "Why would you do something like that?"

"Because my future depended on it. Not that it mattered. Coach didn't let me off the bench anyway." Shame boiled in my stomach that I'd sold out my feelings for Leona to satisfy the coach. The kick to my already bloodied teeth was that it didn't even matter. It almost yanked a humorless laugh from my throat.

"You broke up with her to try to get your spot back on the team." Disappointment radiated from each syllable.

"What other option did I have?" Irritation bristled through me and made my skin itchy.

"Stand up to your coach and tell him where he can shove his loyalty bullshit."

"Like you, Dad? Like when you marched into Steve's office and stood up to him, and he fired you and had you escorted from the building? We almost lost the house. You haven't been able to work as a mechanic in nearly six years. You're dead tired most days." The bitterness of my power-lessness to fix this situation soured my gut.

"And?" He dropped that bomb, which whistled in my ears.

I slammed my hand against the vaguely sticky table, and the salt and pepper shakers by the wall rattled. "And it's bullshit. I've worked hard and was supposed to keep my focus. How do I stand up to Mikelson? He's my coach. I need to play. We need me to play."

His loose fist rapped the table, and his intense expres-sion brimmed with understanding. "Because it's all you've ever wanted to do. We watched games together, and I saw how you busted your ass back in high school to make the team. You love it."

If only it were that easy. "It's not just about loving the game, Dad. There's a plan." I slapped my hand with the back of the other. "I've always had a plan. I'd have more money than I needed. You'd get set up somewhere new. Somewhere better, if you wanted. You'd get your own garage and fuck Steve and the lies he's told people about you. You'd never steal a dime. So it'll all be a big fuck you to every one of them."

He stared at me from across the booth like he wasn't sure who I was. The waitress came back with our food.

The whipped cream smiley face and chocolate chip eyes and nose on my pancake mocked me from the plate.

Dad's head dropped, and he shook it slowly back and forth. "I've failed you, son."

I jerked so hard my stomach hit the table. "What? No, don't say that, Dad. You've been through so much. You haven't failed me. I'm the fuck-up."

He looked up at me with a pained expression. "If that's the lesson you took away from the Steve situation, then I really did. Because what I was trying to show you was that you stand up for what's right. You stood up for that littler kid, and I was never prouder."

"But I lost." With ripped jeans, bleeding knees and a busted lip that everyone on my walk home could see.

"It wasn't about losing—it was about doing what you know is right. The decision you make so you can look yourself in the mirror in the morning. I've never regretted for a day what I did. His son was a bullying little asshole. And I'd go back and confront him in his office a million more times and still never regret it." His Adam's apple bobbed, and his eyes glistened. "I don't regret that decision and haven't regretted any that came after. Were things harder, sure, but I could always hold my head high knowing I showed you how important that was. It's all I've ever wanted for you. To not look back on a profound decision about your life and wish you'd been stronger to make a different choice. For you to live a life without regrets."

The words hit like a sledgehammer to my chest. I couldn't say I'd lived my life that way—not now. Maybe not ever again.

I'd make a choice that felt like I was selling my soul. Before everything had been wrapped up in the game. It had been wrapped up in the attention and the glory. But that was before Leona. That was before she'd buried herself in my soul. The loss I'd been feeling hadn't been the loss of the game. It was losing her.

35

REID

My dad's words had rumbled through my head for almost a week before I got up the nerve to finally make my move. Every night I'd stare up at the ceiling, wishing I had the key to unlock the answer that would fix all this in a snap, but it never came. Everything came crashing down even harder when I opened her Christmas present. A display box made of Lego and glass for my draft hat and jersey with a small plaque with my name and beneath it, "First Found Draft Pick".

I had to take the first step. A leap. I had to do whatever it took to repair what I'd shattered.

The smell of coffee billowed out the open door at the back of The Grind House near the agricultural building. It wasn't as busy as some of the others on campus. Inside, the sounds of the milk frother and steam weren't relaxing at all, but it didn't stop at least fifty students from setting up shop all over the place, mainly congregated around the outlets.

Taylor spotted me before I saw her.

She jumped up and launched herself over the coffee table, rushing to me. "What the hell are you doing here?"

"I wanted to talk to her."

"Like hell." She crossed her arms over her chest before peeking behind her. "It's been almost two weeks since whatever you said to her. You lose and now you show up thinking she'll just what? Forget you broke her heart? I couldn't even watch the game," she spat.

That was monumental for Taylor, and it made me feel even worse. Just when I thought the flood had been set, nope, a new basement door opened.

"She told you." Of course she would've. I deserved it, and at least she had Ashley and Taylor in her corner to back her up, even if it meant they didn't want to be my friends anymore.

"No." She barred her arms across her chest. "She hasn't said a word, but Ashley and I aren't blind."

Even now she was trying to keep things quiet, just like she'd said she would. Hello, new trap door in the floor. "I fucked up." I needed Leona to see I knew that.

"No shit. You should go."

"I need to talk to her. A few minutes is all I'm asking for." Ashley had been in sentry mode when I'd stopped by the apartment earlier. I wouldn't be surprised if they didn't take up tag team guard duty over her. I was glad they were being good friends and also annoyed as hell.

"Unless it's words to a time travel spell, I don't think she wants to hear from you right now."

"Maybe I need to hear it from her." I didn't expect whatever I said to fix everything, but if there was a glimmer of hope, I wasn't going to stop chasing.

"Taylor, apparently that trick only works for you because he charged me for the extra chocolate syrup. I think he might've actually given me less than normal." Leona held up Taylor's iced coffee, staring into the clear plastic cup. Her smile fell when she saw me.

"Hey, Leona." I plunged my hands into my pockets so I didn't reach for her. My heart raced, aching in my chest at being so close to her after so many weeks. I'd set up on the couch in the living room no matter how much anyone grumbled for the chance at a glimpse of her, which hurt even more because I knew she wanted nothing to do with me. And why should she? Staring into her deep brown eyes, I felt like my tongue was made of lead, and my mouth was filled with sand.

"Reid." She gently shook her head and wiped her face of all expression. Holding her hand out, she passed the cup to Taylor, who continued to glare daggers into the side of my face. "Sorry about the playoffs." Her gaze shot to mine, then back down to her cup before she rounded the chairs and sat down.

I moved to follow, and Taylor blocked my path. Frustration rippled through me, and for a split second, I considered picking her up and moving her out of my way. But Leona probably wouldn't like that, and Taylor would scratch the shit out of me.

She jammed her finger into the center of my chest. "I'll give you two minutes. If you make her cry, I'll break both your knees, starting lineup or not." Shoving her straw into her drink, she aggressively sucked it and pointed two fingers at her eyes and back at me. "I'll be right over here, Leona, if you need me."

Leona didn't look up.

I sat on the edge of the seat beside hers.

Her body tensed in the oversized burnt orange chair.

Dread fell over me like a three-hundred-pound lineman.

I hated that I'd made her this uncomfortable. From the first moment we'd run into each other, she'd been smiles and teasing. Even when we were trying to stay apart, there had been a relaxation that was easy to fall into. Now I wondered if I could repair the damage. Unable to take my eyes off her, I searched for the words.

Her hair was tied in two braids that hung over her shoulders just like the first day we'd met. Back when things were so uncomplicated, when she was just her and I was just me. We didn't have the weight of expectations and responsibilities and loyalties holding us back from one another.

A binder and notebook sat on the wide arm of the chair, but she wasn't focused on them.

Her fingers drummed along the top of her cup, and she took a sip, then sucked in a sharp breath.

"Too hot?" I cursed inwardly. That was the best first opener.

She grimaced and made a noise that I chose to believe was a reply.

I scooted forward more. "I—I wanted to come talk to you."

"You said all you had to back in your room." Her throat worked up and down, not in a swallow, but maybe like she was choking down biting words I'd thrown at her all over again.

Anguish at the pain I'd caused her ripped through me, and my throat tightened. "No, I didn't. I was mixed up."

"You seemed to know exactly what you were doing. What you were saying." She leveled her gaze at me, and I met it, not wanting to hide anything from her anymore.

"I fucked up." I cleared my throat, trying to loosen the brick lodged there. "A one hundred percent fuck-up, and I've wished so many times that I could go back and change things. I've wished I had done things differently that night. I never meant to hurt you." I stared at her one hand where it rested just above her knee. Swallowing, I reached across the chasm between us to her hand. Would she even let me?

She sank back in her chair and crossed her leg, putting more space between us.

No, she wouldn't. Grief burrowed its way deep into my chest.

A small huff of a laugh escaped her lips. Her gaze skimmed across the room. "This is the first time we've been out together in public on campus."

I dropped my chin but held her gaze.

Her expression was distant and poised, like she was up on stage beside her dad, waiting for another speech to be over so she could politely clap, then leave.

"It's not nearly as scary as I thought," she said. "No one's even looking. Pretty self-important of me to think anyone would care at all. Like STFU Dirt would be lurking around the corner or stalking me to expose every secret I had." Another huff, and she took a sip of her drink, this time with only a slight grimace. "You should go though." Her gaze was pointed this time and straight at me.

The stalled words came rushing back as I saw my chance with her closing like a slamming door.

"There's nothing I can say to take back what I said."

"No, there isn't."

"But I'd like to show you—"

"Reid, the season is over, but you still have another left. What? Do we keep trying to date in secret? I—" Her mouth snapped shut. "I can't do that anymore with secrets and lies. You've worked hard to get your spot on the team. I complicate that. The plans you have for after graduation are bigger than whatever we had."

"It's that easy for you to walk away?" Defeat blared in my ears so loudly I couldn't even hear my own racing heartbeat.

Her chin jutted out. "I didn't walk out, Reid. You shoved me out and let me know exactly what you thought about what we were doing. Do you want me to get hysterical and fling myself at you, so happy you changed your mind?"

She felt different. Distant. Detached.

I did this. I saw the look in her eyes when I cut her down with my words. I knew they hurt. And how many times since she'd walked out the door had I prayed for the numbness to make it easier?

She was numb now, and it was my fault. Defeated once again, I tried to look for any way to salvage this.

"I only wanted to apologize."

"And you have." The paper-thin smile she flashed showed a crack in the façade. A split second where the mask fell, and I saw what was going on inside. It gave me hope that she hadn't shut me out completely.

"Can we have dinner or a coffee sometime?"

"Why are you doing this?" The words were strained, almost desperate.

"All I want—"

"I don't care what you want. You decided. You treated me like shit, Reid, when all I wanted to do was be there for you. And you told me exactly where I fell in your life's hierarchy of importance. I don't blame you. Me against a contract worth millions—it's no contest. In your position, I probably wouldn't pick me either, so don't try to reverse that decision. You're still a football player trying to get his big break."

I hated myself for making her think my feelings for her

could be reduced to zeros in a bank account. "I shouldn't have snapped at you like that."

"But it was the truth—is the truth. Us being together wasn't a good idea from the beginning." Another humorless laugh. "We agreed and decided we wouldn't, but..." She toyed with the edge of the plastic lid to her cup. "You made your choice, and it was the right one. It hurt. I won't pretend it doesn't—didn't hurt, but I always knew if the choice came down to me or football, it would be football."

"Leona..." That's who I was, wasn't it? It's what I'd repeated to myself. My eye had been on the prize, but it was the wrong one. She was the only prize I wanted. The only one that mattered.

"You've known me for six months. You've been a football player for over six years. It's a dream with a whole lot more zeroes behind it than I could ever hope to make in a life-time, let alone make it worthwhile for you to give up your dream."

"It's not about the money." I could see it all so clearly now. How easy my dad's decision had been. I'd always doubted it and could never understand it. Now I did, only maybe it was too late.

"Then the fame and glory. I saw you at the game. You wanted it. You looked out on the field and saw yourself out there. I can't take that from you. I also can't forget what you said and how you said it." She retreated back into herself. "No hard feelings." Her swallow was audible. There was a sheen in her eyes, and I was at a loss on where to go from here. But from the look on her face, there wasn't anywhere to go right now.

She was closed off to me, and I didn't know how to get her back. Helplessness sucked me into the void left behind when I was shut out of Leona's life—maybe for good.

Taylor hovered over my shoulder.

I shoved up from my seat and marched out of the coffee shop, determined to show her that everything she'd said about football and my future didn't matter. None of that would stop me from wanting her. From needing her. Now I just had to prove it.

36

LEONA

I'd prayed for the numbness to come back after Reid and I spoke. Sitting in the coffee shop across from Taylor, I'd used every ounce of strength not to break down and lose it.

After ten minutes, I gave up on trying to get myself under control and went back to the apartment. Everything shut down, like my brain was protecting me from the intensity of my feelings.

But there was no disconnection now. I couldn't stop feeling everything. Almost like the faucet was cranked from a trickle to a torrent, and I was going to drown in the deluge.

My eyes were bloodshot and puffy. My nose was raw from the three boxes of tissues I'd gone through. My cheeks stung from the tears that had tracked down them for what felt like eons. At least the throbbing in my head had lessened after an hour of holding off the waterworks.

It hadn't helped that Mom called a few times like she could sense what I was going through. I wanted to talk to her. I wanted to listen to the sage words of advice she always seemed to have, but it felt like a betrayal. It felt like everything she was to me was a lie, and I didn't want comfort from a lie. That's what would've happened if I'd agreed to Reid's ask for dinner or a coffee. It would've only been a matter of time before he realized it wasn't worth it, and then I'd be in even deeper than I already was. It was difficult to imagine how much harder I could fall and be hurt, and I didn't want to find out.

Staying in my apartment was slowly unraveling me. Every time I left and walked to my car or the bus over the next few days, I'd catch a glimpse of Reid's house, and it was at least another half hour before I could get the tears to stop.

I'd escaped to my dad's house so Ashley and Taylor wouldn't have to hear me crying all the time. I couldn't handle their helpless and pitying looks anymore. Plus, there were plenty of tubs of ice cream and packages of Oreos in the cabinets at Dad's place.

And at least there I was saved from those seemingly unstoppable breakdowns, but it didn't mean it didn't hurt. It didn't mean it didn't hurt all the time.

Dad was in a ton of meetings and probably wouldn't be back until tonight. Maybe I could get myself together by then. I could muster a smile and be glad his job was safe. Inside, I was happy for him, but it was hard for that ray of sunshine to slice through the fog of despair lodged in my chest.

I lay on my bed in my room, curled up against my pillows. A gentle knock rattled the door. Moving was not an option. Another knock, then the walking knock that happened when the door was being opened.

Dad was giving me maximum cover up time in case I wasn't clothed.

I wiped my face against my pillow as if one look at me wouldn't tell my dad all he needed to know.

So much for having time to put on a brave face.

I should be happy, ecstatic even, that his job was safe now that Reid had lost. And that hurt me. I never wanted Reid to have to lose, but for life to work out for two people I cared about, one of them couldn't win.

"Amy said you came back here and looked upset."

Damn Amy and her keen skills of observation. She'd been coming out of Dad's office and reminded me about the field house groundbreaking ceremony. I figured the sweatshirt hood would've been enough to keep her from seeing my bloodshot eyes as I sprinted up the stairs away from her. I'd been wrong.

"I'm fine." I rubbed at my face with the sleeve of my shirt and winced at the sting. "You're busy, Dad. You don't have to babysit me. I'm good." I tried to keep my voice even rather than an emotional, tear-clogged mess.

The edge of the bed dipped, and a gentle hand rested on my comforter-covered leg. Dad sighed and patted my calf. "It's times like these I wish your mother were here."

"No, Dad!" I shot up with the pillow clutched against my chest and wiped at my eyes. "How could you even say that?"

His eyes widened, scanning my face.

I dropped my chin as if that would somehow shield me from his gaze. From the look on his face, I probably looked like a swollen sea creature that had been decaying on the beach for a week.

He squeezed my leg again. "I'm sure she'd have better advice about this type of thing. I'd imagine it has to do with a boy?"

"Why would I ever want relationship advice from her?" My heart rate spiked with guilt. I hated that I'd missed her earlier. That I'd longed to talk to her so she could help me figure this all out.

He looked at me with sadness in his eyes. "Sometimes people are better at giving great advice than they are at following it themselves."

Taking a few deep breaths, I tried to calm myself. "I can't talk to her right now. I don't know if I ever want to talk to her again."

He sighed and scooted closer. "Leona, I love having you here. I missed you so much for so long, and I didn't ever think we'd get to hang out like we have been. I'm so happy I can get to know the young woman you've become. But I don't want you to cut your mother out of your life out of misguided loyalty to me."

I slammed the pillow onto my lap. "Are you serious? Everything is her fault. She lied and moved continents away. You were here all alone." Anger and guilt hit me with a one-two punch.

His fingers brushed the pattern on my comforter. "What happened between your mother and me in our marriage was between your mother and me." He held my gaze without a trace of bitterness. "It never had anything to do with you, Leona-Loo."

I opened my mouth, ready to launch into another tirade, when he butted in.

"It affected you profoundly, I know that, but your mother has always been a great mother to you."

"It doesn't mean she can just—"

"You punishing her for her mistakes that I forgave a long time ago is only going to hurt you more. I know what it feels like to be on the other end of the shutout, and I wouldn't ever wish it on your mother."

Remorse gnawed through my sternum.

His Adam's apple bobbed. "You made your choices too. I know they were based on incorrect information."

Massive understatement.

"But she never got in the way of us spending time together or speaking. You were a teenager and you made that choice."

A sob caught in my throat.

He covered my hands with his. "I'm not angry with you either. I need you to know that. I'm not angry with you, I don't hate you, and I'm not harboring some deep-seated resentment either. It's in the past, and being angry with your mother to deflect your guilt isn't serving anyone.

"The world isn't nearly as black and white as we'd like it to be, Leona. People make mistakes. People we love make mistakes. But our job as someone who loves them back is to decide if it's forgivable. We have to decide if they've truly changed, and that's scary. It opens us up to hurt again. Sometimes it's a door you need to close for yourself, but sometimes it's a second chance they need."

His capacity for forgiveness blew me away. I'd want to hang onto the anger. I'd want to never give them the satisfaction, but when I saw him, he was happy. Maybe a bit lonely—although with Amy around, I wasn't sure how much longer that would be the case—but things seemed like they rolled off him. I'd always thought maybe that was just the way he was, but making that choice intentionally? It felt infinitely harder, and I didn't know if I had it in me.

"I feel like she stole those years from us."

"I know, Leona." He cupped my cheek. "It was rough, and I can't tell you there weren't times I wasn't angry and so profoundly hurt by what happened. But if I'd let it all eat me up inside or turn me into a bitter shell, what kind of dad would you be coming back to? What kind of man would I have been for the next woman I fell in love with? It hasn't been easy, but I knew you'd come back to me, kiddo, and I know there's a future out there for me that I need to be a better man for."

A sob clawed its way out of my throat. I lunged forward and wrapped my arms around him.

"I'm so sorry, Dad."

He held onto me until my tears soaked through his shirt.

My chest had been cracked open by his words and his forgiveness. I'd always thought that maybe, somewhere deep down, he hated me. And even now, once I told him everything about Reid, I knew he'd be disappointed and probably angry. After all, I'd proven I was more similar to my mom than I'd wanted to admit.

The confession weighed heavy on my chest. "I've been lying to you."

His arms tightened around me for a flash, and he leaned back with shock on his face. "You have?"

I nodded, grabbing the pillow and plopping it in front of me like it would be a barrier against his disappointment. "Yes, I've been dating a football player. The one who flipped you off after the award ceremony last semester. We liked each other, and then we found out who the other was and decided to stop seeing each other and then...well, we started again.

"He didn't realize who you were when he flipped you off and he's actually really nice. The whole team is. They've all been really nice to me. Except their coach, who you already know is a colossal douche. Half the things you think the team has done are all him. They mostly hate him." The words tumbled out of me in a confession avalanche before I could stop them.

He sat in stunned silence, staring at me like I was a stranger.

My stomach roiled. "I didn't mean to keep it from you,

but I knew the trouble the coach was causing, and it seemed like so often when we talked, you were going on about how much the team disrupted campus and how terrible they were and how everyone was so obsessed with the team. I didn't want to disappoint you." As I talked, my shoulders crept higher and higher in a turtle impersonation while I waited for the fallout from my confession.

"Okay, wow." He dropped his arm and stared straight ahead.

"I'm sorry, Dad."

"How long have you two been seeing each other?" He looked over his shoulder.

"Sort of since move-in day, but maybe starting at homecoming. Only we're not together anymore." It still felt raw, like he'd broken up with me a minute ago and five years ago all at once. This was a lot of hurt to cram into the past couple weeks.

Realization dawned on his face, and he glanced over at my nightstand stacked with three dirty bowls. "Hence the tears and the ice cream."

I nodded, trying to keep the tears from my eyes. Why couldn't my tear ducts have an off switch?

His eyebrows furrowed, and he stared at me intently. "Did he hurt you in some way?"

I grabbed his arm and shook my head so hard the pounding throb returned to the center of my forehead. That was the last thing I needed my dad to believe—that Reid might've hurt me physically. He had hurt me emotionally, for sure, pretty much detonated a bomb in my heart, and I still wanted to cover for him. "We broke up after the first play-off game. The coach barged in here and caught us kissing."

"You were kissing here? In this house?" He pointed at the floor with shock-wide eyes.

I cringed. "He snuck in a little before you went to take the present to Amy." What was the point in lying now?

"I see." He sighed again. "And William waltzed into the house once again?"

I nodded, thankful his mind wasn't focused on what Reid and I might've been doing alone in the house. "I was walking Reid to the door. He kissed me. The coach marched in, saw us and benched Reid. It's why we kept things a secret. I didn't want to disappoint you, and he didn't want to get benched, but it's all happened anyway."

"You've been dealing with a lot on your own, huh?" He turned to me with a soft, thoughtful expression.

I rubbed my nose with the back of my hand. "Kind of."

He sighed. "I'm not angry about you dating a football player, and the only disappointment I have is that you felt you had to lie in the first place."

"Sorry," I croaked, overwhelmed with relief that he wasn't angry.

He patted my leg. "You wouldn't be this upset if he didn't mean a lot to you."

I squeezed my lips shut.

"It's a scary thing being in love."

"I—"

"I may not be your mom, but I can see all the signs now. Did you break things off or did he?"

"He did." The words burned my throat.

He tsked, shaking his head. "Maybe he's not as smart as I hoped he was to snag a catch like you." His attempt to drag a smile out of me was transparent and made him the most loveable dad ever.

"He tried to talk to me yesterday. He tried to apologize,

but I didn't want to hear it." Inside, it felt like my heart was being pulled apart, muscle thread by muscle thread.

He made his noise of deep thought.

"I won't say it's not scary, and I'm not saying there's not a chance he'll disappoint you, but it might do you both good to hear him out. You don't have to forgive him and forget he hurt you, but you can't make that choice until you listen to what he's trying to say."

The risk...it already felt like my chest had been sawed apart. What happened if I heard him out, forgave him, fell even harder this time and he broke my heart? "How do I know if I believe he won't hurt me again?" It felt scarier than anything I'd faced before.

He covered my hands with his and gave me a sympathetic pat. "There's always that chance. For any of us. Nothing is ever a guarantee, but you have to decide if what you feel for him is worth that risk."

Dad hugged me again and let me know dinner would be ready in an hour.

I was left to reflect on what he had said. The leap I'd be taking would put my heart on the line once again. It was already battered and bruised, and I didn't know how I'd make it through the pain again. I'd also never felt for anyone what I'd felt for him. It all boiled down to: was I willing to take a risk on Reid again, knowing what I knew now and how I felt about him?

37

LEONA

The wind chapped my cheeks as I stood on the riser in front of the open patch of earth behind us.

I breathed into my hands, having once again forgotten my gloves. It was a reminder of Reid. Of his heater sabotage and attempt at getting closer to me. I hadn't worked up the courage to knock on his door since I talked to my dad a few days ago. My walks into the apartment had been slower, hoping to maybe see him on the street, but at this point, I couldn't fault him for avoiding me. I'd made my stance on letting him say his piece clear. Guilt knocked around inside my chest. "When do they start building?"

Amy leaned closer with her tablet in hand. "April." Other than her rosy cheeks, she looked perfectly put together as always. How did she knot her scarf like that? It perfectly puffed out of the opening in her camel coat and matched her gray gloves.

"Then why are we standing out here freezing our butts off in January?"

Dad tugged my ear with an amused smile. "Because this

was the only slot we could find for the groundbreaking in everyone's schedules."

I gently bounced on the balls of my feet, trying to build warmth, and slid my hands back into my pockets.

Davenport, the board member who'd interrupted Reid and me on the field, droned on from the podium with the school seal on the front. "This new field house for the athletics department will breathe new life into a decades-old facility."

He launched into a story about the building and attending STFU a million years ago and how when he was on the volleyball team that watching the football team on the practice field was some of his fondest memories.

The crowd was restless. Their eyes kept darting to the doors leading to the gym. I'd stolen a couple cookies before we started, but right now, I wanted to get my hands on the hot chocolate. At this point, I'd dunk my hands in it. Inside there was a carnival's worth of food, and I couldn't blame everyone for their expressions that screamed *is this over yet?*

Davenport finished speaking, and it was my dad's turn. I clapped with numb fingers before shoving them back into my pockets.

"As always, we value what the athletics department brings to this campus. The field house will provide five of the athletics teams with upgraded facilities."

Mikelson grumbled loud enough that I could hear him from ten feet away. If it didn't have to do with football, he didn't give a shit.

"While this season didn't end as many of us would've hoped, there's always next year." Dad knew how much it meant to the students, and despite his misgivings about the team and football overshadowing everything else, he hated to see everyone so disappointed. He wanted the STFU community to get their win. He stepped back from the podium and held out his arm, motioning Coach Mikelson forward with a huge grin.

The coach looked over his shoulder and glared at us.

Dad and I linked arms and smiled and waved back. We'd taken the *kill him with kindness* route. Dad had even invited him over for dinner next week to discuss how they might better address the needs of the football players. Mikelson had stood in rigor mortis shock for five seconds before grumbling that he was busy.

Dad leaned closer. "Nothing brings people out like the promise of free food. I'm not above a little bribery." He chuckled.

More students filled the area, and sprinkled among them were some familiar faces. Football players. My heart raced, and I took deep breaths to calm myself. It made sense they'd be here. The coach had probably told them they had to show up. But it also meant there was a chance—

My breath froze in my throat.

Reid arrived with the other guys and slowly inched his way forward through the crowd, his gaze locked onto mine.

Heat rose on my cheeks, and I was pretty sure steam was rolling off me straight out of the collar of my coat.

The speeches were wrapping up, and my eyes kept darting to him. Every time, he'd moved closer like a weeping angel in *Dr. Who*, only I wasn't gripped with an intense and irrational fear by his movements.

My heart skipped like a stone across the lake.

He jogged up the stairs and nodded to my dad, who nodded back.

Shock rocketed through me, and I wobbled a little. What in the ever-loving hell was going on?

"I know you're hungry, so I'll make this quick."

He leaned to the side to look at the line of people behind the podium before settling on Mikelson. "Thank you, Coach Mikelson. I appreciate your dedication to the team and how hard you push us. All I ever wanted to do was be on a team like this, one where the other guys were like my family, and every day we pushed each other to be better."

His gaze swung back to me.

Tingles traced their way along my skin as his eyes filled with moisture.

"But there's also a time when you realize what's truly important and how to live your life without regret. Someone showed me this and they're up here right now. I made a huge mistake. I've never been happier than I've been with you, and you showed me that I can have more than one dream. I promise I'll never take you for granted again and will cherish every moment we have together."

I locked my knees so I didn't go staggering back.

Someone shouted from the crowd. "It's President Oakes, isn't it?"

That got a few laughs.

"Not quite." He grinned before sobering and leaning closer to the mic. "Leona, I have a very important question to ask." With long strides, he left the podium and crossed the stage to me.

Mikelson caught his arm.

I clenched my fists at my sides, wanting to tackle that jerk.

Reid turned to face me fully. "Leona Larson-Oakes, will you be my girlfriend?"

Shocked to soaring, my heart raced like it was running toward him. And the tears I'd thought I'd run out of threatened to spill over, only now they weren't from my ragged wounds, but the soothing balm of Reid's words.

From the inside of his jacket, he pulled out a clear, crinkly package. In his palm, he held out an individually wrapped cookie that usually had a smiley face, but instead of the face, it had the initials L and R iced onto it. I glanced from him back down to the delicately decorated cookie as Reid's image swam in front of my watery eyes.

Mikelson stepped forward and spoke through gritted teeth. "Think very carefully about your future, son."

Reid's gaze didn't waver from mine. Determination and adoration were etched all over his face, from the almost dimples to the gentle lift of the corner of his lips. "I have. And I already have a dad who's taught me everything I need to know about my future."

The wind stung the tears of happiness in my eyes. I couldn't believe he was truly here in front of everyone—in front of his coach—telling them how much I meant to him. Showing me how much I meant to him. My throat clogged from the emotions whirling around inside me.

Voices rose in the crowd. Breaking away from Reid's gaze, I looked toward the ruckus.

The rest of the team, headed by Cole, Hollis, Griff and Ezra, marched onto the stage. Were they here to drag him away for putting his future in jeopardy? Those were the kinds of friends they were. They'd try to save him from himself.

Reid and I exchanged looks. He looked just as confused as I probably did.

"What's going on?" I whispered.

"I have no idea."

Cole stepped forward and handed me an identical cookie to Reid's. "Leona Larson-Oakes, will you be my girlfriend?"

I stared at him, stunned. Next, Hollis repeated the

phrase and handed off another cookie. Each football player stepped up and placed the cookie in the growing pile in my hands—then cradled in my arms when it got to be too many. Some wore amused expressions, others, like Ezra, were more stoic, but they all nodded to Reid when they walked back off the stage and stood out front.

Hollis hopped up on stage and took the mic. "Leona, we're all waiting for your answer."

No longer on the verge of tears, I held back my laughter. Might as well give the campus something to talk about. Juggling my armful of cookies, I marched over to the mic Hollis held out for me and spoke into it as I stared at Reid. "Yes, my answer is yes."

The whole team down below cheered along with the rest of the students.

Behind me, I could hear Mikelson's teeth grinding. I checked over my shoulder to make sure he wasn't poised to shove me off the stage.

Davenport stepped forward and clapped his hand onto Mikelson's shoulder with a big grin. "I'm not sure what's happening, but it's great to see the whole team showing solidarity together, don't you think, Will?"

"It's what I've taught them."

"I'm sure this'll make things easier next season, especially with this young man on the field. You were sorely missed during those last couple games. I'm sure whatever issue there was is all cleared up now, isn't it?" Davenport jostled Mikelson and kept his wide smile. "It's a great team you've got, Will. The board can't wait to see them *all* shine next season."

I'd been around my dad and his meetings enough to know how the game of academic politics was played. Mikelson's ace in the hole with a season win was gone. He was being put on notice, and it couldn't have happened to a nicer guy.

Amy produced a felted container out of nowhere for me to dump the cookies into. Her laughter wasn't completely smothered, and even my dad looked entertained by the whole display.

"I'll make sure these get back to the house." She pinched her lips together, but it couldn't stop the shake of laughter in her chest. Her professional façade cracked a little, and it was great to see her laughing, even if she was trying to pretend she wasn't.

"Thanks, Amy."

I leaned in, whispering in Reid's ear, "You do know now everyone on campus is going to think I'm sleeping with the whole football team."

He gazed at me with his half dimple smile, and my whole body flooded with so much happiness that I nearly floated off the stage. "They can think whatever they want. But I know I've only got eyes for you. I love you, Leona."

I gasped. "I love you too." Wrapping my arms around his neck, I kissed him, finally letting my heart open completely. It was scary, but I trusted that whatever life threw at us in the future, we'd face it together.

A throat cleared right beside us.

We jumped apart, and I covered my mouth with my hand. Oh god, I'd been making out with Reid in front of my dad. I'd just professed my love for the first time ever in front of my dad. I winced and wanted to crawl under the stage. Maybe grab the shovel they'd used for the groundbreaking and bury myself.

Reid didn't let me pull away though. He clasped his hand around mine and held on tight.

My dad stared at us with a hint of amusement flitting

across his face. "If you two are done now, we can get everyone inside for the food." He raised his voice louder for the last part.

We stood on the stage as the crowd dispersed and rushed through the gym doors to the food. Dad and Amy walked off laughing with one another, and his arm reached around to hold her shoulder before he snatched it back.

I wanted him to be happy, and she made him happy. The same went for Amy, who had to be one of the kindest people I knew. Maybe I'd have to see about helping them both along—not that I was a love or relationship expert by any stretch of the imagination.

Mikelson and Davenport were also deep in conversation, headed in the opposite direction.

"Are you sure about this?" I asked Reid as I chewed on the edge of my lip.

"Positive." His eyes shone with certainty, and he gently pressed just below my lip to free it from my teeth.

"Did you know all the guys were going to show up?"

Cole popped up behind Reid and grabbed his shoulders, rocking him back and forth. "He had no clue."

I stared, and my mouth hung open. The frigid breeze whipped around so hard my teeth ached. "You were totally willing to come up here and make that speech all by yourself?" A tingle spread through my chest, warming my whole body.

"I'm all in and I'll never run away from what we could be again, Leona." He pressed his finger against my chin to close my mouth.

"But, Reid—"

"It's done. Unless you want to get rid of me." A flicker of doubt flashed in his eyes.

"No, of course not." I tugged him forward by his jacket

and kissed him again. Letting him go, I looked at the rest of the guys with my cheeks aching from my wide smile.

Hollis pouted with his arms crossed over his chest like a petulant five-year-old. "What about us? We're the ones who pulled this off."

Reid shot him a playful glare. "How did you get everyone here?"

Griff waved an extra cookie in the air. "You had to order a shit load of these to get the custom design. I found the box." He shrugged.

Ezra ripped open another cookie package. "With the promise of free cookies, embarrassing Mikelson and showing him if he wanted to unfairly punish one of us, it meant the whole team wouldn't put up with it, they were all in."

Just when I thought Reid couldn't have a better group of friends, they one-upped it. They all put themselves on the line for him. They rallied the team around us—for him. I kissed all four of them on their cheeks. "Thanks for looking out for Reid. It's great to know he's got friends like you guys backing him up."

They grinned at him and responded in unison, "Always."

"I don't know where my basket of cookies disappeared to. And I'd love one of those cookies. Who wants to share?" I held out my hand, and the four players looked at each other, then jumped off the stage, running away.

"Jerks!"

Reid spun me around.

"Can you believe they won't share?"

He tugged his hand out of his pocket and waved a cookie in front of me.

"You have another one."

He nodded and gently tugged apart the seal. "I'd planned on eating the whole box if you'd said no."

"Does that mean that's for me?"

"That depends," he teased. "What do I get for it?" He tilted his head with his almost dimples doing their thing, and traced the warm backs of his fingers against my cheek.

A coil of heat throbbed between my legs. "I'm sure I can think of something."

He grinned and held the cookie out for me to take a bite.

I took a big chomp and let the buttery, sugary goodness fill my mouth.

"I could watch you eat these all day," he said.

"Then it's a good thing you bought a truckload."

"That's if the guys don't get to them first."

"Then maybe we should go back to your house to keep them safe."

His arm tightened around me, and hunger swirled in his eyes. "I think that's an excellent idea."

We rushed off the stage hand-in-hand. The cold didn't feel nearly as sharp with Reid's fingers curled around mine. And the heat of anticipation gathered under my coat for what he had in mind once he got me alone.

Giant homemade banners were being rolled down the campus buildings as people stood on the roofs, cheering and shouting to one another.

I looked at Reid.

"What other traditions do you have around here?"

"You haven't seen the half of them. And I can't wait to show you them all."

REID

Reid

I pulled the plastic covered stack of cups from the spot we'd stashed the thousand my dad had dropped at the beginning of the school year. "Got them."

The floor above us rumbled with the thump of bass from the music and at least sixty bodies drinking to their hearts' content.

Leona twirled in the middle of the room with her arms out wide. "Why don't you guys use the basement? It's huge and cleaner than half the apartments on campus."

"We only cleaned it out after the season ended. Before that, the landlord had a lot of gear down here. He knocked money off our rent, if we helped move it all out."

"I've got the perfect idea." Her hand shot up, smacking into the single lightbulb swaying from the exposed beams. "Movie theater."

"We've been trying to decide. Ezra and I voted for a weight room."

"Like you guys need to work out more. If you get any

more ripped, you'll give me a complex." She ran her hand down my arm.

I cursed the thermal stopping her from touching my skin. "I'm the one who should have the complex."

She tilted her head. "About what?"

The last few weeks had been magic. No longer feeling like we had to sneak around, every moment we could was spent together. I didn't want to ever have to be apart again. "That you'll get sick of coming to my games and practices, freezing your ass off with Taylor."

"I could never get sick of watching you play."

"Even when we get our asses kicked?"

"Maybe that's a little less fun, but you're doing your thing. I love watching you play. When you take your helmet off and I can see your smile from the stands." Her voice flooded with amazement. "It's the best feeling."

Pressing her back against one of the steel pole supports, I kissed her.

She kissed me back. Her hands looping around my neck. "Make that the second-best feeling."

"I love you. You know that, right?" I kissed her between every word. The certainty of it was imprinted on my bones.

She nodded and tugged at the hair at the nape of my neck. "You show me every day." Her mouth was hungry against mine.

Pressing harder against her, I groaned when she wrapped both legs around me.

"Reid, where are the cups?" Griff shouted down the basement steps.

Leona broke the kiss first. Her chest rose and fell. Her eyes were glazed with longing.

Suddenly, the party felt like a pain in the ass—in the

way of me taking Leona up to my room and not leaving until classes on Monday.

"Coming!" I shouted back although it would be a miracle if he heard me over the growing crowd.

Upstairs, I tossed two bags of cups at Griff and Ezra who were hanging out in the kitchen.

Red, pink and white balloons were taped to the walls in heart and arrow shapes.

"You guys will have a party for any reason." Leona laughed and poured out a handful of pink and red Skittles into her palm from the bags in a massive bowl in the living room.

"You don't think the week after Valentine's Day is a perfect occasion for a party?" I squeezed her from behind and lifted her off the ground.

She squirmed in my arms. "I'm chewing." Her laugh was swallowed by a snort.

I set her down and spun her to face me, kissing her cherry sweet lips. Lucky didn't begin to describe how I felt about being here with her.

Music spilled from the speakers in the living room. Pink streamers with kiss lips had been taped to the ceiling. Ezra had mumbled about the glittery banners when Hollis and I had strung them up. Cleaning duty would suck for him tomorrow. A month left until the countdown for the next game.

A guy ran past in a cupid costume, complete with diaper and bow and foam arrows with red hearts on them. With the season over, we finally had a chance to live up to our house namesake. It was even better having Leona here.

STFU Dirt had posted a few other stupid stories about her, but for the most part she'd been left alone. If I ever figured out who was running that thing, I'd take a bat to their car.

"He's got to be freezing." She watched him run past, shaking her head. "Now I know why this place is called The Zoo."

I set up another round of cups along the edge of the folding table we'd brought up from the basement for the party. "You didn't even get to come to the Halloween party last year, but next year you'll really see how we do it."

This was tame. Way tame, but the partying held less appeal than it had in the past. Not when I wasn't looking to hook up with anyone other than Leona. Good season or bad, she'd be there for me and that was all I needed.

"I'm sure there will be plenty more opportunities between now and then."

"Of course there will be. Spring break, prank war, Signing Day, senior week, Neptune Night."

"Now you're just making those up."

"Wait and see," I teased.

"Do you decorate for all of them?" She ducked under one of the pink and white mini unicorn pinatas twirling above the table.

"Ezra's catering guy said whoever was having their big party left all this crap behind. Paid them to clear it all out and the guy asked Ezra if he wanted any of it along with the candy and fudge."

"That salted caramel fudge is dangerous." She set up the last cup.

"So dangerous you've eaten at least a pound of it."

"That's what I'm talking about. I need to be banned from the house until it's gone."

"Any takers against the Flip Cup champions?" Her voice

was fueled by booze and bragging. Her aim, skill and speed increased with every drink.

"I guess Ashley and Taylor better be ready for me to move-in until then."

"They won't mind as long as you cook for us."

Two new opponents stepped up to the table ready to meet their demise. After three more rounds, we remained undefeated.

Leona pumped her fist in the air at the end of the line of overturned cups. "My flip cup champion." She raised both hands and I high-fived her. "Kennedy's here!"

I shook some Skittles in my hand and downed them.

Cole would have a field day bitching and being a general ass once he knew she was here, whenever he decided to show up.

Picking up her drink, she waved and rocked back, arm above her head, but no longer moving.

"What's wrong?"

I followed her line of sight. My eyes widened and we moved closer to the now closed door like we might fall into quicksand at any moment. Choking on the candy, I grabbed at my throat as my eyes watered.

Leona smacked my back until I regained the ability to breathe.

Cole walked in, but he wasn't alone.

Taylor and Ashley walked down the stairs. Hollis and Ezra came out of the kitchen and everyone had the same looks on their faces.

Cole raised their interlocked hands and kissed the back of hers like they'd been together for years.

Kennedy took her coat off and turned to him. "Thanks, babe."

Taylor's jaw hung open and she screamed. "What the fuck?"

"What?" Kennedy shrugged and looked between our heads with her hand still interlocked with Cole's. "Who's winning at Flip Cup?"

For the next two hours, Cole and Kennedy gave us serious alien invasion vibes. They were making all the right moves and saying all the right things, but damn if we weren't all a little freaked out by the abrupt eighty mile per hour U-turn they'd pulled.

Ezra kicked everyone out at two a.m. to get a jump start on cleaning. Leona and I helped along with some freshmen he'd recruited.

"You guys don't have to stick around." Ezra rammed a stack of cups into the double thick black bag as tall as him.

"I know it's part of the rules, but you've got to be tired after that long trip you took."

"Who said I took a trip?" He straightened with his hand froze halfway to the bag.

"Figured when you disappeared for a whole day and night you weren't on campus." I pushed a broom through the tissue paper and streamer mess on the floor.

Leona waddled in with a bucket filled with soapy water spilling onto the floor. She skidded on the wetness and caught herself against the wall.

Ezra turned to her. "Please take your boyfriend and get out of here."

"You don't want our help?" She set the bucket down, eyes drifting from the mop to Ezra.

"You make it sound like I'm not giving you an invite to my birthday. I'm cutting you both loose. Go have fun or whatever. If you're gone now, maybe you'll be passed out by the time I get upstairs and I won't have to hear your closet

Olympics," he grumbled with his hat shadowing his face as he went back to cleaning up.

The freshmen scurried around pitching in.

I wrapped my arm around Leona's waist and guided her to the stairs. "Thanks, Ezra."

He waved overhead without looking at us.

In my room, Leona sat on the edge of my bed with one leg crossed over the other.

"What are you thinking?" She hooked the hem of my shirt and pulled me closer, so I was staring down at her.

I touched her cheek, tickled by the soft cascade of her hair over my hand. "I'll tell you, but you have to promise you won't make fun of me."

She stared up into my eyes twinkling with playfulness. "Promise."

I held out my pinkie.

Her nose scrunched with amusement and she raised hers.

We linked them and I lifted her hand and kissed her knuckles. "I don't know if I'll ever stop falling for you." Warmth coursed along my skin.

"I'm with you on that same ride."

"Let's make sure it never ends." My chest lurched with one expectant heartbeat.

Her smile widened. "I'm game, if you are."

Thank you for diving into this brand new world with me! There were a few familiar faces and a lot of new ones. Getting to explore this new campus and this new group has been such a fun ride. And there will be loads more stories for you to discover!

First, I wanted to let you know there's a special bonus scene of Reid and Leona, when you're looking for a little more of these two.

Next up, Cole and Kennedy are ready to make their big splash into your hands with their book, The Kiss List. What could possible have brought these two together? Their story is ready for you when you're ready! Grab it now!

EXCERPT FROM THE PERFECT FIRST

Seph - Project De-virginization

The jingle sounded again as the door to the coffee shop swung open. My head snapped up and my bouncing leg froze. The sun shone through the doorway and a figure stood there. He was tall, taller than anyone who'd come in before. His muscles were obvious even under his coat. He paused at the entrance, his head moving from side to side like he knew people would be looking back, like he was giving everyone a chance to soak in his presence. His jet black hair was tousled just right, like he'd been running his fingers through it on the walk over from wherever he'd come from. The jacket fit him perfectly, like it had been tailored just for his body.

I glanced around; I wasn't the only one who'd noticed him walk in. He seemed familiar, but I couldn't place him. He bent forward, and I thought he was going to tie his shoes, but instead he wiped a wet leaf off his pristine white sneaker. Heads turned as he crossed the floor toward me. Squeezing my fingers tighter around the notecards, I reminded myself to breathe.

He glanced around again and spotted me. The green in his eyes was clear even from across the coffee shop. Dark hair with eyes like that wasn't a usual combo. He froze and his lips squeezed together. With his hands shoved into his pockets, he stalked toward me with a *Let's get this over with* look. That didn't bode well. He stood beside the seat on the other side of the booth, staring at me expectantly.

My gaze ran over his face. Square jaw. Hint of stubble on his cheeks and chin. My skin flushed. He had beautiful lips. What would his feel like on my mouth? I ran my finger over my bottom lip. What would they feel like on other parts of me? My body responded and I thanked God I had on a bra, shirt, and blazer or I'd have been flashing him some serious high beams. This was a good sign.

He cleared his throat.

Jumping, I dropped my hand, and the heat in my cheeks turned into a flamethrower on my neck. "Sorry, have a seat." I half stood from my spot in the booth and extended my hand toward the other side across from me. The table dug into my thighs and I fell back into the soft seat.

Sliding in opposite me, he unzipped his coat and put his arm over the back of the shiny booth.

"Hi, very nice to meet you. I'm Seph." I shot my hand out across the table between us. The cuff of my blazer tightened as it rode up my arm.

His eyebrows scrunched together. "Seth?" He leaned in, his forearms resting on the edge of the table. He was nothing like the guys from the math department. They were quiet, sometimes obnoxious, and none of them made my stomach ricochet around inside me like it was trying to win a gold medal in gymnastics at the Olympics.

I tamped down a giggle. I did *not* giggle. The sound came out like a sharp snort, and I resisted the urge to slam my eyes shut and crawl under the table. *Be cool, Seph. Be cool.* "No—Seph. It's short for Persephone."

He lifted one eyebrow.

"Greek goddess of spring. Daughter of Demeter and Zeus. You know what, never mind. I'm glad you agreed to meet with me today."

"Not like I had much choice." He leaned back and ran his knuckles along the table top, rapping out a haphazard rhythm.

I licked my lips and parted them. Not like he had much choice? Had someone put him up to this? Had something in my post made him feel obligated to come? I hadn't been able to bring myself to go back and look at it after posting it.

Shaking my head, I stuck my hand out again. "Nice to meet you..."

He looked down at my hand and back up at me, letting out a bored breath. "Reece. Reece Michaels."

"Very nice to meet you, Reece. I'm Persephone Alexander. I have a few questions we can get started with, if you don't mind."

"The quicker we get started, the quicker we can finish." He looked around like he would have rather been anywhere but there.

Those giddy bubbles soured in my stomach. A server came by with the bottled waters I'd ordered. I arranged them in a neat pyramid at the end of the table.

"Would you like a water?" I held one out to him.

He eyed me like I was offering him an illicit substance, but then reached out. His fingers brushed against the backs of mine and shooting sparks of excitement rushed through me. Pulling the bottle out of my grasp, he cracked it open and took a gulp.

My cheeks heated and I glanced down at my cards, flipping the ones at the front to the back.

"I have a notecard with some information for you to fill out."

Sliding it across the table, I held out a pen for him. He took it from me, careful that our fingers didn't touch this time. I'd have been lying if I'd said I didn't want another touch, just to test whether or not that first one had been something more than static electricity. He filled out the biographical data on the card and handed it back to me.

I scanned it. He was twenty-one. Had a birthday coming up just after the New Year. Good height-to-weight ratio. Grabbing my pen, I scanned over the questions I'd prepared for my meetings.

"Let's get started." *Just rip the Band-Aid off.* Clearing my throat, I tapped the cards on the table. A few heads turned in our direction at the sharp, rapping sound. "When were you last tested for sexually transmitted diseases?"

Setting the bottle down on the table, he stared at me like I was an equation he was suddenly interested in figuring out. And then it was gone. "At the beginning of the season. Clean bill of health." He looked over his shoulder, the boredom back, leaking from every pore. *Wow.* I'd thought guys were all over this whole sex thing, but he looked like he was sitting in the waiting room of a dentist's office.

"When did you last have sexual intercourse?"

His head snapped back to me, eyes bugged out. "What?" I had his full attention now.

"Sex? When did you last have sex?" I tapped my pen against the notecard.

He sputtered and stared back at me. His eyes narrowed and he rested his elbows on the table.

I scooted my neatly lain out cards back toward me, away from him.

"No comment."

"Given the circumstances, it's an appropriate question."

The muscles in his neck tightened and his lips crumpled together. "Fine, at the beginning of the season."

"What season?" I looked up from my pen. That was an odd way to put it. "Like, the beginning of fall?"

"Like football season."

The pieces fit together—the body, the looks from other people around the coffee house. "You play football." That made sense, and he seemed like the perfect all-American person for the job.

"Yes, I play football."

"When did the season start?"

He shook his head like he was trying to clear away a fog and stared back at me like I'd started speaking a different language. "September."

"And..." I ran my hand along the back of my neck. "How long would you say it lasted?"

His eyebrows dipped. "It didn't last. It was a one-night thing. I don't do relationships."

Of course not. He was playing the field. Sowing his oats. Banging his way through as many co-eds as possible. Experienced. Excellent.

I cleared my throat. "No, I didn't mean how long did you date the woman. I meant, how long was the sex?"

The steady drumming on the table stopped. "Are you serious?"

I licked my Sahara-dry lips. "It's a reasonable question. How long did it last?"

"I didn't exactly set a timer, but let's just say we both got our reward."

"Interesting." I made another note on the card.

"These are the types of questions I'm going to be asked for the draft?" He took the lid off the bottled water.

The draft? Pushing ahead, I went to the next line one my card and cringed a bit. "Okay, this might seem a little invasive." I cleared my throat again. "But how big is your penis? Length is fine. I don't need to know the circumference, you know—the girth."

A fine spray of water from his mouth washed over me. "What the hell kind of question is that? I know you're trying to throw me off my game, but holy shit, lady."

∾

Persephone Alexander. Math genius. Lover of blazers. The only girl I know who can make Heidi braids look sexy as hell. And she's on a mission. Lose her virginity by the end of the semester.

I walked in on her interview session for potential candidates (who even does that?) and saw straight through her brave front. She's got a list of Firsts to accomplish like she's only got months to live. I've decided to be her guide for all her firsts except one. Someone's got to keep her out of trouble. I have one rule, no sex. We even shook on it.

I'll help her find the right guy for the job. Someone like her doesn't need someone like me and my massive...baggage for her first time.

Drinking at a bar. Check.

Partying all night. Double check.

Skinny dipping. Triple check.

She's unlike anyone I've ever met. The walls I'd put up around my heart are slowly crumbling with each touch that sets fire to my soul.

I'm the first to bend the rules. One electrifying kiss changes everything and suddenly I don't want to be her first, I want to be her only. But her plan was written before I came onto the scene and now I'm determined to get her to rewrite her future with me.

Grab your copy of The Perfect First or read it for FREE in Kindle Unlimited at https://amzn.to/2ZqEMzl

ALSO BY MAYA HUGHES

Fulton U

The Perfect First - First Time/Friends to Lovers Romance

The Second We Met - Enemies to Lovers Romance

The Third Best Thing - Secret Admirer Romance

Kings of Rittenhouse

Kings of Rittenhouse - FREE

Shameless King - Enemies to Lovers

Reckless King - Off Limits Lover

Ruthless King - Second Chance Romance

Fearless King - Brother's Best Friend Romance

CONNECT WITH MAYA

Sign up for my newsletter to get exclusive bonus content, ARC opportunities, sneak peeks, new release alerts and to find out just what I'm books are coming up next.

Join my reader group for teasers, giveaways and more!

Follow my Amazon author page for new release alerts!

Follow me on Instagram, where I try and fail to take pretty pictures!

Follow me on Twitter, just because :)

I'd love to hear from you! Drop me a line anytime :)
https://www.mayahughes.com/
maya@mayahughes.com